Priya Basil was born in London in 1977. She spent her childhood in Kenya and now divides her time between London and Berlin. *Ishq and Mushq* is her first novel.

Ishq and Mushq

Priya Basil

BLACK SWAN

TRANSWORLD PUBLISHERS
61-63 Uxbridge Road, London W5 5SA
A Random House Group Company
www.rbooks.co.uk

ISHQ AND MUSHQ
A BLACK SWAN BOOK: 9780552773843

First published in Great Britain
in 2007 by Doubleday
a division of Transworld Publishers
Black Swan edition published 2008

Addresses for Random House Group Ltd companies outside the UK can be
found at: www.randomhouse.co.uk
The Random House Group Ltd Reg. No. 954009

The Random House Group Limited supports the Forest Stewardship
Council (FSC), the leading international forest certification
organization. All our titles that are printed on Greenpeace approved
FSC certified paper carry the FSC logo. Our paper procurement
policy can be found at: www.rbooks.co.uk/environment

Typeset in 11/13pt Giovanni Book by
Falcon Oast Graphic Art Ltd.

Printed in the UK by CPI Cox & Wyman, Reading, RG1 8EX.

2 4 6 8 10 9 7 5 3 1

For my family,
who filled me with stories.

And for Matti,
who helped fulfil my desire to write one.

'What trouble is there?' he asked.

'No exact trouble,' said his wife. 'Just the business of two people discovering each other by degrees, and not discovering enough, as they live together.'

Patrick White, *The Tree of Man*

Part One

Part One

1

'Remember, there are only two things you can't hide –
Ishq and Mushq: Love and Smell.' This was the wet
whisper Bibiji sprayed into Sarna's ear before the train
pulled out of Amritsar. Whether this information was
offered as a warning or consolation, Sarna wasn't sure. She
wrapped the purple corner of her chiffon sari over one
finger and rolled it around the inside of her ear to wipe
away the dampness of her mother's farewell. The shrill
echo of Bibiji's words was not so easily erased, but it
began to fade just as her ample old figure waving from the
platform slowly disappeared, and Sarna was filled with
relief. She was finally on her way. Away.

Even when she arrived in Bombay, twenty-six hours and
one thousand four hundred kilometres later, she still had
a way to go. A long, long way. Four thousand, five
hundred and twenty-eight kilometres, to be precise.
Maybe, Sarna hoped, that would be far enough.

The weather, as if in sympathy with all that Sarna
seemed so easily to be leaving behind, was fuming at
45°C. In the heat of the livid June sun, Bombay harbour
sweated reluctant activity. At its fringes a collection of life
hovered inertly: vendors too weary to tout their wares;

idlers too hot to indulge their indolence; and beggars too scorched to advertise their afflictions. The sea looked a sickly grey-green and lolled unsteadily as if it too were suffering a bad case of sunstroke. Between these scenes of heat-beaten resignation was a little hub of action. It was concentrated around the mighty hull of the *Amra*, the creaking hulk of a ship due to sail for Mombasa, Kenya.

Porters hurried back and forth, bent double under vast loads of improvised baggage. Anything that could be filled, folded or knotted seemed to serve as acceptable apparatus for holding things. A steady stream of metal trunks, wooden crates, woven sacks and multicoloured knotted bundles of old saris was slalomed through scattered groups of passengers and those come to see them off. The restless crowd tried to counter the effects of the heat by drinking the lemon water that was being peddled energetically from makeshift wooden carts by skinny men who alone seemed to have the resilience of camels against the sun. Amongst them the odd pickpocket and petty thief trailed listlessly. Their work had been made easy by this heat: people were too preoccupied with fanning it off to be paying the necessary attention to their belongings. But even the small-time crooks were unable to muster the energy to capitalize on the easy targets afforded them.

It was through this bustle that newly-weds Karam and Sarna approached the ship. Karam was not in a good mood. The cramped train journey from Amritsar and the unrelenting heat had worn him down. And now having to manage the transfer of their luggage to the deck through this madness was not doing his humour any favours. Several porters were helping to carry their things, but trying to coordinate the progress of these minions made

Karam feel like a shepherd trying to get his animals across a busy main road. Except he felt less fortunate than a shepherd, because he had no staff to rein in the errant flock. Instead he had to rely on the dexterity of his eyes to keep all four men within his vision at once; on the strength of his voice box to shout the abuse and instructions necessary to keep them all going at an even pace; and on the agility of his body to move quickly through the thick crowd, and the thicker heat, in order to keep up with the nimble porters.

'Idiot!' Karam shouted in the direction of one porter, who'd stopped to dig a finger up his nose. 'Already dreaming of lunch? Pick at yourself in your own time. Right now I'm paying you to pick up my things.'

The impervious man dug away for a bit longer before resuming his duties.

'Slacker! Where are you going?' Karam shrieked at another porter, who seemed to be veering off track to the right when the *Amra* was clearly straight ahead of them.

'Short cut, Sahib,' the porter said, as if it was perfectly natural that he should bypass the back of the queue and cut in somewhere at the front.

'No short cuts, what-not cuts. We go straight. Like everyone else,' Karam decreed. He glanced around and saw Sarna a few steps behind him, protectively carrying the hoard of mangoes she'd insisted on buying at the last minute. The heat, unable to keep its hands off her, had left the red imprints of caresses on her cheeks. Her sharp nose, damp with perspiration, glistened like an expertly cut jewel in her face. Karam's heart contracted sharply. God, she is beautiful, he thought. It was a revelation that had not ceased to stun him.

Still, that didn't put her beyond reproach. He blamed

her for their predicament. It was her stubborn refusal to leave anything behind that had led to this ridiculous situation, with him chasing, like a crazed circus master, through the blistering heat after a bunch of porters. He himself had virtually nothing to take back to Africa – nothing that could be packed into bags, anyway. True, he was taking back more than he'd arrived with – he now had a wife and a stack of unexpected experiences, but these conveniently carried themselves. Sarna, however, had more than made up for his lack of luggage by bundling up everything that had been available for the taking in Amritsar.

'What? Are you planning to open a shop or something?' Karam had watched in astonishment as his wife packed up what looked like a lifetime supply of herbs, spices and other dry foodstuffs.

Sarna laughed and shook her head.

'But why, then?' Karam protested. 'You can get everything there.'

She arched her eyebrows at him and quipped, 'Just in case, S'dharji.'

He noticed the subtle shortening of her address with surprised pleasure. 'Sardharji', the typical address of Sikh wives to their husbands, had not remained intact in Sarna's mouth for long. Karam was aware of the impropriety of the informal address, but he liked it. He took it as a sign of love and he was gratified.

Less pleasing was the 'just in case' that became her explanation for everything. Karam watched helplessly as luggage filled with cooking utensils, yards of fabric for sewing, bags of henna, piles of clothes, nameless tinctures and medicines. He could at least see a purpose for these,

14

though he remained dubious about their value. But there were other things she packed away which left him utterly flabbergasted, even a little worried: bundles of mismatched rags and fabric ends, empty little vials and containers, tiny secondhand baby garments.

Karam had tried different lines of argument to stop Sarna's stockpiling tactics. In his own mind he had a watertight case against her:

'We don't have enough bags. Transportation of so many bundles will be cumbersome. We will be stopped at Customs. There is no storage room in the house in Nairobi. Half the goods will probably break or leak on the way.'

Sarna continued to pack stuff up. Karam had come across bags that seemed to be full of rainbows but were actually crammed with parandas of every conceivable colour, elaborate ribbon-like accessories for the hair. Other bags that glittered with the promise of riches revealed stacks of assorted bindis to adorn Sarna's forehead, and sheets of silver- and gold-leaf paper to decorate the heady Indian sweets, like barfi, that she loved to make.

'*Why?*' Karam stressed. 'Just in case *what*?'

'Just – in – case,' Sarna enunciated mysteriously. No real explanation for the hoarding existed in her mind. It answered the impulse of her heart and therefore made sense. Any further attempt at rationalization would have exposed the three words for the hollow justification they were.

Those words never ceased to antagonize Karam. They were so deliberately and obstinately dismissive, the equivalent of the cryptic 'because' that adults so frequently hand out to children. The words pretended at finality, but were actually, he felt, a precursor to doubt and further questioning. The more he thought about them the more infuriated he became. To him, Sarna's 'just in case' was an in-just case: without substance. In any court of law she wouldn't have stood a chance with her unconvincing mantra. 'Case dismissed,' the judge would have said. But Karam and Sarna were playing preliminary matches in the court of love. There, as we know, certainly in the early stages, considerable allowances are made for irrationality.

In truth, Karam was irritated because Sarna's need for plenty of everything clashed with his own impulse for less. He hated clutter. Anything that lay unused grated on him because it suggested inefficiency and waste. He couldn't accept her obstinate optimism about the inherent usefulness of all things. Better to have a few handy and meaningful items than vast stocks of unnecessary rubbish – that was his philosophy. He also worried that her amassing of things was indicative of materialism. He was concerned about what future implications this might have for his pocket.

In the end, though, the leniency of love won out. Karam resigned himself to Sarna's wishes, and case after case was filled to bursting, 'just in case'. And now here they were, struggling to shift the damn loads, just as he'd predicted. Meanwhile, Madam had impulsively bought three crates of mangoes just before they'd left Amritsar. Of course, Karam had objected, but, as ever, to no avail.

'In that case,' he had said, 'you can carry them yourself.'

Small effort it seems to be costing her, Karam thought – until he glimpsed her moving regally through the crowd in her purple sari, elegant even as she lugged several dozen mangoes. He noticed the admiring glances and entranced stares directed her way, and his exasperation was overridden by another feeling: the desire to press his big nose into her skin, breathe in her gorgeousness and forget the trying demands of the day. Suddenly the idea of Sarna holding her mangoes was stirring other parts of Karam to bigness. However much her words and actions might sometimes antagonize him, when he looked at her he became defenceless.

'Sa-hib!' Karam's attention was snapped back to the porters, who had reached the deck of the ship and were waiting for him to catch up and pay them.

Annoyance twinged in him, like a poorly plucked sitar string, as he considered the wastefulness of having to remunerate four men for carrying unnecessary things. He did a quick mental calculation of what he owed them and then handed out half the required sum. The porters objected vociferously.

'That's all I have.' Karam shrugged.

The porters hung around, scowling in silent accusation. Karam glared at them. They stared back. These were men skilled in expressing outrage. Their livelihood depended on their ability to make any payment seem paltry. Karam couldn't remain indifferent to them for much longer, but he was loath to put his hand back in his pocket. As Sarna stepped up to join them, he leaned over, picked up one of the mango boxes and shoved it towards the porters.

'Share this,' he said.

No sooner had he done so than Sarna dumped the other boxes she was holding, swooped in and snatched the mangoes back. 'No!' She glared at Karam. 'These are *mine*.'

Karam quickly handed out more change. 'Bloody looters,' he muttered at the departing porters – as if it was all their fault. Then, not quite ready to look Sarna in the eye, he busied himself with considering how best to get their luggage from the main deck to the third-class section below. It dawned on him that he would now have to enlist the help of a couple of the ship's porters, who would be twice as expensive as the other ones. He didn't voice his feelings because Sarna's beautiful face was still pouting at him incredulously.

The vast third-class deck beneath the main helm of the *Amra* was heaving with people. In this hollow underbelly of inter-continental travel there was no distinction between man, woman or child. Here baggage was king. The deck operated solely on a baggage bonus basis – the more bags you had, the more territory you could bag for yourself. But the prize for most luggage would have been difficult to award. Karam noticed with some surprise that his and Sarna's hoard looked quite modest in comparison to others'. He glanced at Sarna and, sure enough, her eyes were sending signals of triumph his way. He shook his head indulgently and smiled in spite of himself.

People were boarding with multitudinous supplies, from the exotic to the basic to the bizarre. Their goods made for a fascinating procession: sewing machines, bicycles, sacks of flour, bags of spices, jumbo jars of pickles, large tins of ghee, bundles of bedding tied together with long strips of cotton, ventilated cartons in which fruits and vegetables nestled snugly against each other. Amongst these easily identifiable items an array of more mysterious packages stood out for their sheer size or impenetrability: wooden crates tightly hammered shut with nails, huge iron trunks resolutely locked with giant padlocks. Stranger still were the oddly shaped bundles, wrapped in layers of colourful cloth held together with copious windings of rope, which were moved across the deck like ominous voodoo dolls.

The parade of goods was a spectacle indeed, but the owners of all this bounty were equally enthralling. Shaken to attention by the demands of the rocking deck, they were all on high alert. Like hunters scanning the vicinity for prey, their eyes scrutinized the deck for the optimal space in which to set down their luggage, spread out and stake their territory for the journey. The more cunning families would close ranks and, as a single unit of momentum – heads down and elbows out, force their way through the crowd towards the desired spot.

The trick was to lay out a sheet or mat (or in some cases several sheets and mats) on the floor of the deck, arrange your bags around it and sprawl yourself across the space to claim it. A few perverse souls went a step further and proceeded to fart, burp or cough in an effort to dissuade anyone from setting up camp too close, taking their inspiration from lesser mammals who routinely mark out their territory by urinating to designate borders. And certainly people tried to steer clear of the more fetid encampments.

Installing oneself comfortably for a third-class sea journey was no mean feat. It was a supreme test of baggage-handling capacity, shamelessness and guile. It was not a task to which Karam was naturally suited. Sarna, on the other hand, was in her element in this environment. She looked at her husband courteously giving way to the crowds pushing past them and decided to take control. All of a sudden she rushed ahead of him, coughing and wheezing as she tripped and tumbled her way past scores of people before throwing herself on to an empty patch and proceeding to have what looked like a strange fit. Eyes rolling in sockets, limbs convulsing, she manned the area until Karam and the new brigade of porters caught up. People stared before hurriedly passing by and getting on with securing themselves a spot. When the porters arrived, Sarna briskly instructed them on where to lay out what. Meanwhile, Karam looked on, embarrassed but impressed. The description 'chalaako', with which he had sometimes heard Sarna's sisters taunt her, sprang to his mind and he smiled. She certainly was a cunning one.

Sarna watched the mass of India receding in the distance. How easy it felt just to sail away from the land of her youth. Would that it were as simple to effect an internal migration. Sarna felt the past following her into the future. Karam had worried about the amount of luggage they were taking on board; it was just as well he had no idea about the excess baggage she was carrying in her mind: it was heavy with unwanted memories.

Sarna's impulse for collecting was curiously mirrored in the arrangement of her memories. But there she was less arbiter than victim of what should stay and in what measure. Her memory operated its own cumulative logic, as memory does. It had a penchant for hanging on to the things she most wanted to forget. In an insidious conspiracy, it squeezed in lost love and a shameful mistake with an adroitness Sarna could not counteract. Why is it, she wondered, that we can choose to remember but we cannot choose to forget?

Forgetting occurs across the spectrum of our experience in three distinct ways. At one end are the everyday minutiae of life – like forgetting to buy more salt or get a tax return in on time. We chide ourselves for lapses of this sort. At the opposite end of the spectrum are the most demanding and life-changing experiences. Here forgetting can be the sweetest of reliefs: we can lose all recollection of traumas that once threatened us with a lifetime of hurt or humiliation. Women forget the pain of childbirth and subject themselves again and again to this torturous wonder. Between these two extremes of forgetting is everything else that happens to us: the immeasurable realm of accumulated experience. We take in so much, feel so much, see so much, hear so much, do so much and still want so much more – but where can we keep putting it all? Forgetting creates the space that allows us to keep absorbing.

So forgetting, though essential and advantageous, is its own master, with its own rules of selectivity. And sometimes it lets us down, not permitting us to forget some of the worst things we have done and endured. Perhaps there is a good reason for such recollection, but right now that was not Sarna's concern. She stared at the choppy sea, more preoccupied by the fact that she could not forget than the reason why. 'Why?' is an uncomfortable question. We happily put it to others without a second thought, but how infrequently we turn it on ourselves.

Sarna pulled the end of her sari over her shoulders like a shawl. She reflected on how there are times when you can deliberately choose to forget – like when you see there's only one mango left and you conveniently 'forget' that anyone else might like it. But it was the big issues that bothered her. There was no way of getting around the booming reminders of failure and sadness. No way of tripping them up and tricking them to disappear. They were a stubborn crew, the memories that manned her head. Well nigh impossible to control.

Sarna shook her head irritably, as though the action might dislodge her thoughts. Red garnets glistened at her ears like freshly sucked confectionery. Remembering was so easy, she thought. You could make lists and repeat things until they stuck. If you could make yourself remember, then surely you could make yourself forget? There was so much she needed to erase from the slate of her experience. Shame was curled up within her like a half-formed thought that dared not unfurl to completion. She had disgraced herself and her family, and the consequences were trying to catch up with her, like a huntsman pursuing a deer already grazed by his first bullet.

Sarna squinted with concentration. The ship rocked roughly and made her totter. She grabbed the handrail and steadied herself. All she wanted was to forget, and yet her preoccupation with doing so was making her remember, giving precedence to the very thoughts she wanted to annihilate.

She shifted her attention to the future, and tried to picture what life in Nairobi might be like. But old memories pushed through the veil of her imagination. So she submitted to them for a while, replaying those dreaded scenes in her mind and visualizing an alternative reality in which all the 'what-ifs' of her tortured conscience came to fruition and made for a more bearable outcome.

It struck her suddenly – if she could not forget, then she could choose how to remember. If she was to remain subject to this constant nagging replay of the past, she would revise the details, alter the facts, change the names, and leave out what she didn't like. She would take control until memory submitted to her purpose.

It's the age-old imitation tactic: take the template and alter the specifics. Who knows, you might fool them. You might even fool yourself. It's all a question of time.

*   *   *

'Have one, Dharji,' Sarna encouraged Karam as she slurped at her third mango. He noticed how she kept offering the mangoes without actually giving him one, but he didn't mind. He was almost sated just by watching her eat. She tore off the mango skin with her teeth and fingers and sucked greedily at the soft honeyed flesh. The sound of her eating resembled the smack of bodies making love. Her lips, glazed with amber juice, glowed like sunrise. More juice dribbled down her hands and collected in the valleys between her knuckles like pools of liquid citrine. She lapped it up savouringly.

'I love this bit.' She moved the mango stone in and out of her mouth. When she was satisfied that there was nothing more to be had, she tossed it on to the floor, where the other two stones gleamed hairy white. Then, smiling at Karam, she reached for another mango. 'Have one, Dharji.' She inclined her head towards the boxes of fruit.

'You'll make yourself sick,' Karam reproached. 'You should stop now.' If she paused, maybe he could halt the fantasies driving him wild with desire. Watching Sarna eat in this way gave him a hint of a sensual appetite he'd never seen in her when they made love. So far, sex had been a discreet and hurried act: dark muffled moments of fumbling with clothes on while the rest of the household slept. So Karam had never seen desire in Sarna's eyes, he had never seen her lips wet with want, he had never felt her lick the core of him to gleaming stone.

Sarna ignored Karam and continued eating. Mango was the most satisfying thing she had yet put in her mouth. Every year since she could remember, from June to August, she had gorged herself on the golden palm-sized

23

ambrosia. And, each year, her mother had tried everything to contain Sarna's insatiable consumption. At first Bibiji had tried to scare her off the fruit with health warnings. 'You'll boil up inside and explode! Do you know how much gharmee mangoes make? They'll heat you up inside and give you spots and heavy periods. *Then* who will want you?' When this didn't work, Bibiji bought less of the fruit. But Sarna still managed to get the largest share of any mangoes that came to the house. She would bribe her sisters to give her theirs, or she'd sneak into the kitchen for a midnight mango feast. Eventually Bibiji had declared a moratorium on mangoes altogether. 'None of that fruit in this house until you learn to control yourself.' Bibiji held firmly to her own rather misinformed interpretation of the Ayurvedic theory of 'hot' and 'cold' foods. She had always carefully monitored the amount of 'hot' foods, like grapes, eggs, nuts, dried fruit and chilli, in the diet of her daughters. She believed such foods, if not eaten in strict moderation, could have an unsavoury health impact on the female body. She thought they hastened maturity, but, more seriously, she was convinced they aroused amorous instincts and encouraged immoral behaviour. With any of her other three daughters Bibiji might have been more tolerant of the mango cravings – but Sarna was the most beautiful of the lot, as well as the most independent and sharp-tongued. There had always been friction between her and Bibiji – right from when Sarna, as a baby, had refused to drink her mother's milk. Bibiji had just about managed to keep the wilful girl in check, but with food-induced passions running through her blood there was no telling how far out of hand she might get. So Bibiji had banned the mangoes.

But when they were in season, Sarna was like a woman

possessed. As bees must go to honey, as dogs on heat must find release, she too had to have her mango quota. Her beauty made them easier to access. The servants risked the wrath of their mistress for the flash of her daughter's smile on receipt of a mango. Sometimes Sarna slipped out of the house and made rounds of the fruit stalls, where every vendor eagerly offered her free mangoes for the sheer pleasure of watching her feast on the fruit. Once in a while, Bibiji would notice the sweetness on her daughter's breath, or the stains of yellow flesh beneath her nails, and with fresh indignation she'd reprimand, 'You will bring shame upon us! No self-control, no self-control. Between this mango addiction and the fetish for putting chillies on everything you eat, God only knows what's going on inside you. Soon you'll have mango juice, not blood, flowing in your veins, and then – hai Ruba – I only hope I am not alive to see what you'll get up to.'

Sarna, however, had continued to eat mangoes. When her mistake came to pass and shame descended upon the family, Bibiji had at least one possible explanation for it. 'That girl's vikriti,' she'd pronounced, using the old Sanskrit word meaning *deviated from nature*. 'She has over-heated. Hai Vaheguru! May God protect young girls from the fervour in such fruits.' Then Bibiji had decreed that all her daughters would drink nothing but iced water until the day they were married. Sarna had been put on a month-long diet of iced water and raw vegetables, in the hope that this would put out the flames of her fiery spirit. But water cannot temper one's nature or wash away a mistake.

Karam put out his finger to catch a drop of mango juice that hung precariously at Sarna's chin. He pressed it into her skin and pushed his finger up in a straight line along her lips, over her nose, up to her hairline and back down again. The svelte symmetry of her face delighted him.

Sarna shook her head to dislodge his touch. 'Mmm-mmm, Jee, I'm eating.'

Jee, Karam thought. Now I'm Jee. He was touched by this broken end of a word. It was the sweetest call of love he had yet heard. With every syllable Sarna dropped from his name, their love broke through the barriers of custom. Sardharji, Dharji, Jee. With each abridged endearment Sarna had deepened their intimacy. Karam felt moved that she'd found, and dared to use, this vocal expression for love. He could not think of any appropriate words. And, in any case, he wouldn't have known how to speak them.

Sometimes he said Sarna's name, repeating it in a hundred different intonations, each resounding a distinct note of love. But mostly he used his hands. With his large, powerful hands and strong fingers with neatly trimmed nails, he traced her smallest curves. He would run a finger along Sarna's eyebrow, over the gentle arc of her nostril or around the delicate sinuous cartilage of her ear. And with these touches he said, 'You are my perfection.'

On seeing Sarna, Karam had felt the word 'beauty' for the first time. He remembered it as a sharp piercing at the back of the throat that had made his breath stall somewhere in his chest and his head grow dizzy. The rest of the company present had witnessed this moment and thought Karam was choking. He'd spluttered an orange spray of the ludoo sweet that Sarna's mother had just stuffed into his mouth. It had flown in Sarna's direction, like a shower of confetti.

Karam had always been susceptible to beauty, but he'd rationalized this impulse as an appreciation of order. He had a fascination for precision. He loved mathematics and relished his ability in the subject, drawing a deep satisfaction from the definiteness it could conjure in his mind amidst the uncertainty that surrounded him. In the cramped home where he'd grown up in Nairobi, he had transcended difficult situations by climbing ladders of numbers in his head. At night, in his shared bedroom, when the whispers or snores of his brothers disturbed him, Karam had retreated into the abacus of his mind and fallen asleep to the lullaby of clicking numbers. When Baoji, his father, had grabbed the broom to punish him for some error, Karam would start counting. As each whack struck his legs, Karam would turn it into a calculation and build an equation against pain. So with the first blow he thought '$1 \div 2 =$', and when the second blow came he used the answer to formulate another sum: '$0.5 \times 94 =$'. With the third strike he continued figuring – '47^2' – and so the computation continued – '$2,209 \times 1,010 =$' – the numbers multiplying in proportion to his pain and simultaneously blocking it out – '$2,231,090 \times 100 =$' – the 0s accumulating in his head so that they wouldn't pop as an 'Oooh!' from his mouth.

From this love of numbers it followed that, for Karam, aesthetic pleasure lay in orderliness, in a task well done. In the arrival or departure of someone at a precise agreed hour. In the efficient elegance of the salai, long and metallic like a knitting needle, tucking any straggling hair back under a turban. When he felt this same pleasure intensified at the sight of Sarna, Karam understood it was the appeal of beauty. In Sarna he found his more sensual side. He looked around and saw anew the bend of a tree's branches, the sinuous puffs of the clouds, the arch in the wingspan of a bird. He saw that even the shortest blade of grass will incline towards the sun. He realized that severity had unnaturally pervaded his life. It had seeped into his thoughts, habits, even his sleep. He had slept straight and stiff most of his life, the inevitable result of sharing a bed with too many brothers. Now, in his sleep, he would curl himself up into a foetal pose, or hook himself, like a half moon, around Sarna. This too was beauty.

What is it about staring at the horizon that makes one reflective? Perhaps if we could keep seeing beyond the boundaries of our last glance we could be distracted forever from ourselves. Alas, it is not so, and it was Karam's turn to lapse into thoughtfulness as he took a walk along the deck and looked out to sea. It was impossible for him and Sarna to do this together, because one of them had to keep an eye on the luggage. Yet, in a way, Karam was grateful for the solitude. He had not been alone for months. He felt overwhelmed as this revelation hit him. He was struck by all the experiences he had not yet properly understood and the losses he had not yet fully felt, because he had not had the time, space or capacity to reflect on them.

'Oh-jalebi-jalebi-j'lebi-lebi-lebi-lebi-bi one rupee!' The cries of the jalebi vendor who'd set up shop on the deck distracted Karam. He watched from a distance as the vendor dripped wobbly coils of batter into the boiling oil and drew out gleaming orange spirals, which were dipped in sugar syrup before being laid out to tempt the passers-by. The vendor caught sight of Karam and beckoned to him. 'Oh, Sahib! Come, come and have one. Hot and fresh, just for you.'

Karam's hand went unconsciously to his back pocket, where his money was nestled. After a moment of hesitation, he walked over to the jalebi stand. The vendor wrapped a fresh stack in paper for him.

'That's too much!' Karam raised both hands.

'Not too much, Sahib. They will give you strength, and put a bit of fat on those bones. Too thin, Sahib is really too thin.' The vendor shook his head disapprovingly and his four chins, like a necklace of jalebis, rippled to endorse his criticism. Karam accepted the large bag of sweets and handed over a rupee. Sarna will like them too, he thought.

Karam had been ill and was still underweight, a fact emphasized by his height and his habit of walking tall. His skin had the unhealthy grey hue that comes from too much time spent indoors. Between his thinned black beard and stark white turban his nose reigned supreme on his shrunken face. Time would restore him to handsomeness, but it would never completely erase the shock and disgust he'd felt on seeing the state of himself after the typhoid. He'd glimpsed the withered face of a man excavated from some ancient archaeological ruin. Karam had cried out at the sight. He'd felt as if he was viewing himself stripped of everything except his faults. He would never again look at himself without seeing a flash of that ghost man to which India had reduced him.

Karam had never harboured any illusions about his appearance. His skin was dark, so he had accepted, wrongly, that he was ugly. But he had sought to compensate for this by observing scrupulous cleanliness and neatness in all aspects of his appearance. He used Simco Hair Fix, a potent glue, on his beard and moustache to keep them tidy. He placed a hair net around his beard to contain it, tying the ends in a tight knot over his head under the turban. He suffered for these vanities. The rigidly tied hair net gave him such severe migraines he was forced to stop using it. And though the fixative irritated his skin, he stubbornly stuck to it. Like women whose feet end up gnarled and corn-ridden from being relentlessly thrust into ill-fitting high heels, he was not left unscathed by his habits.

Karam had adapted the style of his turban to a distinctive shape, quite unlike the wide, rounded satellites sported by his contemporaries. Instead, the neat front folds of the turban tapered elegantly to a precise V at the top of his head. Much to Sarna's annoyance, he always preferred a pristine white turban. Even in the dusty heat of Africa, where a white turban needed to be replaced almost every day, he would insist on it. For him its crisp, starched purity was a symbol of integrity and good intention. 'People notice your turban before they see you,' he declared. 'It must speak for itself. A turban is a lighthouse in a sea of heads.' Karam dressed smartly too, in meticulously pressed shirt and trousers. He always wore socks with closed shoes. 'Shoes without socks,' he would say, 'are like a suit without the trousers.' Throughout his life he remained very particular about his appearance. But inside he remained insecure, unable to strip himself of his perceived flaws.

The soft over-sweet warmth of the jalebis was comforting to Karam, but even they could not mask the bitterness he felt. In his mind he was raging against India. He knew he ought to be grateful to her for giving him a bride and the promise of love. But he could only dwell on what Mother India had taken away from him. Karam felt weak with anger. Six months of his life! She had robbed him of half a year and left him with no awareness of what had happened in that time. She had reduced his body to a frail shadow of itself, and she had taken away the one person

30

who held the key to how everything had unravelled.

Karam had left India with his family at the age of six and gone back twenty years later. He had returned without nostalgia for his motherland, without fondness, and perhaps he was even guilty of returning without respect. He had come with only one purpose: to find a bride. He had come to take, as so many have come to India and taken, with no mind that he might have to give something in return. And India had rebuked his presumption. She had taken this child, unversed in her history, sucked him into her belly, dragged him through her tortured guts and finally spat him out: altered but intact.

For a man like Karam, who needed order and logic for peace of mind, the puzzle into which a part of his life had been fractured was disturbing. It would be many months before he could let go of the sense of victimization and draw some lessons from his experiences.

What did it mean? Karam asked himself as he pulled a newspaper cutting from his shirt pocket and unfolded it. On the creased page was a photograph. In the background, bodies lay strewn in various postures of anguish. At the centre of the image, a withered man was staring at the camera, his hand outstretched towards the viewer in a benign plea for mercy. What could it mean?

The storm was unexpected. It destroyed the gentle rhythm into which the *Amra* and her passengers had settled and rattled them relentlessly for three days. On every deck bodies succumbed to sickness and vomiting. Sarna was one of the worst victims. A few hours after the storm hit, she was doubled over, retching. She spewed out the everyday evidence of living – lentils, rice, water and, of course, mango. Hai, the mango! She regretted the waste. She winced in discomfort and groaned with frustration. She did not like being ill.

Karam tried to console her with scientific explanations. 'Don't worry, these are typical symptoms of seasickness. Your body is just confused, it's reacting to contradictory messages about position and movement.'

Sarna looked at him blankly.

'Even if it doesn't seem as though we're bobbing around violently, your inner ear, which is much more sensitive than your eyes, picks up the slightest changes in the angle of the ship. The brain becomes confused by these contradictory perceptions. This is what's causing your nausea and dizziness,' Karam explained.

Sarna clutched her stomach and turned away from her husband.

Karam's analysis was correct. In Sarna, the temporary unsettling of the brain he'd described caused nothing short of chaos. The self-preserving order she had imposed on her mind was upset. In her, the storm was causing seesickness. The reshuffling of her memories, which she'd longed for only a couple of days before, began without her direction: layers of buried consciousness, so vigorously suppressed, were rumpled loose by the agitations the tumultuous ocean caused in her brain. Karam saw her colourful inside life spill out before him – a kaleidoscope on whose medical cause he speculated but whose spiritual significance he didn't fathom. He was surprised that Sarna was sick at all. He had always thought of her as robust, the very essence of life. In the year he had known her she'd never once been ill. *She* had been the unwavering hand of health that had nursed him back to life. Now, as he tended to her, he felt helpless and even a little disappointed.

The second day of the storm brought less frequent but

more forceful ejections from Sarna. She heaved and discharged a yellow bile. It glowed brightly and was foul-smelling. Mushq. A sharp and acrid stench of fear. Karam was convinced it was the mangoes and immediately berated himself for not reining in Sarna's appetite. But the discharge proved more sinister than mango. Its acidity burned holes in the cloth Karam used to clean it, and then it evaporated into thin air. Karam recoiled from the yellow assault and even Sarna seemed to coil up deeper into herself, as if to get away from it. Maybe it's hepatitis, Karam thought, wondering if he should get a doctor. Ah, but the cost. He felt for the diminishing wad of notes in his pocket. However, Sarna seemed to fall asleep and Karam hoped the worst was over.

On day three Sarna stirred, with deep, low moans. Then, slowly, she expended a viscous red-black mucus, dark with unvoiced passion and thick with guilt. Karam was alarmed. She was bleeding! As he tried to clear the pool of liquid it slid away from him, mercurial and elusive. Karam jumped up and shouted for help. The whole deck stared curiously in his direction, keen for any drama that might counter the spectacle of the storm.

'Eh – what are you all looking at?' Karam snapped. 'Someone do something – please!'

A young man obliged by going off to look for a doctor. Eventually Dr Kang, the ship's medical chief, made his way to them. A compact man in his late fifties, with a thick head of greying hair, he was short – just like his temper. He had the impatient aura of someone who has seen everything. The doctor leaned over Sarna, peeled open her eyelids and watched her respond faintly to the call of her name. Then he felt her up. 'Checking for fever,' he explained as his hands slipped from her hot forehead, over her flushed cheeks, down her bare throat and on to her full breasts – where they lingered. 'Heartbeat . . .' he murmured, looking Karam straight in the eye as he cupped and squeezed Sarna's bosom. He was silent for a moment, holding Karam's concerned gaze for as long as possible before pronouncing, '. . . seems to be normal.'

'Normal?'

'Yes. Nothing to worry about. Just a case of seasickness.' Dr Kang's hands clasped each other, as if keen to play out the fantasy of coupling inspired in him by Sarna's fleshy curves. 'The symptoms will pass. Like a fever, they must spend themselves before settling.'

'But is there nothing you can give her? She's vomiting blood,' Karam said.

Dr Kang shook his head. He'd given his verdict, hadn't he? Why was this man questioning his judgement? 'It's not blood. She'll come through.' His hands suddenly sprang apart for an instant, before meeting again for several short, hard claps, suggestive of a climax. Dr Kang's business was done. He waited for Karam's payment, then turned on his heel and departed.

Karam watched helplessly as the doctor walked off, thinking of the fee he'd had to fork out for the useless diagnosis. What is this? Third-class deck, third-class service?

What Dr Kang had predicted came to pass. Sarna stopped vomiting within a few hours of his visit. Her body quietened and a vague consciousness returned to it. She felt emptied, but at the pit of her was a hollow aching. She opened her eyes, but the world was still hazy, distant. Karam's voice filtered through the fuzziness. 'Sarna? Sarna . . . Sarna.' But there was no chance to respond. Her ears began to ring with the cry opening up inside her. She opened her mouth to release a wail so pained that people were knocked back by its force. Several passengers toppled off the low stools on which they were squatting. A young boy, who'd just popped a candy in his mouth, grimaced as the ball of sweetness exploded and splintered into a sour dust of sherbet. People wearing glasses thought the world had fractured, but it was their lenses that had cracked at Sarna's cry. Startled babies shrieked before sobbing quietly into their mothers' breasts. An old lady pressed her hands over her ears and on release found that, for her, life had been permanently muted.

Sarna was transported on the cusp of this wail to a memory of a faraway room where she had not been allowed to weep. Her body started to shudder and palpitate, her howl increased in pitch. Karam desperately looked around for what to do. Other passengers frantically offered advice. Some of it seemed practical: 'Water, water – splash her face!' 'Turn her over.' 'Stuff a scarf in her mouth.' And some of it was useless: 'Take off her clothes!' suggested a leery man who, even in the desperation of the moment, could not put aside the carnal thoughts inspired by the special treatment he'd seen Sarna receive at the hands of Dr Kang. 'Slap her!' snapped a woman who'd had enough of the commotion. Bewildered, Karam followed his instinct and put a hand over Sarna's mouth, but it was forced back by the violence of the noise. He was encouraged to try again by a burly Singh man who intervened. 'That's the way! Shut her up,' the Singh urged, placing his own hands over Karam's in assistance. The wail tried to resist. It needed to get out. Sarna's eyes strained with the effort of shouting, her face felt as though it was splitting, her body seemed ready to burst. But together the palms of Karam and the Singh proved a formidable barrier, and the wail started to sub-side. Just like that, it seemed to curl up and roll back into Sarna. She coughed painfully. Karam thanked the Singh, who was proudly basking in the gratitude being expressed by other passengers. 'Oh, it's nothing, yaar,' he said. 'Just remember in future, Bhraji, nothing like a strong hand to keep a woman in check.'

Sarna had been silenced but her wail continued to echo. It ricocheted around the deck, rolling through the crowd the way an artfully thrown pebble hops along the water's surface before sinking.

'Sooo . . .' Karam breathed in. 'Hmmmm . . .' he exhaled. 'Just one more day, and then we'll be there.' He didn't know what else to say. He didn't know how to ask what she had been through. He felt ashamed for having witnessed her suffering, as if he'd seen something he shouldn't have. So he kept quiet and didn't refer to it again. Sarna didn't say anything either. Through the hand that rested on her stomach, she could feel the knock of the silenced wail pounding inside her like a second heartbeat. It was reminding her that her life would always beat in two different rhythms: in the tempo of the time that was now and in the metre of the moments that might have been.

So they remained, Sarna and Karam: bodies close to each other, thoughts closed from each other. Sarna with the harrowing burden of too many memories, and Karam with the uneasiness of a huge gaping hole in his memory.

'Have a mango,' Karam offered. It was an attempt to recapture the calm before the storm. But the remaining mangoes, which had been so gently ripening to per-fection, had turned black and were a sticky mess of rancidness. In their unexpected putrefaction was a dark premonition of things to come.

2

Karam and Sarna received a quiet reception on arrival in Nairobi. Sarna was disappointed by the welcome. It was nothing like the celebratory extravaganza she'd expected. There was none of the hospitality a bride deserved. The newly married couple had arrived to an ordinary scene of everyday domesticity. No one had dressed up or decorated the house for the occasion. None of the traditional welcoming rituals, like consecrating the main doorway with oil, had been observed. No special meal had been cooked. No guests had been invited and some family members weren't even home. Most gratingly for Sarna, there was an addition to the family about whom she had not known. She had pictured herself arriving as the first daughter-in-law, but she'd been upstaged. In Karam's absence the next-eldest brother, Sukhi, had married, and it seemed as though his wife, Persini, had already become Karam's mother Biji's right hand. For the first time since leaving, Sarna felt a pang of longing for India. She missed her home and family, missed being a part of something. Here she felt like an extra, an appendix to a unit that seemed to be ticking along just fine and wasn't about to alter itself to accommodate her.

*　*　*

Biji seemed to take an instant dislike to Sarna, but Baoji was more positive about his new daughter-in-law. Like most men, he was aware of her physical charms. He especially liked the slight gap between Sarna's two front teeth that seemed to grin cheekily within her smile. It reminded him of the considerably bigger gap in his own mother's teeth, through which, he'd once believed, he and his siblings had come into the world. Baoji's soft spot for Sarna became even more tender when he tasted something made by her hands. The vast stacks of spices she'd brought from India found their first purpose in the making of tea.

Baoji closed his eyes after the first slurp of Sarna's brew and sighed. Eyes still shut, he raised the cup to his lips again, but it missed his mouth and imparted some tea into his beard. The beard, long used to accepting random ejections from Baoji's mouth – the odd lentil, a dribble of chicken curry – seemed gratified with this latest offering. Unperturbed, Baoji opened his eyes and took another sip. 'Best cup of tea I've ever had.'

'Definitely a good cup,' Mandeep, one of Karam's five brothers, said as he drank his tea and eyed Sarna's breasts.

'Oh, she's a very good cook.' Karam squared his shoulders. 'Just wait until you try her ras malai. That's really something.'

Mandeep didn't doubt it. If Sarna's ras malai was anywhere near as milky as her skin, or as voluptuous as her curves, he was sure it'd be a damn fine pudding. He couldn't believe his strict stiff brother had found a wife like her.

Sarna, meanwhile, relished her first success. She clutched gratefully at the compliments. If I can rule in the kitchen, she thought, I will surely win their hearts.

Her mother-in-law's heart, however, was not to be won by culinary conjuring – or any other means. Biji was not sure what to make of Sarna. Outward appearances suggested Karam had chosen well, but Biji was, for the moment, reserving judgement. She remembered her own mother's warning: 'Don't judge by the face, judge by the sense.' Sense aside, Biji already had reservations about Sarna's face. There was no doubt the girl was beautiful, but Biji detected traces of something else in her visage. She couldn't quite put her finger on it. At first, Biji thought the incongruity lay in Sarna's eyes, which alternately signalled innocence, then daring, then guile. There's a certain madness in those eyes, Biji surmised. The more she watched, the better Biji understood what she disliked: it was the self-conscious drama of the girl trying so hard to impress. Biji recognized that anxiety might be the cause of Sarna's erratic behaviour, but she had reservations and resolved to keep a close eye on her.

Sarna's life came to revolve around the kitchen. It was her territory by choice and necessity. By day it was a laboratory dedicated to tastebud titillation. By night a different sort of seduction went on within its walls. On the single mattress dragged into the kitchen each night, and pushed into a slot between the door and the low shelves stacked with flour and rice, Karam and Sarna made quick, quiet and passionate but inept love. Then they slept side by side, slotted together like spoons.

Karam's family had always eaten well. Food was their only luxury – it may not have been cooked to perfection, but there was plenty of it. When Sarna took over the kitchen she raised their epicurean status to that of emperors. And what an empire they enjoyed – though only every other week. In between Sarna's weekly endeavours, Persini turned out her own special brand of Punjabi food, characterized by one word: insipid. When Sarna cooked, the family feasted on her fragrant food and overindulged. Intoxicated by her creations – the tongue-loosening tastes and mood-enhancing smells – they forgot themselves and chattered amicably at the table. After a week of this excess, they guiltily accepted Persini's bland, simple offerings and ate sparingly in penitential silence. The routine worked quite well for their digestive systems: the post-prandial bloat of Sarna's dishes dissipated during the period of Persini's moderate meals.

Sarna wanted her food to be vibrant and varied. She liked bright clothes, jewellery, synthetic flowers. Under Biji's forbidding gaze, however, all colourful expression was severely limited. This impulse against colour was evident in the dreariness of every room in her home: a dullness made more morbid by the spoils of Karam's brother Sukhi's hunting passion, which covered the walls and floor.

The horns of impala, springbok and kongoni deer sprang off the walls like alarmed question marks and caused uneasy pangs in Sarna whenever she saw them. Some horns remained atop the taxidermized heads: those of a greater kudu and an eland stared at each other in resigned despondency from opposite walls of the living room. In one corner, a metre-long elephant tusk leaned in anticipation of the big sale Biji claimed Sukhi would make when he returned from his latest trip to Tsavo. On the floor, the stuffed head of a lion rose ominously from its carpet of a body, limbs akimbo and uncanny in their one-dimensional horizontality. Sarna was horrified by this collection. It filled her with a sense of foreboding. The changing display of dead mammals was like a haunting *danse macabre*. She imagined the medley of body parts assembling themselves into a mutant monster and exacting a terrible revenge on the family.

It was no wonder Sarna needed an antidote to this grimness. She indulged her need for brightness by using food as a colour palette. While the men of the house were at work or school, and Biji went out socializing, Sarna passed some of the long hours of the day experimenting in the kitchen.

Rice, most often served absolutely plain, became a psychedelic medley at Sarna's table. Every day it looked and tasted different. She might fry the raw grains in clarified butter before boiling them, to give the rice a delicate golden fluffiness. Her rice might be lightly spiced with mustard seeds and curry leaves, slightly browned and tangy with tamarind, sharp and yellowed with lemon rind, fragrant with cardamom, cloves and cinnamon, sweetly flecked with peas, or sunny orange with saffron and studded with sultanas and nuts.

As she created these kaleidoscopic variations, the idea that it might be possible to alter memory recurred to Sarna. Through her cooking she discovered that every ingredient can be transformed and almost every flavour can be disguised. Slowly at first – and with trepidation – she began to deconstruct her memories while she constructed her recipes. Thus Sarna concocted new tastes and tales. In a bubbling pot of khudi she tried to boil away the shame of her terrible mistake. In sizzling hot oil, as bhajias fried, she battered her insecurities about Persini being Biji's favourite in a crisp and crunchy coat of indifference. Beneath thick veils of spicy smell she disguised her homesickness for India. 'Only two things you can't hide – Ishq and Mushq: Love and Smell.' Bibiji's words came back to her and she smiled. Already feeling wiser than her old mother, she thought, Actually, maybe you could hide Ishq in Mushq, for Mushq can mask many things.

Sarna did not know that our olfactory receptors are directly connected to the limbic system, the most ancient and primitive part of the brain, thought to be the seat of emotion and memory. It was sheer instinct that led her to choose a perfumed path for the journey of forgetting. Usually smells evoke memory, but Sarna used them to alter it. She wanted to create a scented sphere in which she would be safe from her past, in which the only memories Mushq could trigger were good ones to block out all that had been bad.

'So,' Mandeep asked over dinner one evening, soon after Karam and Sarna had arrived, 'if this is how you were feeding our Karam in India, why wasn't his health better? How come he's still so thin?'

'Thin?' Sarna tossed her head and the little gold chandeliers at her ears tinkled. 'If you think he's thin now, you should have seen him when Amrit-ji brought him to the door of our house in Amritsar. They were withered, both of them. Stick men. Skin and bones, filthy and smelly, turbans lost, hair all over the place. My bibiji screamed and slammed the door shut on them at first. Amrit-ji had to explain who they were before she let them in. Dharji here couldn't even walk. He was unconscious. And light as a baby. Even I could carry him without much effort.'

'What happened exactly?' Mandeep turned to his brother.

'I don't remember much.' Karam was reluctant to speak about his India experiences. He was still trying to come to grips with it all.

'He doesn't remember, but *I* know what happened.' Sarna basked in the attention everyone turned on her.

Biji glared. The audacity of this girl! But Sarna was too glad of the opportunity to speak to notice Biji's disapproval.

'One day he was confirming the marriage proposal and saying he'll be back in two weeks, the next thing I know almost two months have passed and not a word from him. We thought he must have died. It was possible. We saw the violence going on around us. Sikhs killing Muslims, Muslims killing Sikhs, Hindus killing Muslims, Muslims killing Hindus – everyone killing, killing. Even we got caught up in it on the way to our summer house in Kashmir.'

Sarna was too animated to see Persini roll her eyes at Biji, who responded with a quick shake of her head.

'We were stranded in a field in the middle of nowhere for three days, I think it was some distance from Jammu.' She ate while she talked, swiftly chewing and swallowing between words. 'Imagine us, just women, Bibiji, me and my sisters. We thought we were going to die. Anything could have happened. No one had any scruples during that time. If we'd been found by Muslims we might have been raped and murdered like thousands of others. My father was a DSO.' This was one of Sarna's favourite proclamations about her past. The childhood memory of her father in uniform had led her to imagine him as a figure of the highest authority. 'If my baoji knew what we went through he would have risen again from his ashes. In the end we were lucky. Army trucks came and brought us back to Amritsar. The city was in ruins. Lahoran Gali, our street, had been ransacked. Our house had been looted. Everything was gone: jewels, clothes, household goods, food, money – it had all been taken.'

Sarna leaned across the table to spoon some okra on to Karam's plate. In this household, where they had so little privacy, she expressed her love for him by plying him with extra helpings of food. 'The worst thing was my dowry had all been stolen as well.' She had been trying to find an appropriate moment to elaborate on this point ever since she'd handed out gifts to the family after her arrival. She may have transported many things from India, but she knew the offerings she'd brought for Karam's family were meagre. When her dowry had been stolen, Bibiji had not minced her words about what it portended. 'First fiancé vanishes, then dowry disappears – all hopes of a wedding might as well be banished now. It must be your punishment. God knows I've done everything to make things right for you, but if life intends you to suffer for your mistake, what can I do?' When Karam had re-appeared and the wedding looked likely again, Bibiji had relented. She'd bought what little she could to send to Karam's family. No one could say she hadn't done her best, but it wasn't enough, and the other Biji had made that quite clear when, on receipt of the gifts, she had remarked, 'Hmmm, Persini gave me *two* sets.' She had then proceeded to show Sarna the jewellery sets from Persini, commenting pointedly on the fine craftsmanship and the quality of the gold. '*Very heavy*.' Biji had sat there like a weighing scale with the jewellery from one daughter-in-law in each hand. Her right hand, which was holding Sarna's offering, hovered noticeably higher than her left. The scales, which had never been in Sarna's favour, had tipped further against her. Sarna had been itching for an opportunity to justify things.

'It felt like we had lost everything.' She licked a dribble of dhal off her hand. 'We had been pillaged, just like India herself. I'm so glad my father didn't live to see what happened to his country. He was a DSO, you know. *Very* patriotic.'

'What's a DSO?' asked thirteen-year-old Balvinder, the second-youngest brother.

Sarna was taken aback. All of a sudden she realized she had no idea what the letters stood for. 'Um . . .' She looked to Karam for support. But he was wondering about the title himself, trying to recall what Sarna's mother had told him about it.

Persini sucked in her cheeks to stop herself from smiling at Sarna's discomfort. 'Deputy something or other?' Her cheekbones jutted gleefully, ready to leap off her face at the prospect of Sarna's humiliation.

Sarna blushed and tried to think of a suitable come-back. Luckily, Karam spoke. 'Oh no. It's not DSO, it's *SDO*. Yes, yes, SDO – Senior District Officer.'

Sarna smiled in relief and hurried on with her story. 'Yes, Baoji would have been heartbroken to see the state of India. My dear Bibiji tried to keep my spirits up. "These are things, just things," she said. "Things come and go. We will have more again in time." But there was no time. Nothing was normal. You couldn't move around freely. Then when Dharji finally reappeared we were busy night and day trying to keep him alive. Who had time for buying things? We were more concerned with saving lives.'

Biji noted the daring tangent Sarna's story had taken and felt no sympathy. The girl would have done better to keep quiet and practise some humility. Biji disliked this tendency, which she had already observed too often in Sarna, of trying to justify everything. Biji resolved not to tolerate it. She would say something to Karam. That had always been her style – to spot the error, determine the level of offence and then get someone else to mete out the punishment.

A little perturbed by the ominous look on Biji's face, Sarna stood up to refill plates.

'Baoji, have more bhartha.' Without waiting for his response, she piled smoked aubergines cooked with tomatoes and onions on to her father-in-law's plate. 'So it was a really hard time. People did terrible, unimaginable things. I couldn't bear it. I became sick with grief and worry. I lost a fair bit of weight myself.'

It was true that Sarna, like many during the year of India's partition, had been deeply affected by what took place in their country, in their neighbourhoods and often in their own homes. She had indeed become despondent. However, what she didn't explain was how it was, above all, for herself that she'd mourned: for the chance of normality and redemption that Karam had presented, which seemed to have been so cruelly snatched away. She'd lamented the inconsiderateness of India – thoughtlessly erupting into chaos just when she had been about to find a way out of her own personal mess. Sarna didn't elaborate on how her depression had given way to anger. She didn't tell of the curses she'd hurled on Karam for deserting her. That wasn't the story she wanted to be in.

'I prayed for him.' Her finger traced a circle through the orange film of oil on her empty plate. 'I prayed he would be spared, even though I didn't believe it was possible. All around us people were losing brothers, sisters, children, husbands, wives, parents. Who were we to be spared? We tried to help people when we could. Our neighbours were killed. A Hindu family, wiped out by Muslims.'

'But . . .' Balvinder paused midway through his corn on the cob. Its yellow flesh flashed between his teeth as he spoke. 'What about Karam? I thought you were telling us about him.'

Imp, if ever there was one. Sarna felt like tugging at one of the stray hairs sticking out of his pubescent chin. But smiling indulgently she said, 'Oh ho, hurry hurry. Why so impatient? I'm getting there. No story is just the story of one man. Everything that happened to Dharji was because of something else, some other person or event. So that's what I'm telling you. Giving you the full story, nah?'

Poor thing. Persini looked sympathetically at Balvinder. She knew exactly how he felt. This story wasn't just full, it was overflowing with Sarna's sense of self-importance.

'So our Hindu neighbours were killed. Somehow, we still have no idea, their baby daughter survived. The rest of them had all been stabbed to death but the baby was spared. We found her because we heard her crying.' Sarna's hand went to her heart. 'It was a miracle, but also a tragedy. She was just a year old and left with no one in the world. I told Bibiji we had to take her in. What hope was there for her otherwise? If we don't help other people, how can we expect any salvation for ourselves? This is what I said, and so Bibiji adopted her. Her name was Sunaina, because of her beautiful green eyes. Such eyes, I tell you – dark green, like you wouldn't believe. She became our little Nina.' Her eyes welled up. 'Well, any-way . . .' She blinked rapidly. 'They say one good deed deserves another. A few weeks later Amrit brought Dharji back to us.'

Baoji spoke up now. 'Yes, very sad news about Amrit.

We got your letter, Karam. It seems he was a real brother to you, not just a cousin.'

Karam shifted uncomfortably in his chair.

'Amrit-ji felt responsible for Dharji,' Sarna said. 'He told me so. He was the one who accompanied Dharji everywhere from the moment he arrived in India.' She looked at Karam. 'We talked a bit before he died. I was taking care of him, you see. I nursed him day and night, just as I nursed Dharji. He told me Dharji was the best man he had ever known. He was an only child, nah? So Dharji became like a brother to him.'

Karam recoiled from these words. They moved but also burdened him. To his knowledge, he had done nothing special in the time they'd spent together. He had done nothing to deserve Amrit's devotion.

'But how did he get you to Amritsar? That's what I want to know.' Mandeep jabbed a spoon in Karam's direction. 'Amrit was obviously quite ill himself. And what with all the troubles going on, it can't have been easy.'

'I don't know. I can't remember.' Karam pushed his food around his plate.

But Sarna was ready to jump in with an answer. 'Another miracle,' she said, as though miracles were an everyday occurrence to which she had long ago resigned herself. 'They came by rickshaw.'

'Rickshaw!' Balvinder and Mandeep shouted in unison while the rest of the family looked confused or incredulous.

'Rickshaw?' Baoji echoed.

'Rickshaw.' Sarna nodded. 'I couldn't believe it myself. But there it was, sitting outside the house as proof. Amrit-ji said he'd found it outside the refugee camp and just grabbed it and rode for his life. Imagine – he rode all the way from Lahore! That's where you were, nah?' Sarna looked at Karam.

'Yes, yes. DAV College, Lahore.' He was relieved there were some things on which he could still comment with certainty. At least he'd been himself when they'd arrived at the camp. At least he could hold on to that.

'Lahore to Amritsar – on a rickshaw,' Sarna continued. 'That's what? Forty kilometres? Amrit-ji cycled it on his own while Dharji lay unconscious in the back. I asked him, "But how did you get through without anyone stopping you?" In those days it was a risk to move around. There was a curfew. Armed goondas were roaming everywhere. All train stations were patrolled by these gangsters. Buses were stopped by them. "We rode through the air, Bhanji," Amrit said to me. "We came through the air like birds. And no one could touch us because we were flying on the fingers of God." That's what he told me. I'm giving it to you *word for word*,' Sarna emphasized, seeing the doubt on everyone's faces. 'He was already ill by then, though. The ride had taken the last life out of him. He could have been hallucinating. Still, flying or no, that rickshaw story is something. For weeks after they arrived both of them lay in bed. Amrit had said Dharji was suffering from Happytitis. We treated both of them for the disease, but there was no change. Day and night I looked after them. I hardly ate or slept. "Something's not right," I said to Bibiji. So Bibiji called another doctor and he did a blood test. "It's Taffoid," the doctor told us. Just in time they were diagnosed. A few more days and who knows what might have happened? Dharji started to get better. I was with him every minute, helping him back to life. But Amrit-ji got worse. He died two months from the day they came back to Amritsar.' Sarna, moved by the memories and satisfied with the version of events she'd extemporized, wiped the tears from her eyes.

Persini pinched her lips together and raised her eyebrows. She was cynical about Sarna's depiction of herself as victim and heroine of the story, with Karam and Amrit playing supporting roles.

Mandeep wondered how any man could do so much for another. He couldn't imagine acting so selflessly – even for his brothers. Then he wondered what it would feel like to grab, between his index finger and his thumb, the smooth little tyre of milky flesh spilling over Sarna's sari at her waist as she sat forward in her chair.

'So anyway, how long were you in Lahore? What was it like?' Mandeep asked, wiping his plate clean with some chapatti. He had heard great things about Lahore. The Sikhs had prospered there. People spoke about the great wide roads and magnificent gardens.

Karam was rather wearied by all this jumbled reminiscing. 'Well, we ended up in the camp just a few days after leaving Amritsar. We'd been making our way to Gujranwala, to see Amrit's family, when our journey was broken by the troubles. We heard later that the disruptions happened because people were speculating about where the border would be drawn, and were trying to secure certain areas for themselves in advance. Anyway, we were forced off our bus and left stranded. Like Sarna's family, we got on the first military truck that came by. It took us to Lahore. I think the camp was somewhere in the Cantonment area, the Sikhs had a strong presence there. I remember just a few days before I got ill. And then, I don't know. We were there for a long time. Four, six weeks, maybe.'

'I guess we'll never know now, huh?' Mandeep said. The

conversation had taken rather too much of a dreary turn for him. He'd been hoping for a tale of drama and intrigue, instead of this strange patchy picture of self-sacrifice and hardship. 'It's done and gone. The important thing is you're back in one piece, and once you've put on some weight you'll be absolutely fine. There'll be nothing to show what happened out there. Probably one day you'll even forget it.' Mandeep got up to leave the table, but stopped at Sarna's next words.

'We can't completely forget, because we have the photo.'

Karam's hand went to his right ear and began pinching at the long lobe visible under his turban. It was an echo of a childhood reflex in which he'd folded his ears up over themselves whenever he didn't want to hear what was being said around him. The turban sitting over his ears no longer allowed him to turn them into little cartilage seals against the world.

'What photo?' Mandeep's eyes widened under his black monobrow.

'Amrit gave it to me,' Sarna said. 'He saw it printed in a newspaper in Lahore and he kept it. Where is it?' she asked Karam.

He shrugged.

'I'll find it.' She got up. She returned a few minutes later and handed the picture to Baoji, whose dozy eyes focused on it uncertainly. Everyone crowded round and stared at the picture. In the background, bodies lay strewn in various postures of anguish. At the centre of the image a withered man was staring at the camera, his hand out-stretched towards them in a benign plea for mercy.

'Oh my son.' Biji gasped in a rare display of sensitivity. Little could pierce the glinting steel ball-bearing that now passed for her heart, but that picture moved her.

'Khalsa is the chosen of God, victory to God,' Baoji said solemnly.

This was exactly what Karam had dreaded – hollow habitual responses that would undermine the singularity of his experience.

In the end, though, it was not a wasted showing. There was a comment from young Harjeet, whose eyes brightened behind his thick glasses. 'You're in history,' he said. They were studying different sources of historical evidence at school and he was keen to display his new-found knowledge. What he learned at school very rarely had any relevance at home. 'You're a primary source of evidence, your photo is a secondary source.'

No one acknowledged his little contribution because Mandeep was still keen to find a juicier story, a saucier outcome. 'What newspaper was this in?'

'*Eastern Times*, I think,' Karam said.

'Oh.' Mandeep looked disappointed. 'It's probably just a one-off, then. I guess that local paper was the only one which printed the photo. Or –' He hesitated, reluctant to relinquish the possibility of a bigger story. 'Maybe this picture appeared in newspapers all over India,' he suggested enticingly. 'Perhaps your face was printed in the press all around the world! Might be, Bhraji,' he squeezed Karam's arm, 'that you're a bit of a hero after all. Huh?'

3

Karam had not been a hero. Far from it.

To any casual observer it might have been a parade. The trucks were like giant floats, each holding a microcosm of Indian life and colour: a cross-section of class, character and karma united in flight. As the giant vehicles moved forward, soldiers shouted for people to climb on if they needed refuge. In their urgent exhortations a few key words stood out, inflating the drama of the moment. They spoke of a fight and advised Hindus and Sikhs to climb on board, bringing as much food and water as they could. People poured into the street. They came out from half-burned houses, from looted shops, from behind smouldering piles of rubble. Many looked haggard with grief or crumpled from concealment. Some individuals, pale and phantom-like, seemed to rise up out of the ground itself.

Karam and Amrit were sucked into the momentum of escape and propelled on to a nearby truck. It occurred to Karam that they didn't even know where the trucks were heading. He shouted to a nearby soldier, 'Brother, we need to get to Gujranwala! Where are you heading?' The soldier shook his head. 'Stay on this truck or you can forget about ever getting anywhere.' The cryptic fatalism of this remark frightened Karam. They had already been stranded for almost a day waiting for a bus. Karam turned to Amrit. 'We'll keep an eye out for any train or bus stations along the way. We can just jump off and continue in our direction where possible.'

His hope was naive and born of ignorance. It was early in June 1947. In and around Lahore, communal clashes anticipating the Boundary Commission announcement of the partition in India had been rife since March. Violence was escalating as Hindus, Sikhs and Muslims tried to stake their land claims and assert their perceived rights through mutual cruelty. Only the day before Karam and Amrit's arrival, the town where they had stopped to change buses for Gujranwala had been attacked. They had arrived to a scene of desolation and had waited in vain for a bus that was never to come. Transport links around the whole area had been disrupted by hijacks and lootings. They were lucky they didn't get a bus – chances are they wouldn't have got off it alive.

The trucks rolled forward with a deliberate constancy, as though any pause might alter the rhythm of history into which they were drawing the displaced and the dispossessed. People continued to pile on to the moving vehicles. They jumped on and held fast wherever they could, like iron filings attracted to a magnet. As the trucks filled up it became harder for people to alight in groups. They started to split up. Families dispersed to different vehicles. Lovers separated. Children were unparented. Person and possession were divided. The trucks rolled on. Stragglers became frantic. Bundles of provisions fell to the road, discarded by those who realized they would have a better chance of saving themselves without their possessions. At the very back of the convoy a baby was thrown into the air. It flew – spurred on by shouts of love and invocations to God – and fell into the empty arms of a woman whose own child had been murdered in one of the recent massacres. Such were the tragic twists of fortune in that strange and tortured year: the time was out of joint, the country was being disjointed, but in unexpected and undistinguished ways individuals were united.

The army drove their human cargo to DAV College, Lahore, where there were already seventeen thousand people in a building with capacity for three thousand. By the end of that week, the number would rise to thirty thousand. It was a wretched set-up. People were indiscriminately packed into every available space. They occupied the balconies and the lawns, and even on the stairs the desperate struggled to hold on to a diagonal survival. Sanitation was poor, everyone defecated where they wanted – inside or outside, it didn't seem to matter. The Mushq was intolerable, the mood grim. Karam and Amrit were absorbed into the rows of refugees and assumed the communal rhythm of eating, washing, asking for the latest news and then, no better informed, sleeping.

Within the haphazard living arrangements, the Hindu sections were easily identifiable by the bright little deities that had travelled with their owners and were now the recipients of urgent pujas for deliverance from this hellish place. It was, however, coloured turbans that dominated the place. Sikh men, anxious and highly strung, gathered to speculate on how things would develop.

Amidst the chaos, small-scale enterprise was already at work. Pan-wallahs, watch-menders, shoe-shiners, ear-cleaners, hair-cutters – every sort of trader whose tools could be carried on his person, and whose practice required only a limited manual skill, set up shop in a rudimentary way. But the real business was being done by dealers in unreality. Fortune-tellers, homeopathic doctors and priests exercised a lucrative verbal dexterity on crowds let down by logic and anxious for the consolations of myth and magic. The granthis and pandits were busy with a cycle of morning, afternoon, evening, pre-meal, birth and death blessings and prayers. These, together with the demand for extra prayers to guarantee the safety of loved ones, the health of ill ones, the wealth of robbed ones and self-survival, made for a demanding schedule. The camp buzzed with the chanting of different refrains. Sikh affirmations of God's greatness:

Vaheguruji ka Khalsa, Vaheguruji kee fateh . . .

Hindu appeals for deliverance by the universal God:

Om jai Jagdish hare
Swāmi jai Jagdish hare . . .

These aural offerings from within the camp were penetrated every four hours by a powerful 'Alllaaaaaahhhhh Huuu Aaaakbaaarrrrrrrrrr!' from the outside world. This reverberating chord was a chilling reminder of the uncertainty beyond the walls of the college. There was anger and resentment against Muslims festering in the camp, and yet many of the Hindus and Sikhs that populated it were there only because they had been saved by the kindness of Muslims. People told stories of how they had been hidden and protected by

56

Muslim neighbours or friends while the rest of their village had been massacred. Karam heard these tales of gratitude but saw also the doubt in people's eyes. Who could they trust, who could they blame? Who deserved the curses that fell so passionately from anguished lips? Surely a whole religion could not be blamed?

Fortune-tellers studied astrological maps and creased palms with deliberate solemnity. They shook their heads and tutted. They sat and stared into the distance for hours at a time, and on rising would press their hands to their temples with the pained look of men who have the burden of inventing the future. For most of this breed severity is a hallmark of legitimacy, but not so for Achariya. He was a funny-looking man. His round bald head shone like a crystal ball atop a wide bulbous body, and his neck appeared to have sunk out of sight in respectful submission to this rotundity. He also had a funny way of speaking, jovially rounding off everything he said with rhymes:

'There are answers everywhere, everywhere,
But the way to find the right one is through there,
through *there* –'

And he would point to the heart of the person he was addressing. Some people said Achariya had cultivated his extraordinary shape and size in order to have a maximum surface area exposed to the world to receive those 'answers from everywhere'. They insisted that his physique facilitated the refraction of everyone's rays of fate towards his own heart, where they could be expressed as revelations that people were unable or unwilling to find for themselves. If you saw Achariya in action this certainly seemed credible. Despite his size he moved with surprising agility, rolling through crowds, his senses missing nothing, his mouth rapidly predicting everything.

Others believed Achariya carried the world in his belly – that's why it was so large. Perhaps they were right, for at times, while he was thinking, the fortune-teller would sweep his hands horizontally across his stomach in the same way that one might spin the world on a suspended globe – or nurse a bad case of indigestion. And it was not just a world of continents that he spun, but oceans of possibility and impossibility, seas of sickness and health, islands of relief and torment, currents of uncertainty, icebergs of doubt, winds of change, skies of clarity . . . So when his hands suddenly became still on his stomach, supporting it as a mother does her unborn child, you knew that his mouth – if it didn't burp – would give birth to your future.

Rival soothsayers thought Achariya frivolous, a few people found his manner dubious, but, for the most part, his brand of rhyming prophecy proved popular in the camp, where foreboding was plentiful. Sometimes he would release a spray of quick, unsolicited rhymes of advice to individuals he passed – as if he was bursting with premonitions that simply had to be revealed. On one of his turns through the camp he overheard an obese asthmatic lady wheezing nostalgically about eating snacks on the streets of Delhi. Unable to resist, Achariya leaned towards her and pronounced:

> 'Oh lady-ji, forget your thoughts of pani poori
> And see this as an opportunity
> To shed a stone or two or three
> And let your breath flow more freely.'

When she glared at him indignantly, Achariya came closer still and whispered:

'Take care, or this may be the last place that you see . . .'

To a worried Jurnail Singh, who had been separated from his wife and children and didn't know their fate, Achariya offered a different perspective. Drawing inspiration from the Western philosophy he'd read, he advised:

'Dwell not on what might have befallen them,
Hold to this moment – *carpe diem*.
The best that you can do for them is strive
To stay this course and survive.'

Karam was wary of such consolations; he had never believed in people who claimed to know the future. Nor did he set much store by the consolations of religion. So for him there was no source of comfort in the camp, and the relief he'd initially felt at having arrived there safely turned to exasperation. Amrit, by contrast, remained calm. This was not just because he was older than Karam or more experienced in India's strange ways, but because he accepted that little could be done about the situation. Amrit had been travelling around with Karam ever since he'd arrived in India. At first he had escorted his cousin out of obligation. But an easy companionship had developed between the two men and so, after the first few weeks when Karam had become familiar with the towns and the transport links, Amrit had continued to accompany him everywhere.

Karam was moody. He worried about being seen to renege on the marriage promise he had made to Sarna's family – he should have been back with them in Kashmir by now. He fretted about how to get news back to his family in Kenya. Most of all, Karam was upset by the unhygienic conditions. Nothing could mask the mephitic Mushq of too many people crowded together in too little space. Others seemed to become accustomed to the smell, but the relief of odour fatigue was not to be Karam's – every inhalation was a new assault. He felt disgusted by the people around him, and yet, he knew, he himself was becoming increasingly indistinguishable from them. Getting his shoes polished every day made no difference. He'd soon be as helpless, filthy and inconsequential as the next man.

A week after they had arrived in the camp, the water supply was cut off. Rumour had it that Muslims were responsible. For four days no alternative supply was available. Conditions in the camp deteriorated rapidly. The squalor worsened and disease was the inevitable consequence. Typhoid ripped through the building, whose inhabitants were already weakened by displacement, depression and hunger. Outside, the heat raged; inside, people's temperatures rose and one by one they succumbed to fever. While the authorities ineffectually tried to make arrangements for water, thousands of dehydrated bodies were emptied of their vital fluids. 'This bloody country,' Karam raged to Amrit. 'Useless. Not fit for living in.'

Karam was not spared. Disease seemed to ravage him with a particularly insidious aggressiveness. Perhaps he was being punished. He had enjoyed India's bounty without gratitude. He had shown dislike for her people. Now Mother India was giving him a darned good lesson in the folly of prejudice. She would show him that no man was beneath bestiality when his life depended on it. She would teach him that, although he had tried to leave her behind, India was still in him. She set all the stakes against Karam, but like a true mother, kind even in cruelty, she gave him one saving grace – Amrit. By some miracle Amrit avoided illness. As Karam succumbed to fever, it was Amrit's fervour that spared them both. His attention to Karam made him heedless of himself. Indeed, he seemed to draw strength from self-effacement. When palpitations wracked Karam's body, Amrit calmed him with hushed words and cooled him by fanning an old newspaper. Whatever food and water came their way, Amrit gave first to Karam, tirelessly spooning nourishment into his cousin's wasting body. He never left Karam's side except to get something for him. But Karam grew steadily weaker and after a few days he lost consciousness. He would never know how he had lain between corpses hardened with dried excretions and rigor mortised hopes. He would never know that in the midst of foulness and death, people could laugh and dance. He would never know the worst or the best of what happened in the camp, or elsewhere, in those fraught months before Partition.

Amrit was witness to everything. He lined up outside to get water when it was finally available. The heat was intense, the water distribution ineptly manned. One man at the front of the line filled his bucket with water and, unable to wait, dunked his head into the bucket and gulped. The effect made him delirious. He wailed with pleasure and impulsively poured the whole bucket over himself. With that one movement he unleashed the longing of the others. Men, women and children surged around numerous water barrels, stripped down and, side by side, poured the precious liquid over themselves. They laughed, cried and shrieked with delight, their bodies twisting and cavorting in a fluid rush. This sudden carelessness, this waste and extravagance after days of waterless withering, was like a mass self-baptism.

Amidst all this, only Amrit noticed the incredulous SNAP – SNAP – SNAP of a Kodak Brownie flash camera. A photojournalist was recording the strange communal wash before heading into the college building for more shots. SNAP, over the entrance blackened with grime and sewered slime. SNAP – SNAP, past the bodies, hundreds squatting, lying, moaning, dying, dead. SNAP, through streams of vomit, urine and dysentery. SNAP, in a corner, the sun streaming through the window highlighting more rags of bodies soiled with their efforts at life. SNAP, a face rising up from the horizontal stasis, turban hanging loosely above a shrunken face lucid with fantasy, one hand reaching out beyond the photographer's vision to a mirage of water created where the sun had met his delusion. A delirious Karam, unwittingly SNAPPED on to the front page of the *Eastern Times* the following day.

It was only because Amrit followed the man to ask for news, help, hope, *anything*, that it became clear the reporter was after a story. So Amrit put words to the pictures, and in return the journalist promised to leave a copy of the *Eastern Times* with one of the camp guards the next day. When Amrit received the paper, there on the front cover was a picture of the hell he and countless others were living through every day: in the background, bodies lay strewn in various postures of anguish. At the centre of the image Karam was staring at the camera, his hand outstretched towards the viewer in a benign plea for mercy.

Amrit tore out the page to save it. As he tucked it into his pocket, a voice spoke behind him:

> 'Nothing can guarantee immortality,
> Seize the day or risk fatality.
> Find what means you can to go
> From here, for you dare not know
> What end awaits you otherwise –
> I urge you, leave before sunrise.'

Amrit turned and found himself looking into Achariya's unflinching gaze, the eyes bright with premonitions. As Amrit's lips struggled to form a 'what?' or a 'why?', Achariya spoke again:

> 'Your name means nectar
> Your role is protector
> Heed the call of who you are
> And go to your destiny in Amritsar.'

Achariya paused for a moment, as if to let the prophecy sink in. Then he added, 'Oh, and please would you leave me the rest of that newspaper?'

Returning to Karam, Amrit could see that his condition was already worse. The only hope was to act immediately, as Achariya had advised. Later that night, two people slipped out of the camp, one carried in the arms of the other. They requisitioned an abandoned rickshaw and rode away.

4

Persini was all edges and points, her small frame un-softened by feminine padding. Bones protruded shyly at her wrists and collar when she wore short sleeves or a wide neckline. Little breasts poked out from under her kameez like grapes. Above her neck, however, Persini's angularity made for an unusual hard-edged loveliness. Her ears were delicately elfin, her cheekbones sharply chiselled. Her eyebrows were startling and dramatic: inverted Vs over the disturbed depths of her big brown eyes.

These eyes often darted furtively towards Karam and Sarna. Persini noticed enviously how comfortable they seemed with each other. She contrasted this with the slow and awkward acquaintance she and Sukhi were still making. Exclude the occasions on which she'd met Sukhi before their wedding and she could count on her fingers the number of days she'd spent in her husband's company. For most of their married life Sukhi had been chasing other pleasures. He was gone for weeks at a time on wild safaris. He would return loaded with meat – deer, partridge or guinea fowl – and flushed with the triumph of his kills. It was the only time Persini ever saw him worthy of his name – sukhi, happy. Would that he could feel such passion for her, that she could be his happy catch! But after just a few days at home Sukhi became dukhi, unhappy. Finally, moody and restless, he would disappear again.

The days of Sukhi's absence were etched as darkly on Persini's heart as the colour of the red kidney beans she collected to keep count of them. The beans already spilled out of the stainless-steel bowl hidden in her wardrobe. She had started to accumulate them as a consolation to herself, a way of convincing herself that surely he would be back soon, for too many days had elapsed since his departure. Already each bean that Persini dropped into the overflowing bowl was a silent accusation against Sukhi, a sigh against life's injustice. Many years later, when the family packed up to leave that house, they'd find kidney beans everywhere. The satiny maroon ovals would clatter in drawers, they'd fall from the folds of clothes, they'd appear in the toes of socks and the corners of pockets. The family would express puzzlement. Persini would remain silent. She'd watch as the evidence of the thousands of days of Sukhi's absence, and the countless tears she'd cried over them, was gathered up and thrown into the rubbish or scattered in the compound outside. Birds, smelling the sadness on the beans, wouldn't peck at them and the soil, which would eventually cover the beans, could never entice them to sprout. Like the person who'd collected them, they would have shrivelled up and died inside.

Even on the days when Sukhi was home, the two of them weren't really together except at mealtimes. And they were only alone when they went to bed for the night. Still, some would say it's not the quantity of the time together but the quality that counts. Certainly, as far as the family was concerned, it had been quality time – wasn't there a child growing inside Persini to prove it? 'Such a successful union, such a blessing. Record timing, huh, Sukhi? Very good. Like father, like son.'

Baoji's virility had long been a subject of admiration. To have sired eight sons was a feat indeed, even if the high infant-mortality rate of the era had taken the edge off his achievement by allowing only six of them to grow up. People used to joke, 'You just have to wave Fauja Singh's underwear over your head and you'll conceive a boy.' So, to the world, Sukhi the great hunter had now proved his mettle as a husband. Never mind that Persini didn't know what his favourite food was, or that they hadn't held a conversation lasting more than a couple of minutes. All this was peripheral. A baby was on the way. It was a good match.

Persini noticed the way Karam found excuses to brush repeatedly against Sarna. Several times she had seen him, for no apparent reason, ask her for the bunch of keys which were always tucked inside her bra. Karam would take the keys and clasp their warmth tightly in his hand. Once Persini had seen him sniff them, inhaling their Mushq with something approaching reverence.

Persini had never seen romantic love before. For her, all close human relations had been characterized by stern respect and stifling decorum. Karam and Sarna's love was a revelation. She was moved but also hurt by it, because she recognized how far she was from experiencing such a feeling. Jealousy can be so irrational. Although Persini was covetous of the seeming harmony between Karam and Sarna, what really made her green was the sense that it might have been *her* enjoying such marital bliss. *She* could have married Karam. She had known him all her life, they had been playmates as children. If only her parents had approached his family a little earlier, before Karam had left for India . . .

The truth is, things between Karam and Sarna were not as harmonious as Persini perceived – no one ever knows the misunderstandings and silences that bind people to each other. But there is no doubt they were in love. Because of this, Sarna felt confident enough to stand up to Karam. And he, against his better instincts, often felt compelled to indulge her. This was partly what made married life in the family home in Nairobi difficult for him.

Almost nightly, on their mattress in the kitchen, they would argue before making love.

Sarna regularly chided Karam for accepting their relegation to the kitchen. 'How could you agree? You should have said something.'

'It wouldn't have made a difference.' Karam ran his fingers through her hair and the smell of the day's cooking filled his nostrils. 'Biji had already decided and she never changes her mind.'

'Your hunter brother isn't even here most of the time,' Sarna said. 'Months we've been here and hardly any sign of him. Persini's got a bedroom all to herself and we're camping here like second-class citizens.' Sarna raised her head, thinking she'd heard a slight shuffle near the kitchen door, but all was silent. 'You should see Persini's eyeballs every time I go to her room to put something in the trunks. Daggers, I tell you, daggers.'

'That's just the way she looks. She doesn't mean anything.' Karam tried to distract Sarna by kissing the constellation of cuts, nicks and burns – the inevitable side-effects of food experiments – on her hands. He kissed each wound better, and in the doing so tasted its origins. This one on the index finger whispered of chopping raw chicken, another one on the thumb was haunted by the slicing of fresh coriander. A little burn, below the knuckle of the index finger on the right hand, sizzled against his tongue with the memory of hot mustard oil.

Even if Karam succeeded in sidetracking Sarna one night, she was on his case again the next.

'How long are we going to live like this? I can't cope. I'm not used to this. My baoji was a DSO,' Sarna would complain. 'What is this life? Day and night, kitchen kitchen kitchen.'

Karam would listen and hold her until complaints gave way again to kisses.

Then, after a few months, Sarna changed tactics. Instead of highlighting her own victimization she began to emphasize Karam's. 'Hai, Jee, what kind of life is this?' She massaged his scalp to ease a migraine. '*You* are the eldest, *you* pay the bills and *you* sleep on the floor in the kitchen. It's not right. They're making a fool of you.'

Karam was too surprised by this new perspective to respond immediately. He had never chosen to see things in such a way. Nonetheless, Sarna's continued insistence on the injustice of the circumstances began to eat away at him.

'What are you?' Sarna grew bolder in the face of Karam's silence. 'Man or mouse? We'll be out in the backyard soon. What will happen when Mandeep gets married? They're on the lookout for a match, you know. Just think of it, Jee. What will happen when we have children? You have to do something.'

Karam was disturbed. He had always tried to do the

right thing, to act responsibly, and for this to be suddenly deemed the ignominious acquiescence of a dupe was galling.

'You must do something. Promise me you'll do something. Promise me you'll say something.' Sarna arched her body pleadingly into Karam's. 'Promise, Jeeeeee!' she cooed, deliberately lingering on the endearment.

Karam promised, and decided against passing on Biji's complaint that the neckline on Sarna's kameez that day had been a bit too deep-cut and fancy. 'It's shameful,' Biji had said to him. 'Tell her to cover up. This is a house full of men. Decency must be observed. Tell her not to wear it again.' As far as Karam could see, the kameez looked pretty inoffensive. He hadn't said so to Biji, though. Oh no, he had apologized and promised to chastise Sarna. But now he didn't have the energy for the heated debate and tears the criticism was certain to elicit. This became his regular dilemma. He was like a punch bag into which Biji and Sarna pounded their anxieties and grievances. He received the blows, shook suitably in response and then settled back into stationary suspension without revealing anything to either.

Karam continued to make promises of a new life to Sarna, but he had no real idea how things could be changed. He couldn't envisage any sort of confrontation with his parents. He and Sarna couldn't move away – that was out of the question, it just wasn't done. Nor could the whole family move to a bigger house, they couldn't afford it. Karam was pretty much supporting them all. He'd got a job as a clerk at the Treasury just a few days after his return from India. Biji and Baoji had made it clear that things had been tough in Karam's absence. Sukhi's hunting spoils couldn't be depended on, Mandeep's salary was meagre and Guru was still unemployed. So, spurred on by guilt, Karam had taken the first job that came his way. He accepted the burden of supporting the family unquestioningly because he had been doing it since he was fifteen.

Baoji had taken Karam out of school just before he was due to take his O levels. It was not a step Baoji had taken lightly, even though, being uneducated himself, he had little knowledge about the value of education. His concern had always been how to get by. However, he had recognized that his eldest son was gifted. The teachers at Khalsa School sang Karam's praises at every opportunity, and Baoji had noticed that Karam always had his nose in some book. So when the pressures of providing for an ever-growing family became too much for Baoji to manage alone, he was reluctant to do the traditional thing and get the eldest son to start helping him. He'd struggled with himself for weeks and had only managed to make the decision with the aid of Biji's practical reasoning. 'It has to be Karam,' she had insisted. 'What good will Sukhi be? He's old enough, but you know as well as I do that he isn't reliable like Karam. And Mandeep is still too young. No point worrying about it, Sardharji. What has to be has to be.'

So Karam had left school and joined Baoji doing manual work on various construction sites around the country: Kisumu, Machakos, Entebbe, Taveta. They went wherever there was work. Karam had hated every minute of it. He'd found the labour demeaning. He had wanted to be an engineer. But although his dream had been snatched away, he never expressed any regret to his parents. That was not the way he had been brought up. The scars of his disappointment would only show up when he became a father. Then, with unrelenting rigour, he would push his children to excel at school and pursue higher studies.

The courtyard of Khalsa School was empty. The children had gone home for the day, but hints of their presence lingered in the footprints, smudges and streaks that their playing feet had drawn on the murum playground. Karam strode across this artwork, adding his presence to the canvas with oblivious shoe-strokes. Today there was no room for regret in his mind as he moved through this environment, once so longed for and denied. Karam walked around the back of the school and knocked on a closed door, across which, in white, the words LAKHVINDER SINGH – BSc were roughly painted.

A long trail of ants preceded Karam into the room. From a crack in the floor near the doorframe they marched around a stack of paper, under the desk, over the dead black nail on Lakhvinder Singh's big toe and collided, in an orgy of busy greed, around the sticky sweet wrapper beside his sandalled foot.

Lakhvinder Singh was oblivious to this activity. Sucking hard on a lemon sweet, he marked essays and scratched his freckled nose. His bright-blue turban was huge. If it rained while he was supervising recreation the children would crowd around him, pressing close for the umbrella shelter of his headgear. A maroon cardigan stretched tiredly over his wide belly all year round, regardless of the weather. Its baggy pockets were full of sweets. 'Lucky Pick Pockets' his students called them, because whenever you reached in for a sweet you always got your favourite flavour.

'Masterji?' Karam poked his head around the door.

'Karam!' Lahkvinder Singh looked up. 'What a nice surprise. Come in, sit down.' He set about shifting papers off the only other chair in his tiny office, which was crammed with books and pictures of the Sikh gurus. In this room Masterji had been trying to write a treatise on Sikhism for as long as anyone could remember. He stood up and patted Karam's shoulder. He was genuinely pleased to see his old student. Karam had been one of the best pupils he'd ever taught and he'd been sorely disappointed when the boy's parents had opted to take their gifted son out of school. 'I haven't seen you for a while.' Masterji sat down again and tucked the sweet into his left cheek. 'When was the last time? Two, no, almost three years ago? Before you went to India.'

Karam nodded a little awkwardly, ashamed that he had not found the time to visit his mentor since his return.

'Is everything OK? Have you come for more books?' Masterji's tongue rolled over the small protrusion in his cheek.

'I would like more books but I don't have much time to read at the moment,' Karam said. These days he was finding he had less and less space in which to think, let alone read. He felt crowded by people and their endless demands. 'Actually I just wanted to talk to you.' He had come here many times after leaving school. Encouraged by Masterji, he had continued to study, and they had sat together in this very room and talked about his progress. Those had been some of the most prized hours of Karam's adolescence. Even when he grew out of the school textbooks, Karam had continued to call on Masterji. They would discuss religion or politics and Masterji would always lend him some new book to read. This time, though, Karam's visit had a more personal charge to it and he was a little unsure about how to begin.

Sensing this, Masterji offered him a sweet. 'Here.' He pulled at his jumper and held up one of the pockets. When Karam refused, Masterji knew it must be serious.

'I'm married.' Karam traced a finger over the sparkling metal buckle of his belt. He'd spent ten minutes polishing it the day before. 'We've been married over a year now. My wife is pregnant. Due soon.'

'Yes, yes, I've heard. Congratulations.' Masterji quickly crunched his sweet. He noticed the staccato strain into which Karam's speech had fallen and heard the anxiety behind the brusqueness. 'The responsibilities are starting to pile up, I suppose. Family, marriage, children – these things can take over your life. You'll have to struggle to keep a space in your head just for yourself. Now you know why I try to spend so much time here.' Masterji waved a hand around the room. 'I'm lucky I have this place as an escape. It drives my wife mad but it keeps me sane, and long ago I decided it was worth preserving my sanity over hers – after all, who is the one writing the history of Sikhism?'

'I met her in India, you know, my wife.' Karam crossed his legs.

'Your father told me about it at the gurudwara. They were very concerned about you. No one heard from you for months, they kept doing ardaas for you in the temple. I understand you were caught up in the Partition troubles. More recently your Baoji said something to me about your picture appearing in a newspaper there. I was quite intrigued.' Masterji smiled.

Karam pinched his ear and frowned. Was there anyone they hadn't told about that photograph? They'd been announcing it left, right and centre, as though it was a great achievement. 'It was taken in Lahore. I was in a refugee camp, face to face with the worst degradation and humiliation. I was forced to see how people can suffer. Then I became ill and was unconscious for months so I missed the main events. People ask me questions, you know. They expect me to be able to describe things, but I have nothing to say. Communal violence? Don't ask me. The fifteenth of August 1947? I don't have a clue. I was there, but I can't claim to have a grain of knowledge. It's as though I was chosen to suffer, and then allowed to bypass the worst of the suffering, only to be tormented with the fate of trying to piece together some kind of sense from what I half know.'

There was silence. Masterji dug a finger into his mouth to scrape away the last crystals of sugar that were stuck in his back teeth. 'I imagine there are many like you, trying to derive some sense and purpose from what happened,' he said. 'I have been dwelling on it as well, attempting to surmise what it will mean for India and for the Sikhs. It's a futile speculation. It's still too early to know how events will pan out. Things haven't calmed down even yet, from what I hear. And, unfortunately, I find myself more and more inclined to pessimism.' He put his hand over his chin and clasped the thick bulk of his flowing beard into a tail. 'I think we Sikhs have lost out completely. Muslims have their Pakistan, Hindus have their Hindustan. What about us? Where's our Khalistan? Another ill-fated twist in our humiliating history. Gone are the glory days of Maharaja Ranjeet Singh. He foresaw it, you know. As he was dying, he predicted, "The day is not far off when the map of Punjab will be painted red." He was referring to the British, of course. As they approached from Calcutta, they marked all acquisitions in red on the map of India. But Ranjeet Singh's vision has been played out twice: once by the British and now in this bitter bloodbath which has drenched the region in a violent red.' Masterji sighed and shook his head. 'Since Ranjeet Singh it has just been a ghastly descent to in-fighting and self-betrayal for us Sikhs. We've been our own worst enemies.'

Karam had heard parts of this tirade before. The state of Sikh history since Ranjeet Singh was a theme close to Masterji's heart. He had once told Karam that he couldn't bring himself to complete his treatise until he perceived some hope for a change in the fortunes of the Sikh people. Well, Karam now thought, it seems Masterji still has some waiting to do.

'I sometimes feel that my involvement was also a kind of humiliation,' Karam said slowly. 'But then I think – no, it is what I make of it. I just need to understand it better. I feel there must be some greater lesson in what I went through.'

'Why, Karam?' Masterji asked. 'Why must there be a special lesson for you? You were not alone in what you experienced. Many suffered the same, more suffered worse. Have you ever considered that it might just be chance? That you were in the wrong place at the wrong time, but you got lucky and got out.'

'I've thought about chance too, Masterji, but this photograph rules that out for me.' Karam held out the newspaper cutting, which he had brought with him. 'Why me? Why am I the face of a people suffering? I *survived*. Even my cousin who saved me ended up dying. Why am I the hollow record of what happened? You're interested in history, I thought you would help me make sense of it.'

Masterji studied the picture. 'I have no greater grasp on

sense than you, Karam. Any evidence is by its nature partial and incomplete. Even if you remembered what happened in those weeks, your version would be just that – a version. At best, it might make for a more coherent narrative in your own head, but even that I doubt. However things had unfolded, I suspect you would be deliberating on them in this same vein. In the end, as you suggested, it is not the experience itself but the reflection on it and reaction to it that counts. We all want to find some sense of purpose. *You* are looking for it in the experience you had in India.'

'Perhaps so, but that doesn't make it any less valid.' Karam crossed his arms over his chest.

'That is true,' Masterji said gently. 'Your need for reflection and understanding differentiates you from others, who might have seen the same but are content to slot back into the normal rhythm of life and forget what happened. I do not wish to dissuade you from thinking, Karam, I only want to help you do it as clearly as possible. And I offer a word of caution.' Masterji leaned forward. 'Do not expect a single, certain truth to emerge from this, and don't be tempted to conclude that what you went through in India is the most defining experience of your life. You must stay open, much is yet to happen. And often it is not the big events but the smallest ones that are our most defining moments.'

'It's just—' Karam broke off in frustration. 'To have been present at a time of such historical significance, and yet . . . at the same time to have been so conspicuously absent, seems, I don't know – too cruel a twist of fate. I just can't reconcile myself to it.'

'Have you ever considered, Karam,' Masterji proposed, 'that perhaps in your unconsciousness you were, in a way, most profoundly in the moment? Have you thought that the wasting of your flesh, the burning of your fever, the pain that wracked your being, and the delusions that terrorized your mind, echoed the larger-scale affliction that beset India? You were an involuntary mirror of India's turmoil and thereby a tiny speck in her history.'

'But surely to be part of a great moment, to be part of history, you have to feel it in the moment?' Karam's outstretched hand quickly curled into a tight fist as if he'd caught a fly. 'This is my regret and my shame – that I was an ignorant victim and now I am an ignorant survivor.'

Masterji shook his head. 'Perhaps,' he said, 'it is always the case with history that the value of the moment is revealed in retrospect.'

Karam was silent. For the first time, he strongly disagreed with his teacher. He was uncomfortable with this discord, the realization that age and authority didn't have a monopoly on righteousness. But he couldn't bring himself to voice his dissent – he felt guilty just thinking it. Still, he was adamant that you had to feel the momentousness of the moment in the moment. He was sure that to have any claim on history you had to know you were part of it, making it – however small your role. And as he considered this, the first inklings of an idea that was to influence his life came to him. History was being made continuously everywhere. All he had to do was find it. If he could feel a great moment of history, perhaps he would get over the dull sense of anticlimax that had been haunting him ever since he'd returned from India. He would find history. Once, history had caught him unawares; now he would seek out and catch *it*.

5

'Call Mina Masi. Go get Mina Masi,' Persini rushed in and ordered Karam as he sat finishing dinner. That could only mean one thing – Sarna's baby was on its way. He hurried off as directed. Mina Masi lived only about three minutes away, on the other side of the compound. Everyone called her Mina Masi – grandparents, mothers, fathers, children – even her lovers. In the typical Indian way, she was everybody's aunt. Yet the name was more than just a term of address. She had been Mina Masi for so long no one even remembered that she might once have been someone else. Govinda Singh, who worked at the immigration office, claimed that even her passport just said Mina Masi.

Karam had known her when he was growing up. She had helped give birth to his three youngest brothers, who had been born in Kenya, and two other siblings who had died. Karam had never really taken much notice of her – he'd never had cause to. Now, as he explained that she was needed to help with the birth of his own child, he felt embarrassed. He hadn't really considered what it was to be a father until this moment. Suddenly he was on the threshold of the new role and unsure how to behave. So he took refuge in silence as the two of them walked back to the family home together.

On the way, Karam remembered the story he'd heard recently from his friend, Harvinder, who'd just graduated to parenthood himself. Harvinder had said that at the birth of a son men always gave Mina Masi a nose ring and, in turn, they received special favours she reserved only for the fathers of the sons she helped bring into the world. Karam hadn't given much heed to his friend's story – it had seemed too fantastical, somehow, the creation of a man heated up on drink and kept too long from his wife's bed. Besides, Karam thought, she can't still be up to such tricks – she's too old. He glanced at Mina Masi. The elegant body and energetic movements of the dark-skinned, slender woman next to him belied her fifty-plus years. Her hair, in its big tight bun, was still thick and shiny, with deep-orange flashes of henna betraying the strands that must have turned white. She was wearing a turquoise sari with a baby-pink paisley pattern and looked like a hail of good tidings as she walked along. Karam, discomfited at finding her attractive, decided that her attire was rather inappropriate for the task at hand. Surely something less cumbersome and more subdued would be better?

In fact, Mina Masi always wore bright saris. Fuchsia and lime green, yellow and deep purple – such were the vibrant combinations that characterized her. She carried intimations of festivity in her wake because it was fitting for her vocation – what a joyous occasion it is when a baby is brought safely into the world.

Karam snuck another glance in Mina Masi's direction and saw her nose ring wink at him enticingly. Even the dim rays of street light seemed to be cavorting and twisting in their eagerness to pass through the golden loop. He looked away quickly. There was something unsettling about the gleaming ring. It seemed to have a body language of its own and swung suggestively in his direction, like a mujrah dancer, despite its wearer's apparent indifference to him. Karam remembered that it had been the fantasy of the ring Harvinder had raved about. Something about entering the ring and achieving complete satisfaction—

'Oh, juldi, juldi! Hurry, Mina Masi, things are moving too fast, really!' Persini's shrill voice interrupted Karam's thoughts. She had been pacing up and down outside the house waiting for them. Mina Masi hurried after her, and Karam was left with his mysterious recollections of a fetishized nose ring.

As well as her bright clothes, Mina Masi was distinguished by the large gold ring, at least three centimetres wide, which swung from her left nostril. The nose ring was huge by any standards and on Mina Masi's slight frame it looked gigantic. It hung down just over the left corner of her lips and swayed to the tune of her moving mouth. Sometimes if it was getting in the way too much, like when she was eating, Mina Masi would flip it away with a serpentine swirl of her tongue. She did this with a casual grace, as one might flick a strand of hair off one's face. Sometimes she would run her tongue over the rim of the ring slowly and deliberately, as a cat might lick her kittens. The action was charged with sexual suggestion and men had been known to swoon as they watched it.

Mina Masi had sported her pendulous hoop for as long as anyone could remember. But few people knew why she had started to wear it. Early in her career, a delighted

Nirmal Singh Body-Builder (so called because he had the skill of being able to restore any clapped-out vehicle back to newness) had stopped by Mina Masi's house to give her a large gold nose ring. The gift was to thank her for successfully helping with the birth of his first son after seven long sad years which had yielded only five daughters. The nose ring was 4.2 centimetres wide. 'Exactly the circumference of the weapon that has produced the boy,' Body-Builder had told Mina Masi proudly. Not one to be easily embarrassed, she'd jokingly asked him to prove it. The elated Body-Builder had been only too happy to oblige. The ring then proved trickier to get off than it had been to slide on – the subject it encompassed having been alerted in the process. Mina had been obliged to resort to delicate means of lubrication and coaxing to slip it off. While engaged in this endeavour the two of them made an accidental but extraordinary discovery about the possibility of absolute pleasure within the circumference of a ring. In a ring's perfect form all longing is contained, concentrated and satisfied. Body-Builder was hooked. He had returned the next day in the hope that the experience could be repeated. But Mina Masi had had time to consider things. The life of a midwife is not easy. It has many rewards, but it does not bring fortune. Mina Masi determined to break out of this mould. She made it clear to Body-Builder that a repeat performance would have to wait until the birth of his next son – and the presentation of another nose ring. 'Feel free to inform all father-to-be friends,' Mina Masi told him. 'But please make clear – terms and conditions apply.' Body-Builder was taken aback by this boldness and departed in a huff. 'I see it's business before pleasure with you, huh, Mina Masi?'

Initially Body-Builder had resolved not to tell anyone about his little adventure. But it's hard to discover gold and keep the knowledge to yourself. After a few weeks he had savoured his secret to blandness and needed to share it with someone in order to feel again its wonder. So he told his brother and work partner, Chindi Gear-Box, an expert on the intricacies of every kind of gear. Thus the secret was advertised. It passed by word of mouth from one imminent father to the next. Fierce oaths of secrecy had to be sworn and revenge was promised for anyone who compromised the discretion of the set-up. The receipt of 'nath news', nose-ring news, as it was called, was like a rite of passage for men. It was a sort of formal initiation into fatherhood – at the hands, for many, of the very woman who had helped bring them into the world. This was how the men of the Sikh Colony along Ngara Road and Park Road came to develop a fetish for nose rings. Mina Masi ran rings around them with the dexterity of a hoop-thrower at a funfair. Men toiled eagerly to get their wives pregnant, and sons, always coveted in Indian families, became even more prized by their fathers – and all because Mina Masi adhered strictly to her policy of one ring-a-ling-ding per male birth.

Mina Masi was an enterprising businesswoman. She wanted more than a fifty-fifty guarantee of payment at the end of a pregnancy. So she spread another secret through the community of Sikh women – a foolproof formula for the conception of boys. Mina Masi had been instructed in the method by her mother-in-law, Mathaji Sant, who had been the proud mother of fourteen sons. The old lady had begun her lesson by saying, 'The most effective way involves the exercise of some restraint. If menstruation starts in the morning, the woman must wait *fifteen* days. If it starts in the evening, she must wait *sixteen* days.' Mathaji had stressed the numbers as though they were a lifetime. Mina Masi, still innocent and easily shocked in those days, had not known where to look. Dizzy with embarrassment, she had fixed her eyes on a crack in the wall. 'Meanwhile, the man must wait too. No release of any sort is permitted – or it won't work. His seed needs to build up and get stale. The older the seed, the more potent it is,' Mathaji had explained. 'Flavour develops, you see – just like with chicken biriyani – so the man's seed can work better to make boys. That fifteenth or sixteenth day is the crucial window. After that, unless you're first-time lucky, like I always was, complete abstinence or caution must be observed until the following month. Follow my directions and you will make me a happy nani for the grandsons I deserve.'

Where Mathaji had chanced upon this boy-guarantee formula, Mina Masi never had the chance to find out. Nor did she get to test the theory. A few months after their conversation, an epidemic of smallpox had whipped through the village of Harnali where they lived and wiped out the entire family. Mina Masi herself had only been spared because she'd temporarily returned to her own village to attend her father's funeral.

On the strength of that information, Mina Masi was now raking in gold. She had added her own twist to old Mathaji's instructions. While giving the XY germination guidance to women, Mina Masi made them drink a personally concocted brew of herbs. She hinted that the potion would help create the right internal conditions for success. She was unabashedly explicit when explaining the method. If the women to whom she spoke were embarrassed, she pretended not to notice. Sometimes she actually relished their discomfort and mischievously added a further equation to the formula. 'The position of intercourse is crucial if the results are to be successful,' she would whisper confidentially. To the overweight and indolent Madhu, she said, 'He must only enter you from behind.' To prim and prudish Sooraj, she solemnly decreed, 'You must be cross-legged to receive his seed.' Whether or not these women had the courage to relay these scandalous suggestions to their husbands, let alone act them out, will remain a mystery. But they must have followed the essence of Mina Masi's rules because the formula proved robust. Sons were born frequently to the women she'd advised, and she reaped the benefits. A hoard of gold rings is not a fortune to be scoffed at. Men being what they are, and Sikh men being especially keen to appear extra manly, the rings were all rather large. Anxious in case news of the requested ring size might filter from Heeraji, the jeweller, into the public domain, most men tended to order outsized rings. Mina Masi repeatedly advised that the ultimate pleasure was in the ring that fitted most perfectly: 'Best fit, best hit.' But for the men, pride always came before a few extra degrees of pleasure, and in the long term this worked to the benefit of Mina Masi's liquidity.

Arriving in the bedroom where Sarna was in labour, Mina Masi took control.

'Bring some hot water and clarified butter,' she said to Persini, whose daughter, Rupi, she had delivered only months before. When Persini returned, Mina Masi was examining Sarna and asking routine questions. She was a little surprised that things were so far advanced in just a few hours. Sarna was already fully dilated and her contractions were sharp and fast. This was unusual for a first birth.

'When did you say the pains started?' Mina Masi asked Persini.

'Oh, two or three hours ago, I think.'

'No, no,' Sarna panted. 'It was longer.' She took another deep breath. 'All day I could –' she shut her eyes and gasped, '– feel it. I didn't –' she puffed, '– kno-o-ow.'

'This *is* first-time birth for you, no?' Mina Masi asked.

'Of course!' Sarna declared. Then, like clouds suddenly altering the tone of a landscape, pain distorted her face. She cried out and pushed as if the force of her labour was also intended to deliver her from the presumptuous question. In the thrust of this vehement reaction she gave birth to twins.

Oh-ooh, double-disaster! Persini thought with glee. Her own failure to produce a son had been eclipsed by this double-whammy of Sarna's. *Twin girls.* Her worry that Sarna would soon be lording it over her with a son had been set to rest. Persini had also noted Mina Masi's 'first time' question and wondered if there might be something to it. After all, Mina Masi was very experienced. If she had needed to ask such a question, there must be a reason. Persini determined to do some investigation. She was excited at the thought of the discoveries she might make about her sister-in-law. It was therefore with genuine delight that she offered her congratulations and spread news of the birth around the family. If her exclamations of goodwill were a little too loud, and her confirmation of the facts – 'Two girls. *Two*. GIRLS!' – was a little repetitive, it was the euphoric effect of *Schadenfreude*.

For Mina Masi, the delivery was a double disappointment: two girls meant two less rings for her collection. She made a mental note to tell Sarna about her boy-guarantee formula. Karam, on the other hand, was pleased. He had been worrying about the logistics of affording a nose ring for Mina Masi if they had a son. Things were a little tight right now. So when Persini burst into the room with the news, Karam's immediate reaction was relief. This feeling was replaced by pride and embarrassment as his brothers started their felicitations.

'Quite a performance.' Mandeep grinned and punched Karam's arm playfully. 'I think it's the first time we've had twins in this family.'

'Must be all those double helpings Sarna forces on him,' Guru commented dryly.

Mandeep hooted with laughter and added, 'Maybe if she'd fed him a bit more they would have had two boys!'

Karam baulked at the thought. Two boys would have meant two rings.

In the weeks after the birth, Persini had to look after the family single-handedly. Biji and Baoji were in India. They had travelled there in the hope that Baoji's arthritic limbs might find relief in the holy waters that surrounded the Golden Temple in Amritsar. Contrary to expectation, Persini didn't complain. In fact, she seemed to have boundless energy for all her tasks. She tended to Sarna with unprecedented compassion, helping with the twins as well as looking after her own baby daughter. She insisted that Sarna didn't lift a finger and regularly brought her vast quantities of special postnatal strengthening foods.

Before her confinement, Sarna, anticipating that no one would bother with such things on her behalf, had prepared huge quantities of panjeeri, a delicious crumble of semolina, butter, almonds, pistachios, raisins, coconut, aniseed, ginger and unrefined sugar, traditionally deemed to be the ultimate postnatal restorative. Persini brought the panjeeri to Sarna in generous portions. She made her mori rotis, thick chapattis heavy with butter, for breakfast every day. Everything else that she cooked was specially adulterated with fat for Sarna's plate: the dhal was spiked with melting dollops of butter, the vegetables swam in an orange rim of oil. 'Eat, eat,' Persini encouraged. 'You need to get back your strength.'

Sarna was wary of her attentions and convinced that Persini was up to something. She was right. Persini was trying to fatten the lamb for slaughter. As she went about her errands or socialized with the neighbours, she was on high alert for anything that might corroborate Mina Masi's doubt. When Biji and Baoji returned from their India trip three months later, Persini was bursting with news. Little did she know that Biji had already uncovered the same information through her own probings in that other world, thousands of kilometres away, which Sarna had hoped she was leaving behind for ever.

6

For some time now, Karam had not been his usual purposeful, energetic self. His friends thought it was the onset of fatherhood making him sombre and he did not correct them. Easier to let everyone think it was this that was affecting him. He could not have explained the real cause of his malaise.

In this new state of mind, all aspects of life appeared negative to Karam. He was frustrated with the dullness of his lowly office job and felt increasingly stifled by the demands of his family. He often had a sense that he was losing himself in the endless mill of life's responsibilities and obligations. More and more, he longed to break out of the status quo, to go away somewhere, even to be someone else. He'd spent most of his spare hours in the last few months considering his options and trying to find a way forward. He wanted to do something that would temporarily take him away from Nairobi, offer him the chance to learn some new skills and pay him enough to keep supporting his family. He'd gradually discovered that the possibilities were very limited. No job met all his requirements. In fact, nothing came even close. Finally, when he'd almost given up on the idea of getting away, an acquaintance, Dalvir Singh, had told him of an opportunity to study abroad in London. It fulfilled, indeed over-fulfilled, only one of Karam's prerequisites: distance. The course in London would enable him to get away from Nairobi – but for a whole year, which was much longer than he'd anticipated. Still, Karam had leaped at the chance. In desperation he'd convinced himself that a year was but a blip in a man's life, and had decided he'd find a part-time job in London to finance his studies and send money back for his family. He'd applied for, been offered and accepted a place on the course. He'd taken a loan to pay a deposit to the college and cover his travel expenses. Three weeks ago he'd booked his passage to London. He was now due to leave Nairobi the following day and still had not said a word about his plans to the family. He'd been half hoping they'd find out from someone else. But for once, no one in their small community had spilled the beans. Karam knew he had to tell his family tonight, and he was dreading it.

'Bhraji, Bhraji?' Harjeet had to nudge Karam to get his attention. Karam looked up quickly and turned to receive the large bundle being passed to him across the dinner table. Tied up in several thick bright kitchen cloths was a stack of rotis. There must have been at least fifty or sixty, all made in advance, piled up and then insulated in cotton so that the family could eat simultaneously. Karam unwrapped the warm package. The sweet smell of butter on the rotis rose up as he pulled out two of the soft, perfectly round flat-breads. Sarna has made them, he thought, identifying her sleight of hand in their size, symmetry and liberal buttering. His heart contracted with love for such comforting signs of home and the knowledge that he was about to abandon them.

'I was just going to say how nice it is that you're eating with us tonight, but it seems you're here in body only and not in spirit,' Mandeep remarked.

'That's odd, seeing as he's become all *spiritual* these days,' Guru said.

Recently Karam had been spending a good deal of his spare time in the gurudwara. He often went straight to the temple from work and returned home later in the evening when his family had already eaten. Everyone had noticed his increased absence but it was difficult to criticize him. How do you berate a man for spending too much time at the temple? It seemed churlish to do so, especially since Karam was still fulfilling all his regular household duties. Sarna had commented on her husband's increased absences several times, only to be brushed off with un-related criticism about how the collars on his shirts weren't starched stiff enough and the creases in his trousers weren't ironed straight. Though Karam longed to unburden himself, Sarna was the last person he could speak to because so much of what he was going through had to do with her.

'How come you're not at the gurudwara tonight?' Mandeep wondered. Friday evenings were the traditional time for attendance. 'Even Baoji has gone this evening. I think he was expecting to see you there.'

Karam shrugged. It was not religious zeal or a desire to observe ritual that took him to the temple. He went there because it was the one place where he could be still and think. He was always glad to take his place on the floor in the prayer hall, close his eyes and let himself be soothed by the sound of a granthi singing banis. Best of all, Karam liked to be at the temple during an akhand paat. Then there were no hymns sung, just the gentle droning of the granthis' voices as they took it in turn to read the 1,430 pages of the Granth Sahib. The reading is done continuously, without a pause, and can take several days to complete. Karam preferred to be present very early in the morning or late in the evening, when the prayer hall was quite empty and the mild murmuring was almost lost in the large room. What relief he felt in those moments! He relished being able to reflect without interruption. Though his thoughts were often troubled, he always valued the chance to be alone and indulge his musings.

Karam now tuned in to the conversation going on at the table around him and waited for an opening to slip in a few words about his intentions. Thanks to the tongue-loosening effect of Sarna's food, all his brothers seemed to be talking simultaneously. Yet his wife's delectable dishes left him tongue-tied. He savoured each bite and wondered when he would eat such a feast again.

Karam's brothers began discussing plans for the weekend, and still he procrastinated. It was only a chance question that forced him finally to confess. Guru wanted his opinion about a picnic they'd started planning. 'Let's take advantage of this good weather before the rains start and go to Lake Nakuru this Sunday. I'll ask Govinda and his family to come as well, and maybe even the Dariwals. What do you say, Karam?'

'I can't,' Karam said.

'Why? Are you going to the gurudwara?' Guru didn't bother to temper his sarcasm.

'I'm . . . um . . . I'm starting a new job.'

'On a *Sunday*?' Guru said. 'Ha, he really is becoming a granthi!'

Around the table a wave of guffaws and sniggers erupted. Karam saw out of the corner of his eye that Sarna had stopped eating and was staring at him in surprise. Usually she raced through her food as though somebody was hanging over her, threatening to snatch away the plate. All the hours, effort and care she put into cooking her dishes seemed to exhaust her patience when it came to eating. It was as though she'd experienced the essence of the ingredients, the soul of the food, during its preparation and all that remained was for her to ingest the final product as swiftly as possible.

'Stop your joking,' Karam said sharply. The laughter died down but the mood around the table remained jovial.

Guru couldn't resist another jibe. 'As far as I know, only priests work on Sundays.'

Mandeep snorted, the younger brothers giggled, Persini's eyebrows shot up like a pair of volcanos about to erupt.

'Eh-heh! Don't make jokes about the temple!' Biji raised her voice and her hand.

Immediately there was silence, every head bowed penitentially. Biji looked at Karam, shaking her head slowly. He regretted losing his temper and triggering her annoyance. He could feel everyone's attention on him.

With artificial levity he said, 'Sorry to disappoint you all, but I won't be taking up any sort of religious vocation. I have, however, decided on a complete career change. There's no real scope in working for the government here. My job is a dead-end one. These days, people are saying the future is in *re-fridge-eray-shun*.' He gave the word such gravitas it sounded like a new Gold Rush or a far frontier, like space. Despite this, no one looked impressed. Karam perceived a ripple of uncertainty running through the ranks. The Singh family did not have a fridge yet and didn't understand what he meant. Mandeep and Guru exchanged a brief, dubious glance. Biji's forehead creased up like gathers in a curtain. Sarna's hand flew to her throat. Karam saw that his intentions were going to be met with as much resistance as he'd expected.

'You need training before you can work in refrigeration,' he hurried on. 'It's complicated – you have to study physics and chemistry and, er, various processes.' He tried to impress them by convoluting the issue. 'So I'm going to study the subject. It will take one year, but it will set me up for life. I've been accepted on a course – it starts in about a week. I can't come to the picnic because I have to leave – tomorrow. I'm going to London.'

At the far end of the table, Sarna pushed away her near-empty plate.

'London?' Biji echoed.

'You're going to *London*?' The bite of food Mandeep had been about to take hovered at his lips.

'To become a fridge mechanic?' Guru asked through a mouthful of chickpeas.

The words 'fridge mechanic' upset Karam. They diminished his decision. For a moment his resolution wavered. He recalled his old aspirations to qualify as an engineer. The refrigeration course seemed like a pathetic compromise. But what would he do if he stayed? He knew that he had to go, because to remain in Nairobi would be to continue in the same vein as before – a possibility that was insupportable.

'It's not just a mechanic,' Karam said. 'Of course, you learn all the technical aspects, but afterwards you could work in sales, on the factory floor, in maintenance and service.' He rattled off the options as though each of them really thrilled him.

'Oh.' Guru mopped some more chickpeas off his plate with a piece of roti.

'How can you go to London for *one year*?' Biji challenged her son. 'Who will look after the family?'

'Well . . . both Mandeep and Guru are working now. And Sukhi is more successful with his hunts,' Karam said, assuming Biji was referring to the family as a whole. They could probably scrape by if he sent back money regularly.

'But you're a husband – and a father of two. You must honour your obligations.'

'I intend to!' Karam insisted. He realized that Biji was concerned about Sarna and the twins becoming a burden if he wasn't around to support them. He thought it rather mean of his mother to say this when he and Sarna contributed more to the household than any other member. Surely it was not unreasonable for the balance of input to shift from time to time? Wasn't that the real meaning of living in an extended family? 'I'll get a part-time job in London. I'll send money home.'

'Your baoji will not like this. He will *not* like this.' Biji shook her head and her grey chuni slipped off it. 'You should have consulted him. Hai Ruba, how can you drop such a bombshell on us at the last minute?' She glanced at Sarna to see if she might have had a hand in this insurgency. But Sarna's shock and dismay were apparent in her pale face, trembling lips and leftover food.

'It all happened very fast. I had to make snap decisions. There was no time to speak to anyone.' Karam looked at his plate. He'd lost his appetite.

Biji was not having any of it. 'Is that why you've hardly been home these past months? Were you trying to avoid telling us?' She pulled her chuni over her head again. 'Your father might say you can't go. He might refuse.'

'I must go!' Karam exclaimed, putting both hands down firmly on the table. 'I have paid for the course and for the travel. I've resigned from my job. I can't stay now.'

'*Go* – all of you!' Biji suddenly gestured at her sons to leave the table. 'Step outside. Keep a lookout for your father.' She disliked the idea of the brothers watching Karam's rebellion. She felt they'd already witnessed enough disrespect towards her. 'You two – start clearing up in the kitchen,' she told Persini and Sarna. No one should be present to see her being contradicted.

Karam remained silent as everyone departed. His mother's displeasure felt like a clammy hand on his conscience.

'This is very bad, *very bad*. What have you been thinking? If you go off on a whim it's not fair on everyone else. You *must* reconsider.'

'Biji, it's too late for any of that,' Karam managed to say, although his mouth was dry with the fear of crossing her.

'It's too late in your head!' Biji snapped. 'As far as I can see, it's perfectly possible.'

'Everything is arranged. I am going.'

'What's happened to you?' Biji looked searchingly at the son who had always been so responsible. 'Suddenly you don't care about your parents' wishes?'

Karam said nothing and Biji, seeing the determination in his set jaw, stood up abruptly. 'Explain yourself to your baoji!' she said before disappearing into her bedroom.

Baoji was frail. Arthritis had weakened his limbs and a susceptibility to high blood pressure forced him to keep his temper in check. At Biji's instigation, he tried to dissuade his son from going abroad. In principle, he had nothing against Karam getting training to improve his job prospects so long as he continued to fulfil his family responsibilities. However, London was too far away, and a year was a long time, and Baoji said as much. Karam remained firm, insisting that London was the only option and the months would fly by. Baoji quickly recognized the strength of Karam's resolve and his own impotence in the face of it. Even with Biji breathing fumes of fury by his side, he could not work up the stamina for argument. Moreover, Baoji was astute enough to realize that issuing an ultimatum forbidding Karam's departure would not stop his son, but would only cause a deep rift which might never be repaired. So Baoji's questions became less hostile, his rebukes shortened, and Karam became aware that his father was giving up. It made him uncomfortable to see the old man acquiescing. He wished there was some way he could preserve Baoji's authority even as he challenged it – but something was changing irrevocably. Karam could feel the balance of power shifting: the vigour of youth was subjugating the fragility of age. 'So, you have decided. Now it's in Vaheguru's hands,' Baoji concluded. 'But a year is a very long time. A *very* long time.'

Time was also at the heart of Sarna's lament. That night, when everyone had gone to bed, she crept from the room she had been sharing with Persini and the children to the kitchen, where Karam had been sleeping alone since the birth of the twins, Phoolwati and Jugpyari. It was the first time she'd come to him this way. Managing the household chores as well as looking after the twins left her too exhausted to seek out her husband, even though she missed him. She had also been restrained from sneaking to his bed by a sense of propriety, suspecting that Biji would not approve. But Karam had signalled that she should come to him, and knowing that he was about to leave her for a year made Sarna forget tiredness and decorum. 'Dharji?' Her voice was thick with tears.

Karam rose and reached out to hold the trembling figure crouched at the end of the mattress. For hours he held Sarna while she wept and pleaded, pressing her body to his. 'Don't leave me. You can't leave me. *Why?* One year is too long. You can't go for so long. Don't go. *Please.*' Her lips sketched the whispered words on his ears.

Karam could offer her no explanations, no reassurance and no consolation. 'I have to. It's for the best,' he repeated inadequately, until in the end Sarna drew away from him.

'Go then!' she retorted between sobs. 'But don't think it'll be the same when you get back. Vaheguru only knows what will become of us.'

Karam was exhausted by her show of emotion. In a way he felt vindicated for not having broken the news any earlier. He didn't think he could have held out against the appeals of his mother and wife if he'd been subjected to them for much longer.

After Karam left, Biji kept throwing hateful looks at poor swollen-eyed Sarna, as though *she* were somehow to blame for his departure.

'Biji, I had no idea.' Sarna hoped she and Biji might find some solidarity in their mutual sense of betrayal. But Biji did not want to give sympathy, she was looking for a scapegoat.

'What sort of wife has no idea her husband's preparing to run abroad for a year? What sort of woman makes her man flee to another continent?'

7

12 July 1951

Dear Sardharji,

You have only been gone a few weeks, but it already feels like months. Why haven't you been in touch? You said you would write every week. I only know you must be OK because Baoji saw Harnaam Singh at the gurudwara and his son, who has just come back from London, said he saw you at the temple there.

Yesterday I cooked red bean curry, and your favourite smoky aubergines. I ate an extra helping in your name and thought of you with every bite. What are you eating there? Do they even have Indian vegetables in the shops? What is English food like? Do they have curry? Make sure you eat well – you've only just got your health back completely.

It is not easy here. Sukhi is back from his latest trip, so I've had to move out of Persini's room back into the kitchen with the twins. We're on the old single mattress again, all three of us. Just try to imagine that. The only way we fit on it is with Jugpyari sleeping by my feet and Phoolwati by my head. It's so uncomfortable. When I can't sleep I write letters to you in my head. Then I also write your replies to me – these are always full of love, they promise you will come back soon and everything will be better.

The twins are growing so fast! You will be shocked when you see them again. Phoolwati may be the older one but she's much more fragile than Jugpyari. Last week they had their vaccinations and Pyari didn't make a single noise while Phool cried before, during and for hours after. She's so sensitive, I tell you – really delicate, like the flower that is her name. I worry about her. Everything seems to make her cry – a little bit of cold, some noise – anything can get her going. Then Biji's shrieking starts up as well. 'Useless mother, useless children,' she complains. Of course, when Persini's Rupi cries Biji doesn't say anything. It makes me so angry. I feel like screaming sometimes, but there isn't anyone here I can even whisper my problems to.

I keep telling myself it's only for one year and then it will all be different – that was your promise before you left. I live for that promise. It keeps me going. But I would get on better if I knew you were OK. Please write.

Sarna

1 August 1951

Dear Sardharji,

Still no news from you. Why? I am so worried. Now that you're not here your brothers take it in turns to check the post box. I wish they would do it every day, but no one seems as bothered about the post as me. Every day I wait, but there has not been a single letter from you. That Persini kamini, evil incarnate, finds it very funny. 'Don't worry,' she said. 'Bhraji must be too busy sightseeing. New city, nah, Trufulgur Square, Buckinghum Place.' 'He's not there for a holiday,' I told her. 'He's there to study so that he can get a job – a *proper* job, not like *some* people's husbands.' 'At least mine's putting meat on the table,' she said.

It's true, Sukhi has been bringing back deer or birds from his hunts almost every week. He's been selling the poor animals' horns to some muzungus as well. So there is money coming in. But that doesn't stop Biji from making comments about how you haven't sent any money yet. Are you working? Please send something so your family will stop acting like I'm a burden.

I try to make up for everything with my food. Two weeks ago I made a va va good curry with the guineafowl Sukhi brought home. Biji said it tasted so good because Sukhi had shot it. Why, do his bullets have a special flavour? I wanted to ask.

This week, though, I think everyone is fed up with my cooking. Biji said, 'What's happening to you? Can't you even manage a simple dish now? So dry, so dry by the end of the meal my mouth is left parched like a desert.' What could I say? How could I tell her maybe it's because my hope is drying up and *I* feel like a desert inside. Where are you? Why don't you write?

Not a day goes by without some criticism from Biji. Everything I do is wrong. And the twins are in the wrong too, because they're mine. Biji never shows them any affection. The only time she mentions them is to complain. She is all songs and praise for Rupi, of course.

Biji loves to see me humiliated. The other day I saw

her smiling for the first time in ages because Balvinder and Guru were joking about the twins. Mandeep was there as well, but he didn't say anything. 'They should have called them milk chocolate,' Balvinder was saying, 'because one is the colour of milk and the other of chocolate.' Of course, big baba Guru had to try and trump him on the wit front, so he suggested the names Kalajamun and Rasgullah for the twins. Black dumpling and white dumpling! This is what your brothers are up to, inventing multicoloured sweet-inspired names for our daughters. Persini had a good giggle at their comments. I don't know how she can laugh – her Rupi is certainly no beauty queen.

What else can I tell you? This is the sorry state of things. You must return. Please. Forget the course, there must be another way to a better life and a better job. We can find it together. Please come back. We need you. I need you.

Sarna

26 September 1951

Dear Sardharji,

I am beginning to get desperate. If only you would write. Have you stopped caring about us? Do we mean nothing to you? Are you ever going to return? These questions trouble me every night. I can't sleep. What is to become of us? We live in this house but we are destitute. I can't even distract myself by imagining letters from you, because I don't know what to think. What would you say after so many months of silence? You are like a stranger now. When you went on a refrigeration course I didn't know you were going to freeze us out of your life.

I don't even know why I'm bothering to write – does any of this matter to you? Biji's latest hobby is picking on my appearance throughout the day. I am afraid of doing anything because I know she'll find something to criticize. Almost every day she makes me change whatever I put on in the morning. According to her, the colour is too bright, the kameez is too tight or the fabric rustles too loudly when I move. However I wear my chuni she'll order, 'Cover your head.' Even if my head is covered it won't be covered right and I'll have to adjust the chuni to satisfy her. If it happens to fall off while I'm working she'll mumble, 'Shameless.' How I am supposed to cook, clean, look after the twins and keep my chuni in place all the time is beyond me. I'm ready to give up. I tell you I can't go on like this. Your mother wants to drive me mad.

Maybe that's what I'll be by the time you get back. Mad and fit only for a madhouse.

Sarna

4 October 1951

Sardharji,

So you *have* been writing! How could I not have seen it before? I was so upset I've been blind to the obvious. That Persini kamini has been hiding your letters. I found out because Mandeep asked me today what your letter said. The kamini then interrupted a little too loudly, 'He hasn't said anything in months. What's he going to say now?' I asked, 'What letter? Is there a letter?' Mandeep looked at me and then at the kamini and said, 'There was a letter in the post this morning. I gave it to Persini because you were with the twins. I told her to give it to you.' The kamini pretends to be all innocence and exclaims, 'Hai! Oh, I completely forgot. Let me get it now.' I followed her to her room, where she took it out of a drawer. 'You've got the rest of his letters as well, haven't you?' I said. Of course she denied it, but she wouldn't look me in the eye. She must have made Guru and Sukhi give her any letters they collected from the post box. I was so angry I started shouting, 'Kamini! Kamini!' I tried to open the other drawers but she wouldn't let me. Mandeep came and tried to separate us. Then Biji appeared as well. I told Biji that Persini was hiding the letters. Biji asked her if this was true, but of course she said no. Biji looked at me and said, 'It's not true.' I just left the room, went to the kitchen and cried. That Persini, the bitch, will get her dues – I'll make sure of it.

Your letter doesn't say anything about when you're coming back. Haven't you read any of mine? For a moment, I thought maybe Mandeep wasn't sending you my letters as he promised, but when I asked him he was quite offended. 'Bhanji,' he said, 'we are not all the same.' But how do I know? Who can I trust? I rely on people who don't care about me. Now I think even you don't care. What kind of letter have you written? The page is full of words, but it doesn't say anything. The only thing I can tell for sure is that the weather is getting cold there. Very nice, Jee. Do you know how cold it is here? Cold as the stone my heart is becoming. Colder than your London, that's for sure. So cold, you might not be able to stand it when you get back.

I don't know why I keep saying 'when you come back'. You're not coming back, are you? I'm a fool for begging you. But who else can I ask? Who do I have? You are everything to me. You brought me here, away from my country and my family, and now you've left me. I can't go on like this, living in a full house and always feeling alone. It is only the twins that are keeping me going. For myself I have no will to live.

I am asking you one last time. Please come back. Please let us find another way together. I will do whatever you want. Please do not ignore this.

Sarna

18 October 1951

TWIN TRAGEDY. RETURN IMMEDIATELY. SARNA

8

He had gone away intending to change things, and things had changed. But some force larger than his will had been the impetus, and the outcome was not as he had envisaged. No, he could not have foreseen this in his worst nightmares.

The funeral had taken place by the time Karam got back, but the house was still shrouded in the palpable aura of death.

Karam had dreaded returning. He had not hesitated, even for a moment, after he had received the telegram. But with the passing of every mile his reluctance to arrive had grown. He was scared. He knew that it was not just a broken family awaiting him, but the consequences of a broken promise.

Entering the house again, Karam expected shouts and recriminations. He would not have been surprised if Baoji had lifted a cane to strike him. He had acted irresponsibly and he was ready to accept his father's harshest punishment. But the house was full of mourners when he arrived. Karam was grateful for the shielding presence of visitors and for their distracting small talk. 'Tsch, tsch. Sorry for your loss,' relatives, friends, acquaintances tutted.

Karam took refuge in their company and avoided any meaningful dialogue with his family and Sarna. Circumstances conspired to shield him from the confrontation he had dreaded, but as time passed it became harder for him to speak and act naturally.

Sarna did not talk to Karam for three days after his arrival. Most of the time she was busy serving tea and food to the endless procession of people dropping by to express their condolences. Karam was shocked by how much weight she had lost. The fabric of her shalwar kameez, which had once sculpted her body as the wind does the sea, now bagged around her shapelessly. It was her face that disturbed him most. Her jaw pulsed with tension and she was constantly grinding her teeth. Grief had stapled together her eyebrows, throwing her forehead into a confusion of creases and ageing her dramatically. She kept blinking back her tears, her eyelids fluttering like the flap of an ill-pegged tent. Every glance at her was like a moment of reckoning for Karam. She was the embodiment of the misery he had caused.

At night, Karam slept with his brothers in the living room while Sarna and Pyari remained in the kitchen. He had crept into the kitchen during his first night back, his fists clenched as if to hold in the tumult of remorse in his heart. The baby was asleep at the foot of the bed and Sarna was curled up tightly at the top. Karam managed to call out her name, but she didn't reply. She doesn't want to speak to me, he thought. And who can blame her? He had no words for his own failure. Every day since receiving the news he had tied his turban and fixed his beard without a mirror, because he could not bear to look at himself. Yet as he left the kitchen he felt a guilty relief. As long as Sarna avoided him, he wouldn't have to face any questions. He wasn't ready to hear her say, 'Where have you been? Why didn't you listen to my letters?' So he kept away, hoping that time would make things easier. Instead they became harder. With each averted glance, and every avoided conversation, the silence between them became more difficult to bridge. Even when they were reconciled some months later, Phoolwati's death remained something they never discussed. It was too laden with implications of their own shortcomings.

Mandeep told Karam how Phool had died. In the end this sketchy version was the only account he ever heard.

'The child went to sleep and never woke up. That's all I know. Dr Iqbal couldn't find any explanation. He examined the body and said there were no signs of illness, no signs of distress. It was . . .' Mandeep played with the thick steel kara on his wrist. It was hard to find words for the scenes that had followed Phool's death. 'Sarna . . . Her wails woke us all early in the morning.' He couldn't describe those cries. For hours they rose and fell, altering in depth and tempo, sometimes like a maniacal laugh, sometimes a repetitive moan. It had seemed as if the devil himself was plucking at Sarna's guts to make the abominable music. 'She wouldn't let go of Phool. The child had to be wrenched from her arms. And then—' Sarna had screamed and screamed until she fainted. Mandeep remembered her collapsing in the kitchen, her head just missing the jiko where the coals were glowing red. 'And then she wouldn't touch Pyari. As if – I don't know, as if she was afraid of hurting her. You must have noticed she's still very strange with the baby,' he said. 'Before, she was all over the twins all the time – hugging them, spoiling them. Biji didn't like it. But anyway that's . . . tscht . . .'

Karam avoided his brother's gaze. His confused and stifled emotions seemed trifling in comparison to what Sarna was going through.

'Mina Masi reckons it's a saraap. A curse. Mangal da saraap, she called it, because the twins were born on a Tuesday. Apparently that's unlucky. Who knows?' Mandeep said.

Karam felt drawn to this explanation. Normally he would have rejected such superstition outright, but now he was tempted by the cushion of defence it offered. If everyone agreed it was a saraap then he would be absolved of blame for what had happened. But he knew better than to allow himself such leniency, so his reply was un-equivocal. 'Nonsense. There's no such thing.'

Mandeep sucked in his cheeks and chewed them for a moment. Then, without looking at Karam, he said what had been on his mind since his brother's return – what no one else had dared to say. 'You shouldn't have gone away. You were needed here.'

When Mina Masi had uttered her cry of 'Saraap!' Sarna had expected the woman to point a finger of accusation in her direction. For *she* was cursed, was she not? Why else was everything she loved taken from her? But Mina Masi had hung the blame on the T of Tuesday and Sarna had been left to press charges against herself. She had been punished for loving Phoolwati more – just a tiny in-calculable fraction more – than Jugpyari. She had justified keeping Phool in her arms while Pyari slept at her feet by telling herself the narrow mattress necessitated this arrangement. In truth, she wanted the older twin closer: Phool, with her pale skin, her delicate features and her uncanny resemblance to a dream Sarna had been forced to renounce. Now she couldn't look at her surviving daughter. She averted her eyes every time she handled the child, as if the tearful love that was brimming in them might somehow be lethal, just as the love in her breath had been deadly for Phool – because that's where she'd mysteriously died, in the warm shadow of her mother's exhalations. It *was* her fault, wasn't it? There was no other explanation. Even Dr Iqbal hadn't been able to clarify anything.

Maybe I am not meant to love or to be loved, Sarna told herself. So although her arms craved Pyari, she resisted picking her up. When her breasts swelled painfully and leaked milk, Sarna could not feed her. She welcomed the soreness, because it helped counter the other pains that consumed her.

The endless stream of mourners in whom Karam took refuge were a help to Sarna as well – there was always another cup of tea to be made or another stack of dishes to be washed. She needed the distraction of the kitchen. She insisted on resuming her chores, begging to do the cooking even during Persini's weeks on duty. Lost in thought while she chopped ingredients or stirred the contents of a bubbling pot, she was unconscious of the tears that fell from her eyes into the food with a sad dull splat. Only when she tasted a dish would she suddenly be alerted, by the sharp hit of an over-salty mouthful, to the culprit dampness on her cheeks. Sarna took to throwing whole potatoes or clumps of dough into her dhals and curries to absorb the salty excess of her tears. If that didn't work she poured water into the dishes to dilute them. Each day the family sat down to insipid meals which tasted as forlorn as the look on Sarna's face. Or they forced down bitter dishes which echoed the absence of Phool. They put up with it for several days, but then Biji capitulated. 'Hai, hai.' She screwed up her face after an acrid spoonful. 'I know you're upset, but there's no need to poison the rest of us with your gloom and doom. Pull yourself together. You're not the first woman to lose a child.' The words came at Sarna like an assailant, pushing her into the familiar corner of shame, pressing up against her with suffocating, brute force. What kind of woman was Biji? She had endured several miscarriages and two stillbirths, and yet she showed no feeling for another's loss. Had she just become numb to pain? Is that what happened when you suffered too much? Sarna didn't think so. Her own experience suggested that heartache never stops. It wasn't like chicken pox, something you have once and then become immune to. No. It recurs, and when it does it often stirs up old wounds and starts them hurting too.

She noticed the distance Karam kept from her, the way he avoided meeting her eyes. She saw that he couldn't bear to be in the house and envied him his excuses to get out. 'I'm going into town to look for a job,' he'd say and disappear for a few hours. *Come back!* she wanted to shout. *Take me with you. Get me away from here.* She needed the comfort of his presence and at the same time she wanted to lash out at him. If he'd been here she wouldn't have had Phool and Pyari in the bed with her. If he'd been here she wouldn't have woken that night to find her baby's body cold and lifeless under her arm. If he had been here. If only, if . . .

She had heard him the night he'd stood in the kitchen and called out her name. She hadn't replied because she wanted to punish him, to see him suffer. Yet while Karam stood there waiting for her response, she had been silently pleading, *Please touch me. Please. Please tell me it's going to be OK. Hold me. Hold me.* And when she'd heard him walk out of the room, *she* was the one who suffered.

Debilitating thoughts whirled round her head, circling her conscience like a gang of thugs closing in on an un-suspecting target. Just when it seemed they would clobber her to death, her will reared up against them. No! What have I done to deserve this? All she had done was love. Was that a crime – loving? Was she to spend the rest of her life paying for one innocent mistake? No! Sarna's spirit pushed through layers of shame and remorse to reassert itself. It took refuge in the only place that offered solace – victimhood. It was Karam's fault: he should have come back. It was Biji's fault: she shouldn't have forced them to sleep on that mattress in the kitchen. It was Sukhi's fault: he shouldn't have hung the remains of innocent, murdered creatures on the walls of this cursed house. With the adrenalin rush of these internal dramas coursing through her body she had the energy to cook, clean, hold herself together and start breast-feeding Pyari again. Sometimes, in better moments, she wondered if some-thing resembling normal life might again be possible.

Whatever we allow ourselves to become accustomed to can so quickly seem commonplace. As the weeks passed, Karam and Sarna continued to say little to each other during the day and they slept in different rooms at night. Although the burden of this estrangement weighed down on both their hearts, its strain on their nerves diminished. Life clicked on, like a slide projector flicking through various images of the ordinary: Karam returning to his old job at the Treasury; Balvinder and Harjeet rushing in from school and heading to the kitchen to pester Sarna for a snack; Baoji getting everyone to hunt for his walking stick; Persini and Sarna alternately filling the house with the smell of their cooking; Biji's head swaying in its natural rhythm of dismay. Routines and responsibilities were resumed and in the clockwork comfort of these conventions the vestiges of normality were restored. But occasionally, unexpectedly, the slide projector would beam out blankness. Like an unforeseen gap in the slide tray which flashes out an eye-hurting blaze of emptiness, memory would flash up before the family, stark and piercing. It took nothing more than hearing someone accidentally say 'Phoo— Pyari!' as they had all done when Phool had been alive, inconsequentially interchanging the girls' names. Such innocent blunders could now reduce everyone to awkward silence and interrupt Karam's and Sarna's heartbeats.

A new year started. The long rains dragged on, falling heavily as if to wash the world of its woes. Karam began to question his allegiance to his family. He started to make small, seemingly insignificant stands against his parents' wishes, like claiming he was too busy to drive Biji to the market or accompany Baoji to the funeral of an acquaintance.

Meanwhile, Sarna persisted in her selective perspective on events, considering everything that had happened to be everyone else's fault. In this way she dealt with her guilt about Phool's death. But though a snake can free itself from an old skin, Sarna's guilt could not be thus discarded. The only thing she was losing was her grip on reality.

At the beginning of February, Sukhi returned from a hunting trip laden with treasure. Late one afternoon, under Biji's supervision, he put up a new set of kudu horns. They were long, lyre-shaped and majestic. Sukhi was proud. He had killed a marvellous male antelope for those horns and the family had feasted on its flesh for two days. Sarna shuddered at the new addition. The morbidness of this room, this mausoleum for Sukhi's conquests, was more potent than ever. She had become convinced that every new victim on the walls boded another calamity. Hadn't Karam announced that he was leaving for London just after Sukhi had bored a rhino horn into the wall? Hadn't Phool died just after that ridiculous photo of Sukhi with his giant tusk had been hung up in celebration? It was the insulted dead spirits of the animals taking revenge.

Meanwhile, in the compound behind the kitchen, under the damp branches of a jacaranda tree, Persini was busy kneading dough for chapattis. She had gone outside to work as soon as the rain had stopped. She disliked being indoors. The house had become like an echo chamber of sorrow ever since that horrible morning when the sounds of Sarna's misery had made the walls tremble. You never knew when or where the traces of grief might appear. Last week a sob had jumped out at Persini from the depths of a drawer she'd opened. Today she'd reached into the big bag of flour and, as she drew out a bowl full of the milled wholewheat, a sad whimper had emerged in a puff of white air. Better to be outdoors where everything isn't contaminated by that woman, Persini decided, glancing up at the surly grey sky. Yes, better to be outside, even if it did look as if the rain might start again at any minute.

As she worked, Persini chatted animatedly to her new best friend, Juginder, the notorious town secret-spreader and gossip-monger. She had taken some pains to cultivate this acquaintance after Sarna had given birth to the twins, and her efforts had not been in vain.

Juginder watched Persini roll out chapattis and throw them on to the thava to cook. 'Such perfect rotis you make, Persini-ji!' she squeaked with exaggerated admiration. '*And* they're quite big.' She used her hands to measure the diameter of a chapatti. A bit too big, actually, Juginder thought. On closer observation it became clear that the rotis weren't perfect at all. Their circumference was as bumpy and uneven as the Nairobi–Mombasa highway. Still, Juginder did not refrain from oh-ing and ah-ing. She knew that such flattery generally got the results she wanted.

'Yes, I've always made big rotis,' Persini said. 'Men need decent portions. I don't believe in any of the small-small fancy-fancy business. *Some* people –' She glanced around. '*Some* people deliberately make smaller rotis. Really, they give themselves more work so that they can say, "Oh he ate *six* today," trying to prove that their food is really delicious when people are only eating more because they didn't get enough in the first place. I've always believed people will eat according to how hungry they are. Taste doesn't make any difference. Don't you think so?'

Across the yard a magenta curtain of bougainvillea rustled in the breeze. 'Hmm,' Juginder said. 'I know what you mean, but I think if something is really good you will always want to eat more. Me, for example, I can't resist Sarna's gajarela. Oh, that dish is really too good.' She closed her eyes and licked her lips. She was glad of this opportunity to turn her treacherous tongue to Sarna. 'Even if I've already eaten before I come here, no matter how full I am, I can always manage two generous portions of that dessert. I keep meaning to ask her for the recipe. Really, she must do some magic – how else could sweetened carrots taste so good?'

As Juginder had anticipated, Persini got annoyed. Her rolling pin forcefully flew across the dough, making a lopsided oval-shaped chapatti. 'Ask her for the recipe if you want, but don't expect to get it – or not all of it. She's bound to leave out some ingredient or instruction so that you can't make it like her.'

'Well, poor Sarna, I don't suppose she'll be bothered with making desserts for a while after what she's been through . . .'

'You get what you deserve.' Persini tossed the ill-formed chapatti on to the hot blackened steel pan. 'That's what I think, everyone gets what they deserve.' It occurred to Persini that she was the exception to this rule. She deserved a lot better than she got. Still, she was sure the stakes would come out in her favour in the end. They had to.

'Yes, of course,' Juginder said. In the heat of their chatter, neither woman noticed Karam approaching the back door of the kitchen directly behind them.

'I'm not surprised by what's happened,' Persini continued. 'I know Sarna and there's *nothing* she won't stoop to to get her way. I haven't said this to anyone else –' Persini leaned forward and lowered her head, her bun stuck up like an ice-cream cone, 'but a part of me wonders whether she didn't deliberately smother the child to get Karam back from London.'

Juginder's eyes widened.

'Yes, she was desperate and he wasn't responding.' Persini pulled a bit of dough from the big mound on her left and began rubbing it between her hands. 'If it had

115

been Pyari who'd died I would have had no doubts what-soever – that would be just typical of Sarna, to get rid of the ugly one. But still, I can't help wondering, you know?'

Even Juginder, gossip queen and lover of lewd details, was startled. 'Hai, hai, Persini-ji, that's enough. No mother could do that to her own child.'

Something inside Karam snapped. Like an overloaded branch that breaks off a tree, ripping the bark as it falls, his feelings tore out from him. He dropped the bags of groceries he was carrying. At the noise, Persini looked up and gasped. Karam ran into the house. He had never felt so enraged or disgusted. Is this what his family had come to? Harbouring disgraceful thoughts about each other and complaining to strangers? There was a time when they had protected each other, when the humiliation of one was shared by another. What had happened? He knew the answer: Sarna. Since she had come, nothing had been the same, and as long as she stayed things would remain fraught. Karam understood this now and he resented his family. Their disapproval of Sarna was like an indirect rejection of him – because he had chosen her.

In the living room, Karam loosened his tie and roughly undid the collar of his shirt. The button came off into his trembling hands. He tossed it aside and looked around wildly, wondering what to do. He needed to make a statement fit for his anger. Biji and Sukhi, still busy rearranging death on the walls, did not notice him. Karam caught sight of Sukhi's rifle hanging behind the front door, and grabbed it. Just then Sarna came out of the bedroom, where she had been feeding Pyari. Karam took her by the arm and pulled her outside to the compound, where Persini and Juginder were standing and fingering their chunis anxiously. Biji and Sukhi looked at each other in confusion and hurried out as well.

Karam's head throbbed inside his turban. He felt it would explode without the stiff starched casing to hold it intact. Everyone was looking at him and their attention fuelled his resolve. He fired the gun into the air. The shot rang angrily. The sound shattered the lock of fear that had been gripping his heart. After weeks of saying nothing, he was finally able to speak.

'Enough! That's enough!' Karam shouted. Enough silence, enough denial, enough thinly disguised contempt. He could take no more. 'What do you want?' he shouted at Biji and Sukhi, who were entreating him to put down the gun. Around the compound, faces appeared in windows and bodies in doorways: the neighbours were watching.

'Is this what you want?' He pointed the gun at Sarna and looked straight at Biji. She was trembling, but her eyes were beaming him a clear message. They darted towards Juginder and then back to Karam again: What will people say?

Karam understood her coded plea and felt sick. Nothing was going to change. Outward impressions would always be more important than honest expression in this house. 'This *is* what you want,' he said bitterly. 'Only this will make you happy. I'll kill her, I'll kill the child and I'll kill myself. Then you can all rest in peace.' Karam aimed at Sarna again and made as if to fire the gun.

In that instant, with the barrel of the gun pointing at her, Sarna's thoughts became still. People say your whole life flashes before you in the face of death – with her it was the opposite. Everything fell away. It was as though she receded from herself: her senses deserted her and her heartbeat slowed down. She was at peace: light and empty.

It was a feeling she had never experienced before and would never again know – and it was disrupted by Biji's scream as she ran forward and threw herself at Karam's feet. Sukhi also ran up and tried to disarm Karam, urging him to calm down. Persini sobbed – not tears of regret for what she had said, but fat green tears of jealousy at the stand Karam was taking on Sarna's behalf, at the undeniable declaration of love. Juginder watched in delighted disbelief – never in all her days of scandalmongering had she come across anything like this.

Only Sarna and Jugpyari were silent, as if they knew that something was going to change. Karam looked at them and understood what he had to do. He stepped back from Biji's grovelling figure and shoved the gun at Sukhi. He no longer needed its forceful rhetoric. Karam moved closer to Sarna, and when he spoke it was with new conviction. 'Nothing I do is ever good enough for you,' he said to his mother. 'I'm the one who supports everyone, I'm the one who was pulled out of school to put food in your mouths and I've got nothing for it. Nothing.' Karam's voice did not betray his shaking knees or hammering heart. Only his forehead hinted at the strain this confrontation was putting on him: the triangular strip of red fabric peeping out from under the folds of the turban at his forehead had been dampened to black by sweat.

Biji didn't say a word. She had approached Karam in a gesture of submission, assuming the pose usually taken by children to receive an elder's blessing. She'd hoped to appease him and he had rejected her outright.

'I never expected thanks for what I've done. I was doing my duty, it was enough for me to do it well. But,' Karam took a deep breath, 'you didn't even give me any respect. I'm sorry that I never brought home trophies for you to hang on the walls. The only prizes I could have brought home were certificates of merit for studying, and maybe, one day, a graduation photo. But that chance was taken away from me. I'm sorry that all I have been able to do is keep us all fed and clothed and together.'

Still no one said anything.

'Biji,' Karam said. 'This is not what I wanted, but too much has happened. Too much has gone wrong. Enough is enough.' His voice trembled. 'We can't stay here any more. We will move away. It will be better for everyone.'

The next day he asked for a job transfer. A month later, he, Sarna and Pyari moved to Kampala, Uganda.

9

'Take off your clothes. I want to see you,' Karam said. Just a few words, spoken like a caress, made Sarna start wondering. Then a purple stain on her neck made her start doubting – Karam had never given her a love-bite before. It had been so long since they'd had sex. Over a year? Sarna tried to remember. The last time had probably been a few months before the twins were born. Yet the long abstinence alone could not explain Karam's new ardour. Nor could it be justified by the fact that they now had their own home, a bedroom, a proper bed, privacy. There was a new knowingness in Karam's touch, a new confidence in his passion. Gone was the clumsy, hesitating lover of their nights on the mattress in his parents' kitchen.

The request to take off her clothes surprised Sarna. The most she had ever removed in front of Karam was her salwar – and that under the shield of darkness. Sometimes he had hitched her kameez up over her breasts as they lay together, but she'd never actually taken it off. She felt exposed and embarrassed as he ran his hands over her nakedness and she recoiled in alarm when he pressed his nose into her underarms, the soles of her feet, between her

120

legs. What was he doing? Then Karam started to lick and suck and squeeze her and Sarna really panicked. What was he *doing*? Where had he learned all this? Should she ask him to stop? Oh, but it felt so good ... Who had shown him such moves? There must have been someone else. Somewhere ... somehow ... in the last year. Was it in England, while he was supposed to be doing his course on refrigeration? Was that why he wouldn't come back? Suspicion tripped awkwardly through Sarna's mind. No, she tried to convince herself, there couldn't have been anyone else. Perhaps this was just a side of Karam she didn't know, perhaps he had been restrained in that stifling house in Nairobi. But even as she formulated these explanations, Sarna mistrusted them. And during the first weeks of their life in Kampala, her instinct was confirmed.

He wanted to make love in the daytime. Coming home for lunch, he would lead her to the bedroom and start to undress her. He possessed her in the full glare of the sun, while she kept her eyes shut tight against the idea of his betrayal. His new audaciousness led him to make love to her standing up, from behind, sitting with their legs splayed around each other. Sarna assumed each pose without protest: they were nothing compared with the position of humiliation into which Karam's infidelity had put her. Every time their limbs coiled around each other, Sarna's conflicting impulses also met in a tangle of emotion. She wanted to submit to the motions of pleasure and greedily take of the new gratification Karam offered her. She wanted to give him a satisfaction that would eradicate his memory of the other woman. She wanted him just to hold her and tell her he loved her. She wanted to push him away and cry out that she knew he had been unfaithful.

For weeks she did nothing. Her anger at Karam was eclipsed by her even greater outrage at life. Why was it dealing her blow after blow? Pain once again filled her being. She felt the ache of betrayal, anger and sadness, but above all, she felt the agony of Ishq, of love intensified by the intimation of something lost.

Her feelings came through in her cooking during those weeks. Everything was prepared in silky sauces heavy with butter or cream, the richness of the food expressing the weight of Sarna's emotion. And yet concealed in the sensual smoothness of each dish was the fiery kick of chilli that left the mouth burning.

When Sarna was finally able to voice her suspicions, the words came out crudely, contaminated by the unspoken hurts the marriage had accumulated. Karam observed that making love to his wife felt increasingly like doing it to a dummy. He could feel her body responding to him but it was a hollow pleasure, not echoed in her voice or her touch. She remained passive and silent throughout. Thinking that perhaps she needed encouragement or even sanction to express her pleasure, Karam suggested that Sarna should relax a bit, be bolder in bed, say how she was feeling.

'I'm sorry,' she said icily, 'but *I* haven't been on a refrigeration course.'

Karam was startled.

'Yes, Jee.' She wriggled out of his embrace. 'I don't know what kind of refrigeration you were studying, but your fridges must surely have felt more like ovens.'

'I don't know what you're talking about!' Karam protested, but his heart suggested otherwise. It was beating erratically, leaping about like a handful of marbles thrown to the floor.

'No, Jee, talking is not your strong point any more.'

Sarna jabbed Karam in the groin. 'You've become adept at a different language.'

'You'd better watch your tongue, woman.' He was taken aback by her venom.

'Why should I watch my tongue, when yours has been roaming in some London fudhi-land?' Her words came fast and filthy, like a sewer suddenly unblocked, and they smacked Karam's startled face. 'Is that what you were up to all those months when your wife and children were suffering? Were you too busy licking pussies to reply to my letters?'

'You'd better stop now if you know what's good for you. You don't know what you're saying.' Karam was horrified by Sarna's language. Where had she picked up such vulgarities? How dare she speak to him in this way?

'I know what I see.' Sarna got off the bed and reached for her kameez. 'I see you've picked up some sordid habits while you were off "studying". I thought you said you didn't finish the course. It looks to me like you did finish some course. It seems you passed your Karma Sutra course with distinction. What did you think? That I wouldn't notice?' Her voice came from within the orange cotton kameez she was pulling on. 'That you could go from fumbling feroz to hot hot hero without me feeling the difference?' Her head popped into view again as she smoothed her top over her breasts.

'You're talking rubbish! Listen to yourself – you're the obscene one.' Karam pulled the blanket across his lower body. He felt oddly disadvantaged lying on the bed while Sarna stood over him.

Sarna shook her head. 'You're not even man enough to admit the truth. But *I* know what you've been up to, Mr Karam Sutra!'

'Shut up!' Karam raised his hand to scare her into silence. He had no other means to counter her accusations: denial hadn't worked and explanation wasn't possible – she would never understand.

'No, *you* shut up!' Sarna screamed. 'You shut us out. You left us. You left *me*. You were more interested in qualifying as a raunchy raja than in giving your family some quality of life. You didn't send money because you were too busy paying those goris to satisfy your needs. You were so busy lusting after those London ladies that you let your daughter die.'

Slap. Before he knew what he was doing, Karam had leaped out of bed and landed one hand across Sarna's jaw. She fell to the floor. He stared at her for a moment as she lay there, sobbing, and then started pacing the room as if to walk off his action. He was filled with regret, but she just wouldn't stop! If she had calmed down or kept quiet . . . What? What then? Karam's conscience asked. You could hardly have told her the truth.

Karam did have an affair in London. Her name was Maggie. 'Call me Maggie,' she had always said, because he, unused to saying strangers' names without some respectful qualification tagged to the end of them, and not wanting to say Maggie-ji, had not called her anything. He had managed to speak to her for weeks without mentioning her name. She had not been beautiful, but for Karam she'd been a prize catch. Compared with Nairobi, where women stayed at home and were rarely seen around town, London seemed to be bursting with ladies. Karam observed them with a wonder bordering on awe. Brushing past women in the street, sitting beside a woman on the bus or giving his order to a waitress in a café, he felt sensuality, the dance which Sarna had aroused in him, begin to spin around and jerk its joints in a new rhythm. After just a few weeks in London the fluid ballet of desire Sarna inspired had been transformed by fantasy into a pulsing jitterbug of lust.

It was the different revelations of femininity that fascinated Karam: the bounce of short cropped hair, the flash of teeth in a painted red mouth or the sinuous curves of stockinged calves. Yet for all his imaginings, he would never have been able to approach one of these women in reality; he was too aware of their difference and too inhibited by his own insecurities. When Maggie began to show an interest in him, at first he hadn't noticed, then he was surprised and unbelieving – and eventually, flattered, he had succumbed.

Maggie worked in the canteen at India House where Karam had gone to eat almost every day while he was in London. He went there because they served cheap Indian food and it was close to the room he was renting in Museum Street. At first his meals were hasty ones, squeezed between the course he had to attend and the sightseeing that was his relief. Then everything had changed. Only two weeks into the refrigeration course, Karam had realized he couldn't continue. In the first practical class, while doing a simple experiment, he discovered that he was scared of electricity. Glancing around the laboratory he had seen a few sparks flying out from other students' attempts. The sight made him queasy and all of a sudden the very idea of water and electricity working together became intolerable to him. He panicked and rushed out of the class. He was so affected by this fear that for a few days he couldn't even flick on the light switch in his tiny room. He sat in the dark, feeling too ashamed to give the course another try, regretting his decision to come to London and wondering what on earth to do with himself.

Eventually, boredom forced him outdoors again and he went first to India House for a meal. Maggie was serving that day. Something in Karam's downcast demeanour made her take pity on him and give him an extra-large helping. Karam noticed the gesture and smiled at her – he usually found food portions mingy when Sarna wasn't serving him. 'Thank you,' he said. After that she always piled his plate higher than anyone else's. The generous portions were soon accompanied by effusive hellos. These pleasantries advanced to longer exchanges, and after a few weeks, Maggie would serve Karam and conveniently take her 'break' so that she could sit with him as he ate. So, once again, Karam's heart was besieged through an assault on his stomach. Maggie's company was a welcome distraction for him, alone and wretched as he felt. When she offered to show him around the city, he happily agreed; when she took his arm as they strolled, he pretended it was normal; when she came back to his room, he felt privileged; and when she asked him if he was married, he said no.

Whenever they made love, Maggie would talk continuously, issuing instructions or describing what she was feeling. Karam, used to the quick, quiet intimacy that had been necessary at home in Nairobi, tried to block out her voice by thinking of the alphabet – just as he had once thought of numbers when Baoji hit him. The alphabet was simpler, though. It didn't distract him from the experience, in fact it became his silent language of satisfaction. Until Maggie helped him shed his inhibitions, all his pleasure was expressed in the soundproofed

erogenous zone of his mind, in sharp hard consonants
and long, lingering vowels:

aaaaa
aaaaaa
aaaaa
b c d eeeee f g h iiiiiiiii! j k l
m n OOO-OOO-OO p q r s t
uuuuu
uuuuuu
vwxyz

Yes, Maggie had seemed quite unlike all the women
Karam knew. She looked different and she was different in
bed. But Karam had then found that she was the same as
other women. Her eyes had produced tears when he had
abruptly announced that he must go back to Kenya. She
had revealed her insecurities and expressed her need for
love when she had begged him, 'You'll write, won't you?
Promise you'll write. And you'll come back?' Of course, he
had reassured her, of course. But he had known even then
that he would never see Maggie again.

Karam looked at Sarna, who was still sobbing on the floor,
and sighed. He glanced at his watch. He needed to get
back to work. He began to put on his clothes. He knew he
was in the wrong, but dammit, how could he explain anything? His was just one wrong in a series of wrongs that
stretched back further than he could see. As he walked
over to the mirror to put on his turban, Karam noticed
Sarna's salwar lying in the middle of the floor, where he
had thrown it after peeling it off her. He picked it up and,
feeling the softness of the fabric, had an idea.

Later that day, after work, he went to Government Street, or 'Gorment Street' as the Indians called the main thoroughfare of the city. He passed Drapers, the upmarket fabric boutique where only white people shopped, and stepped into Sudan Stores, where all the Indian ladies bought their cloth. Sarna had been itching to come here since moving to Kampala. Looking at the towers of textiles – coloured, patterned, striped, spotted – extending down the length of the shop, Karam felt he was seeing a psychedelic vision of the future and all the possibilities that could still be realized. For once heedless of price, he started to select different fabrics. He chose a dozen. 'Five yards of each,' Karam said, recalling that this was the quantity Sarna always bought for her outfits.

The cotton fabrics were unrolled in undulating seas of brightness, while the silk susurrated sexily. The materials were measured swiftly against yard-long wooden rulers, shorn in the required quantity with giant scissors that murmured in satisfaction at their task, then folded meticulously and popped into brown paper bags. 'Dhaga?' the assistant asked Karam. 'Oh, yes, yes,' he assented. And her eager crew dived into drawers filled with every colour of thread to find a match for the fabrics chosen. 'Chooria?' the assistant enquired, sensing she could probably sell anything to this man. 'Yes, why not?' Karam laughed. And packs of shimmering glass bracelets clinked gently atop the bags already bursting with bounty.

Karam left the shop feeling elated; it was not until the end of the month that his spending spree would pinch his pocket. He carried his purchases carefully – those brown packets were full of promise for the future. Now it was only for Sarna to accept them.

Filled with trepidation and hope, he held the gifts up to

his sullen wife and said, 'I'm sorry.' She saw 'Sudan Stores' on the packages and her face softened. What had he done? Karam tore open the bags and, like a magician drawing an endless array of knotted handkerchiefs from a hat, pulled out fabric after fabric. Sarna met his imploring gaze. Had he really bought all of this? Had he really spent all that money? On *her*? Karam draped the fabrics around her on the sofa. 'Let's forget everything that's happened. Let's leave behind all the dull grey days of sadness. We're in a new place, together. Let's start anew. These are the colours of happiness. I am giving them to you. Please take them.'

Sarna took, stitched and wore them. Her new wardrobe shone like a rainbow in the often clouded and stormy sky of their relationship.

10

The land was magnificent. They had left behind lush, hilly Kampala and were driving along the verdant banks of the Nile. The mythical river must have irrigated the farmland with magic to create this spectacular panoply of green: from lime to the darkest forest green, and with every possible permutation in between, the countryside glowed. Karam, gazing out of the window, remembered the maxim everyone used to pay tribute to Uganda's fertility: 'You can cut off a man's head and plant it in the ground and by the next day his body will have grown back.' He understood what they meant. The richness of this bit of earth was like nothing he had seen before. Its fecundity was palpable. He could smell its sweet, fuggy aroma and feel its hot, damp touch on his skin. This intense physical presence made him think of Sarna and for a moment his pleasure was soured. She'd probably love to cut off my head, he thought, but she'd make kebabs out of me so that there'd be no chance of any resurrection. Their year-long honeymoon in Kampala had been dealt its first big blow by Karam's announcement that he was going to London again.

* * *

'I'm thinking about going to London. Just for a week. I must attend Queen Elizabeth II's coronation. We're British subjects, we should show our support,' Karam had told Sarna as they strolled in their garden one evening. He'd anticipated objection, because he knew any mention of London antagonized her, but he'd hoped that their new harmony could accommodate his decision.

'Excuse me, Jee.' Sarna had narrowed her eyes. '*London?*'

'Yes, I have to go.' Karam, affecting nonchalance, inspected the cuff of his left sleeve.

'But what about this?' Sarna ran a hand over her swollen stomach.

'What about it? You've got three months to go and I'll be back within a week. It's all sorted out.'

Sarna stared at him, her lips twitching with the struggle of what to say. How could he talk so casually about leaving her again? Leaving her with child, and with one small child. Anxiety stung at her eyes and nose the way pollen taunts hayfever sufferers. Her eyes dilated for an instant before scrunching up as she spat, 'How could you?'

Karam pulled out a handkerchief to dab away the saliva that had hit his face, even though Sarna was standing more than a metre from him.

'Again, you've planned everything without telling me.' Sarna was phosphorescent with pregnancy. Behind her a bush of bougainvillea bloomed orange and red, a vermilion tiara crowning her good health. Tiny white flowers protruded, trumpet-like, from each leafy beak of colour.

Karam moved closer to take Sarna's hand. 'I'll be back before you know I'm gone.'

She stepped away. 'You don't *have* to go. I don't want you to. No good will come of it, I can feel it in my blood.'

She clutched her wrist and pressed her thumb down on it like a doctor measuring a heartbeat. 'I can feel it in my stomach.' She pressed her abdomen to stifle the nausea that was rising up in her. 'And,' her nose twitched, 'the whole plan's got a bad Mushq.'

'Calm down, please.' This time he managed to take her hand. 'It's really not such a big deal. Everything is different now. It won't be like last time.'

She responded to his touch, stroking his hand, pressing up to him. 'If it's not such a big deal then don't go. Stay with me.'

'I must go.' This was his chance! He had been considering it since the king's death last year. He had decided then that he would go to the new queen's coronation. Karam had thought a lot about this queen, who might also have been queen of India if the British had not been impelled to sail away on the ebbing tide of history. Were it not for the British, India might not have been parted so violently in 1947, and he might not have ended up in the refugee camp, and therefore never have started to reflect on the importance of history.

Preparations for the coronation had been going on for some sixteen months before the day itself and all the while Karam had also been preparing: saving for and looking forward to the event. By participating in the ceremony in some small way, even as an insignificant observer, he hoped to be a part of the historic occasion. He hadn't said a word about any of this to Sarna until the last minute, because he thought she wouldn't understand – and he had been right. What did she know about history? Not a thing, obviously.

'*Must go?*' Sarna dropped Karam's hand and crossed her arms over her chest. Who did he think he was? Declaring his intentions like some maharaja who'd received a personal invitation to the ceremony. 'So now some queen sheen is more important than family? What about Pyari?' she said as the little girl ran into view with her two braids flying behind her, the green ribbon bows at their ends dancing like fat dragonflies.

'This has nothing to do with family. It's something I have to do. I—' But Karam didn't get a chance to finish.

Sarna turned away, shaking her head. It had everything to do with family! What had happened last time he left them for London? She could not bear to remember. She was afraid of being alone, afraid of herself. How could he go?

'I want to find History.' Karam continued talking to the back of Sarna's head. Her hair glinted midnight blue in the fading evening light. 'A coronation is not an everyday event. I want to see this queen crowned. I won't get another chance.'

Sarna recalled the newspaper pictures of the queen-to-be that Karam had shown her. She wondered if those looks had inspired Karam to lust for his London ladies again. 'I know who your queen is, Mr Karam Sutra. It's that same raath di rani from your last London trip, isn't it? That queen of the night is still ruling your fantasies. The tricks she taught you are still your crowning glory.' She spun around, her hands settling on her hips.

The argument had escalated from there. The two of them squabbled the sun out of the sky and continued to bicker in the darkness against a background of burping crickets. Pyari, hidden in the clasp of the night, crouched by the bougainvillea sucking at the ends of her braids and watching them.

'It's impossible to reason with you!' Karam had finally

lost his patience and left the house. Striding up Kira Road, he wondered why he was trying to explain things to Sarna. What was the point? He didn't have to justify anything. Had Baoji ever asked Biji for permission? Did Sukhi ever ask Persini? Of course not. He was a fool for thinking he could make Sarna understand why he was going to London. She was just too damn high-strung, that woman. And her tongue! He should have kept it in check from the very beginning. He had been naive to allow such liberties. He had let Sarna wield her blade of a tongue against others, and all the while it had just been sharpened for assaults against him. Well, Karam decided, enough was enough. He reached the top of Kira Road and stopped. Looking down the hill he sought out their L-shaped bungalow. It was almost indistinguishable from the surrounding white concrete Ls with their red-tiled, pitched roofs. There was no sign of the conflict that had raged within its walls. Karam's gaze stretched across the Kololo area, where they lived, to the undulating green environs. Kampala was built on seven hills. On one of these, in the distance, Karam could see the illuminated rounded roof of the Bahai temple. Everything looked so peaceful. God only knew what went on inside every home.

Karam had gone back to the house with a renewed sense of his own power. He did not speak about his impending trip again. When Sarna brought it up, he ignored her. His taciturnity indicated that there was nothing more to be said. His decision was final. The days before his departure had been tense. Sarna had tried everything to dissuade him from going away. She'd cried, yelled and given him the silent treatment. She'd cooked his favourite food in an effort to tempt him to stay at home, and when that hadn't worked, she'd served him piping-hot dishes heavily laced with chillies, to punish his mouth for not speaking the words she wanted to hear.

Karam had resisted all her ploys. She must accept what I decide, he told himself. He should have known better.

Sarna was hurt by the injustice of the situation. Where was this London place that was stealing away her husband? What did he get there that she wasn't giving him? She thought of the shillings she'd saved by boiling hot water for their baths on the coals instead of using the geyser, picking cheaper shoes for Pyari and bargaining expertly with the mama boga who sold vegetables. And now all the expenses she had spared Karam had gone towards financing his fantasies. She resolved not to pass on to him any future savings made from her household expenses.

All the time that Karam was away, Sarna's abiding fear was that something else might go terribly wrong. She filled the days with cooking, preparing elaborate teas for the lady friends she invited over. But her nights were sleepless. Either she was waiting for a reassuring kick in her stomach or she was slipping into Pyari's room to check her breathing. Sarna would open the curtains and squint in the moonlight until she saw the rise and fall of her daughter's chest or heard the suck of the child lapping at her thumb as if tasting the sweetest of dreams. She still found it hard to touch Pyari. Most of the motherly actions she performed were painful and therefore perfunctory – a reminder of what had been lost and could be lost again. It was only in feeding and dressing the child that she allowed herself to be indulgent. She sewed or knitted all Pyari's clothes and hoped her feelings might somehow permeate the girl once she put on the garments.

Usually Sarna was nimble at plying Pyari's hair into neat ropes, but in Karam's absence she faltered at the task like a child learning to tie shoelaces. The coloured ribbon she weaved through each braid twisted and slipped out of place as if it was following the direction of her thoughts and not her fingers. Why had he gone? Who was he with? How long would he be away this time?

Outside Karam's window, the landscape began to alter as they travelled north towards Sudan. The fertile farmland gave way to the savannah and by the time they crossed the border the land was arid and desert-like. Nothingness stretched all around them, barren and uninhabitable. Only the wind moved imperviously through this waste-land, sweeping up the sand so that it trailed in the wind's wake like the train of a wedding gown. The road became an unsurfaced dirt track which proceeded hesitatingly, sometimes disappearing altogether for a few hundred metres, as if it had been formed in the ground against its will.

'How much longer?' Karam asked Ngiti, the driver of the minibus.

'Note fah,' Ngiti said. 'Baht the roads are bud. So it teks some hawas from here to Juba. Longa if the weatha is also bud.'

Karam and his fellow passengers groaned. They'd already been on the road for hours. Maybe it wasn't the best way to London, but at least it was the cheapest. Karam just hoped there wouldn't be any delays.

They reached the airport on schedule, only to discover that the flight was postponed. When Karam tried to enquire about the estimated departure time, he was told, 'Sah, we do not know when it wheel depat becos we do not know when it wheel arife.' Is this an airport or a come-and-go-as-luck-will-have-it terminal? Karam thought.

It would soon transpire that luck – that is to say, the absence of it – was indeed to be an integral part of his journey. At two p.m., when they should have been taking off, the passengers were being offered lukewarm 'cold' refreshments. At six p.m., when they should have been halfway to their destination, and Karam's frantic pacing back and forth had probably amounted to an equally for-midable distance, their plane still hadn't arrived. At eight they were told the plane would arrive at ten and depart for London at midnight. Karam did a quick calculation. If things went exactly to plan and there were no more delays, he could still be in central London by mid-morning tomorrow. He might miss some of the action, but he should be able to see most of the coronation ceremony. Karam threw a resentful look at the empty check-in desk: that plane better get here soon.

At ten o'clock no flight arrived. The airport staff did not return to their deserted posts, so Karam still had no one on whom to vent his annoyance. He walked around with his hands slapping slackly against his thighs to dissipate his frustration. Other passengers looked weary at the delay but seemed generally resigned to it. But then, none of them were awaiting the plane for the sole purpose of attending the coronation. None of them were in danger of missing the great event altogether. Were they?

As the hours passed, Karam's outrage began to turn into something more insidious: the chilling premonition of disappointment. At midnight, an attendant surfaced to announce that the flight would not depart until the next morning. He slunk off the moment he'd finished speak-ing, as though he knew he would otherwise be seized as a scapegoat. When Karam heard the announcement, he couldn't even summon the energy to look at the culprit who'd delivered it. The trip was going to be futile: a waste of money and time. The only person who would derive any pleasure from this would be Sarna. Karam could already see her saying, 'I told you so.'

The flight departed from Juba at four a.m. on 2 June 1953. Karam sat fastened into his seat, trying to rein in his new optimism. He had spent the night resigning himself to the fact that he would miss the coronation. Now here it was, just within his reach again. But Karam warned himself, anything was still possible – engine failure, emergency landing, unplanned detour. He was not going to underestimate the possibility of disaster. He kept looking at his watch, willing the pilot to go faster and the tail wind to blow stronger. He regularly glanced out of the window, as though he half expected History's gleeful face to look gloatingly in at him and stick out its tongue before charging ahead and winning their race. But so far, it seemed, Karam and History were keeping pace.

The plane reached maximum altitude and around the world, as if in celebratory tribute to the Queen, the news was breaking that Edmund Hillary and Tensing Norgay had conquered Mount Everest.

The aeroplane cabin was at full capacity. Passengers looked out of the small windows, which glowed like little screens featuring the multi-hued marvel of sunrise. Across England, the front rooms of the privileged few who owned televisions were filling up with excited neighbours. Children sat cross-legged on the floor, adults stood behind them, and together they watched the coronation play out in a scaled-down black and white version which did not diminish its wonder.

The plane's heavy engines roared. In the streets of London, tens of thousands of people cheered the arrival of Queen Elizabeth II at Westminster Abbey.

The voice of the pilot burst over the drone of the engines. 'We are now cruising at an altitude of . . . Estimated time of arrival is . . .' And in the Abbey, the congregation's shouts of 'God save Queen Elizabeth' pierced the drone of the service's prayers, psalms and hymns.

Once again, Karam started to fret that he wouldn't make it on time. What luck, he thought, what bloody bad luck. Meanwhile, during the service at the Abbey, the Queen's left hand kept touching the Irish shamrock embroidered with soft green silk, silver thread, bullion and diamanté on her dress. This emblem, a lucky four-leafed clover, had been added to the left side of the coronation dress by its designer, Norman Hartnell. Maybe that's why fortune was struggling to favour Karam – all its power had been sewn on to the new Queen's side that day. But hold on, could it be that there was a little bit, a tiny loose thread of luck left over for Karam?

Karam jolts awake. The words '. . . save the Queen' escape tunelessly from his mouth. He is unaware of this, nor does he hear the pilot's announcement, 'Ladies and gentlemen, we are about to commence our descent into London Heathrow . . .' because the sudden reduction in cabin pressure is having an unpleasant effect on his ears. Turning away from his fellow passengers, he leans his face against the window, then he pinches his nose, purses his lips and inflates his cheeks. The effect of this tripartite action is similar to that produced when Dorothy clicked the heels of her ruby-red slippers three times: Karam is suddenly in another place. Not home, but somewhere more longed for . . . He watches the clouds outside his window part and suddenly he can see clearly below them. London! His eyes sweep across the cityscape until he finds his bearings when he spots Trafalgar Square. He looks along Whitehall and sees that it is teeming with people. Further up, near the Houses of Parliament, it seems impossible to move at all. The compacted crowd stands waiting. What a view, Karam thinks, just like a bird! He can see everything simultaneously – a perspective that surely even History cannot command. And then, behold, from Westminster Abbey carriages emerge – horses, footmen. The crowd roars, the sea of arms waves like wheat in a field. It's the Queen! Karam is thrilled. He wants to get closer and he tries to sweep down for a better angle, a crumb of the action. But his head hits the window. Hard. The woman next to him shouts for help. The next thing Karam sees is the air hostess bending over him, the letters LIZ glowing white on her name tag. 'You fainted, sir,' she says. 'It must have been the pressure.'

History had outwitted Karam again. Mirage-like, it had beckoned and then disappeared. Even the commemorative coronation teacups that he bought in London and took back to Kampala were cracked or chipped by the time he unpacked them at home. Deep inside, Karam knew that the cups, like his experiences of historic events thus far, were imperfect. Still he insisted on putting the less damaged specimens on display. Positioned so that their flaws were hidden from the glancing eyes of visitors, the cups sat as proud evidence that he had indeed been somewhere.

That collision with Partition in India in 1947 had given

Karam a heightened sense of History, but also left him forever out of step with it. Time after time he was not in time, as Sarna never shrank from highlighting. 'Oh ho, Jee, did you *miss* it?' she would ask in mock sympathy on his return. 'Such a shame, *Mis*ter Karam Sutra. Well, a few things went *amiss* here in your absence. You *missed* your daughter breaking her wrist and your wife having to get a ride home by matatu after the car broke down in town. But what's all that? Just one or two *mis*haps. Nothing for you to worry about. I would ask if you *missed* us, but no doubt you were so busy seeing your London ladies that there was no time. Jee, why do you look so shocked? Have I made some kind of *mis*take?'

Yet Karam's trips were not complete failures. They made for anecdotes to share with people. His friends and brothers loved to hear about his 'almost being there' and 'just missing it'. The story of Karam's attempt to see the coronation remained a firm favourite. It was the way he told it, never quite letting on where reality ended and his imagination took over. 'I opened my eyes and the name LIZ was staring at me from a badge on a woman's blouse. What? I thought. One minute I'm watching her from a distance, the next I'm on nickname terms with the Queen?'

A few days after his return from the coronation trip, Karam was chatting with friends when Paramjeet Singh asked, 'Oh, did you hear about Tan Singh while you were in London?'

'No, I don't think so,' Karam replied. 'Who is he?'

'*Who is he?*' Paramjeet repeated, looking shocked. The other men in their company laughed and shook their heads. 'Oh, Karam bhraji, you went to see the English queen and missed out on our Sikh hero. Tan Singh? He reached the top of Mount Everest with some Englishman the same day as the coronation. The very top. King of the mountain, he is now. We heard it on the radio.'

Now it was Karam's turn to laugh. 'Tan Singh!' He clapped his hands. 'Who told you that? He's not a Sikh. He's a Nepalese Sherpa who climbed with Edmund Hillary. His name is *Ten-zing*. Tensing Norgay!'

His friends listened in surprise.

'Haaaw . . .' Paramjeet's hand covered his mouth. 'We announced it in the gurudwara. We said ardaas for him.'

Karam could barely speak for laughter. Later he considered that if he hadn't been in London he could easily have fallen prey to the same error. Instead he had been spared that folly. He had gone in search of new knowledge and sensations, and the resulting experiences, though imperfect, helped distinguish him from the men around him. Karam liked this feeling and therefore went abroad every few years. The world was his university, London was his history course of choice, and experience was his lecturer. He gave himself up to their tests and imagined that every trip he completed was like graduating in the degree of life.

Sarna never got used to Karam's infatuation with London. Her heart was like a puppet in life's hands and each time Karam went away the strings were pulled tauter. They constricted her breath as if they were attached to her ribs, tugging at the very core of her, where the greatest fears and biggest mistake resided. She could not tell him that every time he was absent she relived the horror of his first desertion, which had culminated in the death of Phool. And the loss of Phool mirrored another loss, which she could never admit to anyone. That's why, left alone with Pyari and their new son, Rajan, Sarna was thrown into a schizophrenic state of love. She was at once over-protective – stuffing them with food, monitoring their heartbeats, hovering as they played in the garden – and distant – unable to squeeze them to the longing expanse of her bosom or gaze lingeringly at their bumbling, chubby little bodies, lest she bring forth the evil eye. It was their dirty clothes that she hugged, clasping the garments to her face and inhaling their child-like smell. It was the phantoms of their presence she caressed, running her hand along the warm imprint left on the sheets when the children turned in their sleep. On sunny afternoons, when they raced ahead of her up a street, Sarna would dance with their long shadows. She could hold the shades of their being to herself without apprehension – because it was not the precious babes themselves receiving the concentrated dose of her accursed adoration.

Unable to articulate her dread about the destructive potential of her love, Sarna tried to dissuade Karam from travelling to London by focusing on his alleged infidelity. She thought she had forgiven his first transgression. But to forgive is to trust again, and Sarna could not do so. The fact that Karam returned again and again to London only increased her certainty that it was the seat of his corruption. United Kingdom indeed – the place had caused nothing but division between her and Karam. The very act of his going to London was like a form of adultery. To imagine then the heinous acts he must be per-petrating there did not require a large leap of imagination. 'History, Shmistry,' she would mutter whenever her husband brought up the subject. She believed history was no more than a front for Karam's carnal sophistry.

At first Karam had responded to her angrily, but over the years he adopted his own language of insinuation.

'So suspicious, always so suspicious. *Why?*' Karam would look hard at her, as though the force of his gaze might bore through her myopia and help her see herself.

'I'm not suspicious. It's *your* record that's suspect – you and your disappearing acts. Every couple of years you get all heated up for that place, rush off without a thought for anyone, come home exhausted and claiming you "missed it" – what am I supposed to think?'

'You don't trust anybody,' Karam would shake his head, 'because you don't trust yourself. I don't know what goes on in that head of yours, but I know that we judge by our own standards, and in your eyes everyone is up to no good.'

Sarna's suspicions about Karam's obsession with London were not entirely baseless. That city remained the prime venue for his hopeful encounters with History. Why did he continue to return there, when the world was full of places where he might more easily have found the drama he sought? Wars, revolutions, carnivals, state funerals – there was no shortage of events. Right on Karam's doorstep a struggle for independence was going on. But he had no regard for that history. Indeed, on 12 December 1963, the day that Kenya was declared a republic, Karam was viewing a house in London and considering its purchase. The British Empire may have been crumbling, but there remained at least one loyal subject who did not want to shake off allegiance to it. When he put in an offer for the house on Elm Road, Balham, Karam made his most concrete bid yet to achieve the status that he had been seeking in all his visits to London: to be part of a nation that was proud of its past and knew how to edify history. He wanted to be uplifted by being aligned with something greater than himself. He craved honour by association. London was the place that satisfied these desires. Just being in the city made him feel connected to history, because he could see the past all around him. From the Houses of Parliament to Nelson's Column to the shabby Victorian stuffiness of the room he rented near India House, everything carried the stamp of the past, everything stood tall with the authority of age. London, Karam believed, was a civilized place. He knew that important things had happened there and he felt it would remain a focal point in the history of the world.

Karam was so caught up in his pursuit of the sensations London offered that he neglected what was happening right in front of him. He did not see that the momentousness of an event is not necessarily determined by its scale. Sarna tried to tell him this, but Karam was disinclined to pay her ranting any heed.

Where was Karam when their house was burgled? Where was he when Sarna miscarried their fourth baby? Where was he when she made the most perfect khatais ever – mini domed marvels that melted in the mouth? Where was he when Pyari won the 'Fastest Maths' prize at school? Where was he when their little Rajan went from having his hair in braids to wearing a putka? Where was he when it mattered? LONDON. The word was like an obstacle to Sarna. When she thought about it, she tumbled into a vortex of doubt. Whenever she said it, the word had to be spat out like bitter coconut milk.

Karam's trips to London translated into a fanaticism about his children's education. He made it clear that, in the future, he wanted both Pyari and Rajan to attend university in England. He supervised their work like a general overseeing a military drill, barking commands: Hurry up! Tidy that handwriting! Fourteen times table? Shakespeare's sonnet number eighteen? Names of the twelve gurus? The instruction 'At Ease' never emerged from Karam's mouth. He did not believe in recreation. The goal was university – the path to it was non-stop study. Only Sarna's pleas for leniency granted the children an occasional reprieve.

Meanwhile, Karam and Sarna became more and more estranged from each other by misunderstanding and silence. Life went on, it had to. And there were happy instances – successes and celebrations. But over time, something was lost: slowly respect disappeared and then tenderness slipped away. One cruel word thrown between lovers can alter their communion. Repeated curses, accusations and threats will eventually destroy love, even though they are often nothing but a desperate cry for it.

When Karam decided he wanted the whole family to emigrate to London, he expected Sarna's reaction to be on another scale altogether. He had been hinting at the possibility for months now. The purchase of the house on Elm Road had been the first clue. He'd justified it as an investment, but he guessed that Sarna knew what he was planning. Mostly she twisted things to fit her own strange logic, but sometimes she saw right to the heart of the matter. She had been responding to his migratory allusions with her usual caustic comments, but lately, he'd noticed, she had been silent when he mentioned London, as if she was mulling over what he said. Nonetheless, when the time came to make his intentions clear, Karam prepared himself for the worst. For a few nights before he spoke to Sarna, his dreams were tormented visions of volcanic eruptions and tidal waves.

Karam explained that they were offering early retirement at the Treasury and that he would be eligible at the end of the year. 'It makes sense,' he said. 'This country won't be the same any more now the British have left. Already the office is filling up with Ugandans. Who knows how things will turn out? Better to get out while we can. And there'll be a good payment, decent pension.' Sarna continued to unpod peas, and taking this as a reassuring sign Karam continued more confidently. 'Pyari will be doing O levels in a few years. It makes sense for her to do them in London. The schools are good and the children's chances of getting into university will be improved.' A pea flew out of its pod and hit Karam on the cheek. Oh Vaheguru help me, she's going to go wild, Karam thought, rubbing the spot where it had landed. He forced himself on. 'It's easy for us now. We have the house, the children are the right age, my pension will mean we have security . . . all I have to do is apply for early retirement.' In fact, he had already applied for and received it.

Sarna's reaction was indeed of a different order. She nodded and said, 'Well, since nothing can keep you from that place, I suppose *we* have to go *there*. Anyway, it's about time we saw this London you've been raving about. I just hope we're not disappointed.'

Surprised and relieved, Karam accepted her support without question. He didn't want to press the issue and risk her changing her mind. Besides, he had already decided. It just made things much easier that Sarna had agreed. Had he probed a little harder or been able to read her thoughts, he might not have felt quite so pleased.

Sarna's agonized ponderings had led her to conclude that going to London might actually be the ultimate chance for her to take control. The problems had arisen because she couldn't stop Karam from heading there, but if they were in London he wouldn't have any reason to go anywhere else. Would he? Sitting here in Kampala, Sarna had no way of checking what her husband got up to in London, no possibility of reining him in. But if she was there, he couldn't just do as he pleased. He couldn't go crawling after his ladies if she was keeping tabs on him. He wouldn't, she was sure, have the gall to try such things when his children were in the same city. Maybe going to London wasn't such a bad idea. Sarna became keen for the challenge of the place. She imagined finally confronting the whore of a land that had seduced her husband. She would grab the kamini by the neck and wring off her head. She would show Karam who was really Queen of London.

11

The rooms on the first and second floor of the house that Karam had bought on Elm Road were rented out. The first floor was occupied by Mr Reynolds, a retired army officer, and his wart-covered wife. They were the controlled tenants who had made the purchase of the house seem like such a bargain to Karam. They turned out to be a moody, xenophobic couple. They'd been living in the house since the end of the Second World War. Like many of the returning demobbed soldiers, Mr Reynolds had been offered rooms in an empty house in the area where he used to live. The rent in these places was controlled by the government, set at a very low fixed rate for the duration of the tenant's life. The Reynoldses had been eking out a quiet existence in Number 4, Elm Road until 'The Singh', as they called Karam, and his family moved in. They felt affronted by the arrival of these 'brownies'. They resented the loud, colourful life that spilt from the ground-floor confines of the Singhs' rooms and rose up to mingle with the first-floor fug of their stale hopes.

Mr Reynolds tutted whenever he saw Karam's freshly starched white turban stretched over the banisters to dry. ''s not a bleed'n' clothes line, y'know', he shouted down the stairs. Mrs Reynolds moaned that the family all had a bath every day. The sound disturbed her, and she thought the ritual was unnecessary anyway, 'No amount o' washin'll make a difference. Darned good dousin' wi' bleach is what they need,' she declared, scratching the hairy mole on her cheek and scowling at her husband. Both of them came to detest the smell of Sarna's cooking. 'Y' can smell it when y' turn into the bloomin' street,' Mr Reynolds complained to Karam, while his wife added, 'Bloomin' smell's in our clothes, our sheets, even our 'air – and there's no gettin' rid of it. Can't be 'ealthy whatever 'tis you're eatin'.'

Naturally, the Singhs gave as good as they got. They worked from the premise that the more the Reynoldses disliked them, the more likely they would be to leave. So instead of curbing the habits that antagonized their tenants, they exaggerated them. Several months after their arrival, Sarna was bold enough to sneak upstairs holding pans sizzling with sharp chillies or onions. She would stand on the landing for a few minutes, while the food's smell and sting invaded the Reynoldses' lodgings. The children were given leave to run up and down the stairs and shriek to disturb any moments of peace. This friction would go on for two years before Mrs Reynolds was eventually driven out. It was not underhand tactics that finally persuaded her to leave, but the fat cheque that Karam grudgingly handed over.

Meanwhile, in the attic room on the second floor there resided a rather different sort of lodger. He had also come with the house, but not in the same controlled capacity as the Reynoldses. The previous owner had recommended that Karam allow Oskar Naver to retain his tenancy. 'He's a good, quiet chap. Been here for years. Pays his rent on time. Won't give you any problems.' Certainly Karam and his family were never given cause to think otherwise. Mostly Oskar kept to himself, but in all his encounters with the family he was polite and friendly. Unlike the Reynoldses, he was intrigued by the Singhs' way of life. He was tempted by the smell of Sarna's food and charmed by the children, who sometimes came up to his room to deliver a tasty snack courtesy of their mother. Over the years, the family warmed to Oskar and regularly invited him to share a meal or have a cup of tea with them. They nicknamed him OK, even though they occasionally doubted that he was, and they would sneak up to his room to tell him things they couldn't mention to each other.

Oskar had an extraordinary capacity for listening. Whatever he focused his ears on was captured verbatim. He could hear the private chatter of his neighbours through the walls of the old Victorian house on Elm Road. In a room full of babble he could zoom in on any conversation with the agility of a radio transistor searching for the correct frequency and select the story to which he wanted to listen. If he concentrated hard, he could even hear what was not said: the unspoken words of private thought. He did not retain this information in a conscious way, but all he had to do was put a pen to paper, and everything he had heard would come pouring out: word after word rendered perfectly on to the page.

While listening, Oskar never asked questions; he never pressed for more information, never imposed himself on what was being said. People opened up to him. They disclosed things they hadn't intended to and revealed truths that surprised them. He accepted a story as it was delivered: the teller's version. Like a priest, he received confessions, but he offered no absolution. Like a researcher, he collected the facts, but never wrote the story.

He just collected stories. Everyone's stories: friends, friends of friends, friends of friends of friends, acquaintances, strangers. True stories, fantasies, newspaper reports, dreams, horoscopes. In all the stories he looked for patterns and connections. He devised elaborate charts on which plots zigzagged across and around each other. He drew graphs, recording the repetition frequency of themes and emotions. He had maps of the world on which stories were plotted in an effort to see how everything came together. What he really wanted was to find a universal tale, a thread linking all humanity, the point at which everyone's tales meet. Then he hoped to write a story.

The Singhs never knew this about Oskar. He was the chronicler of everything and nothing, the pursuer of mirages, the silent thief of other people's words. If asked what he looked like, people would register, in surprise, that they recalled nothing of him. Maybe this anonymity was part of his ability to remain invisible in the face of another person's story. He seemed ageless, because his own story was suspended in the recording of others', so life bypassed him and left him untouched.

Some people believe that God is in the details, but Oskar had begun by assuming that plot is in the details. It was from this premise that he had set about collecting people's stories. He wanted to see if the details would prove infinitely varied and the plots essentially the same. He wondered if perhaps through this search he would find a template for the creation of the ideal story, in which everything happens as it must and everyone finds the answer they want.

Just as the stars, studied through a telescope, reveal their impenetrability, their eternal extension into galaxy after galaxy, so Oskar's all-absorbing ear found more and more stories with more and more variations. At first this had excited him. He collected zealously and catalogued carefully. He used coloured paper to record his work, putting stories into vivid rainbow assortments – thousands of them preserved in colours to which only he had the code. Records of the years extended back as a psychedelic array of hues. He had started with whites and creams and moved on to pale pastels: light pages that glowed with the premonition of an idea eager to be elucidated. He had progressed to extraordinary in-between shades of colour, reflecting doubts about the viability of his intentions. Over the years, the pages had become bolder in colour, darkening as they received the strong cursive black script that marked them. Towards the end of his collecting, when he was beginning to understand the futility of his enterprise, Oskar would use jet-black paper, thus erasing the stories even as he wrote them.

Thousands of stories captured over many years now filled the room in Elm Road where Oskar lived. The papers chronicling his efforts lay stacked in numerous shoeboxes that lined his walls from floor to ceiling. The project had expanded much further than he had anticipated. The details alone had overwhelmed him. He had been forced to accept, in frustration and wonder, that although books fit neatly into their covers, individual stories are not so easily filed into neat compartments. Lives do not adhere to patterns to indulge a theory, feelings spill messily over plots, and the smallest detail can change everything.

Oskar had begun by thinking of his mission as a giant dot-to-dot picture bursting to reveal its simple and surprising image. Now he knew that at some point, long ago or maybe yesterday, he had acquired too many dots and no clear picture could ever emerge. Yet sometimes, he still told himself that the stories were like many pictures layered delicately over each other to give a more credible and deeper reality, a post-modern perspective. Like those three-dimensional pictures which appear as a random confusion of colour, but which when glimpsed from the right angle reveal a clear image.

Oskar had to believe this, because the story collection had become an addiction. It was his only occupation, and yet it was painful because he saw, every day, how it dithered on the brink of futility. Sometimes he stared in horror at all the paper he had accumulated and knew that what remained were not plots or characters, but the sad scraps of obsession. He imagined the stories slowly losing their value and fading to nothing in their boxes. But in moments of absolute stillness, usually in the dead of night, when the house was sleeping and the city rested, a rustling could be detected, a subtle murmuring, as the disparate stories recognized their connections and fluttered with a longing to rearrange themselves. In these moments Oskar found himself validated but tormented, for he could not find the words to piece them together.

Oskar did not allow himself to reflect on this failure. He told himself that his job was only to record. In his dreams he suffered for it, as the question of his responsibility to the stories he collected rose up to challenge him. He wanted no obligation to the characters in his stories. He believed it was his neutrality that ordained the collection; to surrender that would be to jeopardize the whole enterprise. The nature of stories is such that they suck you in, and before you know it you're part of their game. Oskar was very wary of this. He had always resisted becoming involved. And he had succeeded – until the Singhs moved into the house where he lived.

It was so quiet. This was what Sarna found most unbearable, because the silence confirmed that she was alone. Lost were the sounds of their maid Wambui splashing the floor with water as she did the pangusa, or singing her Swahili songs while she washed clothes. Gone were the windows that opened on to bright greenery and the twittering of birds. Sarna could no longer hear children playing outside, shouting as they rode their bikes down the slope of Kira Road. Even the enticing cry of Mama Boga urging customers to buy fresh fruit and vegetables was now just a memory: 'Ndizi! Papai! Matunda!' Sarna felt she would give anything to hear again that familiar call and eat again those everyday fruits – bananas, pawpaw, passion fruit – which here in London had acquired the mystique of the exotic. Passion fruit, Sarna craved longingly. She swallowed as the word triggered the astringent memory of a sweet-sour tang, producing a rush and tingle of saliva in her mouth. She remembered the time when she had scooped out and thrown away all the seeds of the passion fruit, expecting to expose its flesh, only to be left with an empty cup of wrinkled skin. Now the day had come when she herself felt like an empty shell. Everything she cared about had been scooped away and she was left exposed in this new place, London. Here she had no idea where the roads led, she knew no one and didn't speak the language. She was at home all day with only the dramas in her head to occupy her. Life, like a gouged-out passion fruit, glowered ominously at Sarna, daring her to drink its bitter juice. What would she do? How would she arrange and contain the mess of experience and disappointment to make it more palatable? How would she reinvent herself this time?

London was a disappointment. Sarna could not believe this was the same great city Karam had bragged about. He had talked of a place with good tarmac roads flanked by grand old buildings. Sarna could see only long narrow streets full of old houses that clung to each other suffocatingly, the way bhajias do when you put too many into the frying pan at once. The sight of the stark and leafless trees upset Sarna. They looked so unnatural, so meagre compared with the chlorophyll cacophony of Kampala.

It did not help that the first weeks after their arrival in Britain were overshadowed by Winston Churchill's death. The subdued mood of the country confirmed Sarna's impression that she had come to a cold, dull place where no one ever smiled. On 28 January 1965, Karam dragged the family to Westminster Hall to see the great man lying in state. They joined the queue, which stretched right over the Thames and back towards St Thomas's hospital. For four hours, the Singhs huddled under one umbrella, which offered little protection from the bitter wind and sleet. Sarna was impressed by the number of people waiting patiently to pay their respects, even if she could not understand why. She felt completely indifferent to the event, which Karam raved about as 'a moment of history'. When they finally got into the hall, they were all soaked to the bone, their feet and hands numb. For a moment

Sarna was struck by the majesty of the place and the awed silence of the spectators. Then she sneezed and Karam looked at her reproachfully, as if she'd deliberately disrupted the air of reverence. Sarna lost all patience. She scowled at her husband, crossed her arms over her chest and hurried around the catafalque without a glance at Churchill.

Karam had described the British people as welcoming and friendly. No doubt he had been referring to his London ladies, Sarna surmised, for to her the place seemed deserted. While Karam went to work at the tax office, Sarna cautiously explored their neighbourhood. She was disappointed to encounter only old people, who moved so slowly it made her feel the world was about to stop. She regularly passed two elderly ladies, who would stare at her and comment, 'Oh, isn't she pretty? Oooh, what a lovely colour she's wearing!' Sarna would hurry past them, wondering what they were saying, worrying that they might be disapproving of her presence in the street. After all, there seemed to be no other Indians around. The idea of living amongst white people, right next door to them, even in the same house, was so strange to her. In Kampala, the black people, the Indians and the whites had all lived in separate areas with their own kind. Sarna had written to her family in India, portraying her life in this white neighbourhood in London as a step up in her social status, but in reality she did not know what to make of it. She felt like a trespasser, and part of her expected to be caught out and punished. Only after a few years, when other Indians had moved into the area and the security of numbers gave her confidence, would her anxiety go away.

* * *

'All day I'm alone with nothing to do,' Sarna complained one evening as Karam hung up a mirror in the living room. On the opposite wall a big brass clock shaped like Africa was ticking away. It had been a farewell gift from friends in Kampala. 'You go to work, the children go to school and I'm left in this big cold house. Once you came here to do a refrigeration course and now you've brought us to live in a fridge.'

The house was old and draughty and so far they had only managed to put carpets down in Karam and Sarna's bedroom and the 'back room' – a little cupboard at the back of the house behind the kitchen where Pyari and Rajan slept. The only source of heat was a fireplace in the main living room downstairs. Karam claimed he was reluctant to use it for 'safety reasons', but Sarna knew it was the expense he wanted to avoid. Karam had bought paraffin heaters for their bedrooms, but he insisted they should be used only when absolutely necessary. 'It's good for you to get used to the cold. It makes you stronger,' he said. When Karam was out of earshot Sarna had remarked to the children, 'Of course, he wants us to get cold so we become as numb and unfeeling as he is.' Then she had turned the heaters up to maximum.

'You were at home all day in Kampala too.' Karam stepped back to see if the mirror was straight. He noticed with surprise that the top coincidentally cut across the Africa clock right along the equator, thereby reflecting only the bottom half of the continent. He tried to point this out to Sarna but she wasn't interested. She pursed her lips as he came and sat down beside her and took her hand. 'It's just the weather making things seem difficult here. You wait, in a few months it'll be spring. Then you'll see how beautiful it is. So many flowers everywhere, people sitting outside enjoying the sun. You can walk in the park. That's partly why I bought this house, because of the park. I thought it would remind us of Kampala.'

Sarna pulled her hand out of his and began toying with the embroidered red border of her kameez. Karam pointed to the mirror. 'Makes the room look bigger, huh?'

'This place is like a prison!' No quantity of mirrors was going to deceive Sarna about the matchbox of a space Karam had moved them into. 'You said we had a house, but actually we have even less room than in Kampala. You made it sound like a huge palace, Victoria-style or whatever you call it.' Who was this Victoria? One of his London ladies? She must be a very shabby woman indeed. 'The place is almost falling down. Your tenants are the real landlords, living upstairs in all the big rooms while we're squashed on the ground floor. All day I'm stuck in here alone. In Kampala I had a maid, I had the neighbours, I could drive myself to the shops. Here there's nothing for me. I'm stranded. I can't even cook because our shipment of things hasn't arrived.'

Karam observed how forlorn Sarna looked, and yet so vital. Irritation had applied a pinkish coat to her skin, like a light wash. Her eyes, a pointillist's dream, glittered with tears and her hair had loosened from its bun to drape her face in a wispy aura. Karam found himself weakening in her presence, even though her words grated on him. He stroked her cheek. 'It will get better, I promise. If it is too quiet during the day, put on the radio,' he said gently. Then added, 'Not for too long, mind you. Just a few minutes now and then to distract you. And remember to pull out the plug when the radio is off. That stupid machine keeps eating electricity even when it isn't on.'

Sarna turned her head away from Karam so that his

hand slid off her cheek and strayed to the curve of her neck and shoulder, where his fingers started to press into her flesh. She bristled at the intention behind his touch. He could forget about it. If he was going to ration her radio use, there would be restrictions on *his* electricity cable – it too could stay unplugged. She shrugged her shoulders, and when Karam's hand didn't budge she tried to push him away with her words.

'What's the point of the radio when I can't understand anything?'

'That's why I keep telling you – go to the adult English class at the Mary Lawson School. It's just around the corner, it's free and it will give you something to do. You'll meet people and you'll learn English. Problem solved. See how simple it is?' His hand worked down to cup Sarna's breast.

'It's always simple for you.' She stiffened and pushed his hand away. 'The children might walk in.'

'I've been telling you for weeks to go to the classes, but you don't listen. You *must* learn English.' Karam stood up and examined the mirror again. 'If you don't learn it you won't be able to integrate properly. The longer you leave it the harder it will be for you.'

His gruff tone irritated Sarna, but it was the words themselves that really riled her because they were true. She had nothing against the English classes except Karam's constant preaching about them.

'What do you think?' Karam shifted the mirror slightly. 'Is it straight?' He leaned forward as if to adjust it again, but started fiddling with his turban instead.

Such a vain man! Sarna stood up in annoyance. He had always taken longer than her to get dressed and since they'd moved to Britain he was fussier than ever about his appearance. Now he was more interested in preening himself than paying attention to her.

'You don't understand me,' she said to Karam, who had taken a pen out of his shirt pocket and was using it to tuck stray hairs under his turban. 'You've never understood.'

Karam watched her walk out of the room. *She* was the one who didn't understand. Such a hard-headed woman. Nothing was ever enough for her. Well, a hard-headed woman . . . Karam almost smiled as the words of the song played into his thoughts. He felt that nothing truer than Elvis's lyrics about how a stubborn woman could torment a gentle man had ever been spoken. He'd first heard this song on the radio during one of his solo trips to London in the late 1950s. The lyrics had struck a chord, as though they'd been written just for him. While listening, Karam had ceased to be the quiet café customer bent over his paper and tea. He'd become a toe-tapping, head-nodding, finger-rapping man possessed by a tune that was telling his story. The lyrics were etched on Karam's consciousness for ever. In trying moments with Sarna, they rang in his head like a chorus of sympathy.

He put the pen back in his pocket and examined his fingernails. In the heat of Africa he'd trimmed them every third day, but here in London once a week was sufficient. This move was proving more difficult than he'd imagined. He felt he was doing everything possible to make life comfortable for his family. But there were certain factors he couldn't control, like the weather and the speed of the arrival of their things from Kampala.

Ungrateful lot. Karam rubbed his nails along each other as if to buff them. Here they were in a new country, new house, new schools, being taken out for dinner almost every day, and still they weren't happy. Other people would give anything to be in their shoes. His own brothers had looked at him with envy when he'd told them about his plans. They all hoped to follow in his footsteps over the next few years.

'Is there anything to eat for dinner or do we have to go out?' Karam called to his wife.

Her dismayed face popped around the door. 'There's no cooker, no groceries – where is dinner to come from?'

'No,' Karam said quickly. 'I just thought maybe you had made sandwiches. If there's nothing, call the children. Let's go and get something, I'm starving.'

If there's nothing – the words hurt Sarna. She read an implicit criticism in them, an accusation that she could not feed her family. Having an empty kitchen made her feel barren. 'If I had a proper kitchen you could expect a proper meal. Pyari! Rajan! Put on your coats, we're going to get something to eat. I don't know why you can't just buy a cooker. One month we've been waiting for the one from Kampala.'

'It's coming, it's coming.' Karam didn't want to get into another argument. 'I spoke to them yesterday. They said it should arrive in one or two weeks.'

'They said that two weeks ago.' Sarna wrapped her chuni around her neck like a scarf as they walked out of the house.

The absence of a cooker meant the Singh family had been eating out almost every day since arriving in London. At first the outings had been a great novelty. They had never eaten at restaurants before. Balham was dotted with little cafés and takeaways. The family's favourite eateries so far were Kentucky Fried Chicken and Wimpy. Tonight, however, Karam had a new suggestion. 'Let's go to Fry It,' he said as they headed down the street.

* * *

Pyari, Rajan and Sarna would never forget their first taste of fish and chips. 'You'll love it,' Karam predicted as they took their seats at a Formica table. The thick air of the small shop, heavy with the smell and smoke of frying, added to their anticipation – similar conditions at home had often preceded the delights Sarna made. When the warm parcels wrapped in newspaper were placed in front of them, they turned their heads to Karam. Following his example, they unwrapped the layers of steamy paper to reveal gold-crusted fish and a heap of fat chips. Tentatively they tasted. Pyari smiled as the crisp crunch of the batter gave way to soft, flaky flesh. Rajan attacked a chip and then sat bolt upright, his hands waving in front of his face, his mouth alarmed into a pained 'O' by the heat of the freshly fried potato. Sarna ate with interest. She was not surprised that fish and chips were typical English food. Karam's strange attachment to the place had long made her suspect there was something fishy about London. The relish with which Karam tucked into his meal convinced Sarna that, as far as men were concerned, there was an undeniable connection between enjoyment of fish and the pleasures of the flesh. She would consider her hypothesis validated later that night when Karam's ardour was awakened. It would not occur to her that the humble cod might have something to do with the weakening of her resolve to resist him.

Sarna picked at her food. 'It's nice . . . but something is missing.' Adding vinegar lifted the meal, but still she wasn't satisfied. A dollop of tomato ketchup improved things further, and yet she craved another flavour. She dug into her handbag, pulled out a dried red chilli and crumbled this over her food. 'Ah!' She nodded with pleasure. 'Now it tastes good. That's more like it. Mmmm.' She munched away for a few moments before trying to share her condiments with the rest of the family. The children refused. Karam said no and then, a few minutes later, inspired by Sarna's obvious enjoyment, he acquiesced. 'Hmmm. Not bad.'

After six weeks of dining on solid English fare, the attraction of the new food wore off for the whole family. Sarna tried to spice up their diet. She piled cheddar cheese and salad between slices of white bread as she had seen them do at the sandwich shop, and lifted the humble combination by adding various chutneys that she'd had the foresight to bring from Kampala. In years to come, she would assert that she'd been making the ploughman's lunch long before it became ubiquitous across Great Britain.

Without a cooker, Sarna felt impotent. Much of the anxiety aroused in her by the move to London might have been harmlessly dispelled if she'd been able to clear her thoughts through cooking. Once she had tried to make a fire in their back garden with a view to cooking there, but the damp mound of grass and twigs just smoked weakly when set alight. She might have persevered, but Mr Reynolds leaned out of the window upstairs and shouted, 'What y'doin', woman? This ain't Africa, y'know. It ain't the bloomin' jungle! Y'll have us all up in flames if y'don't stop.' Sarna didn't have a clue what he was saying but his harsh tone was deterrent enough, especially since his shouting brought other neighbours to their windows. She was unable to persist with improvised barbecuing under the shadow of those frowning faces.

Stuck in a kitchen without a cooker, Sarna's natural

propensity to churn things over had no outlet. Denied the release of chopping, boiling, frying, melting or colouring her thoughts through food, she was feeling increasingly oppressed and unhappy. But the body always finds some form of release and, bereft of a real-life cooker, Sarna's insides became the hob of creation. She felt the burning in her chest and the bubbling in her belly. She heard the gurgling in her gut and the sizzling in her soul, and she put it down to indigestion. 'Your English food is not agreeing with me,' she began complaining to Karam.

Every process has a result and the outcome of Sarna's bodily brewing was a deadly breed of the humble fart. Foul and sulphurous, these offenders slipped out of her silently and then guiltily disappeared into thin air. But they could not vanish without leaving a potent trace of their rottenness hanging around for several minutes. Sarna was alone at home when the first of these emissions was produced. Despite the relief of its release, she was horrified. She threw open the windows of the living room, where she was sitting, and turned the radio up louder as though that too might help alleviate the awful stench. Inevitably the incident recurred in the presence of Rajan and Pyari. 'Uuuuuugh! Something's died,' Rajan squealed as the smell reached him. Pyari, who never opened a window for fear of letting in the cold, flew to the front door and ducked outside to gulp some fresh air. For the first time since coming to London, Sarna really laughed. She guffawed from sheer embarrassment and perverse delight. Her laughter was hushed and hidden, but violent in its quietness: her body, bent double, shook like a wind-up vibrating toy. When the children saw her, they folded up in giggles too. 'Mee!' Pyari chortled in disgust. By the time they all calmed down the smell had disappeared. Sarna was the first to speak. 'Don't you dare tell your pithaji.' She wagged a finger at the kids.

Pithaji did not need to be told, because a few days later he was unexpectedly treated to the experience. The children were sitting at the table in the living room doing their homework and Sarna was sewing. All of a sudden, Karam looked up from his newspaper and sniffed cautiously. 'Is the gas on?' he asked. Ignoring her impulse to open the window, quelling the heat of shame that was creeping up her neck and stifling the giggle that was tickling her throat, Sarna grabbed the opportunity to say, 'How can the gas be on when there's no cooker?' Karam, too affronted by the smell even to imagine it might have come from anything human, left the room to investigate. Rajan and Pyari collapsed on to their text-books. Sarna glared at them as she threw open the window. When Karam returned, the odour was less noxious. Sarna pointed her nose at the ceiling. 'Must be coming from upstairs. Those Reynoldses of yours are just rotting up there.'

It came as a surprise to Karam when, a few days later, Sarna said she felt ill. She refused to share the exact nature of her symptoms but insisted he take her to the doctor. There, of course, she was obliged to tell Karam what was up, because he had to translate for Dr Thomas.

'Doctor, she says she has whole body pain.'

Dr Thomas had known other Asian ladies who came in with complaints of 'whole body pain'. He'd worked out that this appeal for help sprang from embarrassment at having to describe pain in sensitive areas to a strange man. With a series of discreet questions put through Karam, followed by some creative thinking to deduce the meaning of Sarna's obscure answers, the doctor was forced to concede that he might be faced with an unusual case. It appeared to him that Sarna's pain was indeed of the whole body. She was suffering from an overall feeling of congestion, an all-consuming lethargy, the cause of which was a blockage in her stomach. Dr Thomas diagnosed severe constipation. 'It's a common problem, probably brought on by the change in diet and general readjustment.' He ran a stethoscope over Sarna's stomach. A slow, sluggish sound filled his ears – and behind that, so faint as to be almost imperceptible, was another noise: *da daa, da daa, da daa*. Not quite the rhythm of a heartbeat, but close.

Karam looked at his wife. 'He says you have an upset tummy.'

Sarna nodded, although she was aggrieved by the mildness of the diagnosis. Her symptoms felt much more serious, but she was in no position to dispute what the doctor said. She really did not want to describe her true state through Karam. How could she say that she hadn't been able to use the toilet for two weeks now? How could she explain that she felt as though she was being suffocated from inside? At that moment she resolved to start English classes.

'He said to take two tablets before going to sleep tonight,' Karam said as he got into the car and handed Sarna the medication from the pharmacist. 'He said if it doesn't work by the morning, wait until tomorrow evening to repeat the treatment. He said you should pass a stool within forty-eight hours—' Karam broke off. He hadn't intended to convey the pharmacist's instructions verbatim. He heard Sarna shift uncomfortably in the seat next to him. Quickly he turned the key in the ignition.

'It's your English food that's upsetting me,' Sarna said. A

part of her knew that the afflictions of her mind were agitating the rest of her body. She had felt everything build up inside her until she'd become blocked. But she didn't like acknowledging this – better to put the blame elsewhere.

Sarna recovered somewhat when the tablets did their work a couple of days later, but she knew that full deliverance would only come with the arrival of her cooker. Three weeks later, over two months into their life in London, it finally came. Sarna tried to get cooking straight away, but encountered a new set of problems. The selection of vegetables in the shops here was so pitiful compared with Africa! There was nowhere to buy fresh Indian herbs – not even coriander. Dishes that Sarna had made without a second thought were now impossible. Trip after trip to the shops failed to turn up what she needed. 'Less use than useless,' was her verdict as they left each supermarket or greengrocer's. She imagined they would be doomed to fish and chips or sandwiches for ever. That was her lowest point of their first year in London. Where had Karam brought her? What kind of country didn't have the most basic ingredients in the world? Methi, fenugreek leaves. Karela, bitter gourd. Bhindi, okra. Matoke, green banana. Anar, pomegranate. Mirch, green chilli. Limbri, curry leaves. Pista, pistachio nuts. In her distress, Sarna tugged at the corners of her chunis until the threads came loose and the hems fell open. The chiffon ones suffered most – they ended up as laddered as silk stockings dragged through a thorny bush.

If Karam had not come to the rescue, something terrible might have happened. Instead, with a tenderness reminiscent of the early days of their love, he opened

Sarna's eyes to what was still possible. She had vast stores of all her dry spices, didn't she? She had bags of dhals and pulses that could be cooked a hundred and one ways. She had the essentials, like garlic, onions, tomatoes and potatoes, readily at hand. In England there was an abundance of vegetables they didn't eat so often – carrots, cauliflower, broccoli and cabbage – but Sarna could make them delicious, Karam was sure of it. Thus he coaxed his wife back to optimism. And she rose to the challenge. She had cooked against hate and envy, beyond suspicion and loss. She had cooked herself into love and out of pain. She would overcome the obstacles and cook up a triumph once again.

12

Sarna was not the only one who had difficulty adjusting to life in London. Pyari and Rajan faced their share of challenges. Getting used to the cold was Pyari's greatest trial. At home, during those first years in London before the house was fitted with central heating, she would huddle by the paraffin heaters whenever Karam sanctioned their use. She would have liked to crawl into the metal cylinder and live in its hot glow. Her parents were always warning her to keep a safe distance from the heater. 'But I'm freezing,' Pyari would protest to Sarna – she wouldn't have dared raise any objection to Karam. 'Better to be freezing than blazing,' Sarna would say. 'You get any closer to that thing and you'll go up in flames. Now move away.'

In school, when Pyari was obliged to spend breaktime outside, she didn't join in the skipping or games of hopscotch. Instead she would wrap her heavy braids around her neck and ears, draw her arms up into the sleeves of her coat and just stand there: a handless frozen statue, her knees knocking frantically.

Rajan, meanwhile, had problems of his own. From his first day at school, his mane rolled into a bun and covered by the handkerchief-like putka made him the butt of endless jokes. It had started with overheard whispers and giggles of 'Is that a boy or a girl?'

'If you're a boy, why've you got a top-knot on your 'ead?' asked Daniel, who was to torment Rajan incessantly for the next six months.

'It's because of my religion,' Rajan mumbled.

'What religion's that then?' Daniel asked. 'Doughnut-headism?'

'Sikhism.' Rajan ran a hand over the navy fabric covering his head.

'Never 'eard of it.' Daniel reached out and tugged at the blue putka. ''s not a religion 'ere, that's for sure.'

Rajan's heart started pounding. He looked at the scraggly white faces smirking at him. Unconsciously he took a deep breath and stood taller in an effort to relieve the pressure on his bladder. To his aggressors it looked like a defiant stance, perhaps even a challenge. The school bell rang. Rajan stepped back and turned to walk to the hall. Daniel grabbed the flap of his coat and gave it a sharp tug. ''Ey! Watch out, brown boy.'

Rajan's long hair, which he had never really thought twice about until now, became a cause of endless anxiety. He began to resent his hair, to see it as an invader, a foreign entity that had attached itself to him without permission. Why did his hair have to be long, anyway? He looked at his father's head and no longer found inspiration in the white turban that haloed it. He had once overheard Karam say that when he was in England people treated him like a king. 'Oh yes,' Karam had declared long ago in Kampala. 'They see the turban, they remember pictures they've seen from the British Raj in India and they think, "He's a maharaja." So people are very polite, very respectful.' For all the king-like resonances of his name, Rajan knew his headgear would never make a maharaja of him. He was treated more like a court jester than a king. When Daniel and his crew caught their first glimpse of his turbaned father, Rajan was interrogated about why his dad wore a nappy on his head. 'Is it to keep 'is ears warm? Can't afford a 'at, eh?' Daniel jeered. 'Look at the lot of you, a bunch of rag 'eads.'

Rajan began looking at himself in the mirror every day, suspiciously observing the bulging contours of the putka. It was an alien sitting on his head. Just as a thumping pain gives the impression that the hurting limb is expanding and contracting with every throb, so Rajan was convinced his bun grew and shrank between the torturous hours at school and his time at home. Pointing to the offending object, he asked for Pyari's opinion. 'How much bigger is it?'

'Bigger?' Pyari had noticed Rajan's intense pre-occupation with his appearance and thought it quite ridiculous. Even when she found out about the bullying, it was some time before she connected that to what she initially considered to be Rajan's new-found vanity. 'Of course it's not bigger. Why would it be bigger? And you'd better not let Pithaji catch you primping yourself like that – you know you'll get a fat slap.'

Rajan was not reassured by Pyari's response. At night as he lay in bed he would pull at his hair, giving it forceful, urgent tugs in the hope that it might detach from his scalp for ever.

As if sensing the dislike of its bearer, Rajan's hair retaliated by becoming more difficult to manage. Washing it became arduous because it curled menacingly around his neck as though it wanted to choke him and it poked at his eyes, making them smart. Post-wash hair-combing also became an act of intensive labour because the hair tangled itself into knots and refused to submit to braiding. Unable to manage it himself, Rajan was forced to let Sarna attack and subdue it with her ruthless pulling and brushing and cursing. 'Hai Ram! This is not hair, it's a nightmare. Must be the London water – it's messing up your hair the way it has my stomach.'

If the hair did not actually grow and expand the putka, Rajan's own gradual shrinkage certainly gave the impression that it was getting bigger. No wonder he saw it as a pulsing parasite sucking the life out of him. The impervious knot sat, fat and turgid, atop the boy's gaunt face. As the weeks went by and the bullying at school continued, Rajan lost his appetite for everything: food, studying, playing, winding up Pyari. While changes in his other habits might have gone unnoticed, Rajan's relations with the dinner on his plate did not escape Sarna. 'Why aren't you eating?' she scolded tenderly. At first she had thought he was being picky because he missed her home cooking. She had watched his cravings for Kentucky Fried Chicken, fish and chips and cheese sandwiches diminish with some satisfaction. Like mother, like son. 'That cooker of ours had better get here soon or we'll all waste away to nothing,' she had told Karam. 'This English food of yours is no good for us. Look at my Raja – he's just withering away. He's like me, he needs proper spicy food.'

But even after Sarna's cooker arrived and she made his favourite dishes, chicken curry and masala potatoes, the boy did not eat. That was when Sarna really started to worry. 'Hai Ruba, why aren't you eating? How are you going to study if you don't eat?'

Rajan just shrugged his shoulders and said he wasn't hungry. When Sarna expressed her worries to Karam, he too brushed her off. 'He'll eat when he's hungry. He can't avoid food for ever.'

'Maybe he's ill,' Sarna persisted. 'Remember when Gudo Masi's son Chand stopped eating? He had malaria, he almost *died*. We should take Rajan to the doctor right away.'

'What's wrong with you? This is London, they don't have such illnesses here. Of course Rajan's not ill. He's perfectly well – no fever, no pain. This is some game he's playing. As soon as his stomach starts rumbling he'll eat again.'

Sarna stared at her unfeeling husband in disgust. Such a man, hai, such a man. Only a woman like her could put up with a man like him.

Pyari urged Rajan not to take the bullying to heart, but her pleas had little impact on his tormented mind. Things came to a head at the end of the first term with the arrival of their school reports. Neither report was the glowing article to which Karam had become accustomed in Uganda. The children's workload had increased and the pressure on them was immense. Given the circumstances, Pyari's report was rather good – but not good enough for Karam. He slammed the report fiercely on the table and made it clear that Pyari's Easter holidays must be spent working for A grades in all subjects.

When Rajan's turn came, there was more heavy pounding on the table. Karam couldn't understand it. The boy had been a star student back in Kampala and now all of a sudden, at a good school with superior facilities, he had slipped to less than mediocre. 'Maths, "Shows understanding but no motivation,"' Karam read out and

174

slammed his fist on the table. Bang. 'History, "Must apply himself better." ' Bang. 'French, "Has made little effort to get to grips with the basics." ' Bang, bang. 'Biology, "Must apply himself more." ' Bang. 'WHAT – IS – THIS?' Karam growled, punctuating every word with a threatening rap on the table. Rajan was too terrified to utter any sort of explanation. 'Every night you sit here looking like you're working, but what are you doing, I ask? What on earth have you been DOING?' Karam's voice rolled into a roar so frightening that even Sarna jumped. 'What have I brought you to this country for? For poor results? I don't think so. This is not acceptable.' Karam glared. 'How did this happen? How many times did I tell you to concentrate?' He raised his hand and lowered it forcefully on to Rajan's back. 'How many reminders do you need?' Smack. 'How often do I have to repeat myself?' Slap. Karam's blows were impossible answers to rhetorical questions. As a young boy he had done mental sums to distract himself from pain; now he inflicted pain to the chant of incalculable aggregates.

'Hai! Stop!' Sarna tried to get between them. 'He hasn't eaten. I told you he's not well. If he can't eat it's no wonder he can't study.'

Tears were pouring out of Rajan's eyes, but fear of his father continued to keep any sound suppressed.

'Just get him out of my sight,' Karam ordered. 'Get out, all of you.' This was the usual run of things. If ever Karam raised his hand against any member of the family, he would either leave the room himself or order them out, as though by putting an immediate physical distance between himself and his victim he could separate himself from his actions.

* * *

175

As the weeks passed, Pyari noticed her brother's behaviour become even stranger. The mirror-gazing became more intense. Once Pyari thought she saw Rajan punch at his putka. She wasn't sure, it could simply have been a sharp move to adjust it, but the grim set of Rajan's full lips made her feel the move was not innocent. This, coupled with the new finger-turban game she saw Rajan playing, upset her. When he was a little boy, Rajan had used scraps of fabric left over from Sarna's sewing to make colourful little turbans for his fingers. It had been a way of emulating his father, whom he saw tying a new turban every day. Rajan's finger turbans had really been very skilful and bore a distinct resemblance to Karam's sharp, neat ones. 'He's a true Singh,' Karam had said, pinching his son's arm fondly. Rajan had long since lost interest in making mini-turbans, but he had now resumed the habit. He effortlessly wound perfect turbans around his fingertips and then pulled them off violently, as if he was enacting some vengeful dream of decapitation. Pyari realized she had to tell her parents what was going on. She guessed that no amount of threats or beating would make Rajan's work improve if he continued to feel miserable about school. She told Sarna that Rajan was being bullied and suggested this was at the root of his unusual behaviour and bad results.

'But why are they picking on *him*?' Sarna looked up from the dough she was kneading. Why would anyone have anything against her Raja? 'He's such a nice, good boy. Every day I pack him extra food to share with his friends. Why don't they like him?'

'*Mee*,' Pyari said. 'Not everything has to do with food. It's because he's Indian – you know, a *different colour*.'

'But he doesn't look Indian – such fair skin he has, like

milk. He could pass for English, I tell you.' Sarna squinted at Pyari. *'You're* the real Indian, you're *much* darker than he is.' She stopped kneading and looked at her daughter suspiciously. 'What about *you*? Don't they tease *you*?'

'No, not really.' Pyari was hurt but unsurprised by her mother's comments. The laments about her dark skin had been part of their daily conversation for as long as she could remember, but the criticism had not lost its sting. She did not know that her mother had looked for faults in her children to reassure herself of their imperfections, because perfection had been stolen from her before. Better to love that which was flawed – maybe then no one would be tempted to take it from you.

'Are you sure? They must say something. Your skin hasn't changed one bit since we came here. I was so happy, I thought the English winter would help whiten your face – but no. Not even one tone lighter, not even one shade different.' Sarna examined Pyari's face and pinched her cheeks, leaving trails of flour on them. She allowed herself such liberties – more health checks than caresses, she liked to think. 'Are you using that Motamarphosa cream? Huh? Are you?'

'Ye-es, Mee. Stop it.' Pyari pulled away from Sarna's prying eyes and prodding fingers. 'And it's Metamorphosis, the name of the cream.'

'That's what I said, *Motamarphosas*. I don't think you're using it. Your skin is looking too dark. Hai, what will I do with you?'

Pyari ran her fingers along the plaited length of a braid as if it was a musical instrument. Sarna was right, she hadn't been using that horrid cream. It stung around the eyes and smelled disgusting and she was sure it didn't work anyway. She had seen Persini Chachiji using it on

Rupi and it had made no difference to her. Pyari hated the way Sarna always got the cream's name wrong. She was convinced her mother deliberately mispronounced the word and derived some kind of cruel enjoyment from the twist. Motamarphosa – do a big fat fart, that's what Sarna's version meant. What kind of cream could have such a name? The ideal cream for a daughter with a too-dark face, probably.

'And your nose! Hai Ruba. So big – just like your pithaji's.' Sarna was still ranting. 'Have you been rubbing it like I showed you? Doesn't seem to have made any difference.' She reached for her daughter's nose, trying to file it down between two index fingers. 'If you'd been doing this every day it would have been half the size by now.'

'*Mee!*' Pyari shrieked the middle syllable from Mu*mee*ji that had become her name for Sarna and wriggled out of her mother's yeasty grip. 'What about Rajan?'

'I can't believe it. If they don't say anything to *you*, why should they say anything to Raja?'

'Because –' Pyari gripped a braid in each hand and waved their bushy ends at Sarna. 'Because he's a boy and he's different. He has long hair.'

'Long hair?' Sarna repeated, smacking her lips as though she was tasting the words before deciding on their authenticity.

'Yes, long hair.' Pyari went on to describe the sorts of jibes that Rajan had been suffering.

'Hai, my son.' Sarna's hand went to her heart. 'But why? Don't they know we're Sikhs? Hai vaichara, poor thing, my little Raja. Who are these boys? Call Raja, let me ask him. I'll tell them.' Her speech became sharper and faster with every sentence. '*I'll* teach them a lesson. No one speaks to my son like that. Wait until your father comes home. I'll make him go straight to your school. He will report those boys. Where's Rajan? Call him.'

'Mee, *no*. He doesn't know I'm telling you. He'll be really annoyed. That's not the solution anyway.' She explained about Rajan's recent actions, then whispered the unspeakable. 'I think the only way is to cut his hair.'

'Hai, listen to you.' Sarna gave Pyari a little shove. 'Don't even *think* about that and don't say a word about it in front of your father. Such ideas! Fiteh moon, how stupid. Poor Raja, he has some problems at school and his sister is hatching plans to chop off his hair. Have some respect, *please*.'

When Sarna told Karam about the situation, he did not share her incredulity about the news but was incensed by it. He took it as a personal affront – for was not any criticism of his son's appearance an indirect insult to his own? To speak out against one Sikh is to slander them all. He wished he had arranged Rajan's dastar bhandi before moving to London as had been his original intention. The ceremony to mark Rajan's move from putka to turban was long overdue. If he had been wearing a turban by now, Karam thought, Rajan would look older and smarter and maybe they wouldn't be teasing him at school. Karam couldn't shake off the feeling that he was indirectly responsible for Rajan's bullying. He should have had the dastar bhandi before they came, he should have just done it.

Despite his sympathy for Rajan, Karam's attempt to speak to him about the bullying resulted in another humiliating grilling for the boy. Karam motioned for his son to sit down on the sofa.

'Your mother tells me boys at school are teasing you about your hair. Is that right?'

Rajan, who had not expected the question, looked at his father in bewilderment and accidentally met his gaze.

Karam took the eye contact as a 'yes' and continued, 'They are ignorant good-for-nothings. You should not be intimidated by them. Did you tell them you're a Sikh?'

Rajan nodded and wondered how his father had found out. Pyari must be the culprit. A sneaked glance in her direction revealed her furtively biting her nails.

'But they didn't stop, huh? You should have showed them your kara,' Karam said, raising his own right hand to reveal the glint of the silver bracelet. 'You should have said we Sikhs are kashatriyas, warriors, and this bracelet is our shield. Anyone who speaks against us shall live to regret it.'

Rajan folded his hands between his legs and looked at the floor. How could he say that they had seen his kara and mocked him for wearing jewellery like a girl?

'You should have told them that the Sikhs helped the British maintain order during the Raj in India. They wanted us in their armies because we were the best fighting men. These boys are teasing you because they know *nothing*.'

Sarna nodded approvingly. Good to hear him talking sense for a change. But all of a sudden, Karam changed tack.

'You did not defend yourself or your faith and so they were able to take advantage of you. Just remember,' he wagged a finger, 'if you show weakness or doubt, people will jump in and try to crush you. In the old days you could have pulled out your kirpan and the sight of the sword would have been enough to scare anyone. These days you must have your wits about you. You must stand tall and proud against such fools, and if they bother you too much you should report them immediately to the schoolmaster. Did you do that?'

Rajan shook his head.

'No.' This was the answer Karam had expected. 'So they knew you're a weakling.'

Sarna glared at him.

'Did they beat you?' Karam asked.

Rajan shook his head.

'Did they take your food or books or anything from you?'

Rajan shook his head.

'Just words?'

Rajan nodded.

'You're a weak boy, getting so upset over words. You should ignore them. The more you get upset, the more they will bother you. No more of this moping about – do you hear me? And no more of this not-eating business. I will report those boys to your schoolmaster first thing next week. What are their names?' He pulled a pen out of his shirt pocket and looked around for some paper.

Rajan did not respond. He was terrified by the prospect of naming Daniel.

Karam hovered over his son. 'They have names?'

Rajan shook his head and Karam lost his.

'Look at you! Do you know what Singh means? Huh? Lion! Singhs are lions. And look at you, such a coward you can't even tell your own father who is bothering you. What are you scared of? No wonder they're picking on you. You're a disgrace to the Sikhs. They must have chosen you because they saw the yellow of your eyes.' Then, as if relenting slightly, he said, 'Just give me a name.' He tore a corner from one page of *The Times* and waited, pen poised.

Rajan sat there looking helpless and shaking his head periodically to emphasize his resistance.

Karam watched in disgust. What a stupid boy! He stabbed the pen against the scrap of newspaper. 'Fine. Have it your way. Stay miserable and hungry. But if your school results don't improve, this will not be an acceptable excuse and there will be big trouble.'

'This is what your London has done! I should never have come here. I knew it. I *knew* it. Only such a place could turn a perfectly happy normal boy into a sick ghost of a child,' Sarna wailed.

Karam didn't know what to say. He looked at the Africa clock and wondered if anything like this could have happened there. Two weeks ago, Rajan had come home from school with a bruised cut on the side of his face where a stone intended to hit his putka had widely missed the mark and narrowly missed his eye. Rajan had claimed it was an accident. In truth, the story of William Tell that was told in assembly had inspired Daniel to use Rajan as a target. Karam had wanted to go to the school and wring the necks of the culprits who had hurt his son, but once again Rajan would not give him any names.

Sarna had suggested that perhaps the only way to solve the problem was by cutting Rajan's hair. Karam had made it absolutely clear that a haircut was not an option. 'Over my dead body,' he'd said fiercely. Well, the body now looking near dead was Rajan's. He had fainted in school yesterday and was lying in bed on Dr Thomas's orders, with instructions to rest and eat lots of fruit and vegetables.

'Ejucation. Ejucation.' Sarna repeated the English word she'd heard Karam use so often and raised her hands as though its meaning baffled her. 'What good is studying if it makes you sick? Hai, my Raja, he was such a healthy boy. Hai, my baby boy. What have you done to him? What have you done?'

For the first time since they had come to England, Karam doubted his decision to move. What *had* he done? There had been nothing but strife in the family since they'd arrived and now Rajan was so ill. How could they keep going like this? What could he do? He went to the shops and bought a huge quantity of fruit. Usually the family ate only bananas and apples, because they were cheap. This time Karam piled his basket high with oranges, pears and grapes. He took the bags of shopping straight into the back room, where Rajan was lying in the bottom bunk because he was too weak to climb to the top. 'Look here, lots of fruit for you. You should be back to normal in no time.'

But as soon as he left the room, Sarna cornered him. 'Why have you bought so much fruit? For rotting? Do something useful.' Her hand swept over her head and rested on her bun in a seemingly innocent gesture. 'Do something that will really make a difference.' She had come round to the idea of cutting Rajan's hair. After all, they wouldn't be the first ones to take such an action. Harbans Singh's sons had both had their hair cut because of trouble at school, as well as Tara Singh's son. Karam knew this and still he was being so stubborn. He was worried about those parents of his sitting thousands of miles away. They wouldn't even care, Sarna had told Karam, and when that annoyed him, she'd said that Rajan could just wear a turban every time the family visited. 'Who can tell,' she asked reasonably enough, 'whether hair is long or short under a pugh?'

The days Karam spent deliberating over whether or not to cut Rajan's hair were amongst the most difficult of his life, although in years to come he would become convinced that the turban was actually the least relevant of the Sikh tenets, that without it the religion was not diminished but liberated. 'Sikhism is not a look, it is a way of life,' Karam would one day tell the few liberal-minded friends who could tolerate his arguments, even if they wouldn't endorse them. 'I say let young people follow their fashions and dress how they like. If they value Sikhism, if they live respectable lives and come to the gurudwara once a week, we should be happy.'

In the end, Karam did what he had to. He did it in spite of his own instincts to the contrary and the cautionary advice of the granthi at the temple in Shepherd's Bush. He did it knowing full well that Baoji and Biji would disapprove when they found out. He did it even though the kara on his right arm repeatedly flashed at him in warning, as if desperate to fulfil its function of making the wearer think twice about his actions. It went against everything he had been taught, but finally Karam told Sarna to get Rajan's hair cut. He acted out of necessity, but most of all he was impelled by love, by the desire to give his son the best possible chance in this land of opportunity to which he had brought his family.

Rajan would never forget the sudden sensation of lightness as the braid came away from his head. Simultaneously, all the anxiety and fear that had weighed down on him for months also fell away. He felt as if he had been made new and whole and perfect. Samson may have lost all his power when his locks were chopped off, but Rajan became stronger. The putka had become a tumour for him, and with it cut out Rajan was able to look his persecutors in the eye and the bullies, who had no more ammunition for their attacks, turned their attention to other victims. That year Rajan experienced a sudden growth spurt and shot up several inches. His schoolwork improved and he was soon at the top of his class in almost every subject. His confidence returned and he started to like London. The city began to seduce him just as it had his father, but Rajan's attachment to the place, his connection with it, went much deeper than Karam's, perhaps because he had, in a sense, been reborn there.

Sarna cried as Rajan's long hair was snipped off. She had always indulged him, as if his being a boy gave him some advantage over her and therefore left him less vulnerable to her love. She snivelled all the way home, caressing the clipped braid as though it were a poor wounded creature she could nurse back to health. In her room, the braid was carefully folded away amongst her prized collection of odds and ends. Once the initial drama of the haircut was over, however, she succumbed to vanity. 'Raja looks really English now. So handsome.'

But it was weeks before Karam could look at Rajan without his heart skipping a beat. The first sight of the familiar stranger with short hair brought tears to his eyes. What had he done? In cutting off Rajan's hair, had Karam cut him off from his heritage? Something had changed. He could see it in the revived spark of Rajan's eyes. Karam had wished to see some sign of remorse, but he found only relief, melting like liquid gold, in Rajan's dark-brown eyes. Then Karam knew that something had been lost, never to be retrieved. It was something purer than innocence, something fragile and essential: the father's image of the model son, which was in fact an idealized vision of himself.

It is said that children have a moment of awakening when they realize that their parents are not the perfect gods they imagined them to be. Parents experience such moments about their children, too. But for them the revelation is more excruciating, because it involves an acknowledgement of their own inadequacy and fallibility. It requires the acceptance that we cannot redeem ourselves through our children, and we cannot save our children from becoming what they must be.

13

Rajan knocked on the half-open door before peering around it. 'OK?'

Under the slanting low ceiling of the attic room, Oskar was bent intently over his desk as usual. The sunlight flooding in through the windows in the roof meant that this room was sweltering in the summer. Hot air momentarily clouded Rajan's glasses, but the heat seemed to have no effect on Oskar. Exactly what he was working at Rajan still hadn't figured out, and no one else seemed to know either. Karam and Sarna described Oskar as a student. 'He must be researching for a degree or something, he goes to the British Library all the time,' Karam observed. But just what was it that Oskar was so committed to? What was he doing with the coloured sheaves of paper that always covered his desk? Rajan had never dared to ask. Now, like all things left too long unsaid, this simple question had become difficult. Yet whenever he was in Oskar's room, he looked around for clues. Today, after lifting up his T-shirt to wipe the steam from his glasses, he registered that Oskar was busily writing on dark-green and navy-blue paper. Rajan watched the fast, fluid transcription of words on to the page. He noticed that Oskar did not pause between sentences or hesitate over a single word, but wrote as if his thoughts were fully formed and he was simply taking dictation from them. Rajan leaned closer in admiration and Oskar, who had been too engrossed to hear his knock or call, looked up suddenly.

'My mum sent this for you.' Rajan held out a plate of food. Oskar looked at his watch. It was just after four o'clock in the afternoon. He smiled and thanked Rajan. There was something in his gentle manner that gave Rajan the courage to ask, 'Are you still studying?'

Oskar cast his eyes over the desk and suppressed a sigh. 'Yes, yes. I suppose so.' He nodded vigorously, more to convince himself than to assure the boy.

'How come you have no books, then?' Rajan was eager to know as much as possible now that the subject had finally been broached. His eyes flashed over the walls of the room, three of which were stacked high with shoeboxes. On the fourth wall, above the bed, was a huge map of the world, covered in so many lines that it looked like a hybrid version of the Ordnance Survey maps he had to study at school. Rajan had no idea that the map represented Oskar's version of geography, in which the contours of human stories make up the landscape of the world.

Oskar noticed how Rajan's boyishness was beginning to be thrown into awkwardness by broadening shoulders and a hint of thickening hair on his upper lip. The development was slight and yet so sudden it made Oskar think of the swift passing of time. Rajan still had all the time in the world, and his questions were making Oskar aware of his own wastefulness with that precious commodity: he was frittering time away pursuing a project which he no longer fully believed in.

No books, no books – Oskar forced his thoughts back to Rajan's question. How could he tell this boy that he loved books, but had been obliged to renounce them? Would Rajan understand that the desire to do something often comes from knowing how well it can be done? Should he describe the way a great book inspired him and then reduced him to pieces by making him aware of his own inadequacies? Oh, what was there to say about the absence of books? Where to begin and where to end? Dare he reveal that he sometimes sought solace in the books of forgotten writers, that he took comfort in the unread and uncelebrated?

Yes, Oskar delved into the obscure corners of libraries and drew out neglected books, dusty with age. He loved feeling like a liberator taking these books off the shelves. He relished opening the covers to reveal the last loan date stamped faintly on the library card – perhaps decades before. He felt a power in releasing the pages, so long untouched and unseen, to light and air and acknowledgement.

Realizing that these desperate thoughts could not be shared with anyone, he said, 'Well, I've finished with the books.' He fingered the stack of papers in front of him. 'Now I've moved on to the next stage.'

Rajan seemed to find this perfectly reasonable. 'You mean like when you revise for exams? You have to do all the reading first and then you go and write the paper?'

Oskar smiled. 'Exactly. Exactly like that.'

'I like exams. I think they're the best bit of studying. I mean, it's always a hassle before them – especially,' Rajan's voice dropped, 'with my pithaji. He makes us study like mad. But,' the voice became animated again, 'exams are fun. You get to write down everything you know and then the teacher gives you top marks for it.'

Oskar laughed, his deep-set eyes crinkling beneath the thick brows which hung over them like a ledge of dried palm fronds. Then, raising the plate Rajan had brought and nodding towards the small kitchenette adjacent to the bedroom, he said, 'I'll just put this out there for now.' Rajan remembered his mother's instruction to tell Oskar to eat the food immediately, while it was still hot. He opened his mouth to convey this information, but then changed his mind. Oskar was obviously busy with more important things.

'Bye, then.' Rajan rushed off down the stairs, taking them three at a time with loud, heavy jumps which made the house groan in protest. From the first floor, Mr Reynolds yelled, ''s not a bloomin' playground!'

Before he had tasted Sarna's food, Oskar had never considered the transformative or narrative powers of cooking. He was surprised that fictions could lurk in the thickness of a sauce, the stuffing of a courgette or the tenderness of meat. He, who had been searching out stories for years, experienced for the first time the tantalizing tales that can be transmitted by the taste buds. Where, he wondered, did Sarna's story belong amidst the network of yarns he had already spun together? He felt there was something crucial her story would tell him, if he could only figure it out.

Oskar was used to being alone and getting on with his work. He had lived in the attic of the house on Elm Road for seven years before the Singhs had moved in, and the previous landlord had rarely disturbed him. At first he had been unsettled by Sarna's sudden interruptions, her demands that he eat immediately and her requests for help with English. But his impatience had slowly given way to curiosity, then warmth, and then desire: to taste more of Sarna's food, to savour her beauty, to appreciate the company of a woman. Oskar could not but be drawn into her energetic orbit of extremes and exaggerations. For so many years he had lived only through the overheard stories he'd recorded; now, unwittingly, he was being coaxed into a live story, and its allure was irresistible.

In part, Sarna's benevolence towards Oskar was a way of snubbing the Reynoldses. Not that they cared – the one time Sarna had offered them some homemade potato and pea samosas they had refused. 'Oh no, we won't be havin' none o' that,' Mrs Reynolds had declared, turning her face away as though the sight alone was hazardous. Mr Reynolds had backed her up with some comment about how 'the bloomin' stuff's all round us, no need to be puttin' it inside us as well'. Sarna took the Reynoldses' rejection as a sign of ignorance, and determined that they should live to regret their rebuff. She wanted them to smell her food until they didn't know the scent of their own bodies from the aroma of her creations. She wanted them to salivate at the thought of all the wonders they had forfeited. Therefore she took pleasure in stomping past the Reynoldses' rooms, singing or coughing to alert them to her presence, as she carried a treat upstairs for Oskar. She enjoyed leaving the waft of her goodies lingering on their landing. She hoped that one day the smell of her food would be so irresistible they would capitulate and come to her begging to be forgiven and fed.

Oskar understood that giving him food was also a way for Sarna to escape her loneliness. By bringing something to eat, she gave herself an excuse for a chat. At first, Sarna had said little and her visits had been brief, but when she started learning English she spent more and more time talking to Oskar. 'Is good for praxis,' she claimed.

Sarna loved speaking English. She looked forward to her weekly class at the Mary Lawson School. The isolation of her first months in London had made her insecure; at the school she not only learned English but recovered her self-confidence. In class, Sarna was pleased to find herself amongst fellow Indians, but she was even more delighted to feel superior to them. She had almost forgotten the impact she could make when she dressed up in all her finery and walked into a room. 'You're going to study, not to be studied!' Karam had commented as he'd escorted Sarna to her first class. Dressed in a lilac shalwar kameez, black shoes, red handbag and purple shawl, fully made up and sporting long dangly gold earrings, she was certainly a sight for scrutiny. Amongst her more demurely dressed fellow students, she stood out like a macaw parrot amongst sparrows. 'How wonderful, Mrs Singh,' the teacher declared. 'Shall I compare thee to a summer's day?' Spring, summer, autumn or winter, Sarna's day was always made when she attended English class.

The Wednesday lesson became the focal point of her week. She'd plan what to wear in advance. She made a concerted effort with the exercises students were obliged to complete on their own. And she always cooked some treat to take and share with everyone. She wanted top marks for everything – her cooking, looking *and* talking style. Karam watched her weekly preparations with detached amusement and mild cynicism. There's no predicting anything with this woman, he thought. She goes from one extreme to the next without any logic in between.

Whenever he saw Sarna set off for the class, in a sarcastic salute to his wife, he silently sang a personalized version of Elvis's 'Devil in Disguise'.

Sarna noticed Karam's funny attitude towards her classes and put it down to jealousy. He doesn't like me going out, getting compliments and being independent, she told herself. Well, that wasn't going to stand in her way. If anything, it made her even more determined to excel within the small circle at the Mary Lawson School. She was especially keen to impress her teacher, whom she regarded as the final authority on all matters English.

'She speaks *official* English,' Sarna told Karam proudly.

'What do you mean, *official*? We all speak English because it's the official language.'

'No. She speaks *Queen's*. Queen's official English. And that's what she teaches us.'

Karam tried to explain that there was only one kind of English spoken around the country, with different accents and slang, the Queen's English being at the posh end of the spectrum. Sarna was having none of it. She remained convinced that she was learning a superior type of English, and for that she was grateful to Miss Oaten.

Miss Oaten was a tall, thin, ginger-haired woman with the pained expression of someone who has spent too long listening to what they don't want to hear. The devoted Miss Oaten did not just teach English. She was a custodian of the language, a champion of correct pronunciation, a devoted practitioner of ee-nun-see-ay-shun. Her task was to teach refugees and immigrants the basics of the language. However, her remit did not end there. With the zeal of an over-eager missionary, she sought to guide her students into the sacred ranks of those who could speak the Queen's English. She fervently believed that she

193

could cure them of their foreign accents and lilts of speech. She worked patiently and tirelessly, but unsuccessfully. Years of failure had not weakened her resolve – indeed, the year Sarna joined her class she seemed more determined than ever to root out that most depraved of tendencies, that most offensive of sounds: 'awe'. Nothing was more unbearable for Miss Oaten than hearing the letter 'o' pronounced 'awe' when a word required that it be said as 'oh'.

Any other sort of error Miss Oaten could deal with calmly. She smiled through countless instances of articles dropped: 'This is way', 'I have brother'. Or articles substituted when the right word could not be found: 'I came from the the the . . .', 'They are a a a . . .' She survived the indelicacy of 'f' pronounced as 'p', and had even kept a straight face when one student told her, 'Today I pound pipty pence on ploor.' But Miss Oaten could not abide the awfulness of a mispronounced 'o'. And who could blame her? Who could not but sympathize with the poor lady, whose name innocently emerged from the mouths of her Indian students as Miss Otten. Although she would never have admitted it, this unsoundly adulteration of her name had done much to fuel her campaign to make everyone speak the Queen's English.

She went to great lengths to achieve her objective. Elaborate exercises were conducted in class where the students were instructed to hold a cork between their front teeth while they chanted 'o'-inspired sentences after their teacher. 'Repeat after me.' Miss Oaten's lips pinched tightly around the cork as she recited, 'Oh, please don't ruin the occasion, said the old man over and over again.' Attempts to emulate her were always quite dismal. Eyebrows knitted as students pondered on the meaning and relevance of the statement they were being asked to repeat. Corks fell from mouths led by habit to open in a long round 'awe'.

The corks were supposed to be returned at the end of the lesson, but Sarna had kept one. At home she regularly employed the prop when speaking English. But instead of using it correctly so that it slowed down her speech and improved her diction, she became an expert at briskly rattling on just as she pleased. Far from aiding her language skills, this practice served to impair them.

'You sound ridiculous,' Karam complained. 'I can't understand half of what you're saying.'

'Joo can't be understanding because I speaking *official* English. Joo are not used to.'

If any member of the family expressed uncertainty about what Sarna was trying to say, she'd holler at them, 'How can I be praxising at home when nobody is understanding? Juiceless all of joo, juiceless.'

Sometimes, if they were alone, Karam would tease her, 'I can think of something much more "juiceful" for you to practise on . . .'

By persisting in her own way, Sarna ended up learning a different kind of English, just as she had hoped, but it was a mutant tongue with its own strange rules, accent and inflexions. In her mind she believed this to be 'official' English. Indeed, so convinced was she of its authority that she adopted English as the language for anything important she wanted to say to family or friends. Eventually the family grew weary of her aggressive reaction to being corrected and they gave up interfering. Yet from time to time, Sarna still needed help and this led her to Oskar's door. There she could expect the deference that was necessitated by the landlady-and-tenant relationship.

Initially, Oskar too had tried to correct her linguistic errors, but her sullen response soon brought his efforts to a halt. He understood that she took even innocent comments on grammar as personal criticism. When Sarna explicitly asked for assistance, Oskar obliged. Otherwise, he did nothing to indicate that he even noticed her malapropisms and mispronunciations. He was the only person who could listen to her without correcting or contradicting – no wonder she became so fond of him.

'Joo like son to me,' Sarna told him. Son? Oskar eyed the woman standing in the doorway – for by some un-spoken understanding Sarna never entered his room. One pencil wouldn't have sufficed to draw all her curves as she oscillated in time to her inarticulate arias. Son? Was that why she always came up to his room well dressed and fully made up? Was that why she smiled and blinked and leaned in towards him so suggestively from the door-way? Was that why she valued his approval of her English? Because he was like her *son*? She couldn't be his mother. How old was she? Late thirties? Just over a decade older than him. Son indeed. Although Oskar was not in-different to Sarna's charms, he would never have compromised either of them by letting this show. And so he played the part of a son. Sarna may not have been attracted to him, but Oskar sensed she relished the idea of bewitching him. She wanted him to admire and desire her while she paraded herself under the benign umbrella of surrogate mother. Oh well, Oskar thought, she probably doesn't know about the Oedipus complex.

Having mastered the English language, Sarna decided she wanted to wear English clothes. She had a vision of herself transformed into someone perfect, wearing a new style of clothes and speaking in a new tongue. How she would stand out from the other Indian women! People would look at her in admiration. She would feel so good – all different and new. Hints were dropped to Karam about her aspirations. He ummed and aahed about the cost, necessity and decency, but eventually agreed. Once upon a time she had criticized all London ladies and now she wanted to be one, he noted. Sarna was thrilled. Ha, she thought, now he'll see, I will be the best ever London lady.

Sarna loved wearing Western clothes, even though they were less flattering on her now robust frame than the modest lines of Indian outfits. There weren't too many opportunities to exhibit herself in the new clothes, but trousers and a blouse became her uniform for the family's weekly grocery-shopping excursion. Pyari came to think of her mother's new livery as the garb of guile.

'Get ready. We're going to the supermarket.' Sarna's voice drifted towards Pyari. A moment later, like the rumble that follows lightning, she thundered into the room, sporting brown trousers and a pale-blue blouse. Holding up a book as proof of her busyness, Pyari said, 'Mee, I have too much homework. Please, I can't come.'

'Your father's finishing his tea and then we're going. Hai, look at you.' Sarna was vexed by the sight of her daughter. Pyari's long, skinny brown limbs were flung serpent-like along the bed, just like the snake of a braid flowing down her back. Seventeen years old and still looks like a young boy, Sarna thought. Where are her breasts? She herself was so amply endowed that the idea of a flat-chested daughter seemed impossible. Must be some defect from *his* side of the family. She did not know that Pyari's slouch had been cultivated to hide a perfectly respectable bosom of which she felt ashamed. All the girls at school had bras and Pyari did not know how to ask her mother for one. Sarna had not thought to get one because she could see no evidence of the need. So Pyari persisted in hiding her womanliness, while Sarna worried that she wasn't developing. Even when Pyari had started her periods she'd been too embarrassed to tell her mother. Sarna only discovered the fact several months later, when she noticed her own supply of sanitary towels diminishing at a faster than usual rate. She guessed the truth and was hurt by her daughter's silence, but she was also relieved. She wouldn't have known how to broach the subject either and Pyari's expediency had saved them both any embarrassment.

'Come on now. No excuses.' Sarna snapped her fingers. 'And change into something decent. None of those dull creations of yours. We're not going to a funeral.' She walked out of the room, then reappeared in the doorway for an instant. 'Wear that yellow top with the frills that I made for you, OK?'

I'm not wearing *that*, Pyari thought as she slithered off the bed. She couldn't stand her mother's gaudy taste in clothes. For years Sarna had imposed her style on Pyari – making identical versions of her own clothes for her daughter. From the moment Pyari could thread a needle, sewing had become her language of resistance. These days she made almost all her own clothes. She'd have stitched her own school uniform if it had been allowed. She swung her long braid like a lasso and eyed her wardrobe. It was a subdued assortment of dark earthy hues and black. But hidden, as piping along a hem or lining behind a collar, were vivid flashes of fabric: gold, fuchsia, turquoise. She picked out a long black dress with magenta trimming along the back slit.

'Hai!' Sarna covered her eyes when she saw Pyari. 'Fiteh moon!' Her teeth sank into her lip with the 'fih' sound, making the gap between the front two look bigger than ever. 'Why are you wearing that tent? Hai, you look like a nun, I swear.' She picked up her red handbag and swung it over her shoulder. 'Let's go.'

Pyari hated their trips to the supermarket. Since they had moved to London, food shopping had become a family affair. They all trooped off together as if they were joined at the hip. Pyari wondered how much longer they would keep heading to the shops en masse. It had been this way for almost three years now! Were they supposed to keep it up for the rest of their lives? Every week she tried to get out of the trip and failed. Only once, thanks to a bad bout of flu, had she managed to avoid the ordeal. Rajan had been more successful with his evasion tactics by citing cricket practice and chess club as excuses. He always got away with such things. It was because he was such a good liar, able to invent an after-school activity or project at whim, even under Karam's scrutinizing gaze. She could never make up such excuses, no matter how she tried. In her father's presence her mind would go blank, while her voice stuck in her throat.

It wasn't the supermarket in itself that Pyari found unbearable, but her mother's actions once they were inside. With Karam dutifully pushing the trolley behind her, Sarna would make an agonizingly slow tour of the aisles. She spent longest at the fruit and vegetable counters. She would reach right to the bottom or the back of the stacked goods to make her selection, because, she claimed, 'They are hiding the fresh things.' Unable to follow the try-before-you-buy approach of the markets in Africa, Sarna compensated by prodding, shaking, squeezing and sniffing the produce, before dropping it into the trolley with a grimace and the verdict, 'Less use than useless.'

But it was the final drama at the checkout that Pyari hated most. As the family queued, a thudding dissonance would build up in her chest. She'd glance around, convinced that everyone was staring at them and knew what they were about to do. By the time they reached the checkout Pyari's palms would be sweating, her face would be flushed.

Meanwhile, Sarna did not appear to be suffering any such pangs. Like an actress taking to the stage, she fell into her role with enthusiasm and ease. She was even wearing a special costume for the performance. As she passed the goods from their trolley to the cashier, Pyari would have to stand next to her, acting as a sort of screen, to block the view of their trolley from anyone in the queue behind them. Karam was obliged to wait on the other side of the counter, ready to bag the items after they had been registered on the till. Throughout the exercise, Sarna would chat animatedly in broken English to the cashier: 'Hello, so many thing today. Childrens, joo know, need eating much to grow.' She'd shift things around on the counter, remark aloud that she had forgotten something and then promptly exclaim that she hadn't. She'd fuss around while getting her purse out of her handbag – spinning around and thrusting out her elbows to ensure that the next person in the queue maintained a reasonable distance. She did everything she could to cause a commotion, to distract everyone from the fact that certain items, the more expensive ones, were still sitting in her trolley, destined to sneak past the counter undetected and unpaid for. When Pyari felt Sarna's nudge, she knew it was time to push the trolley forward so that Karam could put in the bags he had already filled with their shopping and conceal the stolen items. In this way the family managed to avoid paying for their weekly rations of chicken, minced lamb and butter. Sometimes, if Sarna was feeling particularly feisty, the odd jar of jam or bottle of oil would join the staple stolen goods. The Singhs had never been caught in their act. (This was before the days of CCTV cameras and curved mirrors at each checkout enabling the cashier to see into a customer's trolley without leaning over the counter.)

Only once had they come close to being discovered. Sarna had impulsively chosen a till manned by an Indian woman. Pyari had begun to push the trolley forward while her mother chattered to the cashier in Hindi. Without warning, the woman had stood up from her chair and peered into the trolley. Sarna's reflex was instant. 'Oi!' she snapped at Pyari. 'What are you going off for? I haven't finished. Those things need to be paid for!' Bewildered, Pyari had stopped and passed the remaining items to Sarna, who continued to chide her as though it was all her fault. 'Fiteh moon! Stupid girl. Not thinking.' Sarna had then explained to the cashier in Hindi, 'I was so busy chatting to you I wasn't even looking what was happening. You know how children are? They don't think.' The cashier had smiled knowingly. Disaster had been averted, but at the price of a blow to Pyari's already fragile self-esteem. She imagined that everyone in the shop had witnessed the episode and had assumed *she* was the one trying to steal. Back in the car on the way home, Sarna had railed viciously against the cashier. 'She did that on purpose, the bitch. I had a funny feeling about her from the start. I should have joined the other queue. May she burn! They're all the same, these people from India – cheats and tricksters. Out to fool each other at every opportunity.'

Karam said nothing while Sarna ranted. Perhaps his silence was born of a reluctance to concede that it was, in part, his frugality that had resulted in such action.

For Pyari, it was a long time before the humiliation of the supermarket saga wore off. Like someone who is forced back on to a horse after falling off, she was dragged back to the shop the following week. Regular trailing of the aisles gradually reconciled her to the place again. In time, someone else would arrive to accompany her on these trips and share her guilt. Someone whose presence would soften the jagged edges of Sarna's rancour and Pyari's reticence, as a flame singes away split ends of hair.

Part Two

Part Two

14

Nina was ten when she first realized there was something wrong with her. She was walking home from school and had just turned into Loharan Gali, the street where she lived. A man stepped up to her. She recognized him – everyone in the gali called him Ramu Mamu. He bent down, looked her in the eye and said, 'Sunaina, I'm your pithaji.' Just like that. No warning, no explanation. Nothing. Nina froze, locked in the certainty of his malachite gaze. Ramu Mamu waited for a response. But Nina could not react. Finally, distracted by the buzz of a fly, his eyes left hers, breaking the dark-green spell, and she ran. She rushed into the house and buried her head in Bibi's lap.

'Hai, Ninu. What's wrong?'

'Ramu Mamu said he's my dad. *You* said my dad's dead.'

'Hai! Cursed man, he's lying. Don't believe anything he says. Hai, may he die! Such a stupid man.' Bibi comforted Nina with more denials. Then, just as the young girl's sobs were beginning to subside, Bibi said, 'Shhh now, Sunaina, my Ninu, my Nina. He's a madman. Didn't you see it in his eyes? He's mad.'

Nina remembered the flashing green irises and all the

relief of Bibi's disavowals was gone. His eyes, you see, they were *her* eyes. She knew she had looked into her own eyes – and she knew that Bibi was the one who was lying. What else had Bibi made up? If Ramu was her pithaji, then who was really her mother?

She did not find that out for another twelve years. After Bibi died, the neighbours started talking and Kalwant was forced to tell Nina everything.

Nina had always thought that Kalwant was her sister, until it was revealed after Bibi's death that she was actually her aunt. In the same way, the three other women whom Nina had grown up calling 'bhanji' also turned out to be 'masi'. However, the redefinition of Nina's relationship to everyone around her could not alter some emotional certainties. 'Whatever blood says, they are my sisters – because that's what my heart says,' she always maintained. But there was one more 'sister', far away in a foreign land, called Sarna, who now turned out to be Nina's mother.

'The best thing would have been to get rid of the child. That's what women who get pregnant outside marriage have to do,' Kalwant told Nina. 'It was dangerous then, some girls even died – but better death than family humiliation. Sadly, we found out about your mother's state too late. Don't look like that, Ninu! You know we love you. Oh Sunaina, my Ninu, my Nina – you know we're happy you're here today. It just would have been better if you'd arrived a different way. Come here, silly nali choochoo.' Kalwant called the teary Nina by her child-hood name, 'runny-nosed one'. She pulled the young woman into her arms. 'Your mother, she was so happy, I tell you, even though Bibi was heaping curses on her and saying she would kill her. Non-stop, your mother cried, because she had lost her love, Ramu – he was our *cousin*.

206

Just imagine! But Sarna was so happy to be having his baby. I thought she was mad, intoxicated by Ishq. I told her she had ruined her life and maybe even ours as well. "It will be better for everyone if the baby dies," I said. I don't know what she hoped – that maybe everyone would change *their* minds. She was waiting for some miracle to make everything OK. Anyway, she learned her lesson for thinking she knew better. Bibi sent her away to Chandighar to have the baby. Bibi's sister, Swaran Masi, was there and agreed to keep her. I wish Bibi hadn't done that. To her dying day, Masi made us feel we were still indebted to her. Even now that son of hers acts like we owe him something.' She shook her head and reached for one of the teardrop-shaped pistachio peras on the nearby tray. 'For five months your mother lived – mmm – there in hiding,' Kalwant continued with the sweet in her mouth. 'She told me later – mmm, very delicious, try, Nina? No? Mmm – Yes, they wouldn't let Sarna go out because they didn't want anyone to see her. All those months, she never left the house and hardly saw the sunlight because they covered up the windows in her room. When you were born, Swaran Masi was the one who delivered you. It was horrible for your mother. She told me how they stuffed her mouth with rags to stop her screaming and how her insides were completely ripped up and bled for weeks after. She suffered for you, no doubt about it. But then we all must pay for our mistakes. She paid the ultimate price when she came back to Amritsar having left you behind. Bibi didn't want any sign of you around, at least until the problem of your mother had been solved.' Kalwant patted Nina's head. 'She just wanted to marry your mother off, to get rid of her in a decent way and save the family name. You should have seen the state of your mother. She wept day and night, wouldn't eat a bite. Of course, she couldn't say openly why she was upset, but she told me that leaving you had killed a part of her.' Kalwant reached for another pera, as though she needed sugar to fuel her through to the sour end of the story. 'Even Bibi felt bad, but she was tough, she refused to let your mother feel sorry for herself. She kept reminding her, "You have no one to blame but yourself. This is all your own fault – the consequence of your crazy Ishq." I thought Sarna would never get over it, but surviving is your mother's speciality. She finally saw that no one was going to save her. When she realized that Ramu wasn't going to defy the world and marry her, she pulled herself together. Just in time, too, because Bibi had found a gullible enough suitor. Karam appeared right in time to save her. Then, while he was caught up in the Partition troubles, Swaran Masi brought you back to us because she couldn't cope with an extra mouth to feed. When Karam returned we told him you were a Partition orphan we'd adopted. He believed it, poor man. He was too in love with Sarna to suspect anything.'

This depiction threw some rays of colour into the impression of Sarna that Nina developed. The rest of the portrait was so harsh, shown as it was through the unforgiving lens of resentment, that Nina could not distinguish her mother from the mistake she had allegedly made. In the end, the mental snapshot Nina had was blurred and imperfect: a profile impression taken in weak light by someone with an unsteady hand. And yet, as can sometimes be the case with amateur photographs, there were elements of beauty which hinted at another truth, something yet to be discovered and understood. The contours of the image suggested fragility, something ever so precariously held together. Most affecting of all was the discreetly averted gaze of the subject that seemed to be the vanishing point of the composition. Its disappearing vortex was characterized by a palpable softness, a hazy yearning aching with guilt and loss.

'Hai, such kismet! Our luck has gone up in flames,' Kalwant wailed. The blue airmail letter slipped from her fingers. Her once pretty features, now softened by plumpness to a sweet sort of plainness, suddenly bloated into a wholly unattractive look of misery. Her heavy breasts shook solemnly in sympathy. From the waist down Kalwant tended to remain immobile, due to the spectacular swelling that had overtaken her body. This largeness, the result of overeating, provided a veritable platform from which the rest of her person could perform. She let her feelings run away with her and her tongue took the exercise of which her limbs were incapable.

'Oh, such bad kismet.' Kalwant slapped her forehead as the blue paper floated to the floor. 'Sarna left her problem with us and is having a great life in London, while we suffer. Even the news of Bibi's death hasn't made her repent. She doesn't say one word here about her old mistake.'

'She always was a chalaako. Knew exactly how to get her way. She was an expert in getting into trouble, but she also knew how to get out of it. A real magician of mischief.' There was a note of admiration and fondness in Harpal's voice. She was a smaller version of Kalwant, just as every sister, except the odd one out who had gone away, was a miniature of the one before.

'Well, she's not getting rid of the problem so easily this time,' Kalwant said. 'For all these years we've looked after

Nina, brought her up, given her a home, fed and clothed her – and without a cent of help or a word of thanks from Memsahib Sarna. We can't do anything more. Our vow of silence was only valid as long as Bibi lived. Now that Nina knows the truth, why should we pretend for Sarna's sake?'

Harpal nodded. Nina looked miserably into her lap.

'It's not your fault, Nina.' Kalwant gestured fondly in her direction, inviting Nina to come and sit by her on the bed in the corner of the room. Chairs were no longer comfortable for Kalwant. It was only on a bed, without the restrictions of back and armrests, that she could really relax. She motioned for Nina to massage her legs. 'But something has to be done. What happened with that Darshan – may he rot in hell – will happen again. Good for nothing, making promises and then breaking them because his mother won't accept you. That woman, her family—' Sensing the decreasing pressure on her legs, Kalwant broke off. 'Oh Ninu, don't cry. All that is over.'

'These lechers will keep wanting Nina, but they won't marry her. That's no life for a girl.' Harpal ran her fingers through the tassels on her shawl.

'This is what I'm saying. She's in the same situation as Sarna was twenty years ago. Exactly the same.'

'Why can't Sarna send money?' Harpal wondered. 'She makes out that she's very well off in the UK. Tell her to send some of her good luck here, share it around.'

'Hai, listen to you, "share it"! Bhanji, what do you think she will share when she doesn't care?' Kalwant placed another pillow behind her head to raise herself up. 'All these years she hasn't come back once. She didn't even turn up for Bibi's funeral. She has forgotten what she owes us. We have brought up her daughter.'

'It was Bibi's wish.'

'Yes, it *was* Bibi's wish. But Bibi is gone. It's up to us now. Sarna will never offer to help – that's clear from her letter. She hasn't said a word about Nina's future. She wants to forget. This is her idea of motherhood.' Another cushion strategically slipped behind her lower back had Kalwant sitting almost upright. 'Oh Nina, use some force,' she said as Nina pressed feebly at her limbs.

Nina hated it when they talked about Sarna in this way. She could never understand why her sisters didn't try to mitigate the facts for her benefit. Why did they have to let her in on every crude detail? They had tried to plug every gap in her consciousness with examples of Sarna's selfishness. It was as though they didn't want to leave any room for Nina to give her mother the benefit of the doubt. They don't like her and they don't want me to like her, Nina thought. But maybe they didn't want her to entertain any romantic notions of reconciliation because they understood that it could never be. Perhaps they told Nina the truth not to hurt but to protect her.

'She always had her head up in the clouds, that one.' The round silver bindi between Harpal's eyebrows glittered.

'Humph.' Kalwant nodded. 'Believed she was top notch with her va va good looks. It's time she faced the facts.'

'But who will tell her?'

'Us. Who else?' Kalwant raised her arms.

'Bibi would not approve.' The bindi bounced as Harpal's eyebrows rose and fell in approbation.

'We swore on Bibi's *life* not to speak, and Bibi is now dead.' Kalwant shot a glance at the picture of Guru Nanak on the wall. May Vaheguru forgive her for speaking of her dead mother this way. 'Like I said, Nina has been told the truth, so why shouldn't Sarna know?'

'Bibi wouldn't like it.'

Kalwant drummed her fingers against each other. She knew Harpal was right. The shadow of that promise still hovered over them all. But still, someone had to do something. Otherwise what kind of life would Nina have? And she would be a burden on them. In time her illegitimate status would affect their own daughters' marriage prospects.

'Maybe Nina could send a message,' Harpal said. '*She* never took any oath.'

Nina's hands froze on Kalwant's ankle.

Kalwant bolted upright. Two cushions, suddenly superfluous, fell to the floor. 'Va va, Bhanji, what an idea! Yes, Nina should tell her.'

Tell what? What will *I* tell? Nina's green eyes widened. Crouched at her sister's feet, her small frame belied her twenty-two years. She looked like a teenager.

'Don't worry, Nina, we will help you.' Harpal came over to reassure the panicked girl.

'Yes, we will help you write a letter.' Kalwant reached over to pick the blue airmail letter off the floor. 'Ohhh,' she huffed, almost falling from the bed. 'A reply to *this*. Telling Sarna everything she doesn't want to know and asking for her help.'

15

Ordinarily, Karam would have turned right out of his office on Millbank and driven alongside the Thames before crossing the river at Chelsea Bridge and heading home towards Balham. Today, he impulsively turned left, proceeding up Whitehall, past Trafalgar Square and on towards Tottenham Court Road. It was a detour he had already taken several times in the last few months. Once again, Karam was feeling discontented with his life. He attributed this unhappiness to dissatisfaction with work. He'd been pleased to land his job so easily when they'd first moved to London. He had thought it a perfectly respectable position: he was a civil servant, an accountant, just as he had been in Africa. He had found the salary reasonable and his colleagues friendly. He had been delighted to be working right in the heart of London – it was a source of inspiration, a daily reminder of how far he had come. When he met acquaintances at the gurudwara, newly arrived immigrants from East Africa, Karam felt good telling them, 'I'm working as a civil servant – right near the Houses of Parliament.' It sounded essential some-how, as if he was part of the engine of England in a way that could not be matched by his contemporaries working at the rubber factory in Southall, owning a corner shop in Norbury or being a cashier at the local branch of the Halifax. But the very aspects of his job that had once pleased him now seemed irrelevant, and invariably he focused on the fact that he worked for someone else. When he reviewed his working life, it seemed that he had always maintained a stable slot in the middle ranks of officedom, always answerable to a higher authority. How had things ended up so? As a young man, he had been determined to work for himself.

This reappraisal of his achievements had started when several of his brothers moved to England. In the last year Mandeep, Sukhi and Guru had come over from Kenya. They had found their jobs and lifestyle threatened by Kenyan Independence and the Africanization that followed it, so they, like Karam, had decided to claim British citizenship.

Sarna had hated the idea of Karam's family, especially Sukhi and Persini, coming to London. 'Why do they have to follow us? I don't want that Persini kamini anywhere near me. If she thinks she can come and stay in my house, she can forget it. I won't have her. Not after all she's done. No way.'

'Calm down,' Karam said. 'They're not coming here, anyway. I explained that we don't have much room.' He had felt so small, making excuses to his brothers. But what choice did he have? Sarna's vehement opposition to their arrival had made Karam realize that he could not help them without seriously compromising his own family life. Sarna had not merely vocalized her intolerance of his family, she had manifested it physically by becoming ill each time the possibility of their arrival was discussed. At first Karam had been inclined to dismiss this as melodrama, but the symptoms – fever, shivering and nausea – appeared so real he could not believe they were being faked. When the doctor prescribed medication, Karam had been forced to accept that the ailments must be authentic. How then could he insist on something which caused his wife so much suffering? Yet he was ashamed that he could not just invite his brothers to stay with him until they found their own places. As the oldest, it was his duty to help his family. Indeed, Karam had anticipated them joining him at some point and he'd hoped to be able to welcome them in style. But they had come sooner than he'd expected, and his own situation had changed more slowly than he'd wanted.

The death of Mr Reynolds had enabled Karam to buy out his wife. This had yielded the Singhs two more rooms on the first floor, but prudence had compelled Karam to rent one of the rooms out again. He and Sarna had moved into the main bedroom upstairs and Pyari and Rajan now each had their own room, but the house still felt too small. And a lot of repair work remained to be done. He knew the bathroom and kitchen needed to be refitted, which was why he'd insisted to Sarna that they get another tenant. 'If you want your new kitchen, we need to rent out a room again. Otherwise, you can forget it for a few years. I just can't afford it.'

Sarna immediately asserted that she would collect the rent from the room herself and save it to put towards her kitchen.

'You don't have a bank account,' Karam had said.

'So? Tenants pay cash anyway and I'll keep it in my safe,' she replied.

'You won't get any interest that way. I will take the rent and put it aside for your kitchen. In six months or so we should be able to put new units in at least. Then slowly we can get a new cooker, put in new flooring. Slowly, slowly, we'll do it.'

But Sarna had collected the new tenant's rent from week one. Five months had passed now and she hadn't said a word about a new kitchen, whereas before she had nagged Karam daily. Now it was he who regularly brought up the subject. 'So, we'd better think about those new units, huh? We must have enough for them now,' he'd say. 'Almost,' she'd reply. Goodness only knew what she was up to. He knew he'd made a mistake when he allowed her to take that rent. In fact, he didn't even recall agreeing, he just knew that when the young Malaysian student moved in, Sarna had fed him dinner and somehow got the chap to digest an arrangement whereby the rent was given to her every week. Since then there had been no turning back. Ah, the bloody tenants. It was really no way to live, having strangers in your house, sharing a bathroom with them.

Sarna refused to have Karam's family anywhere in their neighbourhood, let alone their house. When he made enquiries about property prices for them, she warned him, 'I can't live near those people. If that Persini ends up anywhere around here, I will have to go. I'll leave, I tell you. Even if it means I have to exit this world.' Against such threats, what could Karam do? Well, a hard-headed woman . . . Fortunately, he was spared any difficult decisions because when Persini and Sukhi arrived at Heathrow they went straight to Southall to stay with some of Persini's cousins. When Guru and his wife Sanjeev came several months later, they too ended up in Southall, where they had an open invitation to Persini and Sukhi's new house. It was only Mandeep who imposed on Karam and Sarna, taking over Rajan's bedroom

216

for a few months, before he too moved to Southall.

Each of Karam's brothers started his own business in England. Mandeep began driving a minicab and slowly built up a small taxi company. Persini and Sukhi bought and ran a post office. Karam watched these enterprises being set up with some resentment. He had arrived in this country several years ahead of them and – lo! – they had come and outdone him on his own turf within months. They had made themselves masters of their own destinies, while he was still serving someone else. Above all, Karam was surprised by his brother Guru.

Guru had always been moody and quiet and had showed little enthusiasm for his studies. The whole family had been astonished when he'd landed a job working as a cashier at Kenya National Bank in Nairobi, and Karam had put it down to a stroke of good luck. 'Don't go messing things up now,' he'd warned. Far from messing up, Guru had been making some big bucks. He proved himself something of a financial guru. Over the years he'd amassed a fortune. Exactly how much, no one was sure, but certainly enough to buy himself a brand-new car and a house without a mortgage in Southall. Enough, it seemed, to have loaned Persini and Sukhi the deposit for their house and post office business. Enough, it later emerged, to buy a stake in Mandeep's taxi firm. Enough, the months would show, to be in no rush to find a job. Karam was stunned by his success. His brother had become Guru Big-Bucks and Karam joined the line of siblings who wanted to borrow his cash.

Karam's white Ford Cortina slowed down on Tottenham Court Road, so he could take in the shop fronts and the passing crowds. People walked slowly, for the warm summer evening linked arms with each pedestrian like a lover and pressed up close, smothering them with its humid ardour. Karam noticed the colourful tie-dyed blouses, skirts and dresses hanging in the shop windows of Top Textiles and Bhattia Clothes. He observed the similar attire worn by some of the women in the street: tops with flowing flimsy sleeves, long brightly patterned skirts, flared trousers. It was a toned-down version of what Karam had seen in Carnaby Street a few weeks before. He had been there a couple of times after an acquaintance at the gurudwara had mentioned that his brother in Nottingham was making a fortune importing cheesecloth garments from India. 'He can't get the goods here quickly enough,' Surjit Bhamra had told Karam. 'Demand is too high. He's selling them all over the country, but especially in London. There are quite a few outlets in the West End, he told me, on Carambee Street or something.' Bhamra was not the only person from whom Karam had heard such reports. Several other acquaintances had cited relatives who were benefiting from this new boom in the cheesecloth market. Their stories had got Karam's mind ticking – maybe this was a chance for him. Maybe his route to riches was through the rag trade. So Karam had started checking out potential outlets for which he could become a supplier. He went to Carnaby Street and wandered through the souvenir shops, the leather stores and the Indian garment boutiques. He hung about in the latter, pretending to be a casual customer while secretly making a note of garment ranges and prices. Slowly Karam had begun to imagine himself as the owner of a shop in Carnaby Street.

Starting a new business occupied more and more of his thoughts. Away from the office, he began scanning passers-by to see what they were wearing. Sarna, who had no idea what was going through his head, spotted his roving eye and took it as a sign of the resurgence of his old wayward habits. Hai, such a man. He'd never change. Why was she was born to endure his lustful longings? To Karam she said with mock sweetness, 'Jee, you'd better control the ogling of your eyes or they might fall out of your head.' Karam did not bother to explain that his interest in the passing ladies was purely professional. The clarification would have required him to confess other things to his wife, like the fact that he was unhappy. He didn't want to admit this to Sarna because he knew she would not give him any comfort. Once, shortly after they had first moved to London, when he had grumbled after a difficult day at work, she had responded with an unfeeling, 'Well, you brought us here . . .' and Karam had been left to complete the sentence in his own mind, '. . . so you can't complain.' Perhaps on another day, in a better state of mind, Sarna might have been able to give her husband the support he needed. But Karam was deeply hurt by that one display of indifference, and had vowed not to share any subsequent disappointments with her. But now he remained silent for another reason as well. He was not keen to discuss the new enterprise until he was absolutely sure of things himself.

The details of the project had been working themselves out in Karam's mind, and he felt more confident that he could see it through. His research in London had convinced him that there was indeed a flourishing trade in cheesecloth, and he was fortunate to have some contacts in India. He hoped that Sarna's family would help him establish a good supply base there. They could oversee things at that end and have a cut of the profits. Why shouldn't her family reap the benefits as well? There would be enough money to go around. Even Karam's financial concerns had been laid to rest, as Guru had agreed to loan him the start-up sum he needed. All that remained now was to persuade Sarna. He needed her on his side to get her family involved, but she was a bit funny about them. On one hand, she claimed undying affection for her sisters, she wrote them letters and sent gifts. On the other hand, she charged them with resenting her and being jealous that she had escaped to a better life. Sometimes Sarna blamed Karam for taking her away from her family and isolating her from everything she knew, and yet whenever he had offered to send her to India for a visit she'd refused, accusing Karam of trying to get her out of the way so he could carry on with his ladies. Karam sighed. Talking to his wife was a trying business – more difficult than setting up a new business.

16

The letter was like all those that had preceded it: an innocent blue airmail envelope with the sender's address written neatly in Hindi and that of the recipient inscribed in English with a more halting hand. However, the contents of this missive were to shake Sarna more violently than anything she had read since seeing the date of birth in her passport printed as 1925 – *four* whole years, she claimed, before the actual date. Karam had taken care of all the paperwork for their move to London and Sarna had only really seen her personal documents when she was standing in the queue at immigration after their arrival in London. She had been looking critically at her passport photo (hai, the lighting did no justice to her complexion) when she caught sight of the date, 1925.

'What's this?'

'Date of birth.'

'*Mine?*'

Karam nodded.

'This is *wrong*. I am not –' she used her fingers to calculate, '*so old*!'

Karam shrugged. 'Doesn't matter. Who knows the exact date, anyway? Even mine I had to guess. It's just for the document.' Karam had made up the day and month, as well as the year, of his and Sarna's birth. The information had not been recorded anywhere. Even his mother, Biji, did not remember. How was *he* supposed to know?

Sarna, however, was furious. 'We have to tell them,' she said as they approached the immigration officers. 'This is wrong. You have to change it. I know when I was born, 1929.'

'I'm not a magician who can just transform things in seconds at the click of your fingers.' He couldn't see why she was making such a fuss.

'*They* can change it.' Sarna pointed at the immigration officers. 'It's their job to make sure everything is correct. *I* will tell them.'

'How? You think they speak Punjabi?'

Sarna pursed her lips before retorting, 'It doesn't matter what they speak – everyone can see a date, whether it's in Punjabi, Kiswahili or English!'

'Don't be stupid.' Karam squeezed her arm. 'You make trouble here and they'll lock us up. We'll change it later, OK? The passport expires after a few years anyway.'

So Sarna had been silently forced into London four years older than when she'd left Kampala the day before.

Of course, as Karam had known and Sarna had suspected, changing the date in her passport was never an option, because a birth certificate was demanded to authenticate her youthful claims. Since none could be produced, the old passport had to be relied on for verification and Sarna was doomed to age before her time. She did not grudge the benefits of the mistake, like early receipt of her pension, or the remarks of officials who claimed that she didn't look her age. But she never forgave Karam for the error.

Had Sarna not rushed to open the letter, she might have prepared herself better for its message. Had she hesitated, just for a moment, she might have noticed that the hand-writing was not that of her sister Kalwant, who usually kept in touch. She might have seen that the name of the sender was not K. Tanvir, but S. Tanvir. Instead, Sarna launched into reading:

Dear Sister,

I know the truth.

Since Bibi has died there is no one here to protect me. I am a burden to your sisters. They love me but they do not want me any more. Nobody wants me. No one will marry me. You know why. There is nothing left for me here. So I want to come there to London. Please, I want to come to you. I can start a new life, like you did. It will be safe, it will be easy. No one knows anything there and I will never tell. I promise. But if you don't help me I will shout out the truth. I will tell everyone – your husband, your children, your in-laws and your friends. Don't make me do this. If I come there I will do whatever you say.

Sunaina

That declaration, 'I know the truth', had jolted Sarna's heart into a different beat – erratic and accusing. As though inspired by the rebellion of this core organ, the rest of her body also revolted. Her lungs flogged her with deep and rapid breaths. Her stomach reviled her with waves of nausea. Her conscience broke out in a cold sweat. Her ears rang like sirens declaring a horrible accident. Her thoughts deserted her, leaving behind only a dizzying sense of despair. Her limbs became weak and numb as if they could no longer bear her. Between her legs she felt a familiar discomfiting soreness, as though her very womb was clamouring to slide out. Still clutching the letter, Sarna fell on to the sofa and started to cry. The tears did not flow as a release, but trickled out slowly like drops of poison, concentrated beads of woe. They stung her eyes, burned her skin and left tell-tale trails of sadness like salty seawater deposits across her face.

Sarna, who thought she knew pain well, like an old friend, could not have imagined it had so many components, could strike so unilaterally and hurt in so many different places. All her emotions seemed to be culminating in agony: self-pity, guilt, remorse, love – she felt these only as an intense ache. She had believed she had mastered her old afflictions, when in fact all she'd done was deny them. Like breath, pain must be released or it will suffocate us. For too long Sarna had kept hers all pent up inside. Now Nina's letter had pulled the plug from Sarna's pain compression chamber and misery coursed through her body.

Her ragged breath gave way to distressed moans. She rubbed the letter against her breast and rocked back and forth on the sofa. The sounds of her suffering drifted through the house. The Malaysian tenant, Chan, was startled from his maths formulas by her wretched cries. He tried to block out the noise by continuing with his studies. Oskar, too, was shaken. The sound made him think of a dying animal wrenching the last agonized yelps out of its trapped, wounded body. Oskar slipped down the stairs and walked to the door of the living room. He looked in and saw Sarna unfolding a letter as if to read it again. He watched her flatten the letter on her lap and start stroking it. She ran her fingers along the words gently at first, as if she was caressing them, and then she touched the page more forcefully as though she wanted to rub the words off it. All of a sudden she picked the letter up and pressed it to her face. Oskar saw the wetness of tears pricking through the tissue-thin airmail paper and appearing as blotches of dark blue: like the stains of another story forcing themselves on to the page. Oskar turned away from the sight. If he had nothing to say, he should not stay. He crept slowly back up the stairs.

Sarna lifted the letter off her face and stared at it. She saw the stains of her tears continue to seep across the page like the shadows of dark clouds falling over a bright day. The tears were altering the quality of the paper as well; it was becoming damp and fragile and felt as if it might disintegrate. Oh that it would just disappear and go away! But she knew that no amount of tears could dissolve this problem. If tears really had the power to wash away more than the kohl in your eyes, hers should have flooded out whole worlds by now.

Fear started to take over: the fear of exposure. Once again, Sarna covered her face with Nina's letter, as if her daughter's shame might mask her own. But emotions are not like maths equations, where minuses multiply to make pluses. The negative of Sarna's shame could not be cancelled out by the negative of Nina's.

Sarna reread the letter, but her mind refused to process its message coherently. At a gut level she understood Nina's diplomatic language perfectly. She felt the raw accusation in the letter's address, 'Dear Sister'. She knew what lay behind the assertions 'you know why' and 'I will tell'. Yet Sarna had spent too long convincing herself that

Nina's existence had nothing to do with her. She had deliberately developed a blind spot to her personal history between the ages of fifteen and seventeen. She had trained her thoughts to circumvent this period and had forced her memory to lie about it. Such a deliberate, careful reconstruction cannot easily be undone.

People expect their day of reckoning to come when they die, but Sarna's had come right in the middle of life.

Sarna agitated the day away. When Pyari and Rajan came home from school she was still sitting on the sofa. She hadn't washed the breakfast dishes or cooked anything for dinner. Excluding the couple of months after their arrival in London when they had been without a cooker, Pyari could count on one hand the times when Sarna had failed to cook a fresh meal. Even illness could not prevent her mother from labouring in the kitchen. Something's wrong, Pyari thought. She asked Sarna what they could eat. 'Just look in the fridge. Take something from there.' This was uncharacteristic too. Normally Sarna was very territorial about the kitchen. She got irritated if anyone went unsupervised through her fridge or cupboards. Pyari looked at her mother's swollen face. 'Mee, are you OK?' Sarna shook her head and waved her daughter away.

By the time Karam got home Sarna was in bed, flushed and hot from worrying. She was sweating heavily and her eyes were glazed with the brightness of delirium.

'What's wrong?' Karam felt her hot forehead. 'Flu?'

She shook her head.

'Pain? Stomach? Whole body?' He deliberately used her vocabulary.

She nodded. Yes, a weakening ache, fire and chill was

coursing through her entire body from her heart, where the blue airmail letter was lodged under her bra. She had folded and rolled the paper up so small that it felt like a little bullet against her breast. A bullet fired from the past to hit a target in the present. It was Sarna who had long ago made the bullet and loaded the gun, but she had never imagined the shot would one day fly towards her like this. The bullet had hit her and hurt, but it could not penetrate – because it had not reached the same heart she had once had. It found a heart that was much, much harder. A heart that had spent years bulletproofing itself against this very foe, against Nina – because she was the dearest and therefore the deadliest. Yet however hard a heart appears, at its core, where the truth abides, it is soft and fragile. The impact of Nina's attack was therefore being taken by the rest of Sarna's body, in order to deflect the pain from her heart and thereby preserve it.

Karam looked at Sarna's trembling hands and dry lips, which she repeatedly licked in vain. She was obviously suffering, but he wasn't sure what to make of this latest affliction. She got sick quite regularly these days and he couldn't understand why. They lived well, they ate well – there was really no cause for illness. Yet she was apparently tormented by stomach cramps, stomach bloating, stomach pain, stomach blockage, stomach upset, stomach swelling, stomach burning, stomach boiling . . . Karam had lost track of his wife's distinct stomach sensitivities. He found it strange that all her problems should be concentrated in that area. It was most unfortunate that the stomach was, geographically speaking, so close to a certain other part of the body: the part essential to the closeness of man and woman. Sarna's stomach symptoms had an adverse effect on their love life. When she did occasionally concede to him, it was no longer the same between them.

Sarna's most common complaint was constipation. It had become such a normal condition of her existence that she had lost the embarrassment she'd originally felt at disclosing it to Karam. Indeed, she now blamed him for it. 'It's your fault. You made me live on your English food for too long. It gave me a complete stomach blockage. Ruined my system. I've never recovered.' The regular medication prescribed by Dr Thomas seemed to have little lasting effect. Indeed, the doctor had finally suggested that perhaps the problem was caused by some imbalance in Sarna's diet. Of course, *that* hadn't gone down well. '*Ve* are eating bestest food, Dr Thawmass. Alvays, only, *bestest*.' The doctor had politely demurred. In a way Sarna was right, but the doctor had a point: there was indeed a direct correlation between Sarna's congested bowels and her rich memory-infused food. Sometimes, when she was especially perturbed, the anxieties that she released through her cooking simply re-entered her again when she ate. Then her own dishes sat heavily in her gut, unable to be digested, cramming her bowels with the same sorrows that crowded her head.

Sarna had always been so robust. Karam had seen her strong constitution as a reflection of her strong will. Now he was perplexed by how her will was stronger than ever but her body seemed to be weakening. In moments of exasperation he cynically thought, It's no wonder she's unwell – if I sometimes buckle under the force of her iron will, it's inevitable that she herself will occasionally capitulate.

Karam hoped there was nothing seriously wrong with her this time. He enjoyed the opportunity to look at her without interruption, without impatience or anger distorting her face. She was still so beautiful. That skin! Glossy and smooth like fresh double cream – he longed to kiss it. The pleasure of looking at her had so often got him through the torment of listening to her rants. Had she been crying? Karam studied her more closely. He cleared his throat. 'So just pain then? Nothing else?' As was often the case, his attempts at tact were misunderstood; to Sarna he sounded nonchalant. The words 'just pain' made it seem as though he thought nothing of pain, as if it was the equivalent of a runny nose or a sore throat. She tossed her head. Karam didn't know what to make of the action. 'Hmm, you'd better rest. Must be flu. If it's not better tomorrow we can go to the doctor.'

It was not better the next day, or the day after that.

For three days Sarna remained in bed, unable to stomach anything except tea. That she gulped copiously, sweetening it with spoonfuls of sugar to take away the bitter taste in her mouth. The rest of the time, she lay fretting. What could she do? There was no one. This was the end. It could not be. Enough. No one would believe it. Her, with two grown children – one a daughter of almost marriageable age – she did not deserve this. It was madness! Who had done this? She would show them. Never again.

For three nights, Sarna had nightmares. She was a cliff from which people hurled themselves into the vapoury depths of a void – she facilitated and witnessed these kamikaze leaps, herself unmovable and unmoved. The world was an ear with a naked child sitting on its lobe chanting, 'If you don't I will tell if you don't I will tell if you don't I will tell . . .' A gust of wind gathered the brown dust of Lahoran Gali into its womb, carried it over oceans, and deposited it in a neat pile outside the door of 4 Elm Road. Anyone who walked through the door stepped in the pile of dust and spread it around the house and along the street, leaving a trail of footprints that could not be erased and led to nowhere.

For three days, Karam and the children crept cautiously around Sarna. She was a palpable presence in the house and yet, in different ways, each one of them felt her absence. Karam hungered for the smell of her cooking, welcoming him from outside the front door. He missed the pressure of her icy feet squeezing between his calves for warmth when he got into bed. Now she just lay still, facing away from him, a stiff bundle of tension wrapped in her own hot presence. Rajan, who had always craved silence while he studied, found it harder to concentrate without his mother's chatter and clatter animating the background. Pyari, who was obliged to prepare their meals while Sarna was incapacitated, longed for her mother to get better and reclaim the kitchen. Pyari realized that she had not inherited any of her mother's cooking know-how. Sarna had never asked her to help in the kitchen. Even when she offered, Sarna had refused. 'You'll be cooking for the rest of your life after you get married. You might as well enjoy your freedom now. Go and do some of your sewing, I know you prefer that.' Pyari did like sewing, but she sensed that her exclusion from the kitchen was not intended for *her* benefit. It was Sarna's way of guarding her territory. 'You're so lucky your mum doesn't force you into the kitchen,' Pyari's Indian friends often commented. Yet she did not feel lucky, but neglected – as though she was being denied the basic legacy of knowledge that passes from mothers to daughters. Now, stuck in the kitchen without a clue what to do, this struck her all the more deeply. Is this what Sarna had wanted? That her daughter should one day find herself in a kitchen, alone and overwhelmed? Is this how her mother had wanted her to feel – inadequate and uncertain?

When Sarna eventually emerged from bed, she was no clearer as to how to deal with the threat she'd received, but she could no longer lie still while her whole being agonized over it. Seized by the need to divert her thoughts, she entered the kitchen. Immediately she saw the evidence of someone's hand at work there: the sugar bowl was sitting by the kettle instead of in the cupboard, the tea towel was hanging on the back of a chair and not over the oven handle. Sarna noticed her favourite pan drying amongst the crockery on the dish rack. She picked it up, sniffed the inside and frowned. Hai Ruba, Pyari must have used it for frying those eggs they were eating yesterday. Hai, such a stupid girl, this was her special meat pan! Sarna looked around. Hai, such a family, leave them for a minute and they turn the house upside-down.

As she opened the fridge a strange sight met her eyes: the milk had curdled, the yoghurt had split, the bread had developed mouldy blue growths. Puzzled, she searched for further signs of decay. There was more: the carrots had become soft and bent flaccidly into circles, the ginger was grey and shrivelled, the mint leaves had turned yellow, the onions were spotted with black. Like pectin, which is used as a stabilizer, or ascorbic acid, which acts as a preservative, Sarna's passion for cooking conserved the products in her kitchen. Her withdrawal into herself had catalysed the process of their decay. She picked up all the items and tossed them into the bin. Hai, what had those children and their father been doing these past days? The cupboards were in complete disorder as well. Someone had obviously rummaged for an item and then left everything in a mess. She saw that a brand-new packet of dhal had somehow split and scattered across one shelf. Below it, a small packet of gram flour had fallen on to its side, coating the neighbouring packets in a powdery yellow film.

Then Sarna's heart missed a beat as she caught sight of the lid of her round spice tin lying randomly on the floor as if it had been flung off in some explosion. The container itself was on the shelf. It held a wild array of colourful spices: red paprika, yellow turmeric, withered grass-coloured coriander seeds, grey and white mustard seeds, green cardamom, dark-brown ground cumin, woody cinnamon sticks and black cloves. The spices had spilt out of their individual steel bowls and bled into each other. How? Tears pricked Sarna's eyes. Someone must have mishandled the container. Why? These spices were the foundation of all her cooking. Many of them were impossible to get here, they were precious stocks that she'd requested from friends and relatives coming to London from Kenya or India. Who was responsible?

She leaned heavily against the counter and gazed into the chaos of her spice box. Her tears continued to fall. Through her watery gaze, the dry mess of spices took on the molten liquid intensity of lava. Then a tear splashed into the spice tin, releasing the smell of mingled spices into the air just as rain hitting the ground liberates the smell of the earth. Sarna breathed in deeply, invigorated by the familiar, comforting Mushq. The spicy aromas rose up from the rubble of her life like a promise of redemption. She wiped her eyes. No, she would not give in. She would find a way. She always had, and she would again.

*　*　*

Sarna could not bring herself to discard the jumble in her spice tin, so she put the lid back on and placed it carefully at the back of the cupboard. She would deal with it later. Meanwhile she swept, scrubbed and polished the kitchen. At the end of her Herculean effort the room wasn't sparkling as Sarna would have liked. Hai, she thought, all these years I've been waiting for a decent kitchen and he couldn't even give me that. She thought about the rent money that had accumulated in her safe over the last months. She had been considering telling Karam that they should start looking for some new kitchen units, but now she wasn't sure. There might be other, more urgent uses for that money. It might be required to buy a new lease on life. You never know, Sarna reflected, you just never know.

She recalled her bibiji saying, 'Every grain of rice bears the name of its eater.' As a little girl, Sarna had delved into a huge sack of rice to examine the grains for names. Bibiji had found her sitting in a sea of rice, looking perplexed. 'Bibiji, this rice has no names,' Sarna said. 'Whose is it?' Bibiji had laughed, but Sarna had continued to fret about the nameless rice. Was it just her that couldn't see the names? Or was there something wrong with the rice? Perhaps the names appeared during cooking the way Sarna's name had emerged from her lips when she was just a year old: 'Sa-na.' It became her favourite sound and she would reel it off repeatedly as if confirming the choice. Sarna, meaning 'will' or 'resolve'.

When the children came home from school that day, Sarna was watering the plants in the living room. 'Oh-ho, you useless ones!' Sarna clucked as she pressed freshly baked flatbreads into their palms. 'Your mother falls sick

233

and you let the house fall to pieces around her, huh?' She briskly patted Rajan's head and pretended to straighten Pyari's collar. They looked so well, she needed to touch them to share their vitality, but even this desire could not override the habit of restraint she had long imposed on herself. 'How were you living? Everything's rotting and filthy. What were you doing?'

As soon as Karam returned, she insisted that an immediate trip to the supermarket was in order.

'So, you're feeling better?' he asked. The shine of her hair told Karam it was freshly washed.

'Better shetter.' She rolled her eyes. 'Better or not, what difference does it make? There are things to be done, and it seems only I can do them. Really, I ask myself, Jee, what would you all do without me?'

In the days that followed, Sarna immersed herself in cooking. The craving for sweetness did not abate. She made an abundance of desserts, beginning another as soon as the one before had been cooked. In just one week she made coconut barfi, gajerela, sevia, kheer, prasad, gulab jamun and ras malai. She stayed up for one whole night hovering over eight litres of simmering milk until it had reduced to just a quarter of its original quantity. Sarna loved the way the milk slowly thickened, yellowed and sweetened as the bulk of it evaporated. She wished the weight on her shoulders could be steamed away, that her big problem could be similarly boiled down to a palatable fraction of itself.

Sarna's ruminations were a comfort while she was cooking, and they felt like certainty when she ate, but they provided no lasting relief, because her unresolved ponderings were slowly and painfully reabsorbed into her system. There they fed the fact that she could not find a solution to Nina's threat. She felt the pressure of the dilemma in her stomach, where no amount of her sugary milk could neutralize the burning acidity of anxiety. She felt it in her gut, where her desserts clogged up to create an enormous blockage. And she smelled it everywhere, because her guilty conscience snuck out of her as a mephitic Mushq. She'd had temporary problems with wind before, but the new emissions were of another order entirely. Their potent pong represented the festering sore of truth inside her. A veritable sorceress of smells, Sarna tried, with limited success, to cover her stench with the appealing aromas of food.

Karam, who was initially delighted by the sweet treats, became concerned when their production showed no signs of ceasing. Sarna was turning out desserts faster than they could be eaten. Regular deliveries of goodies to the tenants, Oskar and Chan, did little to disguise the fact that Sarna was cooking more then they needed – and wanted. For several days Pyari and Rajan were sent to school with packs of Indian sweets to share with friends, but the saccharine bites proved too cloyingly sweet even for schoolchildren. In the end, Pyari and Rajan guiltily dropped their mother's creations into the bins near the school gates.

Karam's brothers also became recipients of Sarna's over-production. On Friday, several days into her efforts, as Karam was leaving for the monthly evening of card games that all the brothers participated in, Sarna gave him a big bag of sweets. 'I know Sukhi loves my barfi, and Mandeep is fond of gajerela.' Karam enjoyed being generous when it did not require too much of an output from him. However, the excess of his wife's cooking continued to bother him. It was a waste, but how could he say that to Sarna? She'd been very touchy lately. He was pleased that she seemed to be better again, and he needed her to stay well so that he could broach the subject of his new business plans.

When he returned from his night out at almost midnight and found Sarna still cooking, Karam felt he had to say something. 'What's all this about? Are you planning to open up a sweet factory or something? Are you going to turn this place into Sarna's Sweet House?'

Sarna kept her back to him and continued skinning some blanched almonds.

'I've been thinking about starting a new business myself, but it looks like you've beaten me to it. Can't be cheap, making such rich things with cream and nuts and whatnot – shame you can't sell them. If you're going to keep cooking so much, we need to find some way of making a bit of extra money.'

Sarna turned, her elbows pinned to her sides, her brown-stained fingers looking like freshly dug-up parsnips. 'Everything is just business and money to you, nah? Can't a woman make some treats for her family without being reminded to count the pennies?'

'Oh ho. What are you getting angry for? There's no need. You know I like it when you cook. I'm only asking why you're making more than we can eat. It's like you're cooking for a wedding! Is there something I don't know about?' Despite Karam's jocular tone, Sarna's heart rammed against her ribs like a terrified animal in a cage. 'Are you expecting someone? Are you plannng a celebration? What is all this for?' Karam gestured at the cooker. 'I don't understand.'

Sarna unconsciously put one hand to her heart and felt

for the implicating bullet under her bra. It was still there. 'What are you trying to say?' she snapped.

Karam tucked in his chin, surprised at her sudden belligerence. 'Nothing, just what I said. This is all a bit too much. That's all.'

Sarna decided to test for any signs that he knew. Could Nina already have carried out her threat? 'No, you're implying something else. I don't know what it is, but I don't like it.'

'Oh ho, keep your voice down, you'll wake Rajan,' Karam said. 'I don't know why you're getting so worked up. All I said is I don't understand.'

'Well, it's not for a man to understand what goes on in the kitchen.'

It is when he's paying for it, Karam silently retorted. 'What's that?' he asked all of a sudden, wrinkling up his nose as a rancid smell filled the room. 'Are you sure the milk isn't off?' He grimaced as he peered into the deep pan of boiling white bubbles.

'Nothing is off except your mood,' Sarna responded, holding her breath and clenching her buttocks as if that might prevent the spread of the smell. 'If you don't want to eat more, that's fine. I'm not going to force you.' She was anxious to get Karam out of the room so she could throw open the door to the garden. 'But don't question me about how much I'm cooking. I know what I'm doing.'

Karam raised his hands in defeat and left the kitchen.

After this exchange, he bit his tongue while desserts continued to proliferate. He told himself it was just a phase, that she would come out of it in a few days – and then he intended to speak to her about his plans. However, another week of dessert-manufacturing followed the first one. Even the fruit in the house did not escape: Sarna caramelized it.

'Mee, when are you going to stop all this sweetifying?' Pyari asked her. 'My friends have been telling me I smell like a cupcake. And the smell of my hair on the pillow at night is so sweet it makes me feel sick.'

Rajan, whose room was right behind the kitchen, also pleaded with Sarna to stop. 'You're cooking non-stop these days,' he grumbled. 'There's always noise and smell, I can't concentrate. Why are you going overboard like this?'

For once, Sarna had no retorts for her children. It was so easy for everyone to complain. They had no idea what she was going through – and it was to protect them that she suffered. No one appreciated the sweets of her labours. This was one of the terrible ironies of her anguish – no one could acknowledge it, nobody could laud her for enduring it. Sarna poured a thick sugar syrup over pistachios and sesame seeds for the gujak. She watched the caramel liquid fill the tray of nuts then harden and set, binding everything together. Would that there was something she could pour over her life to hold the disparate pieces together and make things whole, lasting and meaningful. Sarna wished so desperately for a resolution. But there seemed to be no escape this time, no way to sidestep or cover up the existence of Nina. The taste of failure suddenly flooded Sarna's mouth. She shuddered, grabbed a rasgullah and stuffed it into her mouth, sucking the sweetness out of the pale curd dumpling before chewing and swallowing it.

17

Three weeks after the arrival of Nina's letter, Sarna's dessert production slowed down. However, the sugar overdose she was inflicting on her family did not decrease proportionally. Her taste buds had become so accustomed to extreme sweetness that anything even slightly salty tasted bitter to her. She always felt she'd used too much salt and she was compelled to temper it by adding sugar. After a couple of days of quietly pushing food around their plates, the family once again sat down to a simple dinner of dishes that had been ruined by the addition of sugar. Rajan bit hungrily into aloo gobi and almost retched at the taste of honeyed cauliflower. He reached for the yoghurt as an antidote, only to feel it spread like sweet cream in his mouth. Relief finally came with a glass of water.

'Ugh!' Rajan blurted as he set down the glass. 'Everything's so *sweet.*'

'Really, I was thinking the same.' The corners of Karam's mouth turned downwards.

Pyari pulled a face too.

Sarna looked at them in surprise – *she* was enjoying her dinner. 'There must be something wrong with all of you. It tastes absolutely fine to me.'

'How can we all be wrong?' Karam asked. 'If we're all finding the food too sweet, maybe you should accept that it is. Three against one.' He held up three fingers.

Under the table, Rajan kicked Pyari. She glanced at him and saw him raise his eyebrows in code for 'Here we go again.'

Sarna stopped eating. 'Don't force the children to take your side. You always try to turn them against me.'

'What? I haven't said anything! You heard them yourself. Ask them again if you don't believe me.'

Pyari began biting her nails. *Please don't ask, please don't involve us this time*. Even Rajan lowered his eyes to gaze at his plate. This was what both the children dreaded most – to be lined up between their parents and urged to take sides in their quarrels.

'I'm not asking anyone anything.' Sarna stabbed a turmeric-yellowed floret with her fork. 'Taste is personal – you can't check mine and I can't check yours.'

'Mmm-hmm. Well, you'd better check yours because it seems to be turning into Guju taste,' Karam said, using the derogatory term for Gujarati to express his disapproval. 'If you want to have all your food sweetened then keep a pot of sugar on the table and add it as you eat, but please spare the rest of us.' He got up from the table. 'I'm getting some bread.'

Sarna stared at her plate. What was happening? Was this it? Was this how people fell apart? By gradually losing the ability to do things that were once second nature? How could Karam casually say that about a pot of sugar? As if food was as simple a matter as a cup of tea and you could just add milk or sugar to suit yourself after it was made. He had no idea. Tears filled her eyes. What good was she to anyone? She couldn't even serve her family an adequate meal any more. Their rejection hurt her. She did not see it simply as a dislike of the dishes themselves, but as dissatisfaction with *her*. And she could not bear that.

'Hey, are you crying?' remarked Karam as he returned with the bread. He felt concerned and irritated at the same time. 'Oh, come on, there's nothing to cry about.' He couldn't reach out and touch her, not here, not in front of the children. 'It was just a mistake, we all make mistakes. And you haven't been well – that affects the taste buds, you know. It's probably why you've been getting the wrong balance with the spicing.'

Sarna continued to cry. Pyari and Rajan looked on helplessly.

'Oh ho, come on now. What good will tears do? Unless you're trying to salt the food with them. Is that what you're up to? Here, please cry over my plate first then.' Karam moved his plate towards her. Sarna gave him a withering look. Encouraged by this sign of recovery, he continued, 'Here, Pyari, Rajan, pass me your plates. With a sprinkle of tears and a loaf of bread each, we should be able to stomach this meal.' Karam passed some bread to the children and ordered them to finish up. 'See? What's there to cry about? We're all eating.'

Over a month had gone by since the arrival of Nina's threat and Sarna was no clearer on what to do about it. When her frantic drive to cook began to slacken, she sought out other distractions to get through the day. She couldn't be idle, because then the frenzy of her thoughts threatened to paralyse her. It was as though her body and mind were locked in some strange contest, each trying to inhibit the other by its hyperactivity. And more often than not, Sarna's mind triumphed over her body. Several times she had started out for a brisk walk in the park, only to snap out of some intense thought to find herself creeping along slowly, barely moving, longing to sit down exactly where she was and stay there, letting the world go on, as it must. In these moments Sarna felt as if there was nothing she could change. Her world was destined to fall apart. In fact, it had fallen apart long ago and she had somehow been holding it together. She could feel her grip on it slackening – and despite the desire to give up, she dared not let go.

Sarna retrieved her disordered spice tin from the back of the cupboard and attempted to salvage the contents. She spent many hours sifting and picking through them. 'Such a business!' Karam remarked, watching her sort spices one evening. Sarna shook her head. Business, everything was business to him. He saw the world only in terms of pounds and pennies, profit and loss. As the last of the mustard seeds were put into their compartment, Sarna smiled to see the tin once again returned to its former glory. The spices sat in perfect arrangement. They circled like planets within the orbit of the spice tin. Order had been restored.

'Look!' Sarna was unable to resist sharing her delight. 'See? Good as new.'

Karam nodded his approval. 'You're right.' He glanced at what looked like an inseparable mound of mixed spices still sitting in the middle of the table on a pale-blue kitchen towel. 'What are you going to do with that?'

'This will be my garam masala.' Sarna began spooning the mixture into an empty glass jar still bearing the faded label of Robertson's Strawberry Jam.

'Oh-oooh.' Karam pushed aside the household accounts he'd been working on and leaned closer. 'I have some garam masala too.'

'Not tonight.' Sarna's hand went plaintively to her stomach to support her objection.

'*No*, that's not what I meant. I'm talking about serious masala. Hot hot work, *business*, masala.'

Sarna stopped listening. She already knew what his masala was – money. It was the only thing that spiced his thoughts. No doubt he was going to complain about how expensive everything was. Then he'd go on to say that they needed to watch their pockets. But suddenly a word sprang out from the white noise of Karam's speech and clutched at Sarna's ear, pulling, twisting, bending it to attention.

'What?' she interrupted. 'What India? Why India?'

'That's where everyone's getting the stuff. The cheese-cloth costs almost nothing and labour is cheap, so you can get clothes from there and sell them here at a profit.'

'What?' Having missed the first part of Karam's explanation she was completely lost. 'Just start again. Tell me again.'

Aware that he now had his wife's full attention, Karam sat up straighter in his chair and recounted his intentions. He gave Sarna a little background information to support his decision. He cited his brothers' businesses as the main impetus for his new plan. 'Even Sukhi is running his own business – just imagine. Who could have predicted that?'

'Hah, business! The only running he's doing is behind that Persini.' Sarna couldn't resist a chance to have a dig at her sister-in-law. 'He's like a sheep, following all the kamini's orders without question. Back in Kenya he was always off in the jungle on a shikar, and here Persini is the shikari. And what a hunter she is – ruthless, I tell you, ruthless. She likes going for the kill, that much I know. There's a destructive streak in her . . .' Sarna stopped.

Karam's knotted brow underlined the irrelevance of her rant to the subject at hand.

'Well, however they're running it doesn't matter. They're making money! That's the important thing. Everyone's raking it in and I'm still in civil service,' Karam said.

'What everyone? Who's everyone? Mandeep is still hand to mouth since he started that taxi siyapa and—'

'At least he's his own master,' Karam broke in. 'It's always tough at the beginning with a new business, but he'll make it, you just wait and see.'

'Oh, you think that—'

'Will you listen? Will you let *me* tell you what *I* think, or are you going to keep interrupting with your own theories?'

Sarna pressed her lips together and Karam went on to describe the thriving cheesecloth market before elaborating on his intention to capitalize on this boom. 'It's a real opportunity. When you see an opportunity you have to take it. Life doesn't throw such chances at you every day.' He gave her an idea of the potential for profit, speaking energetically in the hope that she might be infected by his enthusiasm. Finally Karam came to the part about India. 'So, the first thing is to get the cloth from India. We have an advantage because we know people there – your family. You always said your sister Kalwant is sharp. She could oversee the supply base.'

Sarna stopped fidgeting with the crotcheted tablecloth and stared at her husband.

'Kalwant could have a cut of the profits,' Karam hurried on. 'That would be a good incentive, I'm sure. You've often said how her husband is a good-for-nothing drunkard who doesn't earn a penny and how she has to break her back with sewing to support the family. Well, now there's

244

another solution.' Sarna remained silent. 'Imagine – you will be closer to your family again! You haven't seen them since we got married – we could go to India together to get the first consignment of cloth—'

'Who will look after the children?' she interrupted.

'The children? They're old enough to look after themselves for a few weeks.' Then, spotting resistance tightening Sarna's features, he said, 'Or something can be arranged. Mandeep could come and stay here while we're gone.'

'I don't want that bachelor boy staying unsupervised in the house with my unmarried daughter,' Sarna said.

'I thought you liked him!'

'Like is one thing, like to look after my kids is another. And anyway, he can't cook. You can't leave children without someone to feed them.'

'Eat! Feed! That's all you think about! If you'd taught your daughter to cook, like normal mothers do, this wouldn't be a problem. But I don't know why you're still pampering her. When you were ill she couldn't make a thing – *I* was better in the kitchen than she was.' What were they arguing about? Karam suddenly wondered. How had they gone off on this ridiculous tangent? 'Anyway, that's the least of my concerns right now. I wanted to talk to you about the India connection. I thought you might have some suggestions on how best to approach your sister about joining the business.'

Sarna shook her head. 'It's no good. You've got the worst combination at the heart of your business plan – family and India.' Then, as if to emphasize the severity of her verdict, she summarized it in English: 'Nothing doing, Jee, nothing doing. Bijness with fame-ily in India eqvals – flop.' She clapped her hands together loudly.

'What do you mean?'

Sarna reverted to Punjabi again. 'Meaning forget your plans. *You* can't do business in India. Number one,' she raised a finger, 'India is full of crooks. You'll be swindled before you know it.'

'Not if your sister is there. She can handle the Indian suppliers.' Karam started pulling at his right ear.

'Number two, that Kalwant is a chalaako – the biggest crook of all. She'll make sure your plan doesn't work. She loves to ruin things. She may seem all sweet and helpful at first, but she'll be biding her time, waiting to stab you in the back. She likes to make everything go bad so that she can look good amidst all the havoc she's wreaked.'

Karam was startled by Sarna's bitterness. He didn't know that the venom in her words was the product of weeks of mental festering, during which she'd convinced herself that Kalwant had masterminded the letter from Nina in order to ruin her life. 'You're too suspicious. How can you talk like that about your own sister? She's family!'

'Exactly! That's my point. Family is always the worst. They mistreat or cheat you without thinking twice, because they expect to get away with it. Look at your family – what have they done to me?'

Karam didn't rise to this. 'If Kalwant has a good incentive for helping with my business, there's no reason for her to do anything underhand. And you know I'm very thorough with accounts. If people know they can't get away with something they won't try it.'

'She's *my* sister!' Sarna pushed the spice box roughly to one side and stood up. 'I know her better than anyone and I'm telling you, this won't work. You can't just go there and expect my family to jump at your offer.'

'Why not? I don't understand you. What do you have

against India? I thought you would like this chance to see your family and help them out.'

'You can't go there!' Sarna stamped her foot.

'Why not?' Karam stood up as well. 'Since when have you been appointed immigration officer, deciding who can and can't go there, huh?'

Sarna searched desperately for another objection. 'Just think what happened the last time you went to India – you almost died. You said you would never go back. You and India don't agree with each other. I have a bad feeling about this. You shouldn't return.'

'Ah, that was ages ago. It was a different time,' he retorted with a wave.

'And . . . and . .' Sarna floundered for a moment, before remembering that money always made her husband think twice. 'How are you planning to pay for this va va grand project of yours? You're always complaining about how tight things are. Where have you got the cash from?'

'That's no problem. I spoke to Guru and he agreed—'

'Oh-oh, very nice, Jee.' Sarna's hands went to her hips. 'So as usual I'm the last to hear about your plans. All the brothers have been told. That Persini kamini probably knows as well. Where else have you announced the news? Does the congregation at the gurudwara know? Why bother informing me at all? Clearly you don't care what I think – even when your plans involve *my* family.'

'No one knows,' Karam said. 'I only spoke to Guru because he's the one who can give the loan. And I've been meaning to tell you for weeks, but you've been ill.'

'I haven't been ill!'

Karam ignored her. 'This is a big chance for us! But you don't see that. You only see the negative, because that's all you look for.'

'So who will you sell these clothes to?'

'Oh, everyone is wearing them.' Karam picked his note-book off the table. He stood beside Sarna and flicked through a few pages, pointing to his neatly written lists. 'English ladies, female tourists from Europe, young girls. In the West End there are lots of small boutiques selling the clothes. That's where I want to supply garments or have a shop – in the heart of London.'

'Hai!' Sarna wailed as her hands flew to her head. 'Why didn't I see that before? Hai, I should have known there was some ulterior motive. You've really surpassed yourself this time. Setting up such a scheme just to satisfy your own desires. Hai, who would have thought?'

Karam snapped the notebook shut. What was she play-ing at now? It all became clear in her next sentence.

'This is all about your London ladies, isn't it? Hai Ruba, may God spare other women from such husbands. Hai, such a business! You might as well be running a brothel! Wanting to involve your wife's family in a plot which gives you endless access to London ladies.'

Karam's nostrils flared. 'That's enough! Listen to your-self, spouting such filth. What goes on in that head of yours? How can everything that enters come out so twisted?' He leaned right up so that his face was just inches from hers. 'I'm not asking your permission to do this. I'm doing it. I had thought you might be able to help, you might get something out of it as well – *that's* why I told you, not because I need your approval. You can either get used to the idea and accept it or sit here feeling miser-able about it. That's the only choice you have – the rest I've already decided.' With that Karam left the room.

Sarna felt dizzy with anger. She looked about her expecting everything to be spinning madly, but all was still. She heard Karam trudge upstairs and slam the door of their bedroom. Then there was silence. She took a couple of unsteady steps towards the dining table and sat down on a chair. This was not what she had expected. Even in her wildest imaginings the scenario of Karam going to India had not occurred to her. She felt as though her whole life was purposefully criss-crossing itself. Fate, like a giant needle and thread, was doggedly darting across time and distance to connect the patchy tapestry of her experience, and she was being hemmed in by its artful stitches.

Sarna looked at the spice container on the table in front of her. The reordered tin, which had given her so much pleasure only a short time ago, now seemed like an aberration. How could everything be so rightfully in place when she felt all out of sorts? At the same time, this image of symmetry quietened Sarna's racing thoughts. It seemed strange that Karam should come up with this India-related business proposal just as she had finished rearranging the jumbled spices. Was there some connection between the two that she was failing to see? For some reason she recalled Karam's words: 'It's a real opportunity. When you see an opportunity you have to take it. Life doesn't throw such chances at you every day.'

The weekend had passed uneventfully, but Karam could not shake off the uncomfortable feeling that something important was waiting to happen. He and Sarna had been studiously avoiding each other. Using Pyari as a mouthpiece, Sarna had cited a new complaint of 'stomach roaring' as grounds for not attending the gurudwara on Saturday. She'd also taken to sleeping on the sofa in the living room since their fight on Friday evening. Quite what point she was trying to make, Karam wasn't sure. She was only inconveniencing herself with such actions. But he wasn't about to say anything. He knew that a confrontation was inevitable. He could not predict when it might come or in what form, he could only prepare himself by expecting it.

On Monday evening, Sarna rejoined her family at the dinner table. She chatted away in the best of spirits, trying to regale them all with stories about the latest developments in Persini's search for a husband for her daughter, Rupi. 'Our neighbour Kamaljit was telling me that the kamini and Rupi have rejected all the eligible boys in England. Just imagine! Such a comment. So shameless! I said, "Since when have all the single boys been queuing outside Rupi's door?" That made Kamaljit do a double-take. Such are the rumours the kamini is spreading, and those who don't know better believe her. She's probably hoping that it will increase Rupi's value or something, make people think her daughter's in demand. Really, Persini has given Rupi such airs – and why? You have to wonder. The girl is hardly a beauty queen and she has no other great qualities to boast of. The poor thing is jinxed even in name – after all, the rupee is one of the weakest currencies. What can you get for one rupee, I ask? A titbit, no more. But this Rupi expects to fetch a handsome husband with a mansion. It's Persini's fault – she always spoilt the girl and that's why Rupi's such a fusspot. This will be the girl's ruin, you mark my words. "Only the best for my Rupi," Persini likes to insist. Hai Ruba, I wish I could tell her that the best is only for the best – and *you* can't tell the best from the rest.'

Sarna paused for a moment to scan everyone's plates. She frowned when she noticed that Pyari was eating the yellow dhal and curried pumpkin but not touching the lamb chops. She tried unsuccessfully to force another roti on to her daughter's plate. 'You're another fussy one. But your pickiness is of another order entirely: you leave the best stuff and go for the rest. What will you do when you're married, huh? What will your mother-in-law and husband think of your vegetarian habits? Come on, eat at least one chop.'

When Pyari refused, Sarna grabbed the bowl and scraped the lamb on to her own plate with her fingers. Licking the thick red-brown sauce off her hand, she turned to Karam and asked, 'Everything OK, Jee? You like it? Have more.' She picked up two rotis and passed them to him, then looked at Pyari again. 'Well, hopefully we won't have any difficulty finding a husband who will tolerate your meat aversion. Apparently the ratio of single boys to single girls is very high – there are just too many boys. No wonder Persini can let Rupi be so choosy.' She turned to Karam. 'Really, Jee. There are too many boys – people are going to India to bring back wives for their sons.'

He shrugged. 'I haven't heard anything about that.'

'No, of course not, this is not men's information. This is all lady-talk – that's why I'm telling you. So you know what's going on. Pretty soon we'll have to be considering such things. Better to be aware – then you can prepare.'

Pyari pulled the collar of her rust-brown blouse up towards her nose. The pearly lining shone up at her from within the top. She would have liked to bury her face in its opaque depths. She hated it when her mother brought up the subject of marriage. It was not that Pyari lacked romantic longings – she just didn't relish the prospect of Sarna being responsible for their fulfilment. If these were the stories that were circulating as Persini sought a

251

suitable boy for Rupi, Pyari dreaded to think what fabrications would characterize her own pre-nuptials. She knew her mother had to outdo Persini on every front. For now, though, it seemed Pyari was to be spared.

'We still have time,' Karam said. 'The girl must finish her studies first, then we'll see about arranging marriage. Don't distract her with such thoughts. This year she has to pass her A levels and get into university – that should be her focus.'

'Oh-ho, Jee, who said anything about distracting? Bear it in mind, is all I'm saying. Who knows how long conditions will remain so favourable for our girls?'

Karam was surprised by Sarna's change of mood. He had thought reconciliation might be in the air when he'd come home from work earlier and the sweet smell of pumpkin had greeted him. But such a positive signal in the current circumstances only heightened his unease. He couldn't believe that Sarna was just calmly acquiescing. She never gave in without a struggle that somehow reworked an issue in her favour. How was she playing things this time? His responses to her friendly overtures remained deliberately cool. He was determined to stay on the alert.

After she'd cleared away the dinner dishes, Sarna came into the living room, where Karam was reading the climate forecasts for major world cities in the newspaper. She sat down and cleared her throat.

'It will be ten degrees again tomorrow. Mild,' Karam said.

Sarna shifted impatiently. It didn't make much difference to her. She was indoors most of the time anyway.

'Winter is nothing really in this country. The rest of Europe is at least ten or twenty degrees colder. Especially the East – Warsaw is minus fifteen. Woooh.' He sucked in air through the funnel of his lips.

Sarna was not interested. There was enough freeze-thaw action going on in her head. It was typical, though, that he was checking conditions elsewhere and ignoring the troubled situation on the home front. 'What about India?' she asked, partly to humour him but mainly to turn the conversation to her desired subject.

'Delhi is sixteen. Pleasant.'

'Hmmm. I've been thinking, Jee, about what you said.' Karam did not move. Through the printed pages of *The Times* it was hard to know if he was even listening. 'You're right about helping family. You know I always like to help everyone. You know how much I do for people. Even from far away I've tried to do what I can for my family. I think of them all the time.'

Behind the paper, Karam narrowed his eyes.

'So today I phoned Kalwant.'

The Times almost dropped out of Karam's hands. It fell away from his face to reveal an expression of utter shock. Phoned Kalwant! What on earth?

'Oh, Jee, my poor sister is not in a good way,' Sarna went on. 'Two weeks ago that drunkard husband of hers, Harbans, broke his leg. He came home drunk and fell down the stairs. So she's now got the hassle of looking after him. That's on top of the problem of her son Jasraj, who's turning out just like his father – a proper good-for-nothing. Between keeping tabs on those two, running her household and sewing to earn some money, poor Kalwant hardly has time to breathe. She's so miserable. She's lucky she gets some support from our sister Sunaina – you remember her, nah? Nina, we called her? She was still a baby when we left India.'

Karam's fingers tightened around *The Times*.

'But now even Sunaina is of a marriageable age.' Sarna knotted and unknotted the corner of her pink chuni. 'And Kalwant has the added problem of trying to find a husband for her.'

'So what?'

'So I said to her, maybe help is on the way. I told her I might have a solution to her problems. I explained your idea to her.' She paused.

'And?'

'Well, Jee, she thought about it.' Sarna started winding the end of her chuni around her wrist like a bandage. 'She wasn't sure, she had doubts – but in the end I convinced her. I told her what a good idea it is and how you are sure it will be a success. Now she's one hundred per cent behind us. She agrees that your business idea could make lots of money. She knows about the cheesecloth boom because people there are talking about it. She'll start making enquiries right away.'

The newspaper slipped from Karam's lap on to the brown carpet.

'I told her that you think most of the big suppliers are in Delhi,' Sarna raced on. Her fingers twiddled rapidly in her lap as if to keep pace with her words. 'She said that's no problem, Harbans has family in Delhi and she goes there sometimes anyway. She also said it might be cheaper to set up a workshop in Amritsar. I told her to check all the options. I asked her to get hold of as many samples as possible. I said you'll probably want to go there and start things within the next three months.'

A wave of resentment washed over Karam. Only a few days ago she had been objecting vehemently to his proposal – now she was meddling and taking over. And yet what could he say? He couldn't complain that she was now on his side. 'I don't know about the timing. You shouldn't just say things like that when you have no idea. I haven't even handed in my resignation yet.'

'I thought the sooner the better, you seemed so keen to start,' Sarna said. 'And if you leave things too long it will be sweltering there – you won't be able to cope with the summer heat. Just remember what it did to you last time. Also, if Kalwant thinks it is happening fast, she'll find things out for us quicker. I told her she'll get some of the profits. "Profit is nothing to me. The real gain is that I get to work with my family. Strong family ties are the real riches in life," she said. Sounds good, nah? She's very eager to be a part of the business. Still, we'll have to watch her – she's a real talker, that one. Got a sweet tongue and a sly mind – always a lethal combination.'

Karam raised his eyebrows – didn't he know it.

'But Kalwant is right, there's nothing more rewarding than helping your family,' Sarna chattered on. Now the chuni was being folded into neat pleats. 'I really want to do more for them. The poor woman has so much on her hands. So I said I would take responsibility for arranging Nina's marriage. I can help with that while Kalwant contributes to your business. Fair and square.'

Sarna's verbal flair only incited Karam to declare: 'Nina? What has she got to do with me? She's not my business.' He kicked *The Times* aside and stood up. 'You can't just make such pacts on my behalf. How do you expect to pull this off? You can't sit in England and arrange a girl's wedding in India. It doesn't make sense. Moreover, Kalwant is not doing me a favour that needs to be reciprocated. This is a business arrangement from which she stands to make real gains. There will be a proper agreement with a guaranteed rate of payment. I want none of this "you do X and I'll do Y and then somehow, somewhere along the line, we'll be even." There's no need for you to get involved.'

'But I am involved!' Sarna's hands danced excitedly in the air. 'It's only thanks to me that Kalwant has agreed to help you. Like I told you, she says the money is less important to her than family ties. I said I would help Nina because that's what she wanted. The girl will come over here and we'll get her married off. It's my duty. The family there have looked after her ever since my bibiji died. Now it's my turn.'

'The girl will come here! *What?*' Karam pinched his ear hard, as if to check it was working. 'Where did *that* come from? Why should she come here? This is all a bit sudden, isn't it?'

'Well, I warned you,' Sarna said. 'Kalwant is a chalaako. She tries to get the most out of every opportunity. She's made my arranging Nina's marriage part of the deal. If I refuse now, she may decide not to help you at all.'

'Why did you have to speak to her?'

'Hai Ruba! So ungrateful! I try to help you and this is what I get in return.'

'You just complicate everything.' He began pacing the room.

Sarna jumped up. 'I am trying to help you! Don't you see? It's good if we have Kalwant by another hook. If we take Nina she'll be indebted to us. Then there's less risk of her doing heraferi and cheating you out of money.'

Karam could not see any logic in Sarna's words. Goodness only knew what roundabout negotiations she'd done with her sister. He'd been correct in anticipating a conflict with his wife, but he had not imagined this would be the order of their clash. He had expected Sarna to engineer a hitch in his plans, but he hadn't suspected that it would involve actually getting someone hitched.

'This is ridiculous, involving the girl,' Karam said. 'We are the ones who'll end up in debt. Have you thought about how you can get her here? Who will pay her airfare? And who will pay for the wedding? Your Kalwant has struck a very clever deal indeed: she throws her expenses into our lap and frees up her hands to take our profits. You're right, I'll have to be wary of her. At this rate *I'll* be the one who's short-changed. Maybe getting her involved is a bad idea after all.'

'No, no, she'll be very useful. I know how to handle her. And don't worry about the money.' She had her savings from the rent, didn't she? That would stretch to the airfare at least. If she could just convince Karam to let Nina come, everything else would fall into place, she was sure of it. She didn't need money – just the chance of matrimony. 'You won't have to pay a penny. I've discussed it all with Kalwant. And coming to the country should also be easy. People are doing it all the time. Remember I was telling you about how there are too many eligible boys and not enough girls for them to marry? Remember?'

Karam recalled her earlier remarks with some dismay. Good God, was *this* why she'd been harping on about marriage during dinner? Had she been plotting away even then, discreetly working on him, laying out the path of capitulation that he was destined to follow? The direction their argument had taken seemed to confirm this. Did Sarna's every word disguise an alternative agenda? And if so, how could a man cope with such guile?

'They choose a wife from India, and then sponsor the girl to get her over,' Sarna went on. 'She arrives, the wedding takes place, the girl becomes a British citizen. Simple as that.' The chuni slipped from Sarna's neck, revealing the bare skin down to her neckline. There was a flutter of pink chiffon – like a rag to a bull – and then the chuni settled around her shoulders. 'If we showed Sunaina's photo at the gurudwara, I'm sure we'd have a suitor within a week. She's an innocent, beautiful girl – the offers will stream in. Just wait and see.'

'I don't know.' Karam sat down again – it was hard to concentrate with Sarna slinking around him so coyly. 'Our own daughter is coming to a marriageable age ... it doesn't seem right to bring another girl into the house and worry about getting her married. I don't like it.'

'Don't worry, you won't even notice Nina is here.'

Karam shook his head and drummed his fingers on the armrest. 'Why Nina? Why now?' He looked into Sarna's eyes, challenging their chestnut stubbornness with his own coffee-bean insistence. 'Just let her be.'

'Hai! I don't understand you!' Sarna's hand went to her heart. 'One minute you're telling me how great it would be to help my family, the next you're warning me off getting too involved with them. What's going on? Am I only allowed to help them when it serves your purpose? You always think only about yourself. Have you ever imagined what it's like for me? Have you even once considered how I've felt all these years, following you from country to country, leaving behind my sisters? No, of course not. Your brothers are here now, you're very comfortable, why should you care about me?' She let her chin fall towards her chest. Sounds of sobbing followed.

'Don't be stupid. Stop playing these games with me. I know how much you've missed your family – so much that you refused every opportunity to go and visit them since we got married.'

The sobs got louder.

Sarna was like a hammer that keeps banging away even after the nail it is hitting has been firmly lodged into the wall. OK, OK, just shut up now, Karam wanted to say. He knew his submission was inevitable, because he did not have the strength to keep arguing. You've got what you want, let her have her way too – it will make life easier, he thought. Yet he could not help feeling that his was a hollow victory. This time Sarna had used his business venture to strike the better bargain.

18

Nina was no ordinary sister, Pyari very quickly understood that much. This sisterly connection was unusual even by Indian standards, where the term 'bhanji' is used habitually in a social context, nominally conferring sisterhood upon friends, acquaintances and even strangers. Pyari sensed some irregularity the moment her mother excitedly announced Nina's impending arrival. 'Your pithaji and I are going to India. He'll be bringing back clothes to start a new business and *I'll* be returning with my sister, Sunaina. You know,' she prompted when her children looked blank, 'the youngest sister – Nina. My little Nina.'

Pyari noticed that Sarna said 'Nina' tenderly, as if the word was sacred. She recalled that the damning accusations and hollow curses which Sarna habitually heaped on her other sisters had never been directed at Nina. All her life, Sarna had railed against her family in India for not appreciating, remembering or caring enough. Pyari knew that much of her mother's ranting was pure drama. Underlying even Sarna's most unsisterly statements was a genuine fondness, which emerged to make conciliatory phone calls and send gifts. Kalwant was the main object of Sarna's denunciations, with Harpal getting an occasional mention, but Nina had never featured at all.

'Will I have to call her Nina Masi?' Pyari asked.

'There's no need for any masi-wasi. She's the same age as you. She'll be more like a sister than an aunt,' Sarna replied without looking up from her crocheting. She was making a multicoloured new cover for the coffee table in their living room. The one on there now was old and faded, like an overused doily.

'So does that mean you've never seen her?' Perhaps Sarna had not mentioned Nina because she didn't really know her.

'What? What "never seen her"?'

'Well, I mean, I was born *after* you left India. So I just thought, if she's the same age . . . maybe you haven't met her.' Pyari toyed with her braid.

'Oh-ho, of course I've met her.' Sarna smiled over the lightning flash of her crochet hook. 'I even looked after her when she was little. I was her favourite. She always wanted to be with me. I would balance her on my hip with one arm and cook or clean with the other. Of course I know her!'

'So how old is she then? She must be older than me.'

'Hai Ruba! I told you – the same as you. One or two years' difference, maybe. The same, really.' A little muscle in Sarna's jaw started twitching.

'But—' Pyari hesitated and then allowed puzzlement to overcome her natural tendency to leave things unsaid. 'I thought your baoji died when you were a little girl. Is Nina . . . did Bibiji, uh, when she was born . . . Who's Nina's pithaji?' she finally spluttered.

'Ooh, that's why you're so interested in her age.' Sarna

was surprised by her daughter's insight. 'The reason is simple.' She put aside her crocheting. 'You can't tell anyone, and especially don't mention it to Nina when she comes.' Sarna beckoned Pyari closer and lowered her voice. 'Nina was adopted by my family during Partition. Oh yes. Goondas came to our area in Amritsar – they burned, looted and massacred in many houses. We thought the end of the world had arrived. Nina's family were our neighbours – very nice people, so good, so kind. They were killed – all of them, wiped out. Somehow she survived. We heard her crying, that's how we found her. *I* found her, actually. Through all the chaos I got her, this perfect baby. And I said to Bibi, "We have to keep her, we have to help. What will become of her otherwise?" She agreed and Nina stayed with us. You can see why I became her favourite. She was only a baby, but she must have sensed who had saved her. So *that's* why Nina is your age. But chup!' Sarna brought a finger to her lips. 'Not a word to anyone. For us, Nina is just like real family.'

'Does Pithaji know?'

'Of course,' Sarna said, as though the very notion of Karam not knowing her deepest secrets was preposterous. 'He was almost dying in some refugee camp in Lahore before I found her. I was praying to God to bring him back, "Oh Vaheguru, Vaheguru, I'll do anything." When I came across Nina I knew it was a test, a choice: life or death. I knew whatever happened to her would decide the fate of your pithaji. That's why I begged Bibi to let us keep her. "One good turn deserves another," I told Bibi. And sure enough, just a short time after I saved Nina, your pithaji was restored to us.'

'So how old is she exactly then?'

'Back to square one? I already told you – the *same* age.

Stop this now.' She took up her crocheting again. 'What is age, huh? Just a number, after all.' A number that was destined to keep changing if Sarna was keeping count.

In front of Karam, Pyari heard her mother maintain that Nina was twenty-four. 'So old?' he said. 'So how come she's not married yet? Is that why Kalwant is sending her here? So we'll be landed with the burden of an old maid?' Sarna became flustered and muttered something about Kalwant being too selfish to bother with the girl. A few days later, Pyari was intrigued to notice that Sarna had revised Nina's age to twenty. Karam frowned. 'I thought you said she was twenty-four.'

'Hai, twenty-four! Listen to the man. Where do you get your figures? Just plucking them out of the air or something? You did that with me, notching up the age in my passport by five or six years. Now you're trying to do the same with my sister. You have something against my family, I swear. You're determined to age us all before our time.'

A ridiculous argument then ensued, during which Sarna fiercely bandied about so many numbers she succeeded in thoroughly confusing Karam and Pyari, who could only watch in horrified amazement as she rattled helter-skelter through time. 'Don't you remember that when you came back from Lahore she was still a baby? Oh, what can *you* recall, you were so sick. I think the Taffoid destroyed your ability to count. It certainly left you looking one hundred years old. When we left India, Nina was starting to walk, taking little steps – one, two, three, four, and then more and more. She ran up to you and pulled at your trousers – remember? She was three years old then, or – no, maybe two. And *you* looked ancient, ninety-nine years old: all thinny-skinny, no hair and pale as death after your illness.

263

People mistook you for my father on the train to Bombay, remember? No? Look at him shaking his head. Of course he doesn't remember *that*. It's only my family's ages that he can summon up – Sarna plus seven, Nina plus six. Wrong, wrong, wrong. Always. And he used to tell me his best subject at school was maths. Va va, Jee, great sums you must have been doing.'

It was only after Nina herself had come to London that Pyari was able to establish her true age. 'I've just turned twenty-three,' she said. Almost five years older than Pyari. It sounded like such a huge gap, but it felt like nothing. From their first meeting, Nina and Pyari felt close to each other: instinctively comfortable, inexplicably familiar – just like sisters. Since the death of her twin, there had been a concave absence traversing Pyari's being. Nina fit that fragile curve as if she had drawn it in the first place. When she confessed to Pyari within days of her arrival that she was actually Sarna's daughter, Pyari was not surprised. It felt absolutely right that Nina was *her* sister. Moreover, the revelation confirmed Pyari's impression that behind Sarna's nervous excitement about Nina's arrival there had been another stronger emotion. There are only two things you can't hide – Ishq and Mushq: Love and Smell. Nina's disclosure made Pyari see what Sarna had been trying to disguise in all her dealings concerning Nina: Love.

Before the trip to India, Pyari had accompanied Sarna on numerous excursions to Oxford Street to find gifts for the family. It was just over twenty years since Sarna had left Amritsar and she wanted to go back in style, laden with presents. The West End expeditions turned into shopping sprees resulting in the acquisition of a whole new wardrobe for Nina. From practical purchases like thermal underwear and thick socks from Woolworths, to the extravagance of a winter coat from C&A and a cardigan from Marks & Spencer, Sarna bought without a second thought. But any pangs of jealousy that Pyari had felt at her mother's strange generosity disappeared the moment Nina said, 'We will share it all.' And they did. Pyari was several inches taller and less curvaceous than Nina, but when they wore each other's clothes you couldn't tell – everything fitted perfectly. Often the young women simultaneously had the same thoughts – especially about Sarna. Even their sleep patterns were similar – both preferred to fall asleep lying on their stomach. During the night they would toss and turn in synchronicity and when they woke they'd be facing the same way.

Sarna expected that it would only be a short while before Nina was married off and she wanted to make the most of the time they had together. She decided to pass on the saucy secrets and spicy tricks she'd spent her life perfecting and guarding. Finally, the legacy was being passed from mother to daughter.

Nina underwent her induction into Sarna's classified cookery cosmos with interest and good humour. She admired Sarna's methods and appreciated her advice. She understood that she was the first person being privileged with this information and yet she could not express the veneration she knew Sarna would have liked to see. In truth, Nina would have preferred not to know any of Sarna's cooking tips if that meant she could say 'mother' to her mother – even if only in private, when they were completely alone. Nina had tried it once in India and Sarna had said, 'I am your sister. You must call me Bhanji.'

So while Pyari and Rajan were at school, while Karam was driving around London selling clothes, Nina was in the kitchen with Sarna, pretending they were sisters, learning what daughters do from mothers. Sarna showed her how to throw a teabag into a bubbling pan of chickpea curry to give a rich red-brown colour. She taught her to coat the rim of a saucepan with oil when cooking rice so that the water doesn't boil over. She advised that cooking turmeric for a minute in hot oil prevents it from staining. She demonstrated how bhajias fry better and come out crispier if a few drops of vinegar are added to the hot oil. She admitted that she often put a quarter of a teaspoon of honey into the cups of those who refused sugar. 'But why, if they don't want it?' Nina asked. 'Aah, people don't know what they want. You give them what's best and they'll like it. Everyone who comes here says, "No one makes tea like Sarna." Don't you tell anyone – this is *our* secret.'

Sarna never suspected that Nina was letting someone else in on these secrets. Every night, when Pyari should have been revising her pure and applied maths or going over her physics, she was committing to memory the cooking skills and techniques Nina had acquired that day. Nina knew that her words were a sort of betrayal, but she did not feel guilty confessing to Pyari. They were sisters, after all, and had a right to each other's knowledge of their mother. In this way the girls drew solace from each other, united in their grievances against a mother who had let them both down in different ways.

Nina was shown off to friends and acquaintances like a prize. 'Look, my sister,' Sarna would say, spinning the girl around and forcing people to appraise the perfection she had brought from India. Shyly Nina would twirl, her head cast down, embarrassment kissing her features with its dripping red brush. She was lovely. No one could deny it. Oskar was stunned when Sarna introduced them. 'Have joo meet my sister?' Sarna pushed Nina forward. 'Meet,' she ordered, enjoying the look of wonder that whispered across his face, turning his grey eyes into spheres of brilliance like brand-new five-pence coins. Nina managed a weak hello, which floated up to Oskar like a soapy bubble before bursting softly against his face.

Even Persini was involuntarily impressed by Nina's outrageously green eyes, set in the sweetest heart of a face above graceful cheekbones and a mouth like a ripe red plum. The girl was a prettier, more refined copy of Sarna. 'Youngest sister, huh? Very funny, isn't it, to have such an age difference between siblings. Twenty years or so, no?' Sarna ignored her and picked up the chuni that had slipped off Nina's stiff shoulders, which were hunching up to her ears in shame.

The Khalsis drove down from Leeds to meet their prospective daughter-in-law. They were one of several families who had expressed an interest in Nina and had offered to sponsor her passage to London. There was much to recommend them as in-laws. They were a fairly progressive Sikh family: well respected, well off, well heeled, well turbaned. But Sarna had eagerly courted their interest for two other reasons: the fact that the families did not know each other – indeed they had few common acquaintances – and that the Khalsis lived several hundred kilometres away in Leeds. 'Pardeep is his name. Oldest son, six foot two, pharmacy degree,' Sarna told everyone proudly, as though this information confirmed that the most stringent criteria had been met.

Pardeep was a little on the heavy side, but well

mannered and affable. It was Nina who fell short of expectations. Her appearance did not disappoint – she looked like the model bride-to-be in a papaya-coloured sari, her thick hair swept tightly into a neat, high bun, gold jewels sparkling at her ears, throat and arms. It was her personality, or rather the apparent lack of it, which let Nina down. The initial charm of her downcast eyes and demure manner was overshadowed by the startled, fearful expression that clouded her features whenever the Khalsis spoke to her. Overwhelmed by the pressure of the meeting, she gave clumsy, stuttered responses to their questions. She knew that her future in England depended on their approval. In her desperate effort not to mess up she came across as foolish and inept. The Khalsis began to converse in English, as though this might somehow bring Nina out of her shell. It had the opposite effect. She, who had hardly been able to get the words out in Punjabi, panicked at the English questions and ran from the room.

'Hai, hai, wery shy girl.' Sarna used her own broken English to try and make a virtue out of Nina's awkward social graces. 'I vas same vhen I coming to this country. Is just innocent, joo know. But she's not innocent or shy in kitchen. Oh no, she is expert cooker. *All* this –' she spread her arms to highlight the bounteous spread, 'all this, *she* making. And cleaning, sewing – she wery good. English just little veak, joo know. Needing praxis. Bhraji, have more tikkis. Here have, eat, eat.'

After the Khalsis departed Nina could not stop shaking. The premonition of rejection was already heavy on her heart. Sure enough, two evenings later the Khalsis phoned to withdraw their marriage offer. They had changed their minds. The girl was too naive. There was too much of the village about her. Sarna argued with them, telling them that their judgement was too hasty, trying to persuade them to meet Nina again. 'Bhraji, one meeting is never enough,' she told Pardeep's father. 'First impressions don't count.'

'Bhanji, when the girl's bangles make more noise than her, one encounter is adequate,' he replied. 'And anyway, Nina is very short. The height difference between her and Pardeep is out of proportion.'

'Hai!' Sarna banged down the phone. 'That's really the limit! Such cheek. Ungrateful wretches.' She went on to repeat all the Khalsis' comments, punctuating them with a generous sprinkling of her own disparagements. 'Who do they think they are? My sister's more than good enough for that fat son of theirs. May they burn! Did you see the size of Pardeep's glasses? Everything is probably magnified fifty times through those giant lenses, no wonder he sees only flaws everywhere. Hai, such a mistake they're making. Well, they can get lost!'

'Easy enough to say, but have you thought about what this means?' Karam's voice emerged from behind the newspaper where he had retreated while Sarna had been on the phone. So far he had remained completely un-involved in all matters concerning Nina. He hardly even spoke to the girl, maintaining a polite distance which suited Sarna just fine – until she needed his help. She'd tried to get Karam to speak to the Khalsis, but he'd refused. He disapproved of her grovelling manner. She'd been too sycophantic when the Khalsis had visited, and just now on the phone it had sounded as if she was begging.

'Those Khalsis have made the biggest mistake of their lives,' Sarna said.

'Be realistic.' Karam put down the newspaper. 'It means

you no longer have anyone to sponsor the girl. She has a three-month visa.' Karam looked at Nina, who was seated cross-legged on the carpet, shoulders drooped, eyes downcast. He almost felt sorry for her now. 'Nine more weeks she can stay here. If she doesn't get married before then, she'll have to go back to India.'

There was silence as his words sank in. Nina bit her lip and hunched over even further. Once again she had not been good enough, once again she had been rejected. It was exactly this sort of repudiation she'd travelled to England to avoid. But, it seems, you cannot escape your fate wherever you go. Nina felt the humiliation of the Khalsis' rebuff, but more than that she was tortured by how this incident might denigrate her in Sarna's eyes. She had let her mother down. She had come to London hoping to make Sarna proud. Instead, she had embarrassed the family.

Sarna was also perturbed by Karam's words. She twisted her wedding ring round and round. Siyapa. What a hassle. She had not anticipated this scenario. After all the hurdles she had negotiated to get Nina here, the last thing she'd expected was rejection by the Khalsis. What right did those fatsos have to be so fussy? Nine weeks was not enough to arrange a wedding. Hai! What had she done to deserve this? After all her efforts, all the risks she had taken, what kind of result was *this*? Aloud she said, 'Ah, nine weeks is plenty. I'll get on the case futa fut, double quick. You wait and see – we'll have this sister of mine married off in no time.'

Pyari was the only person who was relieved by the Khalsis' decision. She was glad that Nina would be with them for longer. She looked forward to more whispered chats late into the night, more strange stories about the world in which Nina had grown up, and more discoveries about how much they had in common, despite their different lives. Pyari had good friends with whom she'd shared doubts, dreams, experiences and clothes, but the bond with Nina was stronger than any other friendships. This was mainly because they could talk about Sarna. Pyari had never shared her mixed feelings about her mother with anyone. Speaking out on the subject had always felt wrong. Moreover, the image her friends had of Sarna was not one that Pyari was confident enough to destroy. 'Your mum's so modern, so well dressed, such a good cook, so funny,' they would say almost enviously. But Nina appeared to have few illusions about Sarna.

'She's dying to get rid of me,' Nina said one night as she watched Pyari comb her freshly washed hair.

'No. She's just worried about finding you a match.' Pyari tugged through the tangles, wincing occasionally.

'I don't know why I thought it would be different here.' Nina climbed into bed. 'All my life, people have just been waiting for me to go.'

'That's not true, Nina. I don't want you to go.' Water dripping from the ends of Pyari's hair had created a landscape of rivulets on her nightie.

Nina pulled the blanket up to her chin. 'I don't blame them,' she said, as if she hadn't heard. 'If my own mother won't have me, why should anyone else?'

'Oh, Nina.' Pyari swept her glossy hair over one shoulder and sat down on the edge of Nina's bed. 'What about all those lovely new clothes she bought you? You have a special place in her heart.'

Nina shook her head. 'If I did she would hold me tightly and say that I'm her daughter.'

'She's never been one for the hugs, Nina. Don't take it

personally. Besides, she fusses over you more than she ever has over me. I've noticed the way she's always fingering your clothes or rearranging your chuni or touching your hair.'

'*Your* hair is so beautiful.' Nina smiled and reached out to touch the long, straight, glistening mass of it. Then she made a face and patted her own thick nest. 'This is my sadness growing out,' she said. 'I can't keep it all here –' She pointed to her heart. 'So it has to go somewhere.' That's what sadness becomes, sometimes: a part of your body, a visible strand in your appearance.

19

The garments Karam brought back from India were sold within a week: six hundred pieces – gone. Karam was surprised. He had never imagined money could be made so easily. He hardly needed to do a sales pitch to get rid of the clothes. From central to north London, from Hendrix-humming shops to patchouli-incensed market stalls, owners were falling over themselves for the items. Karam had expected people to be picky about the designs, testy about prices, cautious about placing orders. But everywhere, it seemed, demand was high, people were eager to buy. From Camden Market to Tottenham Court Road, from Carnaby Street to Kingston, they were calling him up and placing orders, pushing for quick delivery. The next batch of goods, which Karam had pre-ordered while in India, arrived on time three weeks after his return to London. These two thousand pieces were also sold within weeks. Such speedy sales set the trend for Karam's business. He was on the phone to Kalwant regularly, instructing her to dispatch more items, urging her to hurry.

Yet despite these early signs of success, Karam erred on the side of caution and ordered relatively small quantities.

'Bhraji, if they're going so fast why don't I send you ten thousand?' Kalwant repeatedly asked him. 'It might take one or two weeks longer, but it will save you so much hassle. Why take this piecemeal approach when there's a chance to have the full meal, huh? Come on, Bhraji, go for it – have a feast, flood the market, do some *real* business. Slowly, slowly won't win this race. To succeed in business you have to think big, you have to move fast!'

Karam would laugh nervously at her advice, sensing that she was right and yet reluctant to accept her recommendations. 'No, no, it's too risky. Just send three thousand.'

'Bhraji, no risk, no win. You shouldn't worry so much. At least let me send five thousand.'

'No, that's too excessive. No, three is fine. Just send three.'

'Bhraji, excess equals success. I'm sending four thousand. I know you'll thank me for it.'

'No! I can't pay.' Karam would put his hand over the receiver to muffle his voice and say, 'Oh, the line is very bad. I can't hear any more.' And Kalwant would hear a final 'Bhanji? Bhanji, only three thousand, huh? I can't pay for more—' before the connection died.

Like Sarna, Kalwant could go on labouring the same point until the listener gave in. Karam had seen her use this strategy to great effect while he was in India. Together they had travelled to Delhi. Dodging rickshaws, cyclists, pedestrians and cows, they had trawled the shops in Chandni Chowk, Karol Bagh, Lajpat Nagar market and South Extension for different varieties of cheesecloth. Karam had watched Kalwant bargain down the most resolute, ill-tempered or intimidating of shop owners with an extraordinary mix of charm and cunning, promises and lies.

Just before they'd started shopping, Kalwant had said, 'Bhraji, *I'll* do the talking.' At first Karam had been embarrassed when she offered only 25 per cent of the indicated price for some fabric. He'd pulled at his ears until they were red and sore. He had expected negotiations, but to start haggling at such a low price! It felt almost like begging. They'll think we're jokers, Karam wanted to tell his sister-in-law, but he had been ordered not to speak. The shopkeepers rolled their eyes, shook their heads or were outraged at Kalwant's offers. She remained unperturbed. She ordered assistants to unroll length after length of cloth for inspection. The whole shop would be draped with her selections, making it impossible for any other customer to be served. Slowly Karam began to understand the deliberateness of Kalwant's performance, as a variation of the same scenario was played out with every shopkeeper or wholesaler.

Kalwant examined cloth with the seriousness of a pawnbroker assessing the authenticity of a diamond. She ran her hands along the material, held it up to inspect the grain, asked an assistant to carry it outside so that she could see the colour in sunlight, and enquired where the cloth had been manufactured or dyed. She made insidious comparisons: 'Hmmm . . . Talochasons have the *same* cloth, *identical*, and it's *five* rupees *less* per yard.' She passed damning judgements: 'You had this dyed in Jaipur, nah? Useless. We've bought this before and the colours ran in the first wash. People started bringing the clothes back to the shop. London people are *very* fussy. We had to take the range off the shelves. Six thousand pieces turned to dead stock. Imagine the loss we made. I know, it happens, in business you make mistakes. But you must never make the same mistake twice. How can you sell such fabric? Get it away from me.' Kalwant gave the impression of supreme confidence and authority. So when she then repeated her offer – twenty-five per cent of the asking price – the shop owner, sensing she was a serious customer, would decline it all the more indignantly.

'Three hundred rupees for one hundred yards of the tie-dye cloth.' Kalwant would state the sum as though it was a done deal.

'No, no way.' The shop owner would shake his head. 'Impossible. Nothing doing.'

'Why, do you think you'll get a better price? Huh, you think anyone else is going to buy so much in one go? This is a good deal! How can you say no?'

At this point, the shop owner might wave his hands and insist that the price was unacceptable or sternly tell Kalwant to stop playing games. Whatever he did, she would make a point of taking offence. She'd rise up grandly and sweep out of the shop. Usually, just as she and Karam were at the door, they would be halted by a shout of compromise, 'Seven hundred for one hundred!' Kalwant would pause. Then she'd turn around and say, 'Three hundred and fifty.' This was when the bargaining began in earnest.

She'd re-enter the shop and request some tea. 'Where's my chaa? You are like my son,' she'd say, shifting from sharp bargain-hunter to sweet relative. 'Doesn't a son offer his mother tea when she comes to visit?'

Tea would promptly be served, along with sweet nibbles.

Karam would sip tea and watch the drama unfold. He

considered himself to be a patient man, but he doubted he'd have the stamina to see through the long-winded bartering process like Kalwant did. This made Karam all the more grateful for her tenacity. She understood the basic tenet of the clothes business: margins are everything. With each reduction Kalwant secured, Karam would gleefully revise his profit projections.

He could never guess when a deal might be clinched. He was simply alerted to it by the sudden slapping down of notes as Kalwant gestured to the shop assistants to cut the cloth. 'Four hundred rupees for one hundred yards. Final price. Deal done. Agreed.'

'You're killing me,' the shop owner would say.

'*You're* looting *me*!' Kalwant would exclaim, folding a malai poora into her mouth. Kalwant could munch through mountains of sweets as she argued.

'This is less than cost price you're offering. My family will starve. My children will have to go out on the streets and beg.'

'How can that be? You're robbing *me*.' A big orange ludo disappeared.

Some shopkeepers refused to look at Kalwant or her pile of money, as if it was beneath their dignity to deal in such paltry sums. The more conniving ones would even instruct their assistants to start putting away the rolls of cloth to indicate that negotiations were being terminated.

Kalwant would put down more cash. 'Four hundred and fifteen.'

The shop owner would show no signs of having heard.

'Four hundred and *twenty-five*.'

Sometimes, even this was not enough.

'Look at me!' Kalwant would beat her chest. 'I'm like your mother. Is this how you treat a mother? Would you rob your mother? Hai! Such a son! What is the world coming to?'

With this appeal, eye contact, at least, would be restored.

'Take everything! Rob me!' Kalwant would cry, opening her bag and pulling out what seemed to be her last few notes and coins. 'Four hundred and fifty! You want every last penny from me, don't you? Four hundred and – seventy – two. There, that's everything I have in my purse. I told you I was being plundered. What more do you want? Here, take my purse as well! Rob me! Loot me!' She threw her bag towards the pile of cash. 'Shall I start taking off my clothes? Do you want me to leave here with nothing? Is this the way you do business?'

Many a deal had been sealed by such an outpour. The shopkeeper would signal to his assistants that they could cut and pack the cloth, and Kalwant would be all effusion again.

'Well, you can look forward to future business from us. My brother here has three shops in London, he also supplies Holland, France and Germany. Next time I hope you won't try to rip us off so badly.'

On a few occasions Kalwant's acting skills had not been sufficient to secure a purchase. Then she left the shop in a rage: 'Fine! It's your loss. You couldn't sell silk underwear to a naked maharaja. I'll take my custom elsewhere!'

Karam could not bring himself to take the plunge and authorize larger shipments. Better to live off smaller profits than to see money tied up in dead stock, he told himself. Every time he went to the Cargo Terminal at Heathrow Airport to collect a delivery, he heard stories of wholesalers who had overplayed their hand and were now saddled with stock they couldn't shift. Karam's freight-clearing agent, Tom Nesbit, eagerly updated him on the latest failure story. 'Dunman's have packed up,' Tom would say gravely. 'Oh yeah, it's been comin' for months. They got eleven thousand items sittin' back there –' He gestured towards the back of the vast warehouse. 'Been there for weeks. They won't come pick 'em up 'cause they can't pay the release costs. And what's the point of payin' for goods you can't sell, eh? Oh yeah, it's bad.' These rumours spurred Karam to further caution. He didn't take into consideration that the businesses in question were unrelated to the rag trade. In the sorry end of thousands of unsold water pistols, dog collars, aluminium cutlery sets or oriental-style lampshades, Karam read a salutary warning: greed comes before a fall.

Such prudence also made Karam hesitate to take a lease on a boutique of his own. He had been unable to find a suitable site before going to India. Since his return he had continued to look, but whenever a potential let came up he procrastinated, worrying about visibility, customer traffic in the area, the cost of refurbishing, rent and maintenance. A part of him really wanted a tangible place that he could point to and say, 'This is mine. This is how far I've come.' His personal historical landmark. Yet the overheads didn't justify the enterprise. Karam knew he could make more profit by remaining a supplier. He was not entirely happy with himself in this role: it was a vague job with no real description. When people asked what he was doing, he had to explain, 'I'm a wholesale clothes supplier. I provide ladies' garments to various outlets across the country.' It wasn't like doctor, lawyer, pharmacist or even civil servant – professions whose dignity could be conveyed in just one word. There was no doubt that Karam felt happier working for himself, but the change had not brought about the dramatic transformation he'd envisaged. He did not feel more secure or confident. He was the same man, with a different set of worries to juggle.

20

Karam was sitting up in bed when Sarna walked into the room. He was wearing a white vest and reading a history of Victorian Britain. His thinning, greying hair, released from his turban, fell into a natural middle parting and spilled down his back and shoulders. He looked strange undressed, like a creature without its shell: soft, fleshy and vulnerable. Without a glance at her husband, Sarna started pulling the pins from her bun. Her hair was still thick, dark and shiny. She'd recently begun to apply dye to the wisps of grey at her temples and the nape of her neck. Karam watched her flatten the high puff of her beehive hairstyle. She patted it with her hands before carefully running her fingers through the coarsely backcombed hair. He folded over the corner of the page he'd been reading, closed the book and set it down on his lap.

'So, um . . . uhuh,' he cleared his throat. 'How is Nina?'

Sarna turned and narrowed her eyes. Why this direct question about Nina? The only time he'd shown any interest in her was when he'd insisted that she attend English classes at the Mary Lawson School.

'Er, her English is improving, I hope,' he continued. 'At least she will have got something from her time here. Who knows, maybe she can find a use for the language some-where in India.'

'In *India*? She's not going back *there*.' Hairpins dropped on to Sarna's dressing table with a light clatter.

'Mmm hmm, but how can she stay here if no one marries her?' Karam asked. 'There are only three more weeks before her visa expires. What are the chances of a betrothal before then?' Karam paused. 'I was thinking . . . maybe I should reserve a seat for Nina to fly back to India with me.' He was planning a return visit to place new orders.

'That's not necessary! There's still plenty of time. A marriage will be arranged.' Sarna took a deep breath to quash the panic rising up in her. She sat down on the bed, in profile to Karam. Her hands began to twitch in agitation. Nina's words, 'I will tell,' still hung over Sarna's head like a guillotine waiting to drop. Every day she lived with the possibility of this beheading, this shameful and messy exposure. Every day was an effort to avoid this menace – to blunt the blade of Nina's truth. Through the kindnesses she heaped on Nina, Sarna was trying to quieten her. With each loving word and each additional gift, she was muffling her voice. And through marriage, Sarna believed Nina would finally be gagged. For Nina would not just be marrying a man, she would be binding herself to silence – just as her mother had done. Marriage would give Nina the respectability and legitimacy she had hitherto been denied, but its price would be eternal denial about who she really was. Sarna knew this; she realized that, once married, it would be impossible for Nina to carry out any threat without jeopardizing her own life. Sarna felt so close to securing this salvation – time was all she needed, a bit more time.

Things had not turned out quite as Sarna had expected. Despite Nina's beauty, all those single boys keen to marry innocent village girls were not queuing up for her hand. But Sarna believed it was just a matter of time. Everything could be resolved if they didn't have the visa problem looming over them like a bad omen. In truth, everything might already have been sorted out if Sarna hadn't been doggedly screening every family who expressed an interest in Nina. She disregarded any offers from people who lived in London or had more than a passing acquaintance with Karam's family. This meant that most possibilities were ruled out even before an introduction could take place.

Dismayed by the slow progress, Sarna had started considering alternative solutions. She had heard of people who arrived with short-term visas and simply stayed in the country, disappearing into the hinterland of the city to eke out an illegal existence. But she knew that Karam would never agree to such an arrangement. There were others who were said to have paid their way to citizenship. Again this was not an option for Sarna, who did not have the contacts or the means to follow it through. One other idea had occurred to her several weeks ago. It was fraught with uncertainty, but could at least provide a back-up plan. Now she decided that this was the only way forward.

Karam could tell that his wife was having some sort of inner struggle. 'Come on,' he said gently, 'you've done what you can. At least you tried. Let her go now. Let things be.'

Sarna misconstrued his tone, reading the quietness as a threat rather than tenderness. 'But I haven't finished! There's still time. I . . . I can manage something.'

'Time for what?' He didn't know how to make her understand or how to understand her. 'Even *you* can't magic a groom out of nowhere. We have to be realistic. It's better she goes now. And it's good that she can travel with me – she'd be terrified of going on her own.'

'No need to book-shook any seat-suit.' Sarna started braiding her hair with determination. 'Nina is not leaving. I gave my word I would get her married and that's what I intend to do. You don't go back on a promise to family.'

'Ah, you're all talk!' Karam said. 'What do you think you can achieve in three weeks? You can't change the world. *No one is going to marry her.* She's a nice girl, but . . . well, something's not right, is it? I don't want trouble with the authorities. I won't risk our own position by letting her overstay illegally. You can argue with me, but you can't argue with the law.'

'There's no need to argue with anyone. It will all be sorted out.'

'What are you saying?'

'I've got a plan.'

'What plan?' He should have known there'd be something up Sarna's sleeve. He should have guessed she was scheming from the way her fingers had been fiddling furiously in her lap, twiddling away as if tapping out a plot on an invisible typewriter.

'It's an idea that will work.'

Karam frowned. 'I won't break the law. If it's anything short of marriage that girl will be on the first flight to India, with or without me.'

'It's marriage!' Sarna insisted. 'It's just not . . . final.'

'You'd better explain.'

'Why are you suddenly so interested?' She stood up, folded her arms and looked down her nose at Karam. 'For months you want nothing to do with the girl and suddenly you're butting in left, right and centre. *You* said this was my problem and I have to solve it – so let me do that now. You keep out of it. I'll manage something, I always do.'

'You'd better explain,' Karam repeated. His hands tightened around the book on his lap, his knuckles whitening.

Sarna had a horrible feeling that he might hurl the book at her if she didn't give an adequate response. She chose her words carefully. 'There's someone Nina can marry – just to stay here. And then I'll have more time to find a proper husband.'

'What? Who?' The woman was talking in riddles. Where did she come up with such nonsense?

'It's just *someone*. A reliable person – decent, honest. You don't need to know. No one will ever need to know. It will just be a quick marriage, followed by a quick, er, you know, separation . . . and then Nina will be a citizen. And *then* I'll have enough time to find her the perfect match.'

'Are you crazy? Shame on you! Marriage is not a game. You can't play with someone's life like that. Once a woman is divorced, that's it – she's finished!' Karam's hand sliced through the air.

'Hai, hai, but no one will *know*,' Sarna insisted, as if discretion was all that mattered, as if the most heinous of acts could be condoned as long as it was kept hidden. She persisted in the misconception that if no one knows there can be no consequences.

'Ah, don't be so naive. People aren't stupid. What makes you think no one will find out? You can't keep such a secret. Marriage is no handshake agreement. Forget it. You just have to accept that the girl is going back.' Karam tugged at the blanket to expose his hot feet.

'No!' Sarna clutched at her heart. She was only just

getting to know Nina. The way the girl chewed on her bottom lip in anxiety and liked to add extra chilli to her food. How her eyes were darkest green just after she woke in the morning and brightened during the day as if they absorbed the light around them. Around midday their shade almost matched that of the malachite-studded earrings Sarna had bought in Kenya. No, she could not let Nina go. Not yet. And not so far away again. Ever.

'*No.* That's very easy for you to say. Who would agree to such a thing? Only a fool. Maybe if you paid someone enough they would do it, but we don't have that kind of money.' Karam yanked at the blanket unsuccessfully again. It seemed to have been sewn rather than tucked under the mattress.

'I know someone who will do it for nothing and will never say a word.' Sarna plucked agitatedly at the strap of her slip. Its snapping sound matched the tone of her words.

'Who?'

Sarna shook her head. 'Why does it matter? Just accept what I'm saying and stop worrying. I'll fix everything.'

'I will not accept such nonsense. You can't conduct this sort of heraferi under my roof and expect me not to ask questions. If you don't tell me I won't allow you to go ahead. I'll have Nina out of here on a plane before the end of the week.' Karam wriggled his toes – his feet felt like they were on fire.

'And if I tell you?'

'Well . . .' Karam hesitated. 'Then we'll see.'

Sarna looked him straight in the eye. 'It's Oskar.'

'*Oskar?* Has he agreed? Why? What did you say to him? I hope you didn't decrease his rent or anything.'

'I haven't mentioned it to him yet. But I know he'll agree.' She came around to her side of the bed.

'Oh-ho, really, you know, huh? And what if he doesn't agree? What if he packs up and leaves? It'll be up to me to find another tenant – have you thought about that?'

'He *will* agree. He's like family—'

'He's not family – he's a tenant, for God's sake,' Karam interrupted. 'You don't ask tenants to marry your sisters to get them citizenship. For all we know, he could report us for even asking such a thing!'

'He won't.' Sarna pulled back the blanket and got into bed. 'He's lived here with us for five years. Never put a foot wrong, so polite, so nice always. And he won't leave. He obviously wants to stay. He was here years before we came and he's never said a word about going. I don't think he even has anywhere else to go. Where's the hot-water bottle? I asked Rajan to put one here.'

So that's what was burning his feet – a hot-water bottle in June. The woman wasn't just living in her own world, she had her own seasons. Karam kicked the bottle on to her side. 'You can't do that! You can't just drag other people into your private business. Why are you so desperate to keep Nina here? Look at you scheming away, ready to do illegal and underhand things to keep her here. Why?'

'She's my sister!' Sarna jumped out of bed again. 'Hai Ruba! I'm an honourable woman.' Hands on hips, she started lecturing. 'When I give my word, I live up to it. And don't forget, it was for your sake, for your business, that I had to agree to arrange Nina's marriage. It's because of *you* I'm in this mess, and *still* I'm not asking you for anything. I'll do everything myself. You won't even know what's happening.'

'Listen to yourself. My fault! My business! My business will go down the drain if I have to support your whims.

Do you have any idea what all this involves? It costs money, you know. You have to give notice at the registry office for a marriage – you may already be too late for that. You have to pay for the registrar, for the certificate and God knows what else. When I helped Charandas arrange his son's wedding at the registry office, the costs came to almost eighty pounds. Eighty! Just think of that. And then the annulment or whatever – you think that's free? And *then*, let's not forget, you have to pay *again* for the final real wedding – if that ever comes to pass. It's obvious you can't do this without me, and I don't want to be involved. So can we just leave it now?'

'I can't. I won't. I made a promise. This is my duty.' Sarna's chin rose defiantly, as did the pitch of her voice. 'I'll pay whatever is needed – I'll sell my jewellery if I have to.'

Karam turned away from his wife. Her words continued to ring in his ears.

'Your brothers are here. Why can't I have someone close by? You want me to be alone . . . This is the best solution. It will work. I know it. And then you'll see.'

Karam would have liked to put his hands to his ears and tell the woman to shut up. Instead he looked down at his book and contemplated reading to block out her voice. But he was too tense and couldn't concentrate. Sarna's confidence reminded Karam of something he'd come across earlier that evening. It was a comment Disraeli had made about Gladstone, something along the lines of 'He could convince most people of most things and himself of almost anything.' What a great quality to have, Karam had thought. Now he reflected that to have such a capacity was not a quality but a flaw. A terribly advantageous flaw: effective but compromising, powerful but destructive.

Sarna was still barking away at him. There was only one way to shut her up and that was by giving in.

'OK, OK, you can stop now.' He raised his hands as though he was being arrested. 'I've heard it all before. Just be aware that if Nina isn't married by the first week of July, she'll be on the plane to Delhi with me. You've got twenty days. What you do with her in that time is your own concern. I don't want to be involved.'

Oskar couldn't do it. He could not marry Nina – even though Sarna had portrayed the favour as one entirely free of obligation. It would change him beyond recognition. Already he had felt his recording capacity diminished by his own participation in the stories he tried to preserve. He had been denying it to himself, but of course he noticed when his hand wavered as his ear reproduced the incriminating '*you*' – that was him – out of a narrative. The letters came out contorted and illegible each time he wrote words indicating his own embroilment in Sarna's story – as when he had gone with her to see the Christmas lights on Oxford Street, for example. Oskar recalled some of the indicting sentences that had started to alter his fate: '*You* remember last time he said . . .'; '*You* know, *you* were there . . .' He had slipped unwittingly from passive to active witness. He had become answerable for having been present, for having cared. This was why he was reluctant to assist Sarna. It was too great a risk. He wouldn't stake a life's work on a whim of helpfulness. What would he be without his ability to write down other people's tales? He was not prepared to compromise himself in order to save anyone. Not even Nina, whose demure gorgeousness could change the colour of his dreams and interrupt the regimented march of his existence.

Yet there was the hollowness of defeat in his resolution. He continued to struggle with himself. Meanwhile, the household seemed to have fallen quiet in anticipation of his decision. Sarna had taken to whispering and she hissed at the rest of the family to do the same, as if silence would be more conducive to a quick and positive response from Oskar. 'Ssssshhhhhh! Sssshhhh!' It was like living in a pressure cooker that lets off intermittent shrill whistles as a reminder that something is cooking. Something certainly was cooking, and Oskar was under pressure to ensure that the dish turned out right. Sarna had done her bit: she'd finished all the chopping, concocting and spicing. Oskar just had to add the final touch: his 'yes' or 'no', like salt or sugar, would enhance or ruin the recipe.

Oskar had seen very little of Nina since she'd come from India. She managed to remain in the background whenever he was present, discreetly retreating to another room with soft steps and averted gaze. Apart from exchanging shy hellos they had never spoken. Yet in the glimpses he had caught of her, Oskar had seen a grace that entered him like a blessing. Her beauty was like a reflection in moving water – at once tangible and enigmatic. She had seemed unreachable and now her life was in his hands. As Sarna had said, 'I putting her in jour hand, OK. If she stay, if she go – is up to joo.' But Oskar's going or staying was also bound up with Nina's. He noted the undeclared hand of power in Sarna's statement – in the end she was the landlady, she had control. Sensing his precarious position, he found it even harder to arrive at a resolution.

In Sarna's mind, the favour she had asked would cost him nothing. 'OK, no cost for joo, no headache, no anything – just joo sign on paper, OK? Bas.' How could he say that to agree might cost him his existence as he knew it? Sarna believed that it was *her* life that was under threat. She had said as much when she'd wept to him, 'I made promise. I said I vill make Nina's marriage. So this I have to, this I *have* to. She is my sister. In India there is no life. If she suffer, I suffer – that is family. If she go, I *go.'* In the face of such passion, how could Oskar refuse? Yet how could he tell her that his own mind was also tormented, held together by thousands of strange stories that had become a mockery of his own stagnant life?

Though Oskar procrastinated about participating in Sarna's plot, he could feel a story unfolding around him. It breathed heavily outside the door to his room, it tickled him in the shower, it followed him in the curry smell of his clothes, and sometimes he saw it flicker across the walls of his room. This story wanted to claim him and he felt its allure more and more powerfully. He could not deny his excitement when his own name appeared in the incidents he recorded. Along with the doubts there was the thrill of possibilities. The perspectives of this vested interest challenged him in a way no story had before. They made him feel more alive. This led him to consider that Sarna's plan might be an opportunity for productivity, a chance to alter the status quo, to seize the moment and to live.

It was now or never. He could be in the story or become non-existent. Without further reflection, he rushed down to accept. 'Yes,' Oskar announced breathlessly as he knocked on the open living-room door. 'Yes, yes, Mrs Singh. I will do it.'

Oskar and Nina were married two weeks later on 2 July 1970. Despite his purported non-interventionist stance,

Karam had ended up taking responsibility for all the paperwork. Then he'd inevitably landed the role of driving them all to the registry office and accompanying Sarna as a second witness. The ceremony was over in a matter of minutes. Two names were signed, two fates were cleaved.

Before signing the certificate, Nina glanced at Oskar. For the first time he looked into her eyes: pools of malachite brimming with relief and gratitude. In that instant a connection was established between them. Like strangers in a crowd who can identify with each other because they declare allegiance to the same country or sports team, an unspoken understanding was fostered: both of them were supporting the hope of a new life.

As he penned the letters of his name, Oskar Naver had an intimation of what it must be like to create, to write the bidding of his own impulse rather than merely transcribe the thoughts of others. When the sweep of the pen completed the final letter, he had a sense of being born again. For a moment he fancied it was not a marriage certificate he was signing, but his own rebirth certificate.

He sought Nina's eyes again, but she was still staring at the signed and dated certificate as though it might disappear if she looked away. This was a rebirth for Nina as well. It gave her the legitimacy she needed to make a fresh start in Britain.

21

That summer, having completed her A levels, Pyari began to work full time at India Craft on Oxford Street. Nina's married status enabled her to obtain work as well, and she got a job at the Phillips factory in Tooting.

When Pyari brought home her first pay packet, Karam was sitting at the dining-room table doing his accounts. Exhausted by her long day and the hot stuffy Tube ride home, Pyari walked into the living room and collapsed on the sofa.

'Hungry?' Sarna put aside her knitting. 'Shall I get you some biryani?'

Pyari shook her head.

'No? Did you eat something on your way home?'

'I bought some strawberries. I got paid today.' She pulled the envelope of cash out of her bag.

The blood rushed to Karam's ears. He stopped his calculations.

'I knew you must have had something,' said Sarna. 'How can anyone work all day and have no appetite? Your pithaji is always starving when he gets back from work.' She looked at Karam, who had got up and was drumming his fingers on the mantelpiece. 'He needs his food on the table within five minutes of getting home. And Vaheguru help me if I'm a minute late.'

As if on cue, Karam spoke. 'Work – yes, hard work. Bills, bills, bills. One man working, paying all the bills, of course he gets hungry. It's not easy. So many bills . . .' He picked up a letter. 'The gas bill has just arrived.' He waved it ominously. 'Next week there'll be more bills – phone, electricity, water, rates . . .'

Sarna screwed up her face and shot Pyari a look that said, 'There he goes again.'

'Bills, never-ending bills.' Karam did not look at the women, but stared dolefully at his own reflection in the mirror on the opposite wall.

Pyari fingered the envelope of cash. Sensing what she was about to do, Sarna frowned discouragingly. But Pyari stood up and placed the envelope on the mantelpiece. 'Here you are.'

Karam scratched his forehead, attempting to look confused – as if he was unaware of what Pyari meant, as if he had no idea what she'd just done. Sarna crossed her arms over her chest and glowered. Pyari retreated to her bedroom.

A few minutes later, Sarna came in and shut the door behind her. 'Fiteh moon!' she whispered. 'Such idiocy! What did you have to do that for?'

'Do what for?' Pyari was touched by her mother's sympathy.

'Giving your pithaji all your pay! Why? That kanjoos will now suck every last penny from your pockets the way he slurps the last drop of lassi out of his glass. Such a miser, such a tight old . . . hai.' Sarna smacked her forehead. 'And you? Dutifully giving him the money without a word. How could you?'

'It's OK, Mee. It doesn't matter now.' Pyari wound her long braid idly around her arm.

'Listen to you. Doesn't matter! Hai Ruba, don't you see? He'll be waiting for you every month now, sitting there moaning about bills. And what will you do?'

'I guess I'll just give it to him.'

'Va va, such a great answer. Oh Ruba! How did I give birth to such children? So useless! You and your brother are the same, always on your father's side. It didn't occur to you for even one minute to give some of the money to your poor mother, did it? After all I do for you, this is the thanks I get. Every penny you earn goes straight into that miser's hands. Do you know what *I* do for you? Do you know how *I* struggle? Hai, you have no idea.'

Pyari let go of her braid as she realized that Sarna's gripe was not that she'd spinelessly given away all her earnings. What her mother really resented was not being the one to receive the cash.

'You didn't have to give it all to him.' Fury scrubbed at Sarna's cheeks and throat. 'You could have taken out a few pounds – he wouldn't have known. But no, you didn't stop to think. Serves you right. Let's see you work your fingers to the bone to line his pockets.'

Sarna was right. The following month, Pyari came home to grumbles about how the car needed new brake pads. The month after that, the complaint was about the increased price of petrol. After several months she started to put her pay on to the mantelpiece the minute she walked through the door, to spare her father and herself the tension of his tall financial tales.

Determined that Nina should not fall into the same trap, Sarna waited outside for her the day she got paid. 'Let me handle this,' she said, taking Nina's money. Later, when Karam said, 'Nina's been working for a month now. Must be pay day soon,' Sarna was ready. 'Yes, she has given her money to me – to keep for her wedding.'

'Oh.' Karam smoothed his beard. 'But, er, she must contribute to household expenses. The bills are never-ending and they're not getting less, I can tell you.'

'What, it's not enough for you to live off our daughter? Now you want to make a profit from my sister as well?'

Nina and Oskar's secret nuptials seemed to have given a boost to the Indian merger market. The Singh family found themselves caught in a whirl of karmais, mendis, chooras, chunis, weddings and receptions. Invitations showered down on them like confetti, requesting the pleasure of their company at the engagements, henna-painting evenings, bracelet-donning celebrations and bride-veiling ceremonies that precede any Indian wedding. Sarna, who had been looking forward to having a break from matchmaking while Nina's citizenship status became fully established, began to worry again. 'Hai, all the good boys will be taken. By the time you can be married properly, Nina, all the good boys will be gone!' She looked pitifully at Pyari. 'And when we get to *your* turn, there won't be any bad ones left either.'

Any doubts about the marriageability of her daughter were firmly put aside whenever Sarna was in Persini's presence. Then she reeled off the attractions of various suitors as if all the boys in the world were hers for the taking. 'I have someone in mind,' she'd tell Persini. 'He's Sikh, a dentist, very good salary.'

'Oh well, Rupi was introduced to a very nice boy only last week,' Persini would retaliate in a superior tone. 'Six foot three, the father is a banker, family goes to India twice a year.'

Sarna would haughtily raise the stakes. 'I'm in no hurry to get rid of my Pyari, but that Sinder keeps pestering me about her son. Have you seen him? White as milk, has *fourteen* people working under him, drives a Mercedes.'

Persini would raise her eyebrows and open her mouth to describe another of her daughter's distinguished suitors. But Sarna, who had the advantage of two girls she could brag about, would put Persini in her place. 'As for Nina, well, the offers just don't stop. I'm thinking the eldest Sagoo boy might be the one for her – degree in optomuppetry, *own* practice, lives in a *three*-storey house with *four* bathrooms.'

Persini's eyebrows would fly up like two Chinese hats being tossed into the air before falling back down in defeat.

One evening, Sarna was grumbling about marriage prospects as the family ate dinner. 'Ah, stop overreacting,' Karam said. 'You're making a big deal of nothing. There's still lots of time and there'll be plenty of eligible men. This one must get a degree first,' he pointed his spoon at Pyari. 'Then we'll see.'

'Digree-shmigree,' Sarna snorted. Hai Ruba, Pyari was just a girl! With a girl all that mattered was pedigree – *that* was the guarantee for the prize of matrimony. It was just her luck to have a husband obsessed with trivialities like a degree. She didn't dare admit to him that she feared Pyari's scholarly qualifications might be more of a liability than an advantage. Dark-skinned *and* over-educated – who would marry such a girl?

'These things always work out. Even Persini's finally found someone for her fussy Rupi, so we should all take heart,' Karam said.

'What? When? Who? How? Haaaww! This can't be!'
Sarna dropped the green chilli she'd been about to bite
into.

'Well, yes, apparently it's all settled. Sukhi told us last
night while we were playing cards. He said—'

'I knew it!' Sarna interrupted. 'I *knew* that Persini was up
to something. She looked so pleased with herself at the
gurudwara last weekend. I should have guessed she was
up to her tricks.'

'What tricks?' Karam asked. 'What are you talking
about? You know they've been looking for a boy for well
over a year now. Anyway, they seem very happy with the
choice. He is a doctor from a well-to-do family.'

'No,' Sarna said flatly, as though blatant opposition to
the facts might render them untrue. There had been an
undeclared race between her and Persini to find husbands
for Nina and Rupi. She was piqued not only because
Persini had pipped her to the post, but because Karam
had known about it before her. 'No, Jee. It can't be.'

'Yes, it is so.'

'Who's the family? Do we know them?'

'I know of them, but I've never met them. They don't
attend our gurudwara.'

Sarna puckered her lips. 'Which gurudwara *do* they go
to?'

'As far as I know, they don't go anywhere at all.' Karam
was unable to keep the disapproval out of his voice.

Around the table, Pyari, Rajan, Nina and Sarna all looked
at him in surprise. Oskar, who had been invited to join the
meal, watched his dinner companions with interest.

'Ha!' Sarna thumped the table. 'I knew it. So who is this
family? Are they *cut* Sikhs?' she said, as though it was
some terrible disease.

'I don't know.' Karam helped himself to another roti. 'I remember hearing that the father cut his hair years ago. I guess the sons must have as well.'

'The father! Hai Ruba. They must be cut Sikhs.' She raised her glass of water as if to toast the revelation. Then she drank thirstily.

'Well, *we* can't talk. Look at your son.' Karam glanced at Rajan's short hair.

'My son! *Your* son.' Rajan continued to eat, apparently indifferent to the way his parents were casually disowning him. 'He's always my son when you disapprove of something. When there's an opportunity to announce his O-level results then he's very definitely your son. "Oh, nine As, my son has got nine As." Anyway, short hair doesn't matter on a young boy like Raja. So many Sikh boys are cut these days. It's become quite normal. But to have no pugri on a man of *your* age! Na na na na.' Sarna shook her head. 'That is unnatural. Who are these people, anyway? You still haven't said. What's the father's name?'

'The family name is Choda.' There were so many Chodas, Karam doubted she could guess which ones he was referring to without more information. He himself had only realized the truth when Mandeep had alerted him. Karam had been giving his brother a lift home after the card game at which Sukhi had announced the engagement, when Mandeep had said, 'You know which Chodas we will be related to, don't you? Chatta Choda.' Karam couldn't believe it. *That* Choda – the infamous Choda of the Hair! Yes, that one. 'The father is Chatta Choda,' he now told Sarna.

Her mouth dropped open, her eyes widened. 'Hai, hai! No. Hai, hai! Oh ho ho,' she yodelled in shock and delight.

'Is that his real name?' Rajan asked.

'Real or unreal, it's what people call him,' Karam said.

'Why?' Pyari and Rajan asked simultaneously.

'Oh, it's a long story.'

'Tell them,' Sarna urged in a gossipy tone. 'Let them see how this family is being corrupted by your relatives. Hai Ruba, who would have thought we would one day be related to such blasphemers? *Tell* them.' She was keen to hear the story again herself, to have the details refreshed in her memory so that she could repeat them when the opportunity arose – and she would make sure it soon would.

'It's not a story for them.' It was a sordid tale of misguided passion and disrespect. Karam didn't think it was necessary for his children to hear of such things, to know that men – Sikh men – were capable of such acts. Moreover, what would Oskar think? He knew little about Sikhism and Choda's story would hardly be a complimentary introduction to the religion. Although Karam was aware that history was full of much more sinister tales of sacrilege, he was unwilling to relate the incident that had given Chatta Choda his name. There was something altogether disturbing about a heinous crime perpetrated by a member of your local community at a place you frequented regularly.

'Why not tell them, Jee?'

Karam shook his head.

'If they don't hear it from you, they'll hear it from someone else.'

Sarna was right. Before Rupi's marriage, the Singh family heard several versions of her father-in-law-to-be's disgraceful exploit.

* * *

Chatta Choda had cut his own hair before a horrified congregation in the County Hall during his brother's wedding. It was a warm spring evening and Balraj Choda, as he was known before the fateful day, was not in a good mood. He was feeling resentful about his failure to get a scholarship for the doctorate course he wanted to pursue. The hall was alive with colour. Bejewelled women flitted around in embroidered suits and saris like exotic butterflies. Someone was drumming on a tabla and another jingled a tambourine while a group of ladies sang love songs. Men in suits that clashed with their turbans tapped their feet shyly. The bride and groom stole glances at one another. Only Choda could not get into the festive spirit.

'It is the curse of our religion, this turban,' he said to the friend standing beside him. 'It holds us back. We should just get rid of it.'

'Yaar, without the turban we'd be just like everyone else,' the friend said. 'No one could distinguish us from Hindus, Jains or even Muslims. Just imagine that. These British, they can't tell the difference. To them brown is brown.' Murmurs of agreement supported this remark.

'You're right.' Choda nodded. 'To them we're all one mass of foreignness. And us, with the funny hats on our heads and the big beards, we're the most conspicuous. They think we're the most backward subspecies of the lot. And all because of this headdress.' He jabbed his black pugri with his index finger.

'But the turban is our saviour. It sets us apart,' another voice dissented. 'That's what Guru Gobind Singh wanted when he made the turban part of our identity. He said a Sikh should always be easily identified in a crowd.'

'Being identified is one thing.' Choda spread his arms the way he had seen men do at Speaker's Corner in Hyde

Park, near where his family lived. 'Being discriminated against is another. The turban singles us out for the wrong kind of attention. I have to be ten times better than any non-Sikh to get the same recognition. I'm fed up. It shouldn't be about what's on your head, but what's in it.'

There were some hesitant nods of agreement, but a sense of indignation generally prevailed. Somebody called for a granthi, hoping he could set the record straight. The priest was one of the few men at the wedding reception in traditional dress; he wore a cream kurtha pyjama and had a grey shawl thrown over his shoulders. Everyone grew silent as he shared his wisdom.

'My son.' He looked Choda up and down, taking in the shiny black suit with a red carnation pinned to the lapel. From the neck down you couldn't tell Choda was Sikh. Even his kara was hidden under the stiff white fold of a cufflinked sleeve. 'What's on your head *is* a symbol of what's in it. Yes, my son, when people see your pugri they immediately know your values – the Sikh values of honesty, equality, strength and forgiveness. Your turban is a reminder to you, and to them, of what ideals we must live up to. If you take off the turban you will remove this badge of morality. You will be less of a man, less of a Sikh.'

Heads nodded and a rumble of approval went through the men who had gathered around. With an inclination of his maroon turban, the granthi turned to make his way to the buffet table where the wedding banquet was being laid out. He did not expect any further objection.

Choda sensed this. 'I don't agree, Granthi-ji.'

At the same moment Granthi-ji's stomach gurgled its own war cry: the food is ready, it's time to eat! 'Achha? Is that so?' This question may have been addressed to either call. The granthi was certainly unsure about which one to heed first.

'Just wearing a turban does not make you a better Sikh, let alone a good Sikh.' Choda drew himself up to his full height – five feet and seven inches. 'That is no longer a good answer, especially here in Britain. This turban is just a symbol – and symbols should be disposable, because whatever is behind them – ideas, beliefs, feelings – can still endure.' Choda knew he was stepping beyond the limits of propriety. Already he could feel a rise in the temperature around him. The Sikhs are a passionate people. The men especially are quick to court anger.

The granthi blinked hard several times, stroked his long greying beard and shifted slightly on his slippered feet in an effort to prevent the next grumble from rising up in his stomach – this one might not be so conveniently camouflaged by Choda's loud voice. The granthi sighed, the long strained sigh of uncertainty that pious men try to pass off as a sign of wise rumination. He was in no mood for such a discussion. He had just completed a session of reading aloud from the Granth Sahib. His throat was parched, his knees were cramped. The smell of the food was piercing his nostrils provocatively. And now this youth was trying to take him to task about the relevance of the turban. He glanced around. Where was the boy's father? A relative, an uncle? Surely there was someone who could clip the boy's ears and shut him up. But most people were busy celebrating, and around the granthi faces were bursting with the desire to rebuke the upstart for his impertinence. But they were restraining themselves, waiting for *him*, the priest, the voice of reason.

'Puther, a good Sikh looks like a true Sikh. We must live by example. Our dress is the code of our religion. Our religion is our honour. Don't let those who are ignorant threaten this honour. And don't dishonour us with talk of discarding your turban.'

'The true followers of God belong to Him, victory be to God!' someone yelled. The loud cry reached the wider wedding party. People began looking in their direction.

'He who responds will be blessed . . .' the granthi called out – and in a chorus that resounded like a round of applause, everyone in the hall shouted, 'True is the name of God!'

The granthi bowed as if taking credit for a performance. Choda was incensed. What did this granthi know about the trials of wearing a turban in this country? The old priest had probably been transported fresh off the boat from India into the haven of the temple. There he worked and lived. There he was fed and clothed. There people came to him to seek sanctuary from the outside world. This granthi lived in Britain without actually being a part of it. He could hardly speak English, and yet he had the gall to stand around and preach anachronisms. What the bloody hell did the granthi know? Nothing, Choda decided. Granthi-ji hadn't had to deal with being the only one in the class with a strange hat on his head. He hadn't had to worry about whether the girls at college were put off by years' worth of uncut hair that covered his face. He hadn't had to sit through interviews wondering if he was being analysed for tell-tale signs of 'otherness' behind the veneer of his academic achievement. The memories of such indignities rose up hotly in Choda and he rebelled. 'You can't prove anything you've said. If I cut off my hair now I would still be the same man – but with a better chance of success in this country. You can't dispute that.'

He raised his chin defiantly, the bow tie at his neck fluttering like a bird ready to take flight.

Voices rose in anger. Fists flew into the air. From a distance the men looked like a group of dancers doing bhangra to the beat of the tabla.

Choda's father rushed up and tried to break up the disaffected little band. 'Stop this. It's your brother's wedding! Leave these quarrels for another day.' He was always stirring up trouble, this youngest son. Always questioning everything.

Choda wasn't ready to stop. He was just getting into his stride. And the fierce opposition of those around him acted like a strong wind propelling him along the path of contradiction. 'Pithaji, we're just talking. What's wrong with that?'

'You leave this for another day.' Choda's father took him by the arm and tried to steer him away.

'Very good.' The granthi's eyes strayed to the buffet again.

'You don't have a clue!' Choda shrugged out of his father's grip.

'Have some respect! In Vaheguru's name, calm down . . . Oh Ruba, preserve us! . . . Unbelievable, the youth of today . . .' All around Choda, recriminations and pleas for moderation erupted. He felt several hands curl tightly around him.

Choda shook himself free, shouting, 'What? What is it? Why can't we talk about such things without people getting offended?'

The granthi raised his hands and appealed for peace. But by now some wedding guests were too highly charged to take any notice of him. Rebukes were shouted at Choda, wild gestures made, faces turned to thunder.

Choda was immune to them; his fury was still directed at the granthi. ' "Live by example!" What do *you* know? Your example only works in the gurudwara. Out there,' he pointed to the windows, 'you have to adapt. You can't sit around preaching the old ways. If we don't open up to change we'll be left behind.'

A punch landed on Choda's left shoulder, but he hardly felt it. Women were crying out, 'Not at your brother's wedding!' but he didn't hear them. The accumulated rage of years was being unleashed within him. 'I'll show you! I'll show you!' Choda started running towards the kitchen at the other end of the long hall.

There, under the shocked gaze of the women getting ready to serve the food, Choda pulled off his turban and cast it roughly aside. Then, grabbing a large knife still fiery with the smell of recently chopped onions, he yanked at his hair and started to hack it off. Almost simultaneously the wind howled through the open windows as if God was uttering a long low cry of pain. This gust caught Choda's tresses as they fell and scattered them carelessly across the kitchen. The hair flew into the vast pathilas of dhal and chunna that sat boiling on giant gas burners. It fell into open sacks of rice and flour, it slipped into the spaces between work tables and walls, between shelves and refrigerators. Hair disappeared into every available crack and cranny. Then, with poised precision, it landed, like an exotic garnish, on the dishes just readied for his brother's wedding banquet.

Alarmed, the ladies started running around, desperately trying to catch at Choda's chatta and prevent it from contaminating all the food. Men crowded into the kitchen and tried to stop him from wielding the sharp blade. Behind them, shocked grandmothers and excited children tried to get a glimpse of the action. Granthi-ji watched the spectacle in horror. His appetite vanished as he saw Choda's hair sitting on the food like a sprinkling of British seasoning. Finally, Choda raised his shorn head towards the gathered crowd. Remnants of his slashed tresses hung wildly about his face. The carnation at his breast had somehow also been lopped off its stem. Red petals lay scattered at his feet like drops of blood.

'I'll show you!' He brandished a fist. 'There is honour without a turban! There is greater success without a turban. You'll see that it's possible to be a good *cut* Sikh – *then* you'll all eat your words.' With that he left the wedding party.

His father collapsed with shame, his mother wept pitifully and his siblings cowered under the incriminating stares of those who had witnessed the incident. Bride and groom dared not look at each other – what did this bode for their future? The in-laws closed ranks and denounced Choda. Everyone was stunned by the act of barberism that had taken place. Each had his own theory about why it had happened. Some people admonished: this was the result of too much education – it gave people ideas beyond their station. What had Choda senior been thinking when he encouraged his son to pursue degree after degree? Anyone with a double doctorate deserved to be viewed with suspicion. Blaming his turban for the fact that people have a problem with his big head – what a nerve.

Other people commiserated: this country was too free, it was hard for the young to find the right balance – perhaps such eruptions of madness were inevitable. What a shame, such decent parents – they didn't deserve it. Too bad it had happened at the wedding – in this hall. Such a transgression would be hard to forget . . . but at least hair would grow back – maybe there was still hope for the boy . . .

Meanwhile, in the kitchen, the ladies responsible for the buffet were busy picking strands of Choda's hair from the food and off the surfaces. They laboured over the bowls, trays and pans of food, pulling off hair after hair until their backs ached from the effort of bending over and their eyes blurred from the strain of squinting for the fine black slivers of sacrilege. Just when they thought one dish had been salvaged, another hair would suddenly appear. Who would have thought one man could have so much hair? No wonder it had been such a weight on his mind.

Despite the women's best efforts to rescue the meal, everyone who ate at County Hall that day found Choda's hair in their food. Each of them had the experience of dragging a long strand from their mouths, some inevitably flossing their teeth in the process. They may not have been eating their words yet, but Choda had certainly left a very bad taste in their mouths.

Unfortunately, the effects of Choda's exploit were not confined to the day of the incident. People remained shaken, a sense prevailed that the community had been violated, a feeling of helplessness nagged at the granthis and the more orthodox elders. Moreover, the hall itself showed hints of trauma and continued to yield up wisps of hair at future functions. They appeared everywhere, like faint lines of a story that can never be erased. For many years anyone who ate at County Hall had a good chance of finding a stray hair in their food, and those who knew the story of Choda wondered if the chatta was his.

* * *

'I once had hair in my dhal at a wedding there,' Rajan recalled with a hint of dismay when he'd heard the story.

'Me too!' Nina revealed. 'And I've only been there once – and that's more than thirty years after the whole mess.'

'Well, that was probably your own, Nina,' Pyari remarked, looking at her sister's thick mop. That hair was an inappropriate, outsized frame for Nina's exquisite face. 'It can't be *his*. Come on – what are the chances of that?'

'Well, you know, not insignificant . . .' Rajan said, starting to calculate. 'If you consider that the average person has about one hundred thousand hairs, and you imagine Chatta Choda chopping that many loose in the kitchen . . . that's a lot of hair left lying around.'

'Uuuuh.' Pyari shuddered. 'But after so much time there couldn't be any left.'

'Why not? Hair doesn't die or disappear. It's pretty resilient stuff, you know.' Rajan put down his book. 'Hair survives long after other body tissue disintegrates.'

Whether or not Choda's hair was still floating around County Hall after thirty years is debatable. However, hair certainly still trailed his name whenever it was uttered: it was there in a word – chatta. To the end of his life, Choda was identified by the hair he had cut off.

He had left the wedding that day vowing to prove himself, and that's just what he did. He went from success to success, picking up a scholarship here, a doctorate there, a research fellowship here, an award for outstanding contribution there. He made a name for himself in the scientific community by being a key member of the team that developed one of the first male-virility-enhancing drugs, the Viagra of the 1960s, called Osopotent. He acquired a small fortune. From time to time, his name appeared in the newspaper. At the gurudwara, granthis came and went, but cuttings of Choda's latest achievements continued to be posted through the temple letterbox (it was never established who sent these, but if anyone had asked Choda he would have declined to answer). Over the years, his accomplishments accumulated to tip the balance of memory so that more people talked of his current prosperity than of his old misdemeanour. As Choda became a more respected figure in his field, his esteem amongst the Sikhs began to grow again. They basked in his reflected glory and began to refer to him as an example of a Sikh success story in Britain. In time, the black sheep did not appear so dark any more; he had come out of the shadows and was looking fairly pristine in the spotlight of success. Accusations that he was a heathen were mitigated and it was grudgingly conceded that Choda was a 'modern man'. Such gradual revisions of opinion meant that the prodigal son would have been welcomed back into the fold if he had expressed the desire to return and had shown a suitable degree of penitence. But he did not. Choda kept his hair short and maintained a long-distance relationship with Sikhism. He never got to a point where he was genuinely able to assert Britishness as his identity. His whole life was an effort at integration, but he remained too conscious of the effort to relax into the goal.

Sarna was pleased to find that Chatta Choda's old transgression was still the filter through which his whole family was viewed. She was less gratified to note that people also admired the man for his worldly success. Indeed they spoke with a certain awe of his awards and accolades, of his appearance in the local paper, of his three-storey detached house in central London and his four highly educated sons. Sarna preferred to dwell more on the shortcomings of the Choda family.

All through the ten o'clock news on Thursday evening Sarna fidgeted and fussed: her fingers played incessantly with the hem of her kameez, her legs restlessly crossed and uncrossed, a little muscle in her jaw continually twitched as though she was chewing gum. She was desperate to talk about Persini's blunder. When the news was over, she launched energetically into a tirade.

'Hai, when I think of all the things that kamini insisted—' she began, but Karam held up his hand.

'Shhhh! The forecast,' he said.

Sarna scratched the armrest with her nails, up and down, up and down. Pyari and Nina, who were sitting on the floor a few feet away, embroidering one sleeve each of the blouse that lay between them, stifled their giggles.

'Hmmm, should be a warm day again tomorrow. Twenty-six degrees,' Karam said, as though everyone hadn't just heard the television themselves. Then he picked up his newspaper.

'I'm just thinking, you know, Persini said her Rupi's husband must be "fully qualify",' Sarna said, imitating the English expression she recalled Persini using.

'Qualified. Fully *qualified*,' Karam corrected from behind the paper.

'I'm just repeating what *she* said. Persini made a point of telling people that the boy must be pug-wallah, dari-wallah, digree-wallah, good-family wallah. And look what she's ended up with.' Sarna proceeded to list the non-achievements on her fingers. 'No turban, no beard, no reputable family. She must have been really desperate.'

'Well, maybe he has other qualities. You shouldn't judge when you don't know everything. It's never so simple, there's often more to people than you think. Maybe he's a decent boy – he's a doctor, after all.'

'Decent boy! Ha! That woman only goes where she can get an advantage. I just want to know what made her settle on *him*. That's all I want to know . . .'

'It's a real advantage to have a doctor in the family,' Karam said.

'Yes, but he's not a *real* doctor,' Pyari suddenly revealed.

'What?' Sarna leaned forward eagerly. Even Karam's face peered over the edge of his paper.

'He's a professor doctor, not a medical doctor. He teaches Chemistry or something in a university.' Pyari didn't look up from her embroidery.

'I knew it! That would be just like her – to tell everyone he's a doctor—'

'He is. I told you, the whole family is very well educated,' the voice behind *The Times* broke in.

'Maybe, but he's not a *real* doctor, obviously. He probably earns less as well – teachers aren't as well paid as doctors. There's a big difference – and Persini knows it. That's why she's not telling anyone.'

'How do you know she's not telling? You haven't even spoken to her!' Karam rustled the paper irritably. 'Just wait and see. I'm sure everything will be made clear. This isn't the sort of thing you can hide.'

'Oh, a person can hide anything if they try hard enough and Persini is the type to keep such facts to herself. Sukhi didn't clarify things either. But how do *you* know?' Sarna asked Pyari.

'Rupi told me.' Pyari resisted the urge to start biting her fingernails. She'd been trying to grow them since she'd seen the misty egg-shaped opals at the ends of Nina's fingers.

'O-oh. When?'

'At the gurudwara, last weekend.'

'Fiteh moon! How ridiculous! So you knew about the engagement even before your pithaji! You've known all these days and you never told me!'

'She told me not to say anything until her parents had officially announced it.' Pyari tucked a strand of her hair behind her ear. Purple lining peeked out beneath the grey sleeve of her kameez.

'Very nice. Thank you very much. Other girls tell their mothers everything, and this one makes a fool of me by not sharing such important news. What kind of a daughter are you, huh? Just useless. If you told that Rupi anything, you can bet she'd have reported it to her kamini mother before you could draw your next breath.'

I wouldn't tell her anything, Pyari thought.

'I do everything for you and I get nothing back. You don't even talk to me,' Sarna said.

'She asked me not to say anything.' Pyari stopped sewing. 'She made me *promise*.'

Sarna shook her head. 'Other people's promises shouldn't come between mothers and daughters. There should be no secrets between us.'

Pyari looked at her mother in disbelief. What hypocrisy! There was nothing but secrets between them: terrible dark secrets that prohibited the possibility of sharing. And yet Pyari still felt guilty. For though the premise of Sarna's criticism was incorrect, the essence of her charge was true: they were not like a normal mother and daughter. There was something missing between them. Perhaps it wasn't quite as dire as a lack of love, but some of the elements that inform love were certainly absent: there was no trust and no understanding. Pyari's eyes filled with tears. She reached for her braid and used its end, like a paintbrush, to wipe them away.

Karam peeped around his paper. 'Bring me some tea,' he said gently. He could see his daughter was upset.

Gratefully, Pyari left the room. Nina got up and followed, leaving the blouse they'd been sewing on the floor. 'Are you OK?' she asked, giving her sister's braid a gentle tug.

Pyari put the kettle on.

'You know what Mother's like,' Nina said.

'I know. I'm used to it.' Pyari's lips trembled. She threw a teabag into a mug.

'She's unbelievable.' Nina took her hand and squeezed it.

Whenever Nina was talking to Pyari, 'Mother' was now her preferred expression for Sarna. Nina's English classes had given her more confidence in using the language and she regularly peppered her Punjabi with English. She chose 'Mother' as her title for Sarna because the word reflected their true relationship but also sounded stiff and formal. Recently, Nina had begun to call Sarna 'Mother' in a mock-serious, bantering tone in her presence. She'd salute Sarna with a military 'Yes, Mother' if Sarna asked her to do something. Sarna tolerated the transgression, so Nina tried it in front of Pyari and Rajan and once she'd even dared utter it in front of Karam. On that occasion, the momentary tension that settled in the room had been dispelled by Pyari rushing to the rescue with a copycat echo, 'Yes, Mother.'

22

'Oskar has gone, Jee. OK is *gone*.' Sarna walked into the kitchen, a sealed white envelope flapping in her right hand. Her voice was unsteady. Nina stopped washing the dishes and Pyari paused from drying them. Rajan emerged from the back room and stood in the doorway, frowning.

'He's gone,' Sarna repeated. 'Gone!'

There was silence for a moment as the news sank in. The sound of the running tap filled the small kitchen: a gushing harbinger of bad news.

'Turn off the tap,' Karam ordered. Nina's hand flew to it. She felt nervous, as though she were somehow responsible for what had been revealed. Together she and Oskar had fulfilled all the necessary criteria to guarantee her claim for citizenship. Their marriage had remained unconsummated, thereby justifying its invalidation. The annulment had come through less than a week ago. Oskar had stayed long enough to ensure Nina's freedom and then he had gone away. Remorse coursed through her like a stone sinking to the bottom of a deep lake. *She* should have been the one leaving. But she was now waiting for someone else to make a wife of her. She wished she had been able to say goodbye to Oskar. She had never properly thanked him for his life-saving gesture. Her eyes had always beamed emeralds of gratitude, but the words had never come from her lips. They could only smile in his presence, curving unconsciously into the shape that best reflected his kindness, the quiet reassurance of his presence.

'I knew something was wrong,' Sarna said. 'I heard him go out yesterday afternoon and I didn't hear him come back again last night. First I thought maybe he came late while I was asleep. But then I didn't see him around today either. I meant to go up at lunchtime, but I got busy. I just went up now to give him some muhtis to eat, and when I knocked nobody answered.'

'Maybe he's still out. Gone on a trip or something.' Karam put down the shoe polish he'd been about to store in the cellar.

'OK doesn't go on trips, Pithaji. He hasn't spent a night away since the day we moved in,' Rajan said.

'He's definitely gone, I tell you.' Sarna waved the envelope at them. 'I found this in his room.'

'You went into his room?' Karam asked.

'Well, when he didn't answer my knock I had to,' Sarna said. 'And anyway, this is still our house. He's the tenant.'

'*Was*.' Rajan pointed at the envelope.

'What does it say?' Karam reached for the letter.

'I don't know. It has "Mr and Mrs Singh" written on the front. When I saw that, I knew he must have gone – why else would he leave a note?'

'Because he didn't give any notice.' Karam took the envelope from his wife and tore it open. A short letter and several ten-pound notes emerged. 'Mmm-hmm.' Karam affected indifference, but everyone could see relief in his eyes and approval in the slight twitch of his lips. 'He's left three months' rent as compensation for not giving notice.'

Sarna stared jealously at the notes in his hand and wished she'd opened the letter herself. 'What else does he say, Jee?' She squeezed along the counter and edged closer to Karam. It was more cramped than usual with all of them in the kitchen.

Karam read out the letter:

Dear Mr and Mrs Singh, Pyari, Rajan and Nina,

Forgive me for not saying goodbye, but sometimes that is the easiest way to go.

Please do not fret about my departure. I have been your tenant for six years, four months and twenty-three days – a long time that seems to have passed in a flash.

You made me feel like one of the family, but the time has come for me to move on. I take with me the memory of over a thousand wonderful meals – yes, Mrs Singh, you really did indulge me – and countless other acts of kindness.

My subscription to *The Times* is still valid for another fifty-nine issues. Do please read it, Mr Singh, and don't worry about creasing the pages –

'Uh-huh-huh,' Karam cleared his throat. Sometimes at the weekend he'd woken up extra early to read Oskar's newspaper. Then he'd ironed the pages and slipped it back in the post box. 'You certainly fed him a lot.' He pointed a finger at Sarna. Then he continued:

Sorry for not giving you more notice. I enclose the rent for the next three months.

I am glad to have been a part of your lives – in

helping you I was able to help myself. Perhaps one day our paths will cross again.

I wish you all the very best.

Oskar

'Is that all?' Sarna was disappointed. She would have liked to hear something about how she'd been the best landlady ever, and how Oskar would miss her buttery parathas. He hadn't said goodbye properly; it didn't feel right.

Everyone quietly shared the feeling that it wasn't right. Even the ticking of a new wooden India-shaped clock on the wall sounded like a disapproving tut. In the last year Oskar had felt, more than ever before, like one of the family. In order to express her gratitude for his marriage to Nina, Sarna had regularly asked him to join them for a meal. He had mingled amongst them naturally, finding the right words and tone for each family member – except Nina, from whom he had maintained a polite, smiling distance as if to honour the commitment he had made to keep relations with her strictly official. Karam had not been able to resist remarking on their situation, 'I see now the best way to be happily married is to have nothing to do with each other. Don't try it another way, take my word for it.' The funny thing was that Oskar had actually seemed more content after the marriage. They'd all noticed that he was more relaxed and light-hearted, whereas before he'd always looked pensive, weighed down by a world of worries. This was why his disappearance felt all the more unexpected and unnecessary.

'I told you so,' Karam said crossly. 'I told you that your heraferi would result in my having to find a new tenant. Such a hassle. I'll have to put an ad in the paper, put notices up at India House and Malaysia House. As if I haven't got enough to do already.'

'Achah, Jee, why are you blaming me? OK doesn't say it's my fault in his letter. And anyway, you've got three months to find someone before you have to start worrying. But no doubt you'll have someone in there futa fut so you can get a few months of double rent. But what about his things?' A finger rested on her chin. 'All those boxes of his . . .'

'What's in them?' Karam's eyes lit up. 'Shoes?'

'Papers. The room is still full of them, just sitting in those boxes.' Sarna hadn't been able to resist a peek.

'Ah, what? Another hassle. We'll just throw them away. What else can be done?'

'Fiteh moon! How ridiculous! Throw them away! You're always ready to toss out anything. He said he hopes to see us again one day – maybe he'll want his papers.'

'If he wanted them he should have taken them with him. We're not a storage facility. We have no room for all those boxes. The best thing is to get rid of them,' Karam said.

'I'll find a place for them, Jee. He very kindly signed important papers for us, the least we can do is keep his papers. He might need them one day and then I'll have them.'

Karam snorted. Picking up a spoon from the dish rack, he used the long end to tuck a few stray hairs back under his turban. Sarna leaped up and snatched away the spoon. 'Hai, hai! This is for eating.' Of all his bad habits, this was the one she most despised.

Unperturbed, Karam reached into his pocket and fished out his car keys to complete the job. 'It's a shame,' he said. 'It would have been nicer if Oskar had said a proper goodbye, but I guess he had his reasons. Hopefully there are plenty of other people looking for a room to rent. I'll ask that Sun Chi in our middle room to post a notice at his university. They're very decent, these Malaysians. No drinking, no girlfriends. Very quiet, just studying, studying. Yes, yes, that should be fine.' He headed out of the kitchen, stopping in the hallway to examine his appearance in the mirror.

'Heartless,' Sarna said. She pressed her hand to her forehead. 'Did you see the way he stuffed that money into his pocket? Of course everything is fine for him – as long as he's got the cash he's happy. And he's got a free newspaper for some months as well. Why should he care? *I'm* just worried about poor OK.'

'Yeah, I hope he's *OK*.' Rajan looked pointedly at Pyari and Nina.

'Of course he's *not* OK. Something must be wrong,' said Sarna. 'I can't believe he's just left without saying anything. Hai Ruba, what has happened?'

Nina scanned the letter, which Karam had left lying on the counter. There was no address on it, no contact number. She would never be able to find him. Never get to say what ought to have been said: those words, formulaic and inadequate, but more strongly felt than any she had uttered before – thank you.

Oskar's decision wasn't the sudden, dramatic event that Sarna imagined. Since the day he had signed his name on the marriage certificate he had been moving towards this departure. That signature had been his first step towards liberation. A braver man would have taken the next step immediately, put one foot in front of the other and marched towards the unknown in the certainty that it would be better than the fruitless tedium of the known. Not Oskar. His inertia was justified by the fact that circumstances did not permit him to walk away. He was bound to remain where he was for another year because Nina's liberty, her citizenship, depended on his staying put. He accepted this confinement gratefully, the way a guilty defendant might welcome the delay of the inevitable afforded by an appeal. But during that year of self-imposed internment, he took a few small steps to an even greater freedom. He began to write. Not the regurgitation of overheard stories – that facility of his was gone. He had been losing it for months, but it finally gave out on him completely when he'd dared to write out his name and marry Nina without its bidding.

He wrote haltingly at first, without plot, theme or character. As children babble before they speak, so he scrabbled before writing. Like eyes growing accustomed to the dark, his mind gradually became used to having its own thoughts. The words to express them jerked out of him like hiccups and landed nervously on the page. For months, frustrated by the awkward, stilted language that poured out of him, he discarded every completed page. He discovered a freedom in this act, too. After years of accumulating paper and hoarding anything he'd penned, it was a relief to throw things away, to let words go because they were not clear or concise enough. He felt as though he was writing out the clutter of old obsessions. Sarna was wrong to think he left 'without a word'. He may not have said much to the Singhs, but he walked out of their house with the feeling that he'd learned a whole new language.

Nina was his muse. Oskar thought of her that way from the instant he signed his name beside hers on their marriage certificate. He was always aware that she was 'his', on paper anyway, for only a year. He never asked for anything in return for the favour he did the Singh family, but Oskar took a reward without their leave: using Nina as his source, he let his imagination fly. In the registry office, her glance had been like an amphetamine shot of inspiration; back at home, just her presence spurred on his creativity. He unashamedly took his visual and mental fill of her. Each time he passed Nina on the stairs, or sat beside her at the table during a meal with the Singh family, or heard her laughter fill the house, or was graced with her shy smile, Oskar savoured the moment. He lingered over their encounters the way you might take your time eating a perfectly ripe peach: slowly, relishing every bite, enjoying the sensation of juicy sweetness in your mouth, delaying finishing the fruit, sucking the last scraps of flesh from the stone, licking your lips afterwards. Having felt the power of her deep-green eyes on their wedding day, Oskar let himself think that Nina would always have a positive effect on him. He believed she was the impetus of his new energy, his Calliope.

The annulment of their marriage was an uneventful process. All they had to do was sign some more papers and then they would allegedly be left in status quo ante – as they were before the marriage. But it was not so simple. Oskar was not the same as before and no amount of legal validation could alter that.

His intention had been to leave immediately after the annulment, but he delayed for a few days, procrastinating. It was his attachment to Nina that prevented him from going. He realized that he had fallen in love with her – or at any rate with the idea of her, for what did he know of her – except that she had made him feel it was possible to write and to live again?

So he left because there was nothing to stay for. He was not the sort of man Sarna would allow to court or marry Nina. He was fine as a temporary substitute, but he could never be considered for the real thing. It's funny how your own approach to life ultimately governs life's approach to you. Oskar had willingly played the understudy for so long, standing in the wings watching others' dramas, that no one imagined he might want a real part. He recognized that only he could rectify this. If he didn't participate in the world, didn't give himself up to it, he couldn't expect any returns.

23

Sarna's concerns about Pyari and Nina were resolved more successfully than she had expected. Three years after Rupi's engagement, both girls had been married off – both to doctors. 'Real doctors, medical doctors, *turban-wallah* doctors,' Sarna proudly told everyone. 'NOT *professor* doctors.' These were the lepers of the medical establishment. 'Nina's Pritpal is a GP-doctor, and Pyari's Jeevan is a surgeon-doctor.'

Then it was Persini's turn to be scornful. Behind Sarna's back she remarked, 'Never mind that the GP is a widower who's twenty years older than Nina and lives miles away in Manchester – at least Maharani Sarna managed to wash her hands of the girl.'

Karam had no doubts about the credentials of the two men. His own frustrated desire for a good education was partly satisfied by the addition of such learned men to his family. But the moment of real satisfaction had come when Rajan was offered a place at Oxford University to study Law. Karam's pride could not have been greater if he had accomplished this feat himself.

Rajan's success had almost eclipsed Karam's regret that Pyari had not completed her university education. The possibility of marriage had led her to give up her four-year Architecture course halfway through. Karam had tried to prevent this disruption to his daughter's studies, but Sarna had been adamant that such a good match didn't come along every day.

'We can ask Jeevan to wait. It's an honour for a man to have an educated wife,' Karam had said.

'Wait? Hai Ruba! No one waits for anyone these days. I can think of at least ten girls who would marry him futa fut.' Sarna snapped her fingers. 'You and your education! Every man just wants a wife who can cook well and bear him good children. Look at everything I've given you without a degree. Are you saying that's not enough?'

'Ah, I'm not saying anything of the sort. No.' He wagged a finger. 'But times are changing. And anyway, Pyari doesn't even know how to cook yet. You've kept the lid so firmly clamped on all your kitchen secrets that her education is incomplete on all fronts.'

'OK, baba, OK.' Sarna did several exaggerated bows. 'Let her finish whatever tecture-tookture she's doing. But when she's still sitting at home in three years' time with nothing but a degree, don't come complaining to me.'

In the end, Karam had left the decision to Pyari. 'Let the girl decide. It's her life.' He'd passed the buck, thinking that her choice would reflect his desire, but he'd been disappointed. Pyari had been happy to stop studying. She wanted to get married and move to Canada. Karam's immediate instinct had been to overrule her. If Pyari had shown a hint of hesitation he might have done so, but she seemed truly relieved to opt out of her course. Karam did not know that she'd never liked doing the degree. She had chosen Architecture because it seemed like the closest thing to design that she could legitimately study. She had imagined herself creating beautiful interiors for vaguely structured rooms. Instead she had found herself outside in the cold and rain doing boring land surveys, or inside faced with dull mathematical calculations. Her reservations about the course made it easy for Pyari to renounce it when the opportunity arose. 'For once the girl is being reasonable,' Sarna had said. 'Some of her mother's good sense has rubbed off on her, after all.'

Sarna had indeed been an influence on her daughter, but not in the way she thought. The major choices that determine our lives are sometimes informed by the most insignificant details. The bounce of a woman's hair can lead a man to commit adultery; a vow of silence can be taken on the basis of a misunderstood look; and the allure of green eyes can seal the most unlikely nuptials. The word 'Canada' had decided Pyari's fate. She had latched on to its promise of far-away-ness. Yes, it helped that Dr Jeevan Bhatia appeared to be a good catch. But his qualities wouldn't have had such appeal for Pyari if they hadn't been haloed by the prospect of Canada.

Pyari had seen that Sarna's interference in Nina's life had not stopped even after she had married and moved to Manchester. Sarna was always on the phone to Nina, complaining about something or other. Every couple of months the family travelled up to Manchester for a few days, where Sarna rifled through Nina's cupboards and drawers, criticizing the way she stored pickles or stacked dishes or folded linen. Nothing was right if it wasn't done exactly the way Sarna preferred; nothing was good enough if it didn't have her stamp of approval. Nina bore Sarna's meddling with remarkable good humour. 'Yes, Sir Mother,' she'd say. But Pyari was appalled. She dreaded the inspections and remonstrations to which her future home might one day be subjected. Was she to be forever over-shadowed by her mother? It had certainly seemed so until Jeevan came into the picture. His promise of life on another continent was irresistible.

Just as, decades before, Sarna had looked forward to leaving India and starting a new life, Pyari now relished the idea of starting afresh. Their circumstances were completely different, but both women were driven by the same impulse. They were seduced by the possibility of re-invention. Both fell for the illusion that happiness could be found somewhere else – if they could just get to that place. But you take yourself wherever you go – that was the lesson Sarna had never learned and Pyari still had to discover. She thought that by getting away from her meddling mother she would find peace. But it seems you also take your family wherever you go. They are there in the character and habits you've developed, and in the lines that age your face, increasing your resemblance to them. The very blood that pumps through your body carries microscopic traces of family, which may one day be manifested as disease or be born as another child in their likeness. The family is also there in obligations and expectations which, even if never articulated, you know you are responsible for fulfilling. Family can make itself felt from anywhere, as a source of comfort or as a burden.

With the girls married and Rajan away at university, Sarna began to feel lonely and bereft of purpose. She disliked the altered routine of her days. No longer were there favourite dishes to be prepared in time for the children's return from school or work. There were fewer clothes to wash and iron, less mess to clear up, fewer people to complain to and, equally importantly, about. A sense of gloom similar to the one that had descended when she'd first moved to England began to settle on her again. She felt that her whole life had been geared to ensuring her children's safety and happiness. What was there left to do now?

Sarna told herself that she had done her duty by Nina – the girl was now married and safely installed several hundred miles away. But the pain of the silenced truth, the continued fear of some sort of exposure and a lingering sense of failure still abided.

As if to compound all this, Sarna became ill. The problem – 'severe stomach sensitivity', as she called it – had been developing for some months and she had done her best to ignore it. The doctor had advised that an operation was necessary, but she had already refused the procedure once. Since then she had avoided going to the doctor and had tried treating herself by rubbing warm ghee on her abdomen and drinking a hot milky concoction made with butter, saffron and almonds. When these remedies did no good, she was forced to face the possibility of a hysterectomy. The irony of her condition did not escape Sarna: her children had left home and now the very source of her motherhood was also to be taken from her. The birds had flown the nest, and the nest itself was disintegrating.

Pyari did not return from Canada to look after her ill mother. 'I've only just got here. It doesn't make sense to come back just for a few weeks if Nina and Rajan are there anyway,' she said on the phone. Rajan came to the hospital once and also visited Sarna at home twice while she was convalescing, but there was little more he wanted to do. It was Nina who waited with Karam in hospital while the operation was done. It was Nina who held Sarna's hand when she regained consciousness. It was Nina who cooked for Karam while Sarna was in hospital and for several weeks afterwards while she recovered at home. It was Nina who bathed, fed and soothed Sarna through this difficult period. It was Nina, the rejected child of the now ejected womb, who mothered her back to health.

While Sarna was in hospital, Karam and Nina were alone. At first, Karam did not know what to say to the young woman who had been forced on him against his will. While she'd lived with them he had remained politely cool to Nina, never speaking to her unless it was absolutely necessary. For Nina, Karam had been like a stern headmaster who spoke to students only when they had messed up badly or excelled. Luckily, she had never done either. But now she was uneasy about their intimate proximity.

In the car, as they drove between home and hospital, the radio covered the silence between them. But at Elm Road they could not altogether avoid talking. During their first meal together the clatter of their cutlery seemed to get louder and louder, like a drum roll heralding some auspicious moment. Karam stirred his lassi as if trying to unchurn the yoghurt. Nina ate her khichdi quickly, trying to ignore the fact that the buttery broth of lentils and rice was scalding her mouth and turning her tongue to rubber. Karam blew at his steaming bowl and watched her.

'I thought it was chillies you liked, not the blazing heat of a high temperature.'

Nina put down her spoon and took a long sip of water before pressing her fingers to her lips. They were pulsing and red like the flashing emergency light of an ambulance.

'Sarna tells me you have started a nursing course,' Karam said.

Nina nodded.

'People will always need doctors and nurses. You and Pritpal will never be out of a job.'

Nina nodded again before taking another sip of water. 'It was his idea – Pritpal's,' she said.

Her resemblance to Sarna unsettled Karam – it always had done. At the sight of her, sentiment and resentment would race each other through the past to collide painfully in his chest. Even the shape of Nina's hands reminded him of Sarna's – the long thin fingers with elegant oval nails – though Sarna's had now roughened with age and work and their ends were often red and swollen, like baby radishes. Karam gave the khichdi a stir before taking a spoonful. Nina started to eat again. The food was less hot, but she couldn't taste anything through the furry roughness of her burned mouth.

'She has taught you to cook,' Karam said. It sounded like the ultimate compliment.

'Yes, she has,' Nina said. She did not add that Sarna had also left strict instructions on exactly what she was to cook for Karam – and in what order – during her absence. All the dishes were simple, almost penitential dishes, like tonight's broth, as if Sarna was determined that Karam should not overindulge while she was convalescing.

After they had eaten, Nina cleared up while Karam watched the news and then did his accounts in the living room. Coming into the hall to switch off the light, he saw Nina sitting at the foot of the stairs, knees bent and feet turned in, her head bowed over a textbook.

'Why are you sitting here?'

Nina looked up. 'I . . . I didn't want to disturb you.' Or

waste your electricity, she thought. Karam disliked it when everyone disappeared into separate rooms and set the light bulbs blaring to perform tasks that could be done communally in the living room. Nina had thought she'd be safe from reproach here in the hall, where the light was usually kept on until the family went to bed.

Karam was moved by her meekness, the self-effacing shape of her folded up on the steps. She was good and modest, that much he had sensed soon after she had come to live with them. 'Don't be silly,' he said gruffly. 'The light here is too dim for reading anyway.'

Gradually, over the weeks of Sarna's recovery, they became timidly acquainted. 'It was good practice for you,' Karam said when Nina was about to leave. And she understood that he was thanking her.

'Yes, I am glad,' she smiled. Though it had been a demanding time, it had also been an opportunity to show her love in a way that Sarna would normally rebuff.

Nina had acted selflessly, and yet there remained in her heart a secret hope that her actions might prompt Sarna to acknowledge, even if only privately between the two of them, that Nina was her daughter. It did not happen this time. Sarna was grateful, and she did not object when Nina called her 'Mother' more tenderly in everyday conversation, but she never said, 'Thank you, my child.' Yet in the aura of intimacy created by Sarna's vulnerable state, Nina could not help believing they were hovering on the edge of the truth.

It was mainly for this reason that Nina would return again and again over the years to nurse Sarna through various illnesses. 'Who needs the NHS? We have the best medical experts in the family,' Karam would maintain. Sarna agreed. 'Nina really knows how to look after people.

So gentle, so patient, she's really like a saint. You know, they say all people whose names start with an S are very saintly.' This was the most public recognition Nina ever got for her efforts, but she continued to strive for a more personal acknowledgement. It would be a long time before she realized it was not Sarna she got closer to on each visit, but Karam.

As soon as Sarna had recovered from the operation, she was back in the kitchen. She couldn't get into the habit of cooking for just herself and Karam. She ended up making vast amounts of food that neither of them could get through. Much of it went into the freezer, packed into old ice-cream boxes or wrapped in unlabelled plastic bags. Sometimes she phoned Nina and, less frequently, Pyari to grumble about life. But long-distance national calls were expensive and overseas ones extortionate, so Sarna was limited in how much she could say to her daughters. Sometimes she tried calling Rajan at his college, but usually ended up leaving messages with the porter for him to call back: 'Is impotent. Tell him his mother calling impotent.'

Conversations with Rajan were brief.

'Have you eaten? Huh, what did you eat?'

Any reply Rajan gave to this question was unsatisfactory.

'Hai, how can you study properly if you don't eat well? Are you coming home this weekend, my Raja? Come, let me feed you. I've made khatais. And I'm going to make your favourite coconut chicken with potatoes.'

'No, I can't, Mum, I've got too much work.'

'What's this "Mum", huh? Going to English college you're becoming so Englishified already? What's happened to "Mumiji"? You used to say it sweetly. You'd better not let your pithaji hear such talk,' Sarna scolded. 'When are you coming? You haven't been home for *three* weeks.'

'Soon, soon, OK? Look, I have to go now. OK, bye . . . bye.'

Sarna would be left listening to the beep of the receiver, wondering how things could change so fast and feeling powerless to do anything about it.

Rajan had started off by coming home every weekend from Oxford because Karam had insisted on it. But then the excuses had started: too much work, exams . . .

'Can't you work here? You have your room,' Karam said.

'I need the library.'

'Why can't you borrow books and use them here?'

'There's too much. The law manuals are huge and some of them aren't for loan. I need to have everything on hand – for reference – in case. Everyone works in the library. If I don't have access to the same books my grades will be lower.' Rajan fabricated excuses for which he knew his father would have sympathy.

'Really?' Karam acquiesced.

So Rajan came home less and less. Now they were lucky to see him once a month.

Unable to lift herself out of the depression into which she'd descended, Sarna began to turn on Karam. He seemed to be going on with life as though nothing was different. One night he leaned over and started to caress her. She felt his hardness knock knock knocking insistently against her left thigh and was overwhelmed by resentment. The man was in his fifties, how could he still be having such longings? He seemed so potent and vital, while she felt dry and barren. She pushed Karam away more roughly than she had intended. 'Hai Ruba! Have you no shame? I've had such a serious operation and you're having silly ideas.' Confused and embarrassed, Karam moved away. He apologized, mumbling that he thought the doctor had said it should be OK after a few months. 'Everything is not OK!' Sarna's eyes filled with tears. She wished he would just hold her. All she wanted was the simple comfort of closeness she had so long prevented herself from giving to anyone else. But Karam did not try to touch her again – that night or for a while afterwards. Though she was relieved, she also started to fret that she was no longer attractive to him. With the big gash across her abdomen and the emptiness inside it, she had no appeal for anyone.

Overcome by a sense of her own worthlessness, Sarna began to resent Karam's productive work life. His clothes business had grown over the last few years. He now had over a dozen regular clients in London, he supplied several retailers in Birmingham, Manchester and Swindon, and he had even sent a few consignments to Paris and Frankfurt. The fact that Karam continued to run the business single-handedly within the United Kingdom meant that he was always busy. 'No point taking on someone and paying him to do a job I could do better,' he said when anyone suggested that he get some help. At his previous post in the civil service, Karam's working hours had been fixed: he had been at the office from nine to five, with evenings and weekends free. Now his work encroached on every waking moment. If he wasn't collecting orders, making deliveries or taking stock counts at the warehouse he'd rented near by, he was doing the accounts or was on the phone to Kalwant, discussing the next consignment or planning a trip to India. Often he would be working at the weekends, taking his wares to markets like Portobello and Camden.

Sarna had always disliked the unpredictability of Karam's new work. She had no way of knowing where he was and when he would return. There were times when he came home late at night, after ten or eleven, blaming traffic, car problems or a no-show by a client for his delay. Sarna was always sceptical of these excuses. She had become wary about Karam's dealings the minute he'd started receiving phone calls from strange women. 'They're clients!' he told her. 'Just sales assistants in shops chasing up a delivery or a dealer's wife increasing an order. It's *business*.' But how could Sarna be sure? He had betrayed her once and could well do it again. Working in women's fashion, imagining how the clothes would look on young bodies, meeting girls all the time, driving to far-off cities for 'deliveries' – the conditions were conducive to having an affair. The most chaste of men would be hard pressed to resist, so what hope was there for one with proven tendencies for such dalliances? There had been much tension and a few heated confrontations between Karam and Sarna on this issue over the years. She had never found indisputable proof of a transgression by her husband, but suspicion did its work to convince her of his guilt.

One night Karam came in late again, just before eleven. He didn't apologize, but immediately offered an explanation. 'Bloody fool wasn't there! Can you believe it? I had to phone him and he'd forgotten I was coming today. Just imagine! I drive all the way to Swindon and the bloody fellow forgets! So I had to wait a few hours before he turned up. And then the traffic on the way home was terrible. Someone had had an accident.'

'The food is still out. Your plate is on the counter. There's yoghurt in the fridge,' Sarna said without looking away from the television.

'Actually I'm not hungry. I'd better get to bed, I have an early start tomorrow.' He moved towards the doorway.

Not hungry? He spends the whole day out and then comes back claiming he's not hungry! He must have eaten somewhere. But where? 'Did you eat already?' Sarna looked at him closely. He seemed a little dishevelled. Stray hairs were peeping out of his turban at the nape of his neck and his shirt was unusually creased.

'Oh, I had a takeaway.' Karam yawned. 'Just a little bite – but it filled me up, and I'm too tired to eat now anyway.'

'What did you have? Where?' She couldn't believe he would have willingly forked out money to eat at a restaurant.

'I just grabbed some chips from this little place as I was leaving Swindon.' Karam's body ached. He was exhausted by all the driving and waiting around. He wanted to lie down and relax. He could see where Sarna's interrogation was leading and he was determined not to go that way. Tired though he was, Karam could not suppress the in- voluntary jerk of his hips as Elvis's 'Suspicious Minds' started playing in his head. These days, every time Sarna voiced her doubts about his fidelity an invisible finger pressed 'play' in his brain and Elvis would start crooning sympathetically inside him. 'I'm going for a bath and then I need to sleep,' Karam said as he left the room and walked up the stairs.

Sarna, who was analysing his every move, did not miss the pelvic thrust, slight though it was. She interpreted it as an ebbing sign of raunchiness, and wondered who had been complicit in the act of betrayal. She did not suspect, for even a minute, that it might be a man called Elvis.

As Karam mounted the stairs, unpleasant inter-pretations of his words began to play in Sarna's mind. Chips? Did he expect her to believe he was full after some chips? She crept into the hall and heard water running upstairs. She grabbed the car keys and let herself out of the front door. The cold of the November night pierced through her thin shalwar kameez – in her haste she'd for-gotten to put on a coat. She looked around uncertainly, suddenly aware that she didn't know where Karam might have parked. But then she spotted his red Volvo standing outside number eleven, a few doors down from them. That car was his pride and joy, one of the few luxuries he'd allowed himself with the profits from the business. He lavished almost as much attention on its appearance as he did on his own. Sarna hastened to the vehicle, unlocked it and leaped in, sniffing fiercely. There were no signs of chip consumption: not a whiff of oil, not a hint of any greasy remains. No tell-tale Mushq. In the pockets of the door and in the glove compartment Sarna found the wads of stiff, abrasive paper napkins that the family always pinched from McDonald's or Kentucky because it saved having to buy tissues to keep in the car, but there was nothing else to indicate a recent visit to a fast-food joint. In fact, there was nothing in the car to suggest that any-thing untoward had taken place. This did not alleviate her concerns.

Sarna hurried back to the house. He probably hadn't eaten chips at all, she thought. He was making it up, try-ing to throw her off the trail. She simply could not reconcile herself to the idea that Karam could come home from work and not eat – he had never done that, *ever*. It seemed unlikely that he would have eaten before getting back into the car. It was so cold, and it had been raining earlier – who in his right mind would eat a takeaway outside in such weather? A lump formed in Sarna's throat and her eyes filled with tears. She turned off the TV and wondered what to do. Karam was probably in bed by now. His abrupt exit had made it clear to her that confronting him tonight would be messy. He would just deny everything and shout at her.

Oh, what could she do? What could a woman do? Who could she speak to? These were not problems you could share – what would people think? They would wonder what she lacked that made her husband wander from the marriage bed. But it was not her fault, Sarna was adamant about that. She had done everything for this family, made sacrifices along the way, risked her dignity for their benefit. She had secretly sewed clothes for friends, telling them that a professional tailor was doing the work and then pocketing the money herself. She had sworn acquaintances to secrecy before agreeing to make samosas for their festivities in return for paltry sums of money. Generally, her family had not noticed her efforts. None of them had thought to ask how she had financed Nina's wedding without a penny of assistance from Karam. They imagined that Nina's earnings from the Phillips factory had covered the cost. Only Sarna knew how she had scrimped, scrounged, stolen and saved to give the girl a decent wedding.

By the time Sarna came upstairs, Karam was asleep. She lay down next to him reluctantly. When she'd first discovered that Karam had been unfaithful, all those years ago in Kampala, Sarna's love for him had overridden the anger and hurt. Then, she had tried not to believe the truth. She had wanted only to please him, to touch him again and again as if to prove that he was really there with *her* and no one else – she would have done anything for his love. Now she lay next to him, imagining the worst in the face of purely circumstantial evidence. She got out of bed and went to sleep in Pyari's old bedroom. Later she would move all her things out of their room and tell him, 'I can't share a bed with another woman. I feel suffocated by the presence of your mistresses.' Karam would declare that she was mad and accuse her of hallucinating, of living in a different world. Sarna would not relent: 'You commit the crazy crimes, but I'm the mad one!' She would not consider that her reaction might be disproportionate to the facts. It was a relief to find something external that could be held to account for her miserable inner state.

The next day Karam left early and little was said. As soon as he was gone, Sarna picked up the phone and called Nina. There was no answer. Where was she at eight-thirty in the morning? Sarna remembered that she must have left for her nursing course. With a sigh she dialled Pyari's number. The phone rang several times. 'Oh, hello, Pyari? Hello? It's your mumiji. Have you eaten? What did you eat?'

'*Meeeee*, it's almost three o'clock in the morning here,' Pyari's tired, muffled voice answered. 'Is everything OK?'

'Your pithaji didn't come home last night.' Sarna's voice was trembling.

'What? Not at all? Have you called the police?'

'Until almost midnight. At midnight he walks in – hai Ruba. Oh God, help me.' Her voice broke.

'He must have been delayed at work. What did he say? Was he OK?' Pyari asked.

'Work-shirk! Leaving early in the morning, coming

home at midnight – what kind of work is that? Work to drive me berserk!' Sarna wound the telephone wire round her finger. 'He was with another woman. He's up to his old tricks again. Now that you children have all left home, he has nothing to worry about. There's no need to pretend any more. What am I? Just his cook and slave. I know him inside out, so he has nothing left to prove with me.'

'Mee, are you sure?'

'Of course. He didn't want to eat when he came home. Said he wasn't hungry. Just imagine! Hai Vaheguru. The only reason a man isn't hungry when he comes home is because he's been feasting somewhere else.'

'Maybe he really wasn't hungry, Mee. You know people do sometimes lose their appetite if they're exhausted.'

'Fiteh moon! You're always on his side. Never mind how he treats your mother, you keep believing in him.'

Pyari remained silent. What could *she* do? She had moved away from home in order to get away from her parents' traumas and dramas, but they still wouldn't leave her alone. Sarna never asked how she was getting on in her married life. She often asked what Pyari cooked for Jeevan and whether she could buy certain ingredients in Toronto, but she never questioned beyond that. It was as if Sarna believed that as long as Pyari could keep her husband well fed, she would be happy. Why on earth did she think that, when the strategy certainly hadn't worked for her?

'I'm all alone!' Sarna cried down the line. 'Who have I got? You tell me. I have no one. Now I can't even talk to my own children without them turning against me. I don't deserve this.'

'Mee!' Pyari willed her mother to stop.

'What can I do? Huh? What can I do? I can't live like

this. I can feel something going wrong inside me. I'll get sick again, I know it. I need a break. I've spent all my life cooking and cleaning for this man and I've got nothing in return except pain. I'm fed up. I need a change,' Sarna sobbed.

Oh my God, Pyari thought. She's waiting for me to say, 'Come here, Mee.' But Pyari could not get out those words. 'Just take it easy, Mee. Don't make any hasty decisions, OK? Let's see what happens. We'll work something out. I'll call you later, OK? It's the middle of the night here. I'll call in the morning. OK, bye . . . bye.'

Pyari did call later and offered her mother a break in Toronto. But by then Sarna's thoughts had taken a new direction. She'd decided that she would only feel better if Karam gave up his clothes business altogether. As long as he was gallivanting around the country, meeting women on the pretext of selling them clothes, Sarna could have no peace of mind. If he wasn't in her bed, she wanted to ensure he wasn't in anyone's. She resolved to put an end to Karam's philandering once and for all.

Sarna knew that engineering the demise of Kasaka Holdings would not be easy. But her name was at the heart of the enterprise: KAram SArna KAlwant Holdings. She had helped bring it together, so she could wrench it apart. Without her, Kasaka would just be Kaka, which was a Punjabi word for a baby boy – so without her the company would become like an infant: naive and hapless.

341

24

The initial relief of his children leaving home had faded for Karam, because with them had gone his control over their lives. Now he had to watch them take decisions, make mistakes and struggle with the consequences, while he remained powerless to intervene. He saw that they did not want his opinion, and if he gave advice they were unlikely to take it.

Karam sensed that Pyari was not happy in her marriage. Within a couple of years she had started coming back to London regularly without her husband. It must be costing the poor man a fortune, Karam thought sympathetically. Pyari regularly talked of missing London and sometimes hinted at a desire to live there again. Karam disapproved of these veiled admissions of discontent. Uncomfortable about probing the issue, he gave his daughter hints about the irreversibility of marriage. 'That's what the ring symbolizes – a closed circle. You both step in and no one can step out.' Pyari never openly disagreed with him. He was grateful for this; it meant a lot to him that the illusion, at least, of parental authority was retained.

Rajan, on the other hand, did not allow his father the comfort of any illusions. That boy really has a mind of his own, Karam often thought, as though independence of mind was a bad habit which Rajan had, unfortunately, picked up. The first change in their relationship came about during Rajan's third year at university. One weekend he came home, and then said that he would be going out on Saturday evening for a talk at some Law Society, which would be followed by dinner. Naturally, Karam and Sarna were disappointed. Rajan rarely came home during term time and they'd been looking forward to showing him off at the gurudwara. But Rajan insisted that the talk was crucial to an essay he was writing. Reluctantly, his parents yielded. 'When will you be home?' Karam asked. 'Not too late,' Rajan said.

Just after three in the morning, Rajan's key turned in the door. At once Karam was out of bed and on the landing at the top of the stairs, with the front door in full view. Rajan, hearing the stairs creak, felt his heart start to pound furiously. The prospect of having to face his furious father in the dead of the night filled him with apprehension. He wondered how on earth he could explain himself. He was suddenly all too aware of the alcohol on his breath and the smell of smoke on his clothes. I've had it now, he thought, stepping into the dark hallway. All of a sudden, he heard a long, low fart like the indulgent purring of a cat. 'Mum?' Rajan laughed. He could get around Sarna without any problem. But the stairs creaked again, and as his eyes adjusted to the gloom Rajan saw a sheepish-looking Karam walking down. Rajan panicked, and Karam tried to contain his mortification. The ignominy of the moment weighed heavily on him. He had intended to confront Rajan with a threatening snarl – What time do you call *this*? Instead, he found himself enquiring almost cordially, 'So, you got held up?'

Surprised by his father's tone, Rajan discarded the contrite stand he'd been about to take. 'Yes, um, it turned out to be more of a party than a dinner.'

'Uh-huh. Well, better get to bed now,' Karam said.

'Yes, Pithaji.' Rajan deliberately used the Indian word so as not to antagonize his father further.

'Don't forget to lock the door,' Karam ordered before turning around.

Heading back upstairs, Karam had the distinct impression that he'd lost credibility in his son's eyes. Rajan, who should have been the penitent one, trotted to his room in relief, elated to have got off so lightly, and immediately fell into a deep alcohol-induced sleep. Karam trudged to bed feeling like the guilty party. Deep inside, he knew they had reached a turning point: Rajan would no longer be afraid of him.

Three years later, the extent of Rajan's autonomy was made clear to Karam and Sarna in one severe blow from which neither ever really recovered. On an innocent Sunday, during one of Pyari's protracted visits, Karam and Sarna discovered something that permanently altered their perception of their son and redefined their future relations with him.

Karam had noticed an uneasy tension between his son and daughter during and after Sunday lunch. 'What are you two bickering about?' he asked finally, as they sat down to have tea in the living room.

'Always the same.' Sarna aped talking mouths with her hands. 'Kuser kuser. Even when you were small it was the same – kuser kuser. Hiding in corners, whispering, whispering.'

'Nothing,' Rajan said as Pyari simultaneously blurted out, 'Rajan has something to tell you.'

Four parental eyes focused expectantly on him.

'I, er . . . I'm, um . .' Rajan shot Pyari a resentful look. He stood up, clasped his hands behind his back and took a deep breath – just as he used to when reciting at inter-school poetry competitions. Very quickly he said, 'I'mnotalawyer.'

'What?' Karam put down his mug of tea and leaned forward, as though greater proximity might clarify things.

'I'm not a lawyer,' Rajan repeated. The dread of that first utterance was subsiding, but his heart was still racing in anticipation of his father's anger.

'What are you saying?' Karam was genuinely confused. 'Of course you are – we saw you graduate. You are a lawyer.' He pointed at the graduation photo on the mantelpiece.

'You *are* a liar,' Sarna echoed, unconsciously giving the word an ironic twist with her Indian pronunciation. 'A sucsexful liar.'

'Yes, I have a law degree, but I'm not a lawyer. I haven't been doing any of the training – I didn't sit the bar exam.' Rajan felt relief. The thick fog through which he'd been dealing with his family was lifting.

'But you did the exam,' Karam insisted. 'You told us. We didn't see you for weeks because you were too busy studying for it. Did you fail? Is that what this is about?'

Rajan cringed as he prepared to set the record straight. 'I haven't been completely honest with you.' His hands were now clasped in front of him, as if in a silent prayer for understanding. 'I wasn't studying and I never had any intention of doing the exam. I've got another job and I'm happy with that. I'm really enjoying it.'

'I knew it!' Sarna shook her head. 'I could tell something was up. A mother feels these things. You know I—'

'So you've been lying.' Karam cut her short with a brush of the hand. 'All this time I thought you were still living in digs studying. What job is it?'

'I'm an account executive in an advertising agency,' Rajan said.

'An accountant? Can you do that with a law degree?'

'No, not an accountant, Dad,' Rajan said. 'The "account" is the client for whom we do the advertising. I help manage the agency–client relationship.'

'So you're a manager?' Karam scratched his beard.

'Well, not in the senior sense of the word, but yes, that's sort of what I do. I help to manage day-to-day issues.' Rajan faltered as he saw perplexity persist in Karam's face.

'But why can't you be a lawyer? What was the point of the law degree? Everyone thinks you're a lawyer.'

'*I* never wanted to do a law degree, Dad,' Rajan said. 'That's what *you* wanted. It was always doctor, lawyer, accountant, pharmacist. Doctor, lawyer, accountant, pharmacist. That was your litany all through my school life. I accepted law because I had the least resistance to it. But I didn't *choose*, Dad, I never felt like I had a choice.'

Crouched on a little stool by the radiator at one end of the room, Pyari watched this confession with a mixture of surprise and admiration. Why had he been afraid to tell the truth? For months Pyari had been urging Rajan to come clean, but he had resisted, claiming he'd do it 'when he was ready', 'when the time was right', 'when it made sense'. Recently she had started to read his whenever as when *never*. That was why, against her nature, she had put him on the spot.

'But we've told everyone you're a lawyer,' Karam said. 'Everyone thinks that's what you are.'

'Well, you'll just have to *un*-tell them, Dad. Explain that I changed my mind.'

'What will I say? That you write ads?'

'No, don't say that. I don't write ads,' Rajan replied wearily.

'You don't write ads? So what do you do, then?'

Rajan's hands flew to his head. His fingers pressed against his temples then ran through his hair, upsetting the side parting, before clasping momentarily behind his neck. He would have preferred anger to this puzzled quizzing. He knew he wouldn't be able to give Karam a clear idea of what his job entailed. 'Like I said, Dad, I *manage* the *account*, like Coca-Cola or Vauxhall or Persil or whatever it is. I deal with the client – the people who handle the marketing for the brand we advertise.' He hadn't got through to his father and Karam's next question proved it.

'You do Coca-Cola advertising?'

'No, Dad.' Rajan sighed. 'It's a small agency – we don't have any really big brands yet.'

Karam stared at his feet as though his expertly buffed shoes held more promise of enlightenment than his son's pleading eyes. He should never have had the boy's hair cut. He looked up. 'I thought you would be a lawyer,' he said wistfully.

Guilt suddenly attacked Rajan. He shifted awkwardly and said, 'Look, I've got to go.' Pyari shot him a look. But he was staring at the door, as if he was worried this one escape route might disappear.

'No, no.' Sarna readily swapped outrage for blackmail in an effort to hold on to her son. 'Have some tea, and I made your favourite – khatais. You must eat, you'll feel better. I've packed some for you to take as well. Come and sit down.' She stood up and pulled Rajan towards the sofa.

Karam muttered, *'He'll* feel better. Huh, he's just fine. What about us? Who will make us better?'

'I'm not really in the mood, Mum.' Rajan resisted her entreaties to sit.

'What's this mood-shood? Eat food and mood will come.' Sarna thrust a plate of the little dome-shaped, cardamom-scented biscuits towards Rajan.

Meanwhile, Karam turned to Pyari. 'You knew this?'

She looked away without reply. This was what she had feared: being complicit in her brother's mistake.

'Very nice.' Karam had no idea that Pyari had been pressing her brother to tell the truth for months. He couldn't have guessed that the knowledge of Rajan's duplicity had been a burden for her and she'd flown to London this time to force a confession out of him. 'If you don't tell them someone else will, and that'll be worse,' she had insisted. Rajan couldn't see why it mattered so much. He didn't know that Sarna was lauding him as the most eligible bachelor everywhere she went, or that she was sending photos of him as far away as India with full details of his legal qualifications written on the back.

'Very nice,' Karam repeated. 'We're supposed to be a family, but half of us don't have a clue what the other half are up to. Each one is going about his own private business, doing what pleases him without a thought for others. Very good.' Turning to Sarna, he concluded, 'This is family for you.'

'A shame, a crying shame.' Sarna was slightly out of her depth. She'd grasped that Rajan didn't want to be a lawyer, but she was even more confounded than Karam about the alternative job he was pursuing.

'There's something else.' Rajan decided to get everything out now. His initial apprehension had been replaced by a growing sense of indignation at his parents' unwillingness to try and see his point of view. This made him bolder with the truth. 'I've got a place of my own. There are no digs or anything. So I won't be moving back home.'

'But your room is still empty. It's waiting for you,' Sarna said, as though the room itself was pining for Rajan in his absence and would be devastated if he didn't return.

'Well I won't be needing it, Mum. You can rent it out.' Rajan glanced at his father to see if the prospect of more income did anything to placate him. But Karam had stood up and was now inspecting the photograph of Rajan in his graduation gown, as if it might be a forgery. He looked from it to his son, trying to work out which was the real Rajan.

'Hai! So you're going? Is that it now? What about *us*?' Sarna's tone was first accusing and then conciliatory again. 'You can't just leave, this is your home. Tell him, Jee. Tell him.'

'There's nothing to tell. He's made up his mind. If he cared what we thought, he would have asked before acting.'

Rajan stiffened at the unfairness of his father's words. He *did* care what they thought. That was why he hadn't had the heart to tell them about his decision – because he hadn't wanted to hurt them. His parents, on the other hand, had decided that he didn't care, because he wasn't willing to sacrifice his life and happiness to the career they had dreamed of him following.

'That's not fair, Dad,' Rajan said quietly.

'Not fair!' Karam was suddenly mightily irritated by Rajan's replacement of 'Pithaji' with 'Dad'. He regretted that he'd allowed it to happen. He always saw too late that a little bit of lenience allowed people to get carried away. 'What is *fair*?' he shouted, standing directly in front of his son. 'Is it fair that we break our backs to raise you children and all you give us in return is dishonesty? Is it fair that we look like fools at the temple because we did ardaas when you became a lawyer, not knowing you had already decided to become some ad man? Is it fair that we should expect nothing from you except disappointment? What is fair? You tell me.'

It's not fair of you to be angry with me for making choices about my own life, just because they're not the choices you would make, Rajan thought.

'What will people say?' Karam went on. 'What can we tell them? One day you're a lawyer, the next you're this ad guy. People will think we're a family of jokers.' It was clear that Karam thought his son had gone down several ladders in the professional world.

'Hai Ruba! What is happening?' Sarna wrapped her chuni piously around her head. 'Your pithaji is right. What will people say? Who will marry you now? Have you thought about that?'

'No.'

'Fiteh moon! Hai! What will we tell people – "qualified as liar but working as . . . as . . ."?' Sarna waited for someone to fill in the gap, but no one came to her rescue.

'I'm going.' Rajan started for the door.

'Hai! Don't be stupid. Sit down. You can't go now.' She leaped up with the plate of biscuits.

'There's nothing more to be said. You've made

350

yourselves clear. I can see that we're not going to get any closer to understanding each other,' Rajan said.

Without looking at his son, Karam said, 'You know, when I moved out of my father's house it was the hardest decision of my life. Bear in mind that I had good reason to move. I'd been married several years and things were very complicated. There were problems with your mother and ... anyway, when I said I was leaving, my father collapsed in tears. "The pillar of this family has been broken and unity will exist no more," he said. I ignored him, but I saw later that he was right. I left and then it was easy for the rest: one by one, my other brothers moved out and it was never the same again. If you live in one home, and you know you must stay together, you always find a way to work things out, to achieve harmony. But once you move apart, you cannot ever live together again.'

'I'm sorry that I didn't tell you sooner. But I don't regret anything else,' said Rajan as he departed, leaving Pyari to sit, just as she'd dreaded, through the tears and recriminations of their parents.

25

Since the inception of Kasaka Holdings, mistakes had been made in the running of the business. This was inevitable. When you have producers, suppliers and retailers in different countries and cities, a minor error from one party can upset the whole enterprise. Karam had dealt with every sort of problem over the years. Recently he had become concerned that there was something lacking from his collections. Pyari always used to help him come up with winning new designs or a nice twist to some existing fashion. The star garments, which had sold out within days of their arrival from India, had all been created by her. Karam had hoped she would remain involved in the business even after moving to Canada. He had become excited about the prospect of setting up a branch of the company in Toronto. Pyari had responded positively to these suggestions, but had shown no real will to get started on the project since going away.

'What is she doing there all day that she can't stitch a few pieces and send them to her father?' Karam asked Sarna.

Sarna had her own gripes about Pyari's behaviour. She'd already grumbled to Nina, 'The girl has forgotten us.

She doesn't call very often, she's not keen for us to visit – it's like she was dying to get away.' But hearing Karam express similar frustrations did not kindle her sympathy. 'Jee, rather than trying to get Pyari involved with your work, maybe you should be giving it up. It's not right – a man with grown-up children selling clothes for young girls. It doesn't look nice.' The portrayal of Karam's clothes trade as an immoral one had become her new hobbyhorse.

'It doesn't look nice to you because you look in such a twisted way,' he said. 'It's a perfectly respectable profession. At least I'm my own master. This is my job – this is what pays for the life we have. And we still have a son to marry off. Think about what you're saying – don't just spout nonsense.'

Sarna's sabotage started in a seemingly benign manner. Her tendency to imagine or exaggerate things in order to portray herself as a victim was the basis of her stance against Kasaka Holdings. She invented problems for the business in the ultimate hope of drawing attention back to herself: Munchausen by proxy.

She began by not passing on messages relating to business calls. When irate clients finally got through to Karam himself and complained, he was completely taken aback. He was very particular about reliability; to find his credibility repeatedly undermined was galling. He confronted Sarna, carefully suggesting that she might have 'forgotten' to tell him something. But she claimed she hadn't taken any calls for him, let alone messages. 'I've noticed that there's been less interest. I thought business must be going downhill.'

Sarna eventually got to the stage where she no longer

even made a pretence of taking the details of the caller. She'd just say, 'Number is all vrong' or 'Mr Singh is no any more in bijness.' This lost Karam a few orders. He had his suspicions about what was going on, but didn't know what to do. Sarna denied everything and he certainly couldn't sit at home by the phone all day when there was so much to be done elsewhere. He tried speaking to his son. Rajan had a degree in Law, after all, even if he wasn't putting it to any good purpose.

'Try to get her involved in the business, Dad. Give her some responsibility, so she feels a part of it,' Rajan suggested. He had already heard Sarna's version of events – a story in which everyone had deserted the self-sacrificing wife and mother to pursue their own lives.

'She doesn't want anything to do with it!' Karam pulled a handkerchief out of his pocket and began to clean his spectacles. Since getting these several months ago he had become fastidious about keeping the lenses spotless. 'She hates the idea of *me* doing this work. *She* doesn't want to get involved and dirty her hands.'

'Well, I think she's bored and feels neglected. If she was working with you, maybe she wouldn't be so, you know, suspicious of everything.'

'Ah, she's always suspicious.' Karam was annoyed by the intimation that Sarna had expressed doubts about his fidelity. 'Nothing can change that, it's her nature. If she pays for anything, she's convinced she's going to be short-changed. We give the TV to the electrics shop in Tooting for fixing and she suspects them of replacing all the original parts with cheap, new plastic ones. The machine works again, but she's convinced they've done something strange to it. "It makes a different noise," she says. She keeps nagging me to report the shop owner to that

Watchdog programme. Just think of it! You tell her any fact and her instinct is to doubt it. *She* always knows better. She's the type to get suspicious over a missing petal on a flower.'

'I don't know then, Dad.' Rajan sneaked a glance at the Africa clock. 'Can't she just be a sort of secretary for you? Get her to answer the phone and post letters or something.'

'The phone is where the problems started. I don't want her near the phone. She needs to get out of the way and stop interfering.' Karam put his glasses back on.

'Maybe it's time you got a proper office.' The dining table was covered with piles of paper. Several clothes samples were draped over the back of one chair. 'Why don't you rent a small place somewhere? That would make things easier,' Rajan said.

'No, no. That would be too expensive. And I don't need a place, anyway. If your mother could just leave me alone, everything would be fine.' Besides, Sarna would probably see such a move as confirmation that he had something to hide.

'Well, get a telephone line put in at the warehouse.'

'What? In that garage? That's no place for a phone. It would cost too much to install. And anyway, I don't want to drive to Tooting every day to use the phone. It's not practical. Petrol, time – you know everything adds up.'

'Well then, I don't know. I really don't know.' Rajan gave up. His father seemed to want things to change without being willing to budge an inch himself.

In the end, Karam advised customers, 'Don't call me, I'll call you.' But there were inevitably times when people needed to get hold of him and then the problems started. Karam's established clients were more tolerant, but it wasn't easy for newer ones and first-time buyers to trust a supplier who didn't respond to messages or whose telephone number repeatedly rang through to a voice announcing 'vrong number' or 'not in bijness'.

Meanwhile, Sarna's underhand dealings proliferated. If Kalwant called while Karam was out, she alarmed her by dropping hints that he was planning to shut down Kasaka Holdings. 'Business is not so good any more,' Sarna sighed, as though she was genuinely worried. 'Don't say anything, but I think he's having second thoughts about this whole clothes siyapa. I'm telling him to stick with it for a bit longer, but who knows what he'll decide? When did a man ever listen to a woman, huh?'

Kalwant, whose personal and financial interests were now firmly tied up in Kasaka Holdings, was naturally upset by these speculations. She was making a good living from the 25 per cent share Karam cut her. She managed to boost this income by driving even harder bargains with the cloth manufacturers and haberdashery suppliers, so that, unbeknownst to Karam, she could siphon off a fraction of the sum allocated for these expenses.

Although Kalwant felt that Karam had always been honest and fair in his dealings with her, she felt angry that he hadn't told her about the possibility of closing down the business. When she asked him about the state of things, he told her that sales were a bit slow but added that he expected them to pick up. Indeed, Karam's actions did little to back up Sarna's premonitions of doom. He continued to request garments as regularly as before, and he even talked about the next collection and another trip to India. Yet Kalwant couldn't rid herself of the niggling doubts that Sarna had planted. After all, it wasn't just a one-off comment her sister made – there were allusions to the impending meltdown of Kasaka Holdings in almost everything she said. 'The market is flooded . . . Sales are down . . . Stock is dead . . . The end is near.'

Kalwant began to consider how she might cope if the business did fold. She worried about how she would dispose of the back-orders for which fabric, thread and buttons had already been purchased and tailors had been paid to stitch. Karam could just leave her high and dry. It would be easy for him to phone her and call it a day. He didn't have that much to lose at the India end. After much reflection, Kalwant decided she would try to keep things going. She could take over the sewing machines and export the goods on her own. All she needed were a few wholesale buyers like Karam. It couldn't be that difficult. Like her sister, Kalwant was an astute woman. If the risk of ruin lay ahead, she would be sure to have a contingency plan in place.

So, over the months, she began sounding out new contacts and sending styles from Karam's existing line as samples. She was surprised by the immediate interest. Realizing that by supplying directly she could make a much larger margin than the one Karam was currently offering, Kalwant went ahead and signed a big contract with a retailer in Holland. Her intention was to start a sideline of her own, so that when Karam announced that he was backing out she would already be well on her way up in the world of cheesecloth fashion. However, things became complicated when the Dutch company told her they needed their garment order fulfilled immediately. The only way Kalwant could meet their demand was by sending a large consignment that had just been readied for Karam. With a guilty conscience, tempered by the justification that Karam was about to renege on his agreement with her anyway, she sent the goods to Holland.

The delay of this consignment was a real blow to Karam. In an effort to inject some new momentum into the business, he had placed a larger order than usual. Unnerved by his own boldness, he had been working around the clock to line up buyers. Anxious not to let anyone down, he had confirmed and reconfirmed the order with Kalwant, stressing that it must be sent on time. The non-arrival of the goods hit him hard. He was already struggling with disgruntled buyers who had been put off by Sarna's bad telephone practice. Two new clients immediately cancelled their orders. Others turned the situation to their advantage, insisting that they would only take the stock if it was sold to them at a cut price.

Karam was so upset, for over a week his ties didn't match his shirts and he forgot to polish his shoes. He shared his grievances with his brothers, who sympathized but had little consolation to offer. He phoned Rajan, who reminded him that he'd always been cynical of the family-based set-up of the business.

'It's not the first time this has happened, Dad. You should have put different back-up mechanisms in place years ago. No serious business relies on just one supplier – I've told you that before.'

Karam listened carefully, but he felt his son did not make enough allowances for factors like family. Rajan drew conclusions based on logic and long-term efficiency, while Karam's decisions were governed by short-term economies and family sensitivities.

'Yes. But what to do *now*?' He wanted some magical fix for the mess.

'You have to change things. Tell Kalwant that you're

getting another supplier on board. Tell her you're cutting her share by five per cent or whatever to subsidize this loss. That'll shake her up.'

'I can't do that, she's your mother's sister.' Karam twirled a pencil in his fingers.

'You have to do it, Dad. Forget this sister–brother connection. She obviously doesn't let that bother her when she misses a delivery date. Right now she knows you're in a weak position, you need her too much. If you have another supplier it makes for better competition. They'll both be fighting to give you better value so you order from one and not the other. They'll have to be reliable, because they'll know you've got another option if they can't deliver. *And* you'll make much better profits in the long run.' Rajan knew this argument would be closest to his father's heart.

'It's not so simple,' Karam said.

'It *is* simple. You just have to take the decision and then you'll see how simple it is.'

'I can't just cut out Kalwant. She's crucial to operations – her name is even part of the company.' Karam crooked the phone between his ear and shoulder. Raising his hands, he dipped the pencil under the back of his turban, tidying what was already neat. Would that his life could be ordered as easily as his appearance.

'You don't have to cut her out, that's not what I'm saying. And the name doesn't matter – most people don't know what Kasaka stands for. It could just be a made-up word, like Kodak. You could even change the name, you know – it's not that critical to the business.' Rajan had never liked the name Kasaka. It reminded him of the throaty shriek a martial artist might emit as he thrashed his fist through a wall of bricks: *Kaaasakaaa!* 'Anyway.' He read reluctance in Karam's silence. 'You asked me and I've said what I think. You'll do what you want, of course.'

Karam wasn't sure what he wanted. Sarna was quick to capitalize on his uncertainty and stoked the fires of his wrath. 'What a horrible mess! I told you this family business would come to no good. Indian people are all after money. Sisters will rob brothers behind their backs. Kalwant must have sold the goods to someone else for a higher price. I wouldn't be surprised if she's using your machines and tailors to run her own business.' She guessed with an accuracy that confirmed the sentiment 'It takes one to know one.'

'Impossible.' Karam was shocked by the suggestion. 'I'm calling her again.'

'Call her, tell her, show her.' Sarna's lips smacked together like cymbals. She alternately crossed and rubbed her two index fingers against each other in anticipation, as though she was sharpening two knives on each other before use.

The conversation started along the same lines as his previous one with Kalwant: 'I don't understand what's going on there.' Sarna glared at Karam and raised her arms, indicating that he should be more forceful. 'One simple job you have – just one job, and you can't even do that properly. I run around like a fool at this end.' Karam's voice was getting louder. 'I kill myself getting orders, delivering, checking out fashions, balancing the books, and you can't even dispatch a box on time!'

'Bhraji, I'm doing my best here. I'm on my own as well – don't forget that. *And* I have a family to look after,' Kalwant said. 'I work hard to get you the best deals, and that means things sometimes take a bit longer.'

Meanwhile, Sarna was gesturing wildly. Like a

conductor leading an orchestra in a crescendo, she urged him on. Stabbing her finger in the air and hissing violently, she indicated that Karam was not being aggressive enough. Her strange brand of music had an energy that possessed him.

'This could ruin me,' he said. 'This was a *very* important consignment. The delay could ruin me!' He felt the strangeness of his own vehemence. 'When will those clothes get here? I need them within a week.'

'Not a week, Bhraji. I told you, I need longer. Maybe three weeks. I—'

' "*Maybe three weeks*." Are you joking?' Karam interrupted. He tried to wave away Sarna, who was doing a vicious slit-throat action at him. 'What have you been doing? Why isn't the order ready? This will finish me, I tell you, Bhanji. I'll have to just shut up shop and end this goddamned business.'

Sarna raised a fist triumphantly and darted towards the kitchen.

For Kalwant, this threat was a vindication of her fears. She imagined that Karam was using the opportunity to drop the dreaded bombshell which Sarna had warned her about.

'What are you saying, Bhraji?' she asked.

'I'm saying I need that order futa fut.' Karam snapped his fingers. It sounded like a small explosion in Kalwant's ear.

'I told you when you'll have it,' she said.

'Three weeks is not futa fut. I just don't understand the delay.'

Sarna reappeared and began gesticulating again. Karam turned his back to her and faced the wall, as if this might somehow protect him from her ferocious stage directions. The telephone wire curled around his waist.

'Last-minute problems.' Kalwant coughed.

Sarna struck a match and waved it in Karam's face. He looked at her in confusion. What was she doing? She narrowed her eyes as if to say, 'Now is the moment – snuff her out,' and then she extinguished the flame with a sharp blow. Karam pulled a disapproving face and turned around again. The coiled wire of the handset wrapped itself around him once more, pinning his left hand to his side so he could no longer use it against his wife.

Feeling trapped by Sarna's manoeuvring, Karam prepared to try Rajan's strategy instead. 'We might need to find another supplier,' he said. 'So that there's less pressure on you and I can be sure of a delivery. It will be easier. I need peace of mind. There's no room for delays in this business. Of course, you'll still be fully involved, but you'll have more time for your family, like you want. We'll need to renegotiate a lower fee – nothing drastic, you know – no major changes. You're my sister, after all. I would never want to cut you out completely.' Karam became aware of an outraged silence at the other end of the line.

Sarna smacked her forehead. This was not the outcome she wanted.

To Kalwant, Karam's words had tumbled out as an incoherent, contradictory babble of excuses. 'Do you want to end our arrangement?' she asked. 'If that's what you want, speak plainly.'

And suddenly Karam was on the back foot. Alarmed that she might refuse to participate in the business any more, he scrambled to mollify her. All talk of extra suppliers and payment cuts was shelved as he launched into a penitent bid to win her back.

'Of course not, Bhanji. What are you saying? You

misunderstand me. I want nothing of the sort.' All he wanted was a simple open arrangement in which he could have absolute faith. 'I was just thinking of ways to avoid a disaster like this in future. If you are sure you can manage then I have full confidence in you. I have no quibbles. I just want my consignments on time.'

'I think you want me out.' Kalwant played up her advantage.

'Bhanji, stop this now.' Karam moved the phone from his ear for an instant and shook it at Sarna. 'You'll only be out when I'm out. If we go down, we go together.'

That storm of misunderstandings and hasty patch-ups blew over. But those who had weathered it were left shaken: both Karam and Kalwant were more sceptical about each other's motives and the longevity of Kasaka Holdings. They continued to work together, but in the absence of trust their dealings were tetchy and superficial. It did not help that Sarna was still undermining the business in the background. To Kalwant she painted a picture of herself as the noble sister, who was making Karam hold to his obligations by keeping her employed despite his intentions to the contrary. To Karam she portrayed herself as the dutiful, concerned wife by playing up Kalwant's duplicity, swearing that she was taking him for a ride and selling to other buyers behind his back.

'Listen to me, look at me, love me, praise me – I'm helping you. Forget the business, *I'm* here. Me, me, *me*,' this was the silent plea behind Sarna's actions. Perhaps it was not entirely the force of her will that brought things to pass as she'd predicted, but she was certainly key to the breakdown of Kasaka Holdings. Kalwant went on expanding her wholesale supply business and, inevitably, Karam eventually discovered what she was up to. On a trip to India, while visiting the workshop, he found out about some 'Holland dresses' from one of the tailors. Karam had then gone through the stock, through the books, through the dispatch forms and had interviewed all the staff. To Kalwant's credit she did not deny anything, but justified herself by accusing Karam of keeping her in a state of uncertainty for too long and complaining he had never paid her enough. Karam immediately terminated all contact with her. He left written instructions asking her to send the latest order as soon as it was completed, adding that it would be his last. He advised that she should sell or keep the sewing machines as her personal payment for this final batch of work.

He returned to London with a head full of regrets and a horrible feeling of failure in his heart. Nine years after its inception, Kasaka Holdings stopped trading. Karam always blamed himself for its demise. He understood too late that Rajan had been right – if he had run things with a firmer head and a harder heart it might all have turned out differently. But Karam had underestimated the Sarna effect. Her unhappiness was a dark and destructive force, able to insinuate itself into another's existence and poison what was good. Yet Sarna found little consolation in her victory, for destroying the achievements of others does little to diminish the dull ache of one's own failures.

26

Karam had never been one to sit idle. After the fold-up of Kasaka Holdings, he felt too old to start another business of his own and too weary to work for someone else again. Yet after just a few weeks of hanging about the house doing odd repair works, reading or sitting in front of the TV, he became restless.

Sarna, who'd plotted tirelessly to have Karam within her gaze all day, also experienced considerable discomfort now that he was housebound. 'Hai Ruba, he sits at home in his suit all day, doing endless calculations. He constantly wants a snack. I can't stand him wandering into the kitchen every five minutes,' she grumbled to Nina. Sarna had difficulty concentrating on her cooking when her husband was hovering near by: she'd lose track of how much spice had been added to a dish, she'd start fretting about the intensity of the flame on which a saucepan was sitting, she'd chop ingredients the wrong size, and, several times, she accidentally sliced at her own fingers. Karam noticed this unease. He saw her pull faces and shake her hips impatiently, as though he was encroaching on her private space.

Sarna was surprised by how much Karam's presence

irritated her. He seemed to be in the way whatever she wanted to do: when she was hoovering, his legs were stretched out like an obstacle in her path; when she went to wipe the table, his papers were strewn all over it; when she needed the toilet, he was already in there; when she wanted to use the phone, he'd be on it. Meanwhile, Karam found it extremely odd that she always needed to fuss around in the exact spot of the house he happened to be occupying: he might be reading quietly in his bedroom and all of a sudden the vacuum cleaner would be thrusting its nose under the chair on which he was seated and prodding impatiently at his feet. Like magnets, Karam and Sarna's opposite habits drew them together for an inevitable clash of wills.

Eventually, Karam started going to the gurudwara more regularly. In the past he'd made a point of attending the main service on a Saturday evening, but now he was at the temple several times a week. It was a great place for socializing. After sitting through the soothing kirtan, where the granthis played the harmonium and tabla and sang hymns, Karam would join the other devotees for a good meal in the dining room. The crowd at the temple often included a couple of his brothers and many friends or acquaintances. Sarna did not approve of these regular visits. Such a man, she thought scornfully. Spent his youth getting up to all sorts of shenanigans and then turns to the temple in old age.

The gurudwara provided a legitimate reason for Karam to be away from Sarna, and eventually he became involved in the administration of the place. He initially joined the committee as treasurer, moved on to secretary, then vice-president, and finally president. He held this post every alternate year for six terms before temple politics and rivalries became too unbearable for him. It was widely acknowledged within the temple community that he was the most effective president ever. Karam took the voluntary post seriously, recommending more efficient ways to do everything from running the accounts to taking bookings for weddings. Until his presidency, women had only been involved in the temple kitchen. But he invited them to join the gurudwara committee, giving them a more critical role in the running of the place. Not all these changes were accepted easily, nor did they necessarily go down well. Sarna was unenthusiastic about the new liberties granted to her sex. 'Typical,' she grumbled to Nina. 'He can't keep his hands off women. Has to find ways to be with them, even in the temple.'

She was not the only one who was displeased. Until Karam took over, the temple had been run under a rotating presidency system dominated by two families, the Babras and the Gills. They were related through marriage, but separated by hate. No one knew the exact cause of their dispute. It was rumoured to stem from an infidelity, a money swindle and an eruption of temper that had almost ended in murder. The intense, long-running rivalry of the families, whose members comprised 90 per cent of the temple committee, had meant that consensus was rarely achieved on any issue. Not surprisingly, this had resulted in a rather slap-dash, ineffectual admin-istration at the gurudwara. In fact, Karam had only gained the presidency when the Babras and Gills had suddenly reached a total impasse, refused to speak to each other and vengefully elected an 'outsider' as president. Each family imagined they'd have greater influence with Karam and would be able to stage-manage his actions from behind the scenes. Both parties came in for a big shock when he proved amenable to neither. They were put out by his rigorous, commonsense approach to everything. Behind his back they called him the Iron Man, because he was a fan of Margaret Thatcher and seemed to share her no-nonsense approach. He quashed lazy committee members the way she did the trade unions.

With a grant from the local council, Karam founded and became president of a Senior Citizens' Group – which in fact meant most temple attendees. This group became a forum for education and entertainment. They got together in the gurudwara hall on the last Friday of every month. These evenings, arranged by Karam, began with a talk given by a professional and were followed by dinner. At first, the themes were mainly medical and were delivered by Sikh doctors, including Nina's husband, Pritpal. They spoke on 'Thyroid Problems', 'Heart Disease', 'The Importance of a Good Diet', 'Depression', 'Incontinence'. Then came a month when Karam could find no available speaker. He tried to persuade Nina to speak on the advantages and disadvantages of being a nurse. She was terrified by the prospect and had to say no, although she hated having to refuse anyone anything. 'I can't, B-ji,' she apologized, swallowing the address 'brother' as always. She felt embarrassed using the term for Karam; it rang so false in her ears that she was sure its bogus clang must grate on everyone else too.

As the date for the next meeting approached, Karam realized the only solution was for *him* to do the talk. He decided to interview Nina and give a lecture based on her experiences. 'Who cares what Nina's work is like?' Sarna asked. 'It's not about her, it's about being a nurse. It will give people an insight into another kind of life,' Karam said. But in the end it *was* about Nina, because everything he learned came through the filter of her kindness, leaving him with the impression that nursing was a most noble profession. 'My goodness, that's quite a job she does,' Karam said to Sarna afterwards. She shrugged as though she had known all along. 'My sisters and I have never shirked from hard work. We've always put others before ourselves.'

Before the talk, Karam repeatedly practised his speech in front of the mirror. It was his first attempt at public speaking and although it would take place in familiar surroundings, in front of friendly faces, he was nervous. On the day, he ironed his shirt twice and changed his tie three times. Sarna mocked his efforts. 'Look at you! President of the gurudwara and jittery as a school boy.' The evening was a success. Friends and family congratulated Karam and some people said he should do it again. And so, from a simple need to fill a gap in the gurudwara's monthly calendar, Karam's public-speaking career was born.

He began to talk regularly at the Senior Citizens' Group. Over the years, Karam pursued many different topics: religious, social, historical. He chose subjects which interested him and, having read widely around each one, was able to deliver passionate, informative speeches. Once he'd become more comfortable in his role as lecturer, he began to expound more abstract themes. Amongst other things, he spoke on the nature of love, the importance of family and the folly of greed. People responded well to his talks, but Karam was never entirely satisfied with his efforts because the real audience he addressed – the crowd of one – didn't appreciate the significance of his words.

* * *

Rajan, who had long been meaning to come and hear his father's lectures, made it to the gurudwara on an evening when Karam's topic was 'Anger'. He sat tucked into the middle of the sixty-strong crowd, next to his mother. His Punjabi had weakened through lack of use, but he could still understand the speech.

Karam took in his audience and then looked at his notes. 'We all get angry,' he started. 'I like what Emerson said: "We all boil at different degrees."' For the next minute he read from his notes, while self-consciously adjusting his glasses. 'If you don't manage anger properly, it can affect your job, your relationships, and, most of all,' he glanced at Sarna, 'your health.' He started reading again. 'I was very surprised by George Bernard Shaw's words: "The test of a man or woman's breeding is how they behave in a quarrel." How true!' He ventured another glimpse at his wife. His brow furrowed into rounded Ws that looked like birds flying towards the peak of his turban. 'Buddha tells us to beware of anger, because "The thought manifests as the word. The word manifests as the deed. The deed develops into habit. And the habit hardens into character."' A quick peek at Sarna. '"So watch the thought and its ways with care." When I read that I almost gave up writing this speech. I considered giving you all a copy of Buddha's words and saying, "Let's just sit quietly and think about this for half an hour." But many great people have spoken wisely about anger and I wanted to mention their ideas as well.' Karam read on. His own comments were just asides or links between quotations. He was impressed by the insight of others and his sense of inferiority was apparent in the way he hid between the gaps of their words. 'While I was researching this subject I came across something Eleanor Roosevelt said, which I really like.' He paused. ' "A woman is like a teabag. You never know how strong she is until she gets into hot water." ' The audience laughed. Even the few who were consulting their watches managed a smile. One man who'd dozed off woke suddenly, his head nodding jerkily off his chest. Only Sarna was oblivious. She hadn't been listening to Karam anyway, so how could she understand the subtext of his words? She was staring into her lap, her fingers fidgeting away on the invisible typewriter of fantasy.

Rajan noticed her self-absorption and reflected on the difference between his parents. Karam, who had always been curious about history and the world, was still exploring life, still keen for knowledge. Though now in his sixties, he stood strong and tall – all those years of sitting up straight so as not to crease his shirt were paying dividends. Sarna, by contrast, had been debilitated by a different kind of knowledge. She had spent a lifetime trying, unsuccessfully, to exorcize and forget old ghosts. While Karam sought out the stimulus of travel, social contact or books, she'd retreated into a closed world of cookery, through which she'd tried to reinvent her life. Her lips had thinned and drooped ever so slightly at the edges, as though wearied by a lifetime of complaining. Her eyes had sunk deeper into her face, as if in retreat from a world that had not altered itself adequately to fit her perceptions. The dullness of her once seductive brown gaze suggested she had found no respite from her demons. It was a sad face, Rajan realized. And yet it was regal, proud and stubborn. Sarna's skin was still flawless and remarkably unwrinkled. Although she was now padded out with surplus weight, there was no doubt that Sarna was still the best looking of all the older women in the gurudwara. She dressed with care and flair, refusing to opt for the more subdued colours and styles favoured by her contemporaries. This diminished but could not entirely hide the damage wrought by the passage of time and the burden of erroneous choices. 'Well,' Karam was saying, 'I will finish with some good advice to all of you – courtesy of Thomas Jefferson. "When angry, count to ten before you speak. If very angry, count to one hundred."'

'That was great, Dad. I really enjoyed it.' Rajan went up to his father as the crowd dispersed for dinner.

Unable to acknowledge the compliment, Karam evaded it. 'Oh, *you* would be very good. You're the educated one. I've asked you so many times, come and talk here. Tell people about some aspect of Law.'

Immediately, Rajan was annoyed. 'I'm not really qualified to speak about the Law any more,' he said through gritted teeth.

'Or advertising.' Karam tried to make amends. 'Come and talk on advertising.'

Rajan quickly changed the subject. 'I noticed a lot of what you said was very relevant to Mum.'

'Did she say anything? Do you think she got it?'

'I don't think so. She seemed very . . . preoccupied the whole time.'

'Ah, she never takes anything from these talks,' Karam said regretfully. How often had he planned a whole speech around her? Trying to tell her the things he could not say privately. 'She's not interested. I don't know where her thoughts are. The talks on depression, healthy diet, pride – she could have benefited from all of them.' He rolled his notes up into a tube. '"You would do well to pay attention to this," I've told her time and again, but it makes no difference. She sits there and doesn't seem to take in a word. The talks are in Punjabi, the ideas are accessible – why doesn't she try to learn something? I don't understand.' Karam tapped the paper tube against the palm of one hand. He felt more estranged from his wife than ever.

27

Oh-ho, Maharani has laid out a red carpet for herself, Persini noted as she stepped through the front door of 4 Elm Road. 'Expecting royalty?' She grinned at Sarna, who was standing at the entrance to welcome them.

'I knew *you* were coming,' Sarna said with an even more forced smile.

How glossy her hair looked, Persini thought, as if she polished each strand individually. Persini entered the house and snuck a glance in the mirror on the wall. The low lighting in the hall – Karam tried not to use any bulb stronger than forty watts – was quite flattering, but it didn't show her own brittle hair to any advantage. She made a mental note to have a rummage in the bathroom and try to find the brand and shade of Sarna's hair dye. Quickly she licked a finger and smoothed it over her eyebrows, as if to emphasize their impressive pointedness. Then she walked into the living room. 'Looks like the King and Queen of the UK live here now, huh, Bhraji?' She looked from the carpet to Karam.

'We are still living like paupers,' he said, thinking of the tenants. 'But it was time for a change and Sarna wanted a red carpet.'

He still loves her, Persini thought, watching him gently stroke the deep-blood wool with the tip of his shiny left shoe. She shivered with envy.

'Yes.' Karam smiled. 'She's been set on red ever since seeing Prince Charles and Lady Diana's wedding on TV.'

The rest of the family trooped in. First Sukhi, then his son-in-law Dr Surveet Choda, fondly known as Sveetie, and Rupi, holding her four-month-old son, Gemjeet. Then came Rupi's plump nine-year-old twin daughters, Ruby and Pearl, shyly reacquainting themselves with Pyari's sons, Amar and Arjun. The boys had recently moved to new schools in London.

In the hallway Sarna whispered to her daughters, 'Have you seen the size of those twins? "The jewels in my Rupi's crown", the kamini calls them. They look more like footballs than precious stones. Forget Ruby and Pearl, they should be called Roly and Poly.'

'Mee! Shhhh,' Pyari said, while Nina giggled and hung coats on the banister.

'What's the new son's name again?' Nina asked.

'Gemjeet,' Sarna snorted, before going in to her guests.

'They call him Gem for short,' Pyari said. 'If he ends up looking like his sisters, Rupi can call her troop The Rolling Stones.'

This particular lunch was long overdue. In line with family tradition, Karam and Sarna were required to invite the newborn relative's family over for a meal to give their blessing. After the requisite six weeks, during which mother and baby do not leave the house for social visits, Sarna had proposed a date. By rights Karam, as the eldest brother, should have been first to receive a visit. But Persini had procrastinated. For over two months she had come up with excuses: little baby Gemjeet wasn't well,

375

Sveetie was away for a conference, Sukhi was having problems with his car, then Rupi was suffering from flu and after that Sukhi's arthritis flared up. Meanwhile, none of these alleged 'problems' prevented Persini from doing the rounds at Karam's brothers' homes. Finally, when all other family obligations had been fulfilled, Persini had condescended to confirm a date with her old rival.

The only aspect of the meal on which Persini commented was dessert, because she guessed that the orange-scented almond cake was the one dish Sarna had not made.

'Very nice cake. Did *you* make it, Pyari?' Persini asked.

'Oh yes,' Sarna answered for her. 'She could make cakes before she knew how to cook dhal.'

'Rupi is *very* good at desserts. Really, Bhabiji, she makes things I couldn't have imagined were possible.' Persini always bragged about her daughter's achievements. She'd been inflating Rupi's qualities since the day that Sarna had given birth to twins in Nairobi; as if to prove that Rupi alone was as good as Sarna's two.

'I definitely love eating cakes.' Rupi flicked her long blond tresses off her fat cheeks. She'd begun highlighting her hair when she married. Perhaps she was trying, in her own way, to keep up the Chodas' tradition of hair exploits.

'These girls have advantages. Pyari has done *courses* where they teach you to make desserts. She has *books* about cooking, she follows *recipes*. We had none of this. Everything we learned we had to figure out for ourselves. I've never even looked at a cookbook. I didn't know there were such things.' Sarna thought consulting a recipe was a serious shortcoming.

'We had our mothers – they taught us.' Persini smiled fondly at her daughter. 'I told Rupi everything I know about food, but now she's overtaken me. That's how it should be.'

Sarna wanted to say that it would be easy for an ant to overtake Persini on the culinary front. Instead she replied, 'If the girls want to learn from their mothers, well and good. But some aren't interested and then they move to foreign countries and have to go on courses.'

'What about you, Nina?' Persini looked at her. Still so pretty, but then those green eyes could turn a donkey into a stallion. Persini crossed one arm over her chest and raised the other to support her sharp chin. 'Who taught you to cook?'

Caught off guard by the question, Nina replied without thinking. 'Mother.' Immediately she realized her mistake.

'*Mother?*' Persini's eyebrows shot up and hit her hairline. She looked at Sarna, before turning back to Nina. 'Oh, so she's your mother now? That's quite a development.'

Sarna jumped to the rescue. 'What other word is there for a sister who does everything?' She glanced at Karam, who was sitting at the dining table with the men, while the ladies and children were spread out on the sofas. She was relieved to see him engrossed in eating cake. Shifting her attention back to Persini, she went on, 'When someone goes out of their way for you, brings you from India, looks after you, teaches you to cook, marries you off *and* pays for everything, you feel the same gratitude you would towards a mother. I've made Nina's life. She has no other family near by. Here I'm everything to her – sister, brother, father *and* mother.'

'Of course.' Persini stroked her chin. 'We all know you two have a very *special* relationship.'

Sarna was put into another uncomfortable position a

short while later, when the conversation turned to children and Persini remarked on how lucky Rupi was to have twins and now a son. 'Such good kismet. A son after all these years. Dear Vaheguru, what more could a woman ask for?'

'No doubt Rupi got her good luck from Surveet's side of the family,' replied Sarna, taking a thinly veiled dig at Persini's inability to have more than one child.

'Twins are such a blessing. With Vaheguru's grace the girls are growing up. God gives and takes away as he sees fit, wouldn't you agree, Bhabiji?' Persini smiled her thin, pointy smile – the lips creasing up rather than spreading wide.

Sarna went pale. Life's digits twiddled and pulled the strings of her heart into a convoluted, constricting pattern. She ached with the memory of a lost twin to which she had never reconciled herself. She got up and hastily left the room.

When she returned, Persini was commenting on Nina's appearance. She had lost weight and was looking very tired. The change had come about in the last year – since Pritpal's death from a heart attack the previous summer.

'You must take care, Nina. Don't lose your health,' Persini said.

'Jes.' Sarna spoke in English, as if this would help her regain the upper hand. 'Health is Vealth. Health is Vealth. No dowt bout tit.' She settled back into the roomy arm-chair reserved for her on account of 'back pain'.

On the sofa, where Rupi, Pyari and Nina were squashed up, Pyari pressed her knee sympathetically against her sister's. Nina had not yet recovered from Pritpal's un-expected demise. It was less his absence than the awful implications of being alone to which she could not reconcile herself. They had had no children. On Pritpal's side there was no extended family for Nina to look after. For the first time in her life, Nina only had to take care of herself – and she did not need to struggle. She was comfortably well off, secure, employed. She was also desperately lonely.

'I thought Nina would have moved here to be with you by now,' Persini said. 'It doesn't make sense, staying on her own up there in Manchester. You should make her come.' She looked at Sarna. 'I'm sure you two have a lot to catch up on.'

This time Pyari's whole thigh pressed hard against Nina, who pressed hers back. It still surprised her that she had managed to resist Sarna's wishes. What a lucky escape. She had spent the three months after Pritpal's death in London. During that time, Sarna had tried to cook creamy foods to comfort Nina, but her efforts had had the opposite effect. Love could not sit easily in Nina's stomach while the evidence of her eyes and ears continued to contradict it. Sarna still gave no acknowledgement of who Nina was. If she could not manage it when Nina was so low, would she ever? The intuition that she probably wouldn't had made Nina return to Manchester.

'Yes, I wanted her to come.' It was still a sore point for Sarna. 'I need help. But the youngsters of today, they don't care about their elders. "I have my own life," they say. Nina wants to stay in Manchester. She says her job is there, her house is there. So?' Sarna threw up her arms. 'What can I do? I can't force her. My door has always been open.'

Persini couldn't leave it there and said, 'Well, it must be nice for you that Pyari is around so much now.'

'Oh yes,' Sarna replied, although the fact that her daughter had recently moved back to London hadn't really altered how often they saw each other. Pyari, like everyone else Sarna now wanted to be close to, was busy with her own life.

'I still haven't seen the house you've bought. It's not far from here, is it?' Persini asked Pyari. And then, without waiting for an answer, she went on, 'Funny that you and the boys have ended up here. And Jeevan is alone in Canada. Doesn't he mind?'

Pyari swallowed, unsure about how to counter the insinuation.

Irritation struck Sarna's features like lightning. 'Of course he doesn't mind,' she snapped. 'Pyari is here for the sake of the children, to make sure they get a good British education.' Sarna tugged at her chuni. Its chiffon folds billowed at her throat, grey as storm clouds.

Persini saw her adversary's anger and backed off.

After Persini and her family departed, Pyari and Nina began to clear up. Sarna, her insides bubbling with rage, headed upstairs for a rest, vowing, as she always did after such an event, never to have 'that kamini' in her house again.

Nina had been feeling sick and chewing vigorously at her lower lip since she'd made the 'Mother' blunder. She fully expected Sarna's wrath to rain down on her for this slip. But Sarna had just railed about Persini before going for a nap.

'Stop worrying about it,' Pyari said. 'It was just a mistake, for goodness' sake. And it's not as if you actually said anything wrong – you told the truth.'

'She must be furious with me. She probably thinks I did it on purpose.' Nina handed Pyari a plate to dry.

'Nina! Maybe *I* should do the washing.' Pyari pointed at an oily stain.

Nina put the plate back into the soapy water that filled the sink. On the wall behind her, above the oven, the wooden clock in the shape of India ticked loudly but told the wrong time: eleven o'clock. It had been hanging on that spot for years and was stained by the fumes of Sarna's cookery. She'd bought it in India during the trip to bring Nina back. Perhaps it was intended to rival the great brass clock in the living room, to signal that India had been as important a place in their lives as Africa. The UK time had been accurate when Karam had originally hung it up, but it had gradually subverted to Sarna time and was now stuck in the past.

'Mee's cooking is getting so heavy it's an effort to get it off the plate,' said Pyari, trying to liven Nina up. When this didn't work, she became serious again. 'Come on, Nina. She doesn't blame you at all. You heard the way she started moaning about Persini the minute after they left. If she's angry with anyone, it's *her*. They've had this ridiculous rivalry for years now.'

'Do you think Mother suspects that Persini knows?' Nina asked.

'No . . . I don't know.' Pyari hesitated. 'We'll probably never find out. I'm certainly not going to ask her, and I doubt she'd ever say.'

Pyari thought back to a couple of years before, when Rupi had divulged that she knew the truth about Nina's parentage – Persini had told her. Of course, Pyari had feigned shock at the news. 'I can't believe you had no idea. Everyone *else* knows,' Rupi had said. Pyari had asked who everyone was. 'Everyone . . . *everyone*.' Rupi said that all Karam's brothers and their wives knew, and most of the

Sikhs at their temple who'd come from East Africa had heard the rumours. Pyari couldn't believe that so many people knew and, to her knowledge, not one had said a word. It made Sarna's denial seem like such a farce. What old customs and codes of conduct led their Sikh community to keep silent? 'Nina must know. I'm surprised she's never told you,' Rupi had commented. Pyari had not said much during the conversation, wishing neither to deny nor confirm anything.

Later she had repeated it to Nina, who'd been more pragmatic. 'Well, everyone in India knew. The only difference here is that people don't *act* like they know – apart from Persini with her rude hints. You can't hide such things. If one person knows, you can bet a whole lot of others do too.'

'That's what I don't understand – why hasn't anyone spoken up? Especially when you consider how self-righteous Mee always is,' Pyari had wondered.

'Well, *you* haven't told her that you know. Rajan hasn't been able to acknowledge the truth to me, although it's been years since you told him. If her own flesh and blood can't confront the truth, why should anyone else? I wonder how much your pithaji knows,' Nina had said.

'*Nothing*. He doesn't know anything. *No way*. I'm sure of it. He could never be quiet about something like this, especially when Mee's always accusing him of awful things.' Pyari had been adamant. 'Sometimes I wish I could tell him, just so that he could put her in her place.'

Later that evening, Pyari went out to meet a friend and Nina ventured upstairs to check on Sarna. She was still in bed and did not mention Nina's mistake, but complained bitterly about Persini. Her stomach echoed the oral indignation, fizzing and popping as though a whole packet of Eno salts had been poured into her gut. Nina advised her to have an early night and managed to slip away. She went into the living room, keen for some relief from the wearying repetition of Sarna's laments.

'Where's Sarna?' Karam asked, looking up from the Sunday paper. His legs were stretched out and crossed at the ankles. The top three buttons of his striped brown shirt were undone, exposing a flash of white vest and scrub of grey hair at his throat.

'Still resting,' said Nina as she settled down. 'She's not feeling well.'

'Oh. Stomach?'

Nina nodded. 'Seething.'

'Tsch, tsch. That Persini . . .' Karam shook his head and folded the paper as though he'd finished with it. He removed his glasses and rubbed his eyes. The skin around them crinkled violet grey under the rough graze of his fingers. He blinked a few times as if this might bring definition to the blur before him.

'What's the forecast for tomorrow?' Nina asked, giving him something on which to focus.

'Oooh.' Karam laughed and swayed his head mysteriously. 'Depends where you are.' Like a rainmaker preparing for the rituals of his trade, he readied himself to answer Nina's question. His glasses were replaced, his collar straightened, the paper shuffled open and then rustled to the right page. Nina smiled in anticipation. For her, he *was* the rainmaker in this house, always temperate amidst the highs and lows of Sarna's unpredictable fluctuations. To be alone with him was to experience a welcome change of atmosphere.

'Tomorrow it will be one degree in Manchester and

minus two here. Very strange – you'd think it would be colder further north, especially in January. Mind you, they're predicted rain and we'll have sun. Unlike Moscow – minus nineteen! Oooh.' Karam's shoulders stiffened as though he was experiencing the freeze. 'Bangkok's the place to be right now – twenty-eight degrees.' He relaxed and shut his eyes for a moment as if the sun was shining on his face. 'No, too cloudy, actually, and humid. Sydney is better, twenty-six but clear.'

The events of the day receded as Nina followed him on the meteorological journey. She had never left England since arriving, but, thanks to Karam's fascination with the weather, she'd discovered new countries by imagining their climates. She didn't feel the forecast as intensely as Karam appeared to. Once, on a mild spring day, she fancied his breath had emerged in a mist as he said, 'Ulan Bator, minus thirty-two.' Some months back, while they were strolling on the common, he'd recounted the details of a flood in Bangladesh and had stepped cautiously around the puddles in their path as if he feared the water might gush forth and sweep him away. (Nina didn't realize he was just trying not to soil his shoes.) When she couldn't recognize the names of the locations he mentioned, she searched for them in his atlas. Slowly, her idea of the world, which had consisted of just a handful of countries, took on the shape of the globe.

Karam continued to read through the forecasts for major cities. So many places, so many variations, so much he would never experience. Floods, droughts, hurricanes – the weather affected the history of the earth and was also the unpredictable impetus shaping the lives of the earth's inhabitants. He followed its patterns the way a person who longs to fly chases the sweep of a bird with his eyes.

Karam finished his report and took off his glasses again. 'Do you want this?' He flapped the paper at Nina.

She shook her head. Fat waves of hair bounced around her face, emphasizing its gaunt angularity. She was a slow reader at her freshest and now she was too tired to concentrate on the task. Reading was still an effort for her. Sheer will had got her through her nursing textbooks, and since then she had not picked up another English book. If she now flicked through a newspaper quite regularly, it was due to Karam. 'You can't rely on the telly for all your information,' he'd said during one of her early post-marriage visits to care for Sarna. His disapproval had spurred her to pick up *The Times* whenever she was at Elm Road. Even Pritpal had approved. 'So it's not just nursing skills you practise down there – you're turning into a little scholar,' he'd teased when she'd taken up his *Daily Telegraph*. Now that Pritpal was gone, she'd started a subscription to *The Times*. Karam would have been pleased, but she never told him. They were still not close enough to make even the smallest confession to each other. And yet they had begun to slide by one another harmoniously whenever Sarna's poor health catapulted them into the same space. The reserved register of Karam's words, his quiet presence behind the newspaper, his pleasure in sharing knowledge were the ideal antidote to Nina's encounters with Sarna. In the same way, Nina's readiness to listen, her capacity for stillness, the generous smile that spread across her face as easily as butter were soothing to Karam.

He stood up and stretched, before easing off his white turban. The hair beneath it, thinning and grey, was pulled into a tiny knot. With the inch-thick red cotton band of cloth still tied around his forehead, he looked like the denizen of some ancient tribe. Nina could tell that he was looking at himself in the mirror behind her, even though he was pretending not to. He pulled off the red ribbon and tried to rub away the imprint it had left on his skin. He wondered how he might comment on Nina's unbecoming weight loss without making it sound too much like criticism. Then his stomach rumbled and solved the dilemma for him.

'Would you like dinner now?' Nina asked.

'No, no.' He was still digesting lunch. But then he changed his mind. 'Maybe a small bite – if you'll have some too?'

'Oh, I'm so full.' Nina exhaled heavily. Sarna's rich meal had left her feeling as if she couldn't eat again for at least three days. Her food was like her presence now – you could only take it in small doses. 'But I can serve you. It's no problem. There's so much left over, I'll just heat up a bit in the microwave.'

'Mmm, I don't want to eat alone. Normally Sarna is always there . . .'

'Well, I can sit with you. I'm just not hungry.' Nina stood up.

'You have to eat more.' Karam looked into the starched white turban cupped in his hands, its folds neat and timeless as the ribs on a shell. 'You have not been looking well since Pritpal passed away. There's no point coming to help Sarna and fading to nothing yourself.'

Nina chewed at her lip, embarrassed that her appearance so indiscreetly told of her grief. She could not get used to being alone. The feeling ate away at everything, including her appetite. The only thing that had kept her going since Pritpal's death was her work. It was like scaffolding holding her together while she repaired and refitted herself for new circumstances. 'OK.' Nina's green eyes darkened. 'I will join you.'

Karam nodded in approval as she headed to the kitchen to fetch their food. Her presence, once disturbing to him, had become benign. She had done more for him and Sarna than their own children. More than she would ever know.

28

Karam had always longed to see more of the world. He'd dreamed of visiting historic sites: the Pyramids, the Great Wall of China, the Colosseum, the Eiffel Tower. Since his early attempts at trailing history through the streets of London, he'd made less of an effort to get involved with momentous occasions. He had joined the crowds at Churchill's funeral and to commemorate Prince Charles and Lady Diana's wedding, but beyond that his only tie to great events had been the newspaper, radio or television. Family responsibilities, work pressures and financial constraints had prevented him from taking off at whim to witness history in the making. Indeed, the urge to do so had abated: the practical demands of middle age had eclipsed the aspirations of youth.

The receipt of his old Masterji's treatise on Sikhism had also curbed Karam's desire to hunt history. Soon after closing down Kasaka Holdings, Karam had been given Masterji's uncompleted work. In a long letter that accompanied the posthumous gift, Masterji explained that Karam was the only person he knew who might be interested in continuing his legacy. 'Perhaps you will finish what I cannot,' Masterji had hoped. Karam started to spend a lot of time reading and thinking about Sikhism. He liked the idea of working on a record of his people.

As air travel became cheaper, Karam decided he too could afford it. The first trip he made, accompanied by Sarna, was to Egypt, where he managed to get a good deal on flights and a hotel. Karam had taken his wife along because he did not know how he could go alone without her causing a commotion. The experience was enough to make him vow never to travel with her again.

It had all started to go downhill from the moment Sarna saw that their room contained a double bed. Hai Ruba, she thought, the miser got such a cheap deal that they only gave one bed. With a man like *him*, sleeping in *one* bed can only mean *one* thing . . . Sarna's suspicions were confirmed when, shortly after they went to bed on the first night, Karam's hand reached over and stroked her arm. She slapped him away as if she was swatting a fly and then turned over so that her broad back faced up to him squarely like a barrier.

The next morning, Karam awoke to the stilted whirr of the ceiling fan paddling dejectedly – and ineffectually – through hot, humid air. Wiping the dampness from his brow with the bed sheet, Karam looked at Sarna. She was still facing away from him, her black, glossy hair spread over the pillow. From beneath the lemony notes of the citronella oil she had rubbed over herself to ward off mosquitoes came a sweet whiff of caramelized onions and fennel. Leaning closer to breathe in that smell, Karam noticed the grey roots of hair at the nape of Sarna's neck and behind her ears. His fingers crept out to stroke this evidence of age – as though the grey might somehow feel different from the youthfulness he still remembered.

Sarna pretended to be asleep. She had forgotten how it felt to caress and be caressed. Only her grandsons got close to her now, giving her the short, self-conscious hugs of young teenagers. How she loved to hold them. But she was still afraid of the consequences of her embraces – too often, the closer she had held love the more painfully it had ended – so she always quickly released the boys from her grip. Now, as Karam started nuzzling her neck, Sarna rolled out of bed shouting, 'Oh ho! No!' Why did he assume he could just slip into her arms again without a word of endearment or apology? How come he still had such longings, when she no longer felt even a hint of sexual desire?

'What's wrong with you? We're still husband and wife,' he said.

'Ah ha ha! When you need cooking, cleaning or sexing I'm the wife. In between, I'm nothing. *Nothing.*'

Karam shook his head, already regretting that they'd come away together.

Sarna was seduced by the city's juice bars – their ceilings strung with bananas and bags of oranges, their counters heaving under pyramids of coconuts, sugar cane and mangoes. Every couple of hours she would duck into one of the dark fruity caves with façades tiled like a chessboard and order a fresh juice. Her sweet drink would turn sour for a moment as Karam paid and complained about being overcharged.

While Karam marvelled at the thousand minarets of Cairo's skyline, Sarna walked with her head bowed, giving a running commentary on the state of the streets, which were slimy with mud, donkey droppings and water leaking from burst mains. 'Hai, so dirty. What a place.

Such a stink!' She covered her nose with her chuni.

'You're acting like you've lived in England all your life. Think of Nairobi or Kampala – think of *Delhi*,' Karam said.

'This is *worse*. Hai Ram, I'm going to faint. Hai, juice, juice!'

She seemed to have no curiosity for new experiences. 'But we went *that* way before,' she'd say, pointing in the opposite direction, if Karam took a different route from the hotel when they went sightseeing.

'Yes, I know, but it's nice to try another way and maybe see something else, discover something new.'

If they got lost, she blamed Karam.

'Look, I don't know these streets. I've never been here before!' He waved the map at her.

'You've got no sense of direction, that's the problem. Hai Ruba! It's too hot. I need mango juice.' Sarna fanned herself with her hand.

The days passed in a haze of bickering.

At night, in their hotel room, Karam no longer dared to touch his wife. She would fall into bed complaining that her feet were aching, her back was breaking and her stomach was groaning. No wonder, Karam thought, with all the fruit juice she'd consumed. He stayed up, trying to read a history of ancient Egypt, but his thoughts kept straying to Sarna. He recalled the time when they had found comfort and delight in each other's arms. Now he slept right beside her, but kept his thoughts, feelings and hands to himself. There was so much he wanted to say that could never be said. Eventually he fell asleep to the lullaby of indigestion gurgled by Sarna's stomach.

Yet Cairo did unexpectedly throw the couple closer together. As they walked along the Muski, one of the narrow, congested streets of the city, Sarna kept crying out:

'Ouch! ... Hai! ... Oh!' At first Karam thought these sounds were melodramatic complaints that would soon be followed by requests for more expensive beverages. When he realized Sarna was being pinched and prodded by invisible Egyptian fingers, he was outraged. 'Eh! Get away! Stop it!' he'd shout, waving his hands and pressing up against her after an attack. He'd scan passers-by for the culprit and glare at all the men who were staring at Sarna. She liked the protectiveness of his stance – strong, comforting and without sexual intention. A few times she pretended to have been pinched just to have him fuss over her. Karam started walking right behind or beside her to avert wandering hands. Slightly intoxicated by the apple-tobacco smell of sheeshas pervading the thick air of the streets, he had to resist the urge to tweak her flesh himself. He could see what other men found attractive. Extra fat had staved off some of the wrinkling and sagging that comes with age and had, instead, enhanced all Sarna's curves. She was superbly voluptuous, her breasts and bottom the more impressive for their bigness. Karam allowed himself to enjoy the frequent bumping of their bodies as they dodged donkey carts or were jostled by the crowd. So they moved in an ephemeral dance of harmony whose music would not outlast the moment.

Sarna got some pleasure from the city's souks, with their towers of vegetables and baskets of pulses. She noticed the old-fashioned lead hexagons used for weighing – like the ones used in the markets of her youth. She was enchanted by the array of dates that sat on vast copper platters – from pale-yellow, dry little nuggets to fat, mahogany-coloured, sticky ones. As she pored over the wares and haggled with vendors using broken English and sign language, Karam stood guard like a Beefeater. Sarna stole glances at him and felt proud of his appearance. Even Cairo's humidity couldn't dampen the crispness of his white shirt or the neat crease of his trousers. She found herself admiring the sharp folds of his turban. She preferred it to the little caps or bulky turbans worn by the Islamic men. All her hard work ironing and starching his clothes was worth it, after all.

In the Souk al-Attarin, Sarna had her only half-hour of pure enjoyment. She moved with delighted, deep inhalations through the stalls of spices, incense, herbal cures and perfume. Though she could not read the Arabic signs indicating which spice was which, she had no trouble sniffing her way through the stocks. The pungency of the cinnamon made her want to moan, the freshness of the cumin made her long to cook. As the vendor packed up everything she'd chosen, Sarna tugged at Karam's sleeve and asked him to pay.

'So much? I'm not a bank, you know. And how will we take all this back? What if we get stopped at Customs?' His nose twitched as he surveyed the kilos of spices she'd selected.

'Ouch!' Sarna suddenly shrieked and flattened herself against him.

'Oi!' He reached out to push away the men crowding around her and his arms unwittingly encircled her for a moment. Their hearts flip-flopped in tune to the slapping slippers of passers-by. Embarrassed, Sarna moved away and pulled her rust-coloured cotton chuni over her head. The vendor looked at them disapprovingly. Karam paid him quickly and picked up Sarna's purchases, while mumbling about extortion.

Their last day was spent at Giza. They approached the pyramids in the glare of the midday sun. Karam, stunned by the grandeur of the site, hardly noticed the heat. But Sarna quickly drew his attention to it. 'Hai, you could at least have brought me when the shade was on this side. They don't even sell juice here.' She held her arms up as a shield against the sun, despite the fact that she was wearing sunglasses and a hat.

Karam ignored her and kept walking. All of a sudden he heard a thud. Turning, he saw Sarna sinking to her knees in the sand. The gesture seemed fitting to him, an appropriate act of devotion in response to the majesty of the pyramids. Sarna, however, was not awestruck but sunstruck. Dizzy and tearful, she lay on the ground begging Karam to take her home.

'I'm thirsty! Just take me back. Take me to London, to Elm Road. Take me back to my kitchen. I want to go home.'

'But . . .' Karam turned to look at the great triangles of stone standing imperiously behind him. 'We're here now. Can't we just go a bit closer?'

'No! Take me home.' Sarna writhed in the sand, sending waves of warm gold over Karam's shoes.

Onlookers wearing dishdashes and disingenuous grins pressed around. 'Taxi? Taxi? . . . Water? . . . Umbrella?'

Karam tried to send the men away. 'It's OK. No problem. You go.' He flicked a hand at them. They did not budge. Karam helped Sarna up. Her hair and clothes were covered with sand, which glinted like glitter in the sun. She could have been an incarnation of the goddess Sehkmet rising from the desert. Together she and Karam brushed off the shimmering aura. He steered her to face the pyramids, as if the sight of them might persuade her to stay. 'It's not far. We can go slowly. I'll help you. Please . . . *try*.'

Sarna closed her eyes and sagged towards the ground again. 'Hai . . . hai . . .'

Karam steadied her and, after a longing last glance at the wonder he was about to miss out on, steered her towards the bus stop. When they got back to the hotel he realized that, somewhere along the way, he had also managed to lose his camera. The only evidence of the trip was the sand in his shoes.

They returned to London thoroughly fed up with each other. Karam cut Sarna out of his future itinerary and she reciprocated by cutting him out of her vocabulary. She stopped referring to him as 'Jee', and when talking to other people she either referred to Karam as 'he' or bitingly called him 'the father'. He noticed the change, but did not comment. He hoped it was just a phase. He thought about how the years had altered her way of addressing him. Long ago, in direct proportion to the growth of her love, she had endearingly abridged his name from Sardharji to Dharji to Jee. Perhaps it was fitting, now love had seemingly ended, that he be reduced to namelessness.

Part Three

Part Three

29

Oskar leaned on the railings outside the Lowry at Salford Quays and looked at the Manchester Ship Canal. It was a Sunday afternoon in June. The sky was bright blue but streaked with a delicate veil of white, as though someone up there was languorously smoking a cigarette.

The four-day stubble that gave Oskar's face the illusion of toughness was tempered by a smile. His silvery hair was attractively dishevelled and curled softly over his small ears. His grey eyes, narrowly set, squinted across the North Bay, trying to see if any new development was being done there. He took a few steps back to get a better view.

'Ouch!' he heard a second later. He had stepped on someone's foot. Turning, he saw a small woman in a coffee-coloured cotton shalwar kameez, bent over and rubbing the exposed toes in her brown sandals. For an instant he thought she was bleeding, but then he realized it was polish on her toenails: glossy maroon with a hint of pink. If desire had a colour – that would be it.

'I'm sorry.' He hovered over her, unsure what to do.

''t's OK.' Her voice was muffled. Then she looked up and he saw the green eyes: two dark pools of malachite. A flash of contradictions met in their gaze – recognition and ignorance, pleasure and shame, warmth and the cold chill of anxiety.

Oskar wished he'd shaved. There was no way she'd recognize him. He spoke, and as he formed the words he realized she was saying exactly the same ones, 'I should have looked where I was going—'

They broke off abruptly and stared at each other. Her skin was beautiful and ever so gently creased, like the delicate wrinkled membrane that forms on heated milk. He smiled. She sort of half smiled back and then looked away shyly. He was so manly. That wasn't how she remembered him. But then, she wasn't sure *how* she remembered him. No past picture resurfaced to counter the intense physical presence of him now. Nina was embarrassed by the sudden gallop of her heart. She looked down and twiddled her still-smarting big toe.

She doesn't recognize me, he thought. Age had not been so kind to him. It had done its work with the rushed hand of an unskilled carpenter who arrives late for a job and is in a hurry to be off again. 'Nina?' It was like a test question.

'Hello, Oskar.' Her eyes flashed over him, noting his eyebrows. Bold as the stripes on a badger, but with a silver sheen, as though they'd been glossed over with spray paint. She chewed her lip and wondered how to behave. She had once been married to this man.

She remembers! He wanted to laugh. There was so much to tell, so much to ask. His lips twitched in their eagerness to speak. 'Do you live here?'

'I've lived here for years.' She smiled and her glance skimmed his features again, picking out the eyes which matched the colour of his brows, just as the sea follows the sky's dress code. 'Since my marriage – I mean,' she flushed, 'my second marriage.'

'You're married?'

'I was.' She pretended to look for something in her bag. He was so close she could smell him. She wanted to slap herself for liking the smell. 'I . . . my husband – Pritpal – he passed away.'

'Oh. I'm sorry.' He lowered his head and Nina saw how the sides of his nose extended from the narrow bridge like the wings of a moth in mid-flight. She was piecing Oskar together bit by bit and the impression was awakening a desire she had felt many years before. The wish to say thank you.

'Long time go. He had a heart-t-tack.'

Oskar loved the inflexions of her speech. He wanted to pluck the sounds off her like grapes and pop their plumpness in his own mouth.

'He liked it here.' She gestured at the quays. 'It's different now. Used to be so quiet, nothing, no one round.'

Oskar nodded. He knew what she meant. He had seen the quays in their heyday when his father worked at the docks. He had seen them decline into wasteland and now he was witnessing their regeneration.

'He liked water.' She turned to face the canal. 'We used to come here and walk.' She didn't know where all this talk about Pritpal was coming from. She had never said much to anyone except Pyari about him. Yet it felt strangely natural opening up to Oskar. 'Now I come all on my lone, sometimes. Just to think.'

He stepped forward and joined her at the railing. 'I love the water too.' He reached into the pocket of his jeans and felt for the malachite marble he carried everywhere. He had seen it while travelling in Kenya years ago. He'd bought it immediately, certain it was the colour of her eyes. He resisted the urge to take it out now and match it to her irises.

His closeness made Nina's heart bolt again. She clutched at the railing to steady herself. She told herself to say goodbye and was a little surprised to find herself asking, 'Do *you* live here?'

'I grew up here.' Why didn't she look at him? 'And I moved back about two years ago.'

He didn't know why he'd returned. Manchester was a bleak city, the Ship Canal its only great feature. Yet something had pulled him back to his old home town and now, seeing Nina, he understood what it was.

They watched the water for a while in silence. Both were thinking about the coincidence of their meeting, wondering what it meant, where it might lead.

'I can't believe we've met.' Nina dared to look at him for a few seconds. And she realized what had changed his face so much. The hairline had receded: a headland of grey curls jutted into his forehead flanked by two deep bays. 'I never thought I'd see you again.'

'I can't believe you recognized me,' he said.

'Of course I recognized you.' Her eyes met, and held, his. 'I'm here – in this country, living this life, standing here – thanks to you. How could I forget *you*?'

30

Money remained one of the biggest issues of contention between Karam and Sarna. Rajan was the only one who did not tolerate either one's complaints on this subject. 'You're better off than most people, Dad. You're just not used to spending money.'

Of course, Karam disagreed with this, but he didn't argue. He knew that Rajan had a different way of thinking. Sarna, who wasn't practised in biting her tongue, often ended up rowing with her son. Taking him into the kitchen after he had come round for dinner one Friday night, she turned up the radio and, to background noise of Sunrise Radio's endless ads, launched into one of her diatribes.

'I'm fed up. Enough is enough.' The words whistled through the gap between her two front teeth. 'Your pithaji's never given me a penny. He's so mean, *so mean*. Haven't you ever wondered how I've survived all these years? Do you think everything can come from the weekly rent of one tenant? All the food, my clothes, Pyari's and Nina's weddings, everything you wanted as children – you don't know how I've managed. I'm fed up to *here*,' she sliced her hand across her forehead as if in salute, 'and he's planning another trip abroad. At his age!'

Actually, Rajan had a faint idea of how his mother had managed, but he wasn't inclined to explore the issue. 'Well, luckily you also have your pension.' He glanced at the wooden India clock on the wall and frowned. 'Is that the time?'

'No, that is.' Sarna pointed to the electric green digits flashing 9:53 on the microwave.

'So what's this doing?' Rajan reached over the oven towards the clock, which claimed it was half past eight.

'Leave it.' Sarna pulled at his shirt.

'I'll put it back, just let me reset—'

'No. Don't mess around. It's the right time for me,' Sarna said. 'If you want to be helpful, listen to what I'm saying.'

The right time for me. Rajan shook his head. She really was in another time zone.

'Do you know how much food costs? I buy every bite we eat in this house – and *he* has no small appetite, I tell you. But you have no idea how I suffer. No one knows what I've gone through, what sacrifices I've made.' Sarna began transferring dinner leftovers into empty ice-cream tubs, jam jars and plastic bags.

Rajan decided to evade her melodramatic appeals. 'Don't forget that Dad pays all the bills, Mum. He pays for the maintenance of the house and the upkeep of his car—'

'*Car?*' Sarna dropped a spoon back into the dhal with a splat. 'What have I to do with that car? It can catch fire for all I care. He gives it more attention than he gives me. The way he washes it twice a week and polishes—'

'Oh, be reasonable, Mum. I—'

'You have no idea. *No idea*,' Sarna cut in again as she

knotted a bag of saag. It looked like the algae Rajan had collected at school for science experiments.

'You're always blaming and accusing,' Rajan said. 'Why don't you just get down to the real issue?'

'What? What real issue?'

'Whatever it is that's troubling you,' Rajan said cagily.

'*You* are troubling me.' She walked over to the freezer and shoved in two warm fat bundles of food. 'You have an answer for everything and you never listen. Talking to your sister is no better, I might as well speak to a wall. Who can I turn to? Who do I have?' Her voice broke. 'No one. I'm alone. Suffering alone.'

Rajan took the onset of tears as a cue to leave. 'Well, I won't trouble you any more. I was about to go anyway.' He made a move towards the door.

Sarna pressed the corner of her chuni to her eyes and tossed her head at him indifferently.

'You shouldn't get so upset, Mum. It's not necessary.' Rajan spoke gently in an attempt at reconciliation.

Sarna glared at him with renewed vigour. 'You wait!' She wagged her finger. 'Just you wait!' Then she trooped past him out of the kitchen and Rajan heard her climbing up the stairs. He returned to the living room determined not to wait, but to say his goodbyes and go.

'How can you just walk away?' Pyari asked almost enviously. She'd heard Sarna's angry stomping and guessed there had been an argument.

'I don't know. But staying doesn't make any difference.'

'No, but how can you leave knowing people are still hurt or angry?'

Rajan shrugged. 'Look, it's not me that starts the god-damn arguments. I come to see Mum and Dad, hoping for a civilized catch-up, and instead I get caught in some irresolvable debate. Sometimes the best way to preserve everyone's feelings is by leaving.'

'I don't know why you have to rise to the bait anyway,' Pyari remarked.

'So should I just sit there quietly like you?' He headed to the door. 'OK, I'm off,' he said. 'Dad, I'm going,' he called out more loudly to get his father's attention. Karam was watching his grandsons play a game of chess. He got up to say goodbye. 'Off already, huh? Well, I hope it won't be months before we see you again.'

'No, I'll be in touch soon. I'll phone.' Rajan could hear Sarna thumping on the stairs again and was keen to leave before she got down.

Too late.

His mother flounced in, laden with bulging plastic bags.

'So I'm the stingy one!' She waved the bags excitedly in the air. There must have been at least half a dozen in each hand.

The family stared in bewilderment. Amar and Arjun looked up from their game, distracted by the rustling, hustling spectacle of their grandmother.

'Would a stingy person spend this much on her family?' She held up the bags as if their fullness reflected the voluptuousness of her own generosity. 'Would a stingy mother go to any lengths to give her children the best? You have no idea what I've done for you. See for yourselves! See for yourselves what I am!' She flung the bags into the air. They flew up like white balloons, some plain and anonymous, others bearing the names of Sarna's preferred shops – Tesco, Marks & Spencer, Asda. As they floated towards the floor, the bags expelled their contents: hundreds and hundreds of receipts flew out and rained

406

down on the family. Dumbstruck, they gawped as Sarna's alleged munificence showered upon them. 'See!' Sarna, impressed by her own show, was triumphant. 'Try adding *that* up.'

Receipts continued to fall. They brushed past the noses of those present, tickled the tips of their ears, settled on their hair and shoulders and teased their eyes with fleeting glimpses of faded numbers. Amar and Arjun, wide-eyed, gazed in perplexed wonder at the paper storm their grandmother had unleashed. Pyari looked away, despairing that her sons were being exposed to this display. Rajan was rendered momentarily speechless. Each time he thought he'd seen the worst of his mother she managed to surprise him by doing something even more disgraceful. Karam was almost impressed by the barrage of bills and all the payments they implied, but the feeling was quickly overridden by dismay at his wife's ugly ostentation. He too was an assiduous keeper of financial records – but this? He had a shelf full of files in which decades of bank statements and years of credit-card bills were meticulously stored away – but this?

'My goodness. You really are something else.' Karam broke the silence.

'You don't know what I am,' Sarna retorted. 'None of you knows. See here, see here,' she gestured at the rug of receipts now covering the floor. '*This is all me.*' As though she was the sum of all the parts she'd ever paid for. 'Everything I've bought is accounted for here: food, clothes, air fares, weddings . . . And all of it done without a penny from *him.*'

'And just where did you get all the cash if it wasn't from Dad?' Rajan found his voice.

'Yes, *where?*' Karam demanded.

'Where-share – what does anyone care? I did what I had to because *he* was unfair.' Sarna pointed at Karam. 'I knew one day I would prove how *mean* he is.'

'And what a great way to do it, Mum.' Rajan kicked up some receipts. 'How interesting that the evidence you use to pit against Dad is nothing but a testament of your own stinginess.'

'Don't use that word for me!' Sarna shouted. 'I have given up everything. I have given up *myself* for all of you!'

'Why do you do this?' Rajan asked. 'What do you want from us? You want gratitude? Of course we're grateful. But you can't look to us to make up for whatever's missing in you. We're just your kids, you know, we're not the answer to your problems.'

'No, you're not the answer.' The tears started. '*You* are the problem. *You are the problem.*'

'Fine then. I'll go and then there won't be a problem any more.' He walked towards the door, a crackle of paper under each step.

'Oh Raj, don't leave,' Pyari said.

'You can't go now,' Karam agreed.

'Why not? I won't be bullied into feeling bad,' Rajan said. 'You should walk out too. This is no way for anyone to be treated.'

'Walk out! This isn't a factory – it's a family,' Karam said.

Well, it feels more like a factory, Rajan wanted to reply. It feels like a little production house of secrets and lies. But he shrugged his shoulders and left.

Sarna wept furiously while Pyari, Karam and the boys collected and rebagged the mess of receipts. For every three bags the others filled, Karam managed only one. He read each receipt carefully before putting it away, as if by reviewing his wife's past spending he might work out how things had gone so wrong between them. But the retail record told him no more than what he already sensed – that their past was spent. And all they could do for the present was endure.

31

From the day of their meeting at Salford Quays, Nina and Oskar quickly became inseparable. He was happy to arrange himself around her schedule at Trafford General Hospital. They spent hours that summer in Piccadilly Gardens, talking and lounging on the wide benches. Nina loved being there in the daytime, when it was full of people and children pulled off their shoes to skip in the fountains. Oskar preferred it when the stone square was less crowded and was bathed in the purple light of early evening. He looked forward to the moment when subdued lime-tinged lights came on under the benches and trees, making the place feel magical.

In the beginning they couldn't go to Nina's house in case someone she knew saw them together. 'People will talk,' she said. 'You know how people are, they always think the worse.' She wouldn't go to his flat either, because that also seemed inappropriate. 'Sorry,' she'd say as they took refuge in the City Art Gallery café or some other coffee shop. 'It's just not what women should do. Is it?' Should do, shouldn't do – these were the concerns that ruled her actions. She was always conscientious about doing the 'right' thing – what other people would approve of. But sometimes even a hundred rights can't undo a wrong, and Nina could never rid herself of the feeling that she was an error: an irrevocable mistake.

She told Oskar everything about her past. He listened as no one had before – impartially and without interrupting. Even to Pyari, who was her closest confidante, Nina had been unable to articulate the deepening schism between her and Sarna, because Pyari, for all her sympathy, was the acknowledged daughter. Oskar was always on Nina's side. She was surprised by how much he knew about the circumstances of her life and the places she mentioned. 'I've been there,' he said. Amritsar, Lahore, Delhi, Nairobi, Kampala – he had travelled to all these cities because they were somehow connected to her. 'After I left Elm Road, I went abroad. I had spent so long just hearing about other people's lives. I wanted to go and see things for myself.' Though even in this quest for independent experience he had followed the lines of another story. He had traced the passages of Nina's destiny, which was so bound up with her mother's. They were a part of him now, like the tracks of his own veins. 'I fell in love with you while we were married.' He felt the absurdity of the statement.

A pink chrysanthemum appeared on the side of Nina's neck.

'With the way you looked, your unassuming gorgeousness, your eyes.' He paused as the chrysanthemums continued to flower. One by one, the buds unfurled along her throat and cheeks. 'Marrying you helped me slip out of my old ways.' He explained how he'd started to write and why he had left so abruptly. Since then he had travelled the world, written guides and articles, but had remained essentially unfulfilled. 'In all my journeys I was looking for you, trying to get to know you better – even though I thought I could never have you.'

Nina, radiant in her bouquet of feeling, looked down. A tear splashed on to the hands folded in her lap. No one had ever spoken to her this way. Not even Pritpal, who had been so kind and cared for her so well. She felt a piercing within – at that spot where the ribs join up, just below the breast. It was the most exquisite ache she had ever known.

I've scared her, Oskar thought, looking at her drooping head. He wanted to kiss the nape of her neck, where the top vertebrae had come to protrude gently because of her bad posture. He shouldn't have declared himself so soon – they had met again only two weeks ago.

Another tear plopped on to her hands. It was so big he heard it. 'I'm sorry, Nina. I . . . I didn't meant to upset you. I . . .'

She shook her head to halt his apology and more tears jolted out of her eyes. 'Don't be sorry.'

He reached for her hand, and she did not resist. He pressed the damp fingers to his lips and tasted her sadness: salty soya sauce. 'I love you,' he said.

She wondered why. What was there to love? She was illegitimate, in her forties and had a terrible haircut. What did he love? And yet the words felt like a gift. She reached into her bulky black handbag for a tissue, opening zip after zip on pocket after pocket before she finally found one. She wiped her eyes and wondered if the buzz in her head was the sound of happiness. She had something to say too. For years it had resided within her, the way a gemstone is held in the metal fingers of a solitaire ring. 'Thank you.' She had never imagined she'd be able to bring that precious gratitude to light and place it before her benefactor. 'For marrying me. I was able to have a good life because of what you did.'

Oskar put a hand into the pocket of his shorts. Nina glanced at his hairy legs. She had never known a man who wore shorts. Together with his thin T-shirt, they gave her the impression that he was almost naked by her side. The fading blossoms on her face flashed scarlet for an instant as she moved away. An inch.

'Look.' He opened his hand and a green marble rolled in his palm. She understood what it meant. 'I've had it for twenty years. I take it everywhere,' he said. He had selected this stone from the range of seven hundred and sixty-four that had been presented to him. She picked up the warm malachite ball and caressed it with her fingers. It *was* the colour of her eyes – and of something else. 'Mother has earrings of this stone – also from Kenya. She says they are her favourites, but she never wears them. Just keeps them on her dressing table to look at every day.'

'So both of us want a piece of you near us, always.'

'She doesn't want me.' Nina tapped her small, sharp nose with the marble. 'She never wanted me.'

'She wanted you, she just couldn't have you.' He stroked her cheek. I want you, can I have you?

'Three-eyed monster!' She leaned her head to one side, pulled a face and held the marble at her forehead. She used such tricks in the hospital to distract sick children from unpleasantness. Now it was herself she diverted from the disagreeable.

Oskar laughed in surprise. Nina smiled and handed back the marble.

'I'm hungary,' she said, as if it was the country. 'Let's get something to eat.'

They went for a pizza and Nina ordered hers with extra

chilli and then asked for Tabasco as well. 'Nina, do you know chillies are the most addictive spice? The more you eat, the more you need. You should start cutting down.' Oskar was astonished by how much heat she could take. They had eaten just a few meals together, but she'd invariably asked for extra chilli on her food.

'Even Pritpal thought I ate too much chilli.' Nina giggled. She only liked food that could sear her tongue and make her ears smoke. Oskar watched in amazement as she ate her Tabasco-drenched pizza without shooting off her seat.

Later, when they kissed, his mouth blazed from the residue of chilli in hers. She kissed his eyes and left them smarting. He blinked away the tears. 'I'm all for burning passion, Nina, but at this rate I'll soon be a pile of ashes.' Nina hid her face in her hands and laughed.

32

'Hai . . . hai. Nina . . . Nina?'

Nina stirred as the plea for help penetrated her sleep. Still groggy, she rose from her makeshift bed on the floor and fumbled for the light switch. Even before the light flashed on, she had ascertained the reason for Sarna's call: a heavy iron-like Mushq filled her nostrils. Sarna had had another accident.

In the miraculously efficient and unobtrusive manner of the best nurses, Nina managed to strip the dirty sheet from the bed and half fix a clean one in place while Sarna was still lying down. Nina couldn't help noticing, again, how the linen here felt so worn and flimsy compared to the stiff, crisp sheets at the hospital where she worked. Sarna's old, yellowed sheets slipped and fluttered across the mattress, refusing efforts to tuck and fold them. Just like their owner, Nina thought, trying to flatten out some creases, they'd only fit as suited them.

'Mother, you'll have to sit up for a second while I finish the bed,' Nina whispered.

'Aaahhh,' Sarna groaned weakly.

'Just for a second. Come on, I'll help you.' She put her arms around Sarna's torso to assist her.

'I can't sit. I can't sit.' Sarna dreaded the thought of putting any weight on her groin, which was still pulsing painfully from the operation she'd had almost a week ago.

'OK, OK! Just get up and lean the other way so I can adjust the sheet.' Nina manoeuvred her mother gently, and within seconds she had Sarna lying down the right way again.

Sarna closed her eyes and exhaled with relief. Nina suddenly felt exhausted. The whole procedure could not have taken more than ten minutes, but it seemed to have used up her last reserves of strength. Sinking down to the tumble of duvets and blankets that served as her bed on the floor, she wondered, Why am I here again? Since Pritpal's death, she'd been helping Sarna out more than ever. Yet every time she'd come to support her, through sickness or health, she'd gone away feeling disappointed because Sarna never reciprocated in the only way that mattered: she'd never been moved to say 'Thank you, my child.' Instead, she took Nina for granted. She'd even suggested that Nina ought to be glad of the chance to help. 'Poor Nina, no husband, no children – no one has any need for you. It's good that you can still come to me sometimes and feel useful, no? Still feel like family, huh?'

Sarna had just undergone surgery for one of her 'severe sensitivities'. She had been suffering from the condition for years – 'since my first child', she maintained. Whether, in her own mind, that first child was Nina or Phoolwati or Pyari would never be clear, but Nina certainly felt implicated by the assertion. She knew the consequences of poor birthing practices and it upset her to think of the primitive, clandestine circumstances in which Sarna might have given birth to her. She imagined a forced delivery in

416

which she was impatiently and inexpertly wrenched from Sarna's womb. She guessed that Sarna, out of fear and shame, had not said a word to anyone about the physical consequences of that labour.

Nina may have had only a vague impression of what caused Sarna's problem, but she was pretty well informed about its effects. Over the years, she was the only person with whom Sarna shared the gruesome details of her ailment. These mishaps were altogether different from the mischance of farting in public – for Sarna had long become an expert at polluting without imputing: she could let off a stink without a blink. The silence of her olfactory emissions made Sarna feel relatively safe in any environment. Her victims might become obliged to hold their breath or run from the room, but Sarna was always secure in her feigned oblivion of the Mushq, because the Law of Farting indisputably dictates that 'he who smelt it dealt it'. But the humiliations Sarna had suffered as a result of the other 'sensitivities' were less easy for her to ignore.

'It's not your fault, Mother. It's a sickness many women have – for some it's more serious than others,' Nina had often reassured Sarna. But Sarna preferred to see the condition as further confirmation that she had been singled out to endure more than other women. 'No one can have it worse than me. Sometimes I wonder if all my organs are going to give up on me. Heart, lungs, kidneys? Who knows what will go next.' Nina had felt like asking, What about the truth? Any chance that could come next? She didn't consider that all Sarna's physical problems might be an expression of truth. The body is evidence. Whatever yarns the mind spins, the body can always betray.

* * *

Seated on the floor of the bedroom that night, Nina could not muster any good feeling towards Sarna. She felt angry that she was still trying to ingratiate herself with her own mother. Why? She'd survived a lifetime without a mother, what difference would it make now to have the acknowledgement of the troubled woman on the bed?

Sarna let out a moan and the deep crease between her brows deepened. Nina looked at her watch. It was almost six a.m. The early sun was rising. It slunk through the gap in the curtains and teased the walls with whispers of yellow.

'You'll have to wait at least another hour before taking more painkillers,' Nina said.

'Don't play the professional with me,' Sarna said. 'One hour makes no difference.'

'It does.'

'Ah, you just want me to suffer!'

Nina was familiar with such emotional blackmail. Usually she ignored it, but just then the tactic enraged her. She sprang up from the floor and stood over her mother. 'How can you say that? Do you really think I'm here to make you feel bad? Is that why you beg me to come and help you time after time – so that you can get worse under my care?'

Surprised by this uncharacteristically bold reaction, Sarna raised a hand to urge restraint.

'Do I sleep at the foot of your bed, on the hard floor, night after night because I want you to suffer? Do I clean up your blood and shit because I want you to suffer? Do I bathe you and dress you and feed you because I want you to suffer?'

'Bas! Be quiet.' The vibrations of Nina's voice were

resonating in Sarna's wound: every word felt like a stab.

'The way I look after you now – that's how a mother takes care of her child,' Nina said.

Sarna grimaced. It was difficult to tell whether she was about to shout or burst into tears. 'Enough. This is no way to speak,' she spluttered.

Nina fell to her knees beside the bed and threw her head into her hands. She looked like a desperate petitioner in a pew, struggling to strike a final bargain with the Almighty. 'Is this all I'm good for? Cleaning up after you? All my life I've had just poor scraps of you. Am I only worthy of your leftovers? Your old, weak body to nurse? Your hard, shrivelled heart to love? Do I only deserve your mean, angry words?'

Sarna's expression remained tortured.

'Mother, why won't you say I'm your daughter? Please? Why can't you just say it? Please, *please*.'

Sarna closed her eyes; tears streamed from under their lids.

'That's all I've ever wanted to hear. Please, say it just once. Let me be what I am for one moment. Let me know what it feels like to have a mother – just for a minute. That's all I need.'

Sarna opened her eyes and looked straight at her. Through a haze of agony, fatigue and misery she whispered, 'Yes, beti. Yes, you are my daughter.'

The world didn't move at the announcement. Joy didn't burst Nina's heart, she didn't feel light enough to fly. Instead, everything seemed to fall still. The curtains, which had been shivering slightly in the breeze from the open window, stopped moving. And the two women, who had spent a lifetime yearning, in their own way, for reconciliation, became frozen in time as well. Neither reached out to touch or hold the other. Instead, both bowed their heads and wept, hugging themselves in their own sadness. Speaking the truth, however much effort it demands, is not enough to make a difference. Change only comes about through living the truth.

In the hours that followed, Sarna claimed that her pain was worsening. It was unclear whether she was more troubled by the after-effects of the operation or the confession. Eventually the doctor had to be called to administer a shot of morphine.

'I don't know what that Dr Jasgul injected Mother with, but it didn't just wipe out the pain – it erased her memory as well,' Nina would later tell Oskar when she returned to Manchester. He suggested that the doctor might have given Sarna memoryphine.

While Sarna recovered, mother and daughter did not speak of what had passed between them. Then, one night before leaving London, Nina raised the subject again. She felt nervous broaching the issue, but was compelled to have the disclosure witnessed by someone else. There was something too dreamlike about that brief exchange between her and Sarna in the early hours of the morning. Nina believed that if the truth could be confirmed in front of Pyari, it would feel more real. She decided to propose this to her mother. She didn't realize even an admission to the whole world can't make motherhood an actuality. Relationships are determined by what is invested in them, not by the words used to define them.

'Mother, I . . . I want you to tell Pyari about me,' Nina said. 'Just her, no one else. Please will you do that? Please?'

Sarna, propped up by several pillows in mismatched cases, looked blankly at her daughter.

'About me being your daughter.'

'What rubbish are you talking?'

Nina took a step back from the bed. 'What . . . what you said to me the other night. That I'm your daughter.'

'Hai! May you fade to nothing!' Sarna's hand went to her temple. 'What a notion! Don't you go repeating such nonsense elsewhere.'

'But . . . but you said it. You admitted . . .' Nina faltered as Sarna's eyes flashed angrily.

'Why would I say that? It's not true.'

Nina stared, confounded.

'I don't know where you got such an idea. Watch what you say, Nina, or you'll shame us all.' Sarna tried to sit up, but winced in pain and resigned herself to remaining semi-reclined.

'I don't understand,' Nina started. 'You *know* – and then you actually *told* me—'

'*You* don't understand! Huh!' Sarna interrupted. 'Hai Ruba, *I* don't understand.' She pressed a palm to her breast. 'You've always been my sister, and now you want to be my daughter. I know I've always treated you like one, and sometimes I wish you *were* – you're such a good girl. Vaheguru knows you even call me Mother, but simply saying something doesn't make it a fact.'

Nina staggered back and fell against the wall for support.

'You can't change ancestry. You can't just jump from one branch to another on the family tree,' Sarna went on.

'Mother.' Nina's voice was hoarse. She felt as though she was being picked apart, segment by segment, like a tangerine.

'Enough of this wishful thinking!' Sarna turned her face away from the tearful Nina. 'I don't want to hear it again. I'm a sick woman. I can't cope with your strange ideas. I'm very upset, Nina. Just stop now, please *stop*.'

Nina left the next day, vowing she'd never return. Sarna's behaviour over the following months only served to reinforce this determination. As she recovered physically, Sarna seemed intent on recovering the moral high ground she'd lost the night she'd succumbed to Nina. The whole family noticed a change in her attitude. She appeared more confident and self-righteous than ever, and she brazenly praised herself at every opportunity.

To Nina, she portrayed herself as a woman who was not – indeed, could not be – the mother of an unacknowledged child. Once she phoned Nina after a story about an abandoned baby hit the headlines. 'Did you hear about it? So terrible. Horrible, just horrible. How could a mother do such a thing? How can any woman abandon her own child? It's inhuman. Hai Ruba, I can't bear it.' At other times she'd call up in tears, having seen a report about children orphaned because of war or AIDS or some other preventable disaster. 'Hai, Nina, hai,' she'd weep down the line. 'My heart is breaking for all these children who are left completely alone in the world. Such an injustice. Such a shame. Hai Ruba, where are You? Oh, where is God, I ask? This world is too cruel.' Sarna also let Nina know that she was sponsoring an orphan in Africa and sending money to UNICEF. 'I must do my bit, I must help where I can. It is a mother's duty to help a child in need – whether it is her own child or another's.'

Nina was deeply hurt by this hypocrisy. For the first time, she developed real coldness towards Sarna. 'I won't be her little sick-time slave,' she often told Oskar, as if repeating the intention would give her the courage to follow it through.

A small test of her willpower came four months after the night of the confession, when Sarna came down with food poisoning. 'Goodness knows what has caused the problem. It's only her own food she's been eating. Can you come and help for a few days?' Karam phoned to ask. After hours of agonizing, Nina rang back and excused herself, saying she couldn't get the time off work at such short notice. Weeks of guilt followed. Nina had trouble sleeping because she felt so bad. Sarna seemed to sense she'd been snubbed and said as much in endless self-pitying phone monologues.

Keeping her distance from Sarna was not a real solution, and Nina knew it. But she felt compelled to make her pain heard in the only way she knew how – by withholding her love. But those who love truly cannot hide it. Familial love, even when it is tried and tested, let down and unreciprocated, is perhaps the most abiding of all love, because it is bound so inextricably with obligation, nostalgia and identity. That does not mean this love is always adequately expressed. Too often, it is not. But time can reveal its constancy.

33

Rajan broke the news to his parents that Pyari was getting divorced.

'Hai! Hai Ruba, no.' Sarna collapsed on to their new three-seater leather sofa, as if she'd been dealt a physical blow.

Simultaneously, Karam shot up as though something had exploded under him. His turban was temporarily pushed up at the back, so that it didn't cover his head but sat atop it like a chef's hat, trembling precariously above his ears as if it too had been shaken.

'I know this must be hard for you, but just remember it's even harder for Pyari. She needs our support and understanding. We have to be strong for her,' Rajan said.

'But . . .' Karam shifted unsteadily on his feet before sitting down again and taking a deep breath.

Meanwhile, Sarna continued to writhe and moan on the sofa, 'Hai, satyanaas! Oh disaster! Hai Ruba, preserve us!'

Rajan, sitting crosslegged in an armchair, looked on incredulously. No wonder Pyari hadn't wanted to tell them. It was bad enough dealing with a marriage break-up without having to watch your parents' breakdown. What the hell was he doing here? Why did it always fall to him to break bad news or direct difficult decisions? He felt like a trouble-shooter who was drafted in at times of crisis.

'Look, nothing's really going to change.' Rajan tried to reassure his parents. 'Pyari will stay here with the boys, and Jeevan will carry on in Canada. On the surface nothing will be different. They've been leading separate lives for a long time.'

'If nothing's going to change, why does she have to do it?' Karam asked.

'It's her decision. She says everything is over between her and Jeevan. You know divorce is not such a big a deal these days,' Rajan said.

'Humpf!' Sarna snorted and sat up. 'Such a silly girl, such a stupid move. No woman should give up her husband so easily. How is she going to survive?'

'Mum, will you just put aside your old-fashioned ideas for a moment and show some compassion? It's much, much easier to stay stuck in a bad marriage. It takes courage to break out of one—' Rajan began.

'Oh ho ho, look who's the expert on marriage now, Mr Never-been-married Rajan who seems to have a new girl-friend every six months.' Sarna's hand waved at him like an eraser trying to rub him out. ' "Easier to stay", my foot. What do you know about staying, huh? You haven't got the staying power of a bullet. Always off like a shot. Even when you visit your parents you're looking at your watch, counting the seconds before you rush off. Hai, just look at you, even now checking the time—'

'That's because I do actually have to get to a meeting,' Rajan said, taking his eyes off the brass Africa-shaped clock. Its ticking black hands told him he had ten more minutes.

'Hah! Your life seems to be one big meeting. Even *we* are just a slot in your schedule. You show up to see us maybe once in two months and then you're skipping to the tune of "meetings". It's true! Ask—' Sarna inclined her head towards Karam. His lack of acknowledgement did not discourage her. 'You're always in such a hurry, you can't even sit still.'

'This wasn't supposed to be about me.' Rajan clenched and unclenched his fists. 'We should finish talking about Pyari, because I have to go soon.'

'Yes, yes, go, go.' Sarna flicked her hands as though she was brushing crumbs off her chest. 'See how easy it is to leave? You just pick up your bag and you're out. Let me tell you, to *stay* in a marriage is the hardest thing. Ask *me*. You have no idea what I've put up with. You can't even begin to imagine. I have suffered for my children – and to what end? To hear them lecture me on how easy it is to leave? Raja, have some respect. You think all your modern-shodern ways are best, but families like ours wouldn't survive if it wasn't for mothers like me who have *never* taken the easy way.'

Rajan, a little chastened by this outburst, did not say anything.

'Maybe there's a chance we could talk Pyari out of this . . . idea.' Karam brought the conversation back on track. He was unable to utter the word 'divorce'.

'I don't think so, Dad. They've already started the ball rolling on the legal front,' Rajan said.

Still, Karam and Sarna spoke to Pyari, attempting, in their own way, to pressurize her into reconsidering.

'Has Jeevan done something? Can I speak to him?' Karam asked when he managed to catch his daughter alone.

'No, Pithaji, he hasn't done anything,' Pyari said, silently adding, *and that's the problem*. Jeevan had always been more dedicated to his job than to his family. Pyari had gradually perceived that he was a workaholic, and then, even more slowly, she'd understood she could not change him. Finally she had admitted defeat and returned to London with her sons.

'Achah? Really? So why then? Why the need to separate?' Karam was unable to reconcile the extremity of Pyari's divorce with its seemingly innocuous causes.

'There's nothing left between us. The marriage is pointless. It's just a show,' Pyari said.

'But what a great show!' Karam clapped. 'He's in Canada, you're here. You have the children, you never see him, he pays all your expenses. Just think about what you're doing. So many people live together for show and it's a complete flop. Look at your mother and me – what kind of show is that? With you and Jeevan, the set-up is perfect. You get to be apart under the respectable stamp of marriage. I always said the most successful marriages are the ones where the partners don't have to see each other. You've managed to live here alone for so long – why call it a day now? Nobody will care if you don't get on with your husband, but everyone will talk if you decide to leave him. This is not the done thing for us people,' Karam said. '*Please*, will you rethink?'

'Pithaji, it's too late now.' Although Karam's views hurt Pyari, she did not resent his expressing them. She understood that he was concerned and was trying to help in the only way he knew how – by highlighting the values he had upheld throughout his life.

In Sarna's words, however, there seemed to be a deliberate intent to wound. She routinely seated herself beside Pyari on the cream leather sofa in the living room and lectured her. 'This life is not easy. To be a woman is to suffer. To *suffer*. Once you see that, everything is easier to accept.' Sarna regularly invoked the sad plight of women to support her arguments, but she did not use the word in the collective sense. When she said 'women' she was really just referring, in a grandiose way, to herself. Yes, she would have conceded, other women did suffer. But *she* had experienced an earthquake of agony, while the rest of her sex merely felt the tremors. This perception had enabled Sarna to cope with life. When she'd realized that her choices had made hardship inevitable, she'd decided to embrace it. Keen to play the martyr, she courted, welcomed and invented distress. It was easier to tolerate her world if she cast herself as its victim. 'Look at me. After all your pithaji has done, I'm still here by his side, cooking and cleaning for him. If I could put up with it, why can't you? Huh, why?'

Pyari never understood how Sarna could offer up her own marriage as a model to be emulated. Normal parents counselled their children against making the same mistakes that they had, but Karam and Sarna, despite their avowed dislike of being together, hailed the fact that they were still married as a great achievement.

'Did Jeevan beat you?'

Pyari shook her head.

'Did he abuse you? Was he unfaithful?'

Again Pyari shook her head.

'No? Hai! Think of the poor women like Nina who become widows – and you are throwing away a perfectly decent man,' Sarna said.

Pyari looked at her mother and wondered if she'd understand that neglect was a kind of betrayal, and that the absence of love can be a form of death. So far, only Nina had instinctively realized. She had sensed long before Pyari had said anything that the marriage was not working. And she had comforted Pyari with quiet reassurances that everything would be all right.

'How could you ask for such a thing? How could you even say that word, let alone do it? Do you know that in the world's eyes a woman is nothing without a man? Why do you think I've stayed with your father?' Sarna grabbed a cushion and began fiddling with the embroidered mirror-work on its cover.

'It was Jeevan's choice as well,' Pyari said.

'Oooh!' A whole new light had been thrown on the subject. 'Well, what do you expect if you leave a man to his own devices for so long? He's found someone else.'

'He's too busy working to find anyone.'

'Hah! Work!' She pounded the cushion with her fist. 'That's what they all say, but work for them is an excuse for play. How many times did I warn you about the tricks these men get up to? Every time you said, "He's working," I asked, "Are you sure?" Do you remember? This is what happens when you ignore your mother. Hai! What a mess you've got yourself into. Hai, my heart is breaking, really my heart is breaking.' Sarna started sobbing. All her suffering would be in vain if the shadow of shame descended on her daughter.

Pyari crossed her arms and legs. Why was *her* heart breaking? Why was *she* the one crying? Not once had Sarna asked how Pyari was feeling or coping. Not once had Sarna tried to tell her that everything would be fine.

Sarna pulled a tissue out of her bra, then dried her eyes and blew her nose with it. 'I'm sure, if you went back to him he would accept. If you apologized and moved back to Canada, he would agree.'

Pyari stared. 'What are you saying? Why should *I* apologize?'

'For leaving him alone,' Sarna said, as if she was imparting the most reasonable advice in the world. 'A woman's place is by her husband's side. Your life is over now. What are you without a man? Men don't want worn-out middle-aged women with teenage sons, they want tight young girls—'

'Mee, *please*—'

'No, you must listen. You have to hear the truth.' Sarna put a hand on her daughter's leg, as if to hold her down while she expounded further.

The truth! Pyari moved away. Who was she to talk about truth?

'I know that in this country people think to be alone is nothing. But for us it is still a curse. Lucky you don't have any daughters, otherwise you could forget about finding decent husbands for them. No one wants to marry into a family with –' Sarna paused, and then whispered, '*diworce*. It's bad luck.'

Pyari looked at the neatly repaired gash in the leather of the armrest to her right – the fault that had enabled her parents to get an extra discount on this shop-display model. The rip on the sofa was sacred – Vaheguru help you if you touched it in Sarna's presence. The wounds of her daughter, on the other hand, were not so carefully handled.

'And children can't be relied on, sons especially. Now Amar and Arjun keep you busy, but soon they'll be off to university. Then they'll have jobs and girlfriends and not a spare minute for you. Ask me. I know. Look at your brother. Ah, the big baba.' Sarna shook her head, but she was unable to keep a hint of fondness out of her voice.

'They all leave you in the end. Whatever you do, you lose them. No one knows that better than me. That's why I'm telling you to think about your future. You've seen how Nina struggles. Recently she's been so busy working, she can't even come down here for a few days. Have *you* thought about how *you're* going to make a living?' Sarna plumped up the cushion and put it, like a gift, in Pyari's lap, as if it might provide the softness and support that she could not.

Pyari ignored the cushion. '*Yes*. I want to build up my sewing business—'

'Hai! You're living in a dream world. Fiteh moon! Your father tried the clothes business and look where it got him – he was stripped of his dignity.'

Sarna could see Pyari withdrawing, shrinking back into the sofa. She might have hugged her daughter if she'd been practised in such tenderness. But words and spices were her means of expression. And illness – although that was often a monologue her body recited against her will.

'Think of your father and me,' Sarna tried again. 'Think of all we have done for you children – and *then* think of what *you* have done for this family. Your brother has disgraced us by not getting married. All the time people speculate about the reason why. I won't even start to tell you the disgusting theories they have. And now you, *you* are getting *diworce*.' The sound 'warse' hissed out of the gap between her two front teeth like a missile. 'What will people say? Hai, they will have a field day. I know, all these years you've been going around on your own and no one has said anything. But that's because they all knew you were *married*. As soon as the news that you're not is out, they will talk about you, make up stories, invent affairs, maybe even imagine *boyfriends*.' She could already

431

see Persini gloating, 'Hai, such a shame. Now there are no more doctors in your family.'

It hurt Pyari that Sarna conjectured endlessly about Jeevan's carnal prospects and condemned her to a solitary life of celibacy. Am I really so awful that she can't imagine anyone wanting me? she wondered.

'This is not the age,' Sarna went on. 'Look at you.' She prodded Pyari and sized her up critically. To Sarna, Pyari's slim body was unhealthy, her elegant face haggard, her short hairstyle ridiculous, and the gentle lines around her eyes were sinister crow's feet. 'Who will have you now? Tuck your greying tail between your legs and scuttle back to Jeevan before it's too late. Otherwise, let me tell you, he will find someone half your age and twice as pretty. Meanwhile, you will be rotting here, struggling to pay the bills and wondering why you didn't listen to your mother.' All her concern had tumbled out as criticism – that self-taught tendency she could not unlearn. A curdled mix of her better intentions.

Pyari started to cry. She fell forward on to the cushion – the mirrors on its surface fractured her teary face into tiny pieces. Sarna, moved by this sudden display of emotion, hurried from the room and returned shortly with a warm bowl of sevia. With some difficulty she knelt before her daughter and offered up the translucent vermicelli noodles in their sweet creamy sauce. Pyari pushed her away.

Time passed by, people forgot about Pyari's situation as other more rancorous divorces began to shake the ranks of her generation, but still Sarna could not get over her daughter's separation. It was an unsightly blot on the spotless image she'd worked so hard to cultivate. She had hoped to bask in the bright light of her children's achievements. Instead, their mistakes were an unwanted reminder of her own immutable fallibility. A reminder Sarna refused to accept.

However, time brought about a subtle alteration in her attitude to divorce. She was confronted with the reality that single women could survive post-marriage. Seeing these women coping admirably and, in some cases, looking happier, threw into question her opinion that 'a woman is nothing without a man'. Over the years, Sarna observed divorced women being more easily accepted even in their Sikh community, and saw some of them successfully remarry. On TV, she watched divorced or single women portrayed as heroines. It was strange for her to view what she regarded as mistakes dressed as accomplishments, and what she believed was failure paraded as triumph. The fact that Sarna's own life had been an amalgam of identical trompe l'oeils did not make her any more amenable to these developments. The change in public perception regarding the role of women threatened her cosy security as the long-suffering wife. She realized that Rajan, Pyari and maybe even Nina considered that she had been weak to stay on in her marriage. Her son had already said as much. Sarna could not bear it. Weakness was not the impression she intended to leave to posterity. She, who had altered and discarded so much of herself in order to survive, would not be undermined by some newfangled notion of women's rights.

So Sarna slightly revised her views on divorce. 'I wish I had left years ago, when the thought first occurred to me,' she began saying to her daughters. 'I would have. I was this close to it –' She'd press her thumb and index finger together really hard, so that there was no gap between them. 'But I couldn't do it because of you children. I always put you first.' When asked where she would have gone, Sarna replied without hesitation, 'To India, of course. I could have had a home there with any of my sisters. They would have welcomed me with open arms.'

Only Rajan managed temporarily to throw her. 'Why don't you do it now, Mum? You're not happy, Dad's not happy. It's not too late.' They were standing in the kitchen, where Sarna had cornered Rajan on the pretext of 'helping', while she prattled on about how dismal life was.

Dumbstruck by the question, Sarna busied herself with rapidly stirring the steaming rice she'd just taken out of the microwave. Why couldn't she leave Karam now? And the answer in her heart was the same one which had always prevented her from even considering such a course of action: because she was afraid. Because, despite all her criticism of him, Karam was her guardian angel. He had started as her passport back to an ordinary life, and he had become a convenient password for all her miseries. She couldn't imagine herself without him. But she couldn't admit this. So she nimbly did a 180-degree turn of thought and looked defiantly at Rajan. 'Hai Ruba, what kind of son puts a death wish on his father?' she admonished. 'Have some pity, Raja. Your father couldn't survive without me now. I am committing an act of charity by staying with him.'

Rajan opened his mouth to say something, but Sarna briskly cut him off. 'Anyway,' she tapped her temple, 'in my head, which is where it counts, I am already divorced.'

Indeed she was, Rajan thought. Divorced from reality.

34

'Why didn't you and Pritpal have children?' Oskar asked Nina.

She looked uneasy. 'It wasn't possible. We tried, but there were problems – with him and also with me. The doctors said there was no hope.'

'Oh.'

'I always wanted to have lots of kids – at least five or six.' She stood up and went to the window. Her house was opposite a kindergarten.

'It must have been really hard for you.'

'Yes – specially after Pritpal died. I felt so lone. I kept on wishing there had just been one child, you know, just *one*. Just one person to need me still.' The swell of her hair around her delicate face was like a tumultuous black sea before a storm. 'I'm so glad I had my work. That was the best thing Pritpal did, forcing me to study nursing.'

Oskar went and stood behind her and slipped his arms around her waist. She was so much shorter than him, he had to bend to rest his chin on her head.

'Mother was so disappointed. She tried to give me all sort of tips. Nothing worked.'

'What sort of tips?' He imagined Sarna cooking up buttery fertility foods for Nina.

'She had this formula for producing a boy – a special *way*. A midwife in Kenya, Mina Masi, told Mother how to do it.' She was glad Oskar couldn't see her face. Just the thought of the method was making her blush.

'Ha!' Oskar laughed. 'Come on, Nina, you're a nurse, you have some scientific understanding of these things. The only way you can predetermine the sex of a child is by some sort of genetic manipulation.'

'But this really works. It's how Mother says she had Rajan.'

'What do you mean by a *way*?' Oskar was suddenly curious. He twisted Nina around in his arms so she was facing him. 'Are you referring to a sexual position?'

She wriggled out of his embrace and busied herself with rearranging the net curtain.

Oskar pestered her to share the secret. Finally she gave in, on the condition that he closed his eyes while she spoke.

'Hhhmmm.' He opened them again, unconvinced. 'So is that how Pyari had both her sons?'

'No. Mother never told her the trick.' Nina took a seat on the blue sofa. Behind her on the wall was a picture of Pritpal. The frame was draped in a garland of fake flowers.

'How odd, how unfair,' Oskar said.

'I asked Pyari about it and she had no idea.' Her words rolled into each other in that funny way he loved. 'I think she felt bad that I knew. "You don't need tricks, you found your own way. If you'd had only daughters, Mother would have told you," I said. I don't know if that made her feel better.'

'She's a funny one, is Sarna. I can't work her out.' He sat

opposite Nina and then, disconcerted by her dead husband's unblinking gaze levelled at him from the wall, he moved and settled down beside her. 'I'm surprised you didn't end up with her in London after Pritpal died.'

'I went there after the funeral. I lived with her for almost three months. That was enough.' She shook her head. 'More than enough. First I thought, maybe she'll have me now, maybe I can finally be her daughter. But then I saw she didn't want *me*. Not who I really am. She wanted to keep pretending we were sisters.' Nina had not been able to bear the thought of living indefinitely under the same roof as that resolute denial. The deception diminished her even when she kept a distance; to stay at its source would have been devastating. Like sitting parched at a spring, hour after hour, while it gushed away from you, resisting your attempts to drink. 'Mother didn't understand how I felt, being so lone again,' Nina said. 'She tried telling me I was lucky. "Pritpal's left you well off, with a house and decent income – he even spared you the burden of children." I don't care about money. I only wanted someone to love who also loves me. That's all.' She chewed her lip. 'So Pyari and Rajan helped me make scuses to come back. And here I am.' Before Oskar could respond, she jumped up. 'Will you have some tea?'

He nodded enthusiastically.

'I'll bring it out,' she said as she disappeared into the kitchen.

He loved her tea. He'd switched from buying Earl Grey to PG Tips when he saw those were the teabags she used, but in his hands these made a bitter cup. He'd asked her how she made it taste so good, but she was always evasive. He walked into the kitchen just as Nina was dolloping a quarter-teaspoon of honey into his tea. 'I don't take sugar, remember!'

She looked annoyed. 'I said I'd bring it out.'

'Or is that yours?' He smiled.

'No, baba, it's for you – and now you've seen the magic it won't taste the same.' She stirred the tea impatiently.

He took a sip – it still tasted wonderful and he told her so. He liked the idea of her secretly sweetening his tea, the way she was secretly sweetening his life. 'You know, in some countries in the Middle East you compliment your guests by the amount of sugar you put in their tea. The more you like the person, the sweeter you make their drink. And the guest has to drain the glass, no matter how sugary the taste, otherwise you risk giving offence.'

'Too bad if you're diabetic, huh?' Nina picked up the pot of honey that was three-quarters full and looked at him shyly. 'Even if I poured all this into your cup, it wouldn't be a sweet enough compliment.'

'Even though that would taste horrible I would drink it up and be the happiest man in the world.'

35

Rajan stepped down the wooden stairs into his parents' cellar. The dark underground cave of a room was full, stuffed with all manner of things. On the left, near the foot of the steps, stood Karam's narrow work-table. It was covered with trays of tools, tins of shoe polish and a box full of shoe brushes and buffers. Beneath it were half-used pots of Dulux. Rajan's eyes scanned around for the tinned tomatoes Sarna had sent him down to find. He noticed the excess ends of red carpet rolled up and resting against the wall. And beyond these, towards the back of the cellar, he spotted untidy stacks of shoeboxes lying neglected and dusty. Oskar's boxes, still there decades after he'd left.

'Hey, Raja? Have you found them? Look – just *there*,' Sarna said, as if *there* was a specific direction, like right or left. Her voice, travelling down into the cold cellar, offered little more illumination than the weak bulb that lit the room.

Rajan negotiated the narrow space between all the clutter towards a large shelving unit laden with food. He took several tins of tomatoes from the shelf. Everything was so inefficiently arranged down here. Why were the tomatoes right on the bottom shelf, when they were probably needed quite regularly, while the fat bottles of oil sat higher up, ready to fall over and make a mess? Filled with a sudden urge to sort things out, Rajan put the tins down again and proceeded to reorganize Sarna's makeshift larder. Crash. Something behind, where he couldn't see or reach, had broken. It sounded like glass or porcelain. Shit, Rajan thought. Reaching his arm behind the stacked shelf, he discovered – what? Another shelf?

'Something broken?' Sarna's sharp ears never missed a thing.

'No, no, nothing. It's OK,' Rajan blurted out, as his eyes fell on something he wished he hadn't seen.

'Why are you taking so long? It's just the tins I want.'

'Yeah, Mum. I'm coming.' Rajan was feeling a little sick. 'I'm just putting things . . .'

'You're not supposed to be *putting*, just *bringing*.'

'OK.'

Rajan had noticed that the deep shelf, which ostensibly held only the dry ingredients for Sarna's cooking, was in fact a double shelf. Like everything in his family, it had a hidden side. While moving the tinned tomatoes, Rajan had jostled the shelf enough to cause something to slide off the back, fall and break. It was a mug that had been destroyed. Crouching on the floor, Rajan drew out the broken pieces from between the wall and the shelf. Even before he'd gathered them together he could see it was a mug emblazoned with the British flag. Rajan knew where he had seen that mug, years before. It was one of the many such receptacles that lay littered around Chachaji Guru's house, holding all the coins he received but couldn't bear to touch.

Guru Big-Bucks couldn't abide coins. The idea of

holding a piece of metal after it had circulated in unknown quarters and passed through countless strange hands, which may have indulged in any number of obscene activities, was repellent to him. Therefore, he avoided using coins and relegated any he received to the barren hold of a cup. Over the years the cups had accumulated, and although Guru was too repulsed to touch them, he remained unable to get rid of them, because he said, 'Whatever state it comes in, you can't throw money away.' Cups full of coins were littered all around his house. And Sarna had occasionally helped herself to one when visiting.

Rajan grabbed the torch hanging over Karam's worktable and shone it over the back shelf. He spotted more of the stolen mugs. His vision blurred for a moment. *Shit*. Blindly he kicked the fragments of broken mug behind the shelf again. He wiped his hands roughly across his eyes, but he could do nothing to stem the memories that were assaulting his conscience.

Forgotten moments of innocence now flooded back as corrupt incidents of complicity. Taking Sarna's heavy handbag to the car in the middle of a visit to Chachaji Guru. Walking into Sarna's room proudly waving his O-level results, only to be shooed out by a panicked mother who was counting the coins in a green and white polka-dot mug. Everything came back to Rajan with painful clarity. The time – oh, why was he remembering this? His twenty-first birthday, when Sarna had given him a hundred pounds and made him swear not to tell anyone. He had wondered where the money had come from. He'd even asked. 'Don't worry where it's from,' Sarna assured him. 'Just take it. Your mother is a clever woman, she always does what she needs to for her children.' Rajan had suspected that he should not take the money, but he'd accepted it anyway. Now the taint of that gift sent another wave of nausea through him. He thought of all the past confrontations when Sarna had accused him, and everyone else, of not caring about her and not appreciating the lengths to which she had gone for her family. Each time he'd had an inkling of what his mother was referring to, but he had not allowed himself to see the truth. Even now, when the evidence had crashed in front of his eyes, he'd shoved it aside and tried to conceal it.

'Raja?' The impatient call nudged him from his thoughts.

'Coming!'

Rajan wondered if never saying anything had been a mistake. Perhaps his discovery of Chachaji Guru's empty coin mugs was fate's way of shoving him towards a real showdown. Maybe he had to break the silence in which they'd all colluded for too long.

He picked up the tins of tomatoes and climbed out of the dark cellar. The kitchen was heavy with the mingling smells of different dishes. Damp aromas hit Rajan's face like the wet heat of a steam room. He was engulfed by Mushq's enticing arms, curling around him soft as ribbons, trying to pull him from the pains of the past to the palatable pleasures of the present. Rajan's stomach purred approvingly and his dry mouth flooded with an anticipatory spray of saliva, but then he heard his mother's voice and the spell of the smell was broken: 'Taking so long. Did something break?'

Rajan did not look at her. 'I don't think so.' He handed the tins to Pyari, avoiding her gaze as well. 'You have too many things down there. What are you keeping – the rubbish of centuries? I don't know why you don't throw anything away. It's made me feel ill. This place is becoming more and more oppressive. I can't stand it any more. I'm going out, I need some fresh air.'

'But food is ready!' Sarna waved at all her bubbling pots and pans.

Why had he lied? Rajan wondered as he walked briskly across the road and on to the Common. It would have been so easy to say something without being explicit. He could have said, 'Yes, I think a cup broke. Some old mug from God knows where. There's all this rubbish behind that shelf, Mum, you should get rid of it.' There, easy. He would have casually intimated what he knew and eased his own conscience without hurting his mother. Or he could have been harsher. Shown her the broken mug and said, 'Mum, this is Chachaji Guru's mug. I broke it accidentally. I saw more of his mugs in the cellar. I can guess how you got them. I understand why you took them, but what you did was wrong. The way you involved me was also wrong. And you can stop pretending now, because I know, and it's all right. You're still my mother and I love you.' But he hadn't said anything. Worse, he had lied and then gone silent. Just like her.

Why had she made him party to her petty crimes? *She* could so conveniently forget everything and masquerade as an oppressed saint, while the rest of them were stuck in reality and continued to remember. Rajan was furious, because he was still attached to her by some invisible cord that prevented him from treating her as he would anyone else who behaved as she did. With his legal mind, trained in the rigours of assessing evidence and pronouncing judgement, he could easily pass the verdict – guilty. But his heart complicated matters. His heart stood in the way and told him to try and understand and to have mercy. But Rajan could not completely trust his heart, because he'd heeded it before and been disappointed. It was his heart, anxious to please his father, that had let him be forced into studying Law. His heart had made him feel that by pursuing the profession he might be absolved of the deception that had tainted his youth. In the end, though, Rajan's nature had not tolerated the strictures of the law. His heart had rebelled against the discipline – although that did not prevent it from aching for years at its own disenchantment and the disappointment of his family.

It had once made Rajan laugh that Sarna always pronounced the word 'lawyer' as 'liar'. No amount of correction could make her change. Now it grated on him. No wonder she says 'liar' – that's the only kind of law she knows, he thought. Rajan strode across the damp grass on the Common. It had never occurred to him that Sarna might be part of the reason why he'd ended up in the murky world of advertising, where most things existed in the grey area between true and false.

He reached the park cricket nets. How many summers he had spent practising here. That was before everything became so complicated. He turned back. As he neared the side of the Common in front of their house, he saw Sarna standing in the street waiting for him. The sight of her, looking perfectly normal when he was in such turmoil, reignited his fury.

'Food is ready. Come and eat.'

'Yeah, I'm coming, Mum,' Rajan said, while his body proceeded to contradict his voice by turning and walking the other way.

'*Coming?* Looks like you're *going*!'

Rajan continued to walk on.

'The food is getting *cold*!'

Rajan ignored her.

'Oh ho, somebody tell this boy.'

He wandered sullenly around the Common. From time to time he looked across the subdued wet greenery at his parents' house and scowled. Normally, when he walked out of the house he could forget the dramas played out there, pretend they didn't exist. Today, the austere brick Victorian façade loomed stubbornly at the periphery of his vision. The chilly November afternoon was still cloaked in that morning's downpour. Everywhere branches and blades of grass shook off their coats of water with tiny quivers, drop by drop. Rajan's lightweight leather-soled trainers began to feel damp and he shivered. In his haste to get outside, he'd forgotten to grab his coat, and now he was braving it against the elements in a thin long-sleeved T-shirt. He looked at the house again and saw Pyari approaching. She crossed the Common, a full wine glass in motion, swathes of a burgundy shawl spilling over the stem of her trousered black legs.

'Can I walk with you?'

Rajan shrugged. As they turned away from the house again, she spoke. 'Is this because of Chachaji Guru's mug?'

Rajan stopped and looked at her. 'You know?'

'Rajan, she's my mother too. I've had my own experience of her . . . habits. I've been her accomplice and her beneficiary.'

Rajan felt slightly relieved. Here was someone who not only knew the truth but was implicated by the knowledge in the same way. 'You never said anything.'

'*You* never said anything! I suppose she placed the fear of God in you as well.' Pyari shook her head.

'But how did you guess now?'

'I didn't guess. She sent me down after you went out to check if you'd broken anything.'

'I can't believe her! She thought *I* was lying!'

Pyari looked at him. 'You *were* lying.'

'Yeah, but for her to *assume*. I mean, the hypocrisy! I thought I was sparing her by not saying anything. I was trying to do us all a favour. I can't believe her. So did you tell her?'

'What do you think? Of course not.'

'I don't know why I kept my mouth shut.' Rajan slammed a fist into his palm. 'We all creep around trying to spare her feelings, while she doesn't think twice about suspecting the worst of us. I can't believe she sent you down to check! She's such a . . . such a . . . !' Several ugly words hung on the tip of his tongue.

'Rajan!' Pyari interrupted.

'It's true. She's spent her life accusing Dad of penny-pinching, while she herself has been pinching mugs of money left, right and centre. For all we know, she could still be at it. Next time she hands Amar or Arjun a tenner just ask yourself whether they shouldn't be thanking Guru Big-Bucks instead.'

Pyari could tell he needed to let off steam.

'I bet you Mum's in the cellar right now.' He pointed towards the ground. 'I can guarantee she's poking around to confirm her suspicions, despite what we have both told her. Well, good! I hope she finds the goddamned mug. I wish I'd left its broken pieces lying right where they fell. In fact, I wish I'd broken more. I'd like to smash all of the mugs to the floor and expose her falsehood with a big crash. You know, I'm sick of this pussyfooting around her all the time. She's got everyone dancing to her warped tune and I'm not doing it any more. We're the ones who will end up paying for all her antics if we don't do anything about them. I'm going to tell her.'

'What?' Pyari wrapped the shawl more tightly around herself. It smelled of Sarna's fennel chicken. 'What will you tell her? About the mugs? About Nina? Where will you begin? And where will you stop if you start? What about Pithaji? Will you tell him while you're at it?'

Now Rajan was silent. That was the difficulty. No issue in this family was intact. Each problem spilled messily into another one that involved someone else.

'I'll just tell her I know everything.' He put his hands into his pockets.

'Oh, good one, Raj,' Pyari congratulated. 'And what difference do you think that will make? *She's* the only one who knows. *She* has the right version. The rest of us are poor misinformed fools.'

They turned back towards the house in silence. The scent of Sarna's cooking drifted down to them like a messenger sent to remind them she was waiting. Rajan sniffed rapidly several times and his stomach growled in anticipation again. This time Karam was waiting outside.

'You'd better come in now,' he said. 'The food is getting cold and your mother is getting all heated up.'

36

Nina stood under the sycamore tree in her back garden and rolled her shoulders. The hot July sun penetrated the thick canopy of leaves and hit the ground in a dazzling dapple of disco. Nina, speckled by this glitter-ball glare, reached up and interlaced her fingers so that her arms, like the strap of a bag, lifted her whole body. Half an hour of gardening and she felt as if she'd done an afternoon of gymnastics. Rising on to her toes, she arched her back and sighed. She might have been a bird of paradise performing a ritual mating dance. Oskar would have been aroused by the sight of her – all curvaceous and swaying to the rhythm of her own thoughts. But he was curled casually over the fire-like flaming dahlias, using twine to give them extra support. His white T-shirt was pulled taut across his back, revealing the bumpy road of his spine, each vertebra a sleeping policeman waiting to be traversed by her touch.

Nina had completely neglected the garden after Pritpal's death. Not that he had been blessed with a green thumb, but at least he'd trimmed the lawn regularly. She'd let it grow into a jungle – which had its charms, but was hardly conducive to enjoying the space on warmer days, which Oskar loved to do. Since leaving behind his introverted existence, he'd developed a passion for the outdoors. He had spent the last year subjugating and transforming Nina's wild back garden. He'd involved her in the process too, showing her how to recognize weeds, pointing out which flowers to dead-head, letting her choose the seeds they would plant together. Nina could not have believed she'd get so much pleasure from such messy, earthy work. She still shrieked at the sight of slugs and worms, but she enjoyed pottering outside with Oskar. She delighted in the results of their labours, exclaiming over each new bud as though it was a world created for the first time. With Oskar she ventured beyond the padded perimeters of her lonely routines and found experience waiting seductively at every corner. Even her daily walk to the bus-stop became like a stroll on an exotic beach when he was with her.

Nina looked around the garden and smiled. The marigolds were still a scattering of yellow in their narrow bed. She couldn't wait to see them all in bloom, spelling out the shape in which she'd arranged the seeds: OK. His name emblazoned in gold across her garden, the way it was across her destiny. She imagined the two of them here year after year. For ever. But then a spasm of guilt tempered the fantasy. She had still not told any of the family about Oskar, not even Pyari. It was partly that she did not know what to say, and partly that she did not *want* to say. So now she, who was a secret, had a secret. She had begun to understand the burden of the deceiver, which is different to that of the deceived. The banal questions of daily discourse had become traps. How are you? What did you do at the weekend? Why haven't you phoned? When will you visit again? Fine. The usual. Busy. Soon. Even her vaguenesses were loaded with falsehood. She was startled by her capacity for insincerity, pained by it. She *would* tell them. But not yet.

'Mother's ill,' Nina said, walking into the garden. It was another blistering day in the hottest July she could remember.

'Again?' Oskar frowned.

Nina loved the crease in his forehead, it looked like a V for victory. 'Yes, but this time it's serious. She has a lump in her throat.'

'Oh.'

'She's been complaining to me about soreness and a hoarse voice for some weeks now, and I just brushed it off, saying it was probably a cold or something.'

'Well, you couldn't know. She shouldn't be asking you anyway, you're not a doctor.' Oskar continued watering the plants.

'I know, I know. I wish I'd . . . I . . .' Nina broke off.

'What is it?' Oskar put down the hosepipe and stepped over to her.

'She has to have another operation.'

'Why? I mean, what kind of operation? What sort of lump? It's not . . . it's not – cancer?'

'She thinks so.' Nina chewed her trembling bottom lip.

'*She* thinks so? Well, what does the doctor say?'

'Yes . . . no – I don't know. We just spoke on the phone. When she said "cancer" I got really upset, and then she started crying and then I couldn't think straight—'

'Look, hold on.' Oskar took her hand. 'Don't start jumping to conclusions. You know she's diagnosed herself with cancer before and all that came to nothing.'

A couple of years ago, Sarna had had a few falls, which left her bruised and bedridden. Unable to find a suitably

450

serious-sounding medical term for what was really a combination of old age, carelessness and being overweight, she'd suggested that she might have cancer. She'd heard of endless manifestations of the disease: head, stomach, breast, skin, even finger. So it didn't seem improbable that she could have 'falling-down cancer'. Everyone had expressed some degree of indignation at this insinuation. Her daughters pointed out that she hadn't experienced any of the weight loss normally associated with the illness. Karam reminded her of how malaria had always been the default malady of the ignorant when they'd lived in Africa. Malaria ya tumbo, malaria ya kichwa, malaria ya muguu – stomach ache, headache, foot ache – it was all malaria. But Sarna only dropped the diagnosis after Rajan had told her off for trivializing cancer.

'Remember all that business about falling-down cancer? You're the one who told me about it,' Oskar prompted. 'And anyway, how has she gone straight to the operation stage? Has she had a biopsy yet? Sorry, but this seems like another case of her attention-seeking.'

'But she was so upset on the phone. And she just kept begging me to go and help her. She wouldn't just do that—'

'Yes she would. She's trying to manipulate you, as usual. Just calm down and think about it properly, Nina. No doubt she's noticed you've kept a bit of a distance from her. She probably thinks the only way to draw you there is on some really serious pretext. I'm sure she's trying to make you feel guilty so you'll go running over there to nurse her. She's—'

'Your water,' Nina said suddenly.

'What?'

'The pipe, the pipe! You need to turn it off,' she gestured.

'Oh God!' Water was gushing over the Love Lies Bleeding, licking lustily at its thick crimson braids, drowning them in adoration. The excess of this passion was trickling down the garden path towards the back door of the house.

Oskar grabbed the hosepipe, intending to aim it elsewhere, but it slithered petulantly in his hand and sprayed Nina. She yelped. Oskar laughed and then rushed to turn off the tap. When he returned, Nina was looking calmer.

'You're right, it sounds odd,' she admitted, seemingly oblivious to the soaked shirt clinging to her torso. 'But *something*'s wrong, because her voice sounds terrible, and she's got a date for an operation.'

'Well, call back. Ask some more questions. Maybe speak to Karam – that's probably the best way to get a clearer picture,' Oskar said.

Karam answered the phone and, when he realized who it was, immediately commented on the heatwave and announced that it was almost thirty degrees in London. 'How hot is it there?' he asked a little competitively. For once Nina ignored his weather wanderings and instead bluntly enquired about what exactly was wrong with Sarna.

'I'm not sure about the details,' he said. 'She just goes into the surgery on her own these days, I stay in the waiting room. I only know what she tells me. Apparently there's some growth in her throat and they have to remove it. A nodule or something, they call it. Wait, she's waving at me – she wants to speak to you.'

'But just a minute, Br-ji. Is it very serious? Is it something like – cancer?' Nina asked.

'*Cancer?* Good God, no! I think it's a minor problem. She goes in one day, has the operation and comes out the next. Here, wait – she's grabbing the phone—'

'Silly girl, she's overreacting,' Nina heard Karam say before Sarna's voice scratched down the line, 'Are you coming or not, then?'

'Mother, I'm worried. You scared me when you said cancer. What's going on?'

'Why are you asking? Will you decide whether to show up depending on how serious it is? Unless I have cancer nobody can be bothered, huh? Is that how it is now?' Even being vocally challenged couldn't take the commanding edge off her words.

'No, Mother, of course not.' She fell right into Sarna's trap.

'Fine, don't come,' Sarna rasped. 'I don't need anyone. I'll cope on my own. I always have and, I guess, I always will.'

'*I'm coming,*' Nina emphasized. At Oskar's prompting she went on, 'That wasn't the question. I just wanted to understand exactly what was wrong.'

'Everything's wrong!' Sarna screeched, forgetting that her vocal capacity was impaired. The exertion made her break into a coughing fit.

Nina looked at Oskar despairingly.

'All I said was that it *feels* like cancer,' Sarna croaked.

'I don't want to go,' Nina said as she put down the receiver.

'Then don't. I thought you'd decided never to help again after the last time,' Oskar said.

Nina pursed her lips at the reminder. All her biting had left them swollen and bruised, like overripe cherries. 'I know. But how can I not?'

'Easy. Just say no.'

'It's not so simple. I feel bad . . . guilty,' she said. But he could see a list of unspoken words in her eyes: unworthy, sad, afraid, angry, fed up. 'I can't ignore her if she says she needs me.'

Misguided as Sarna's claim to have cancer was, it reflected a metaphorical truth. She was host to a terrible lie. A lie of that magnitude, perpetuated over a lifetime, festers in the psyche and can corrupt all that is good and true. Because a lie is not just a statement of untruth, but a compound of the emotions triggered by it: guilt, shame, anger and fear. To be constantly in the grip of such potent feelings can be debilitating. In Sarna these emotions had ceased to ebb and flow as they do in normal individuals. Instead they had become her dominant sensations and, like cancer cells, they grew rapidly, assumed abnormal shapes and sizes, and eventually spread to infect every part of her. Every thought, every action, every spoken word and every physical pain had its origin in her existential lie. She had fought against her past as if it was an infection, something to be overcome and eradicated, but in the process she had exposed herself to another virus: the deadly disease of denial. And now that disease had metastasized and claimed her very soul.

While Sarna was in hospital, her family discovered the real significance of the node that was removed from her throat. She was still under the influence of sedatives when the surgeon popped by during his ward round. Sarna appeared barely conscious. She was lying semi-upright, propped up by several pillows. Her hair was pulled back severely in a ponytail, exacerbating the austerity of her pale face. She remained motionless during the surgeon's brief examination – except for her eyes, which rolled drowsily under their lids and flickered occasionally. Nina found this eye action quite sinister. It seemed as if Sarna was trying to fight off the effect of the drugs and witness the scene unfolding around her bed.

The surgeon gave the family a quick update. 'The anaesthetic hasn't worn off yet, but everything went well. She'll be fine. We'll discharge her tomorrow.' He scribbled something on his clipboard. 'It's best if she refrains from speaking for a few days. Some initial hoarseness may be experienced when speech is resumed, but this should clear up of its own accord. We expect full vocal recovery within a few weeks.'

'Just a few weeks?' Karam adjusted his tie.

'Oh yes, Mrs Singh is very fortunate. In her case the damage was quite minor. She's not a singer by any chance, is she?' the surgeon asked.

'That, Doctor, would depend on your definition of singing,' Karam said. 'She does regularly raise her voice to a high pitch, if that's what you mean.'

The surgeon suppressed a smile. 'I just meant that this is more commonly a problem amongst singers, usually opera singers. That's why the condition is referred to as "singer's nodes". And, obviously, in such cases, the removal of a node can have more serious implications.'

A little baffled by this information, Karam asked him to elaborate. It emerged that the node was a sort of lesion resulting from strain on the voice box.

'Do you mean to say my wife might have developed this node from talking too much?' The corners of his mouth stretched with *Schadenfreude*.

'Well, Mr Singh, I couldn't possibly comment.' This time the surgeon was unable to hide his smile. 'I don't know your wife or her vocal ... habits, shall we say. But certainly, these nodes do arise from excessive use of the vocal cords.'

Karam grinned and almost clapped his hands in delight. The two men shook hands and the surgeon moved down the ward. Karam turned to Nina and Pyari, who were sitting on either side of Sarna's bed looking equally amused by the surgeon's comments. Nina quickly straightened her face when she saw Sarna's eyes bulge under their lids, ready to burst out in repudiation.

'I always wondered how she could yell away like she does without suffering any consequences. For years I half expected her tongue to fall out, because of the way it flapped about in her mouth.' Karam moved closer and peered at Sarna's throat.

'No wonder she was so vague about what Dr Jasgul told her. She probably didn't want us to know,' Pyari said.

'Exactly!' Karam tapped the steel frame of the bed. 'I have to tell her. You know the way she thinks she's never raised her voice, and she always accuses *me* of shouting. This should teach her a lesson.'

'She probably won't believe you, Pithaji.'

'I'll ask the doctor again – in front of her,' Karam said.

Unfortunately, the surgeon did not reappear on the ward during the family's visit, which meant there was no opportunity for the exposé Karam wanted. Then during her first two days back home Sarna appeared to be in a lot of pain, so again Karam could not accost her. 'I don't understand why she's in such a state. You'd think she'd just had a triple bypass *and* hip-replacement surgery from the way she's behaving,' he said to Pyari and Nina, echoing their own thoughts.

The impulse to speak was so strong in Sarna that she

kept trying to talk. Her voice would start off as a weak whisper and taper off into a fit of coughing. 'Mother! You're not supposed to say anything for a few days,' Nina kept admonishing. Karam thrust a pen and paper into her hands and suggested she write things down. Sarna was forced to heed their advice, but she expediently found another way around her vocal limitations. Using the remote control, she'd turn the TV up to maximum volume whenever she wanted attention.

After three days, unable to contain himself any longer, Karam broached the subject of the self-induced nature of her throat problem. Sarna was resting in her preferred position on the sofa: flat on her back, legs crossed over each other. In one hand, which rested over her torso, she held the TV remote control; the other hand lay protectively around her throat, stroking and probing, as if feeling for signs of recovery.

From the kitchen, where she was preparing soup for lunch, Nina overheard Karam begin to relate his conversation with the surgeon. She wished Pyari was also around, it was easier to cope with such situations when they were together. But Pyari and her sons had left that morning for a holiday in Italy. Hoping that her presence might help keep things calm, she slipped back into the living room on the pretext of laying the table. Karam recounted the surgeon's verdict, embellishing a little so that in his version the surgeon said, 'Your wife must have been talking too much.' Sarna scowled fiercely, her nose twitching like a rabbit's. Knowing she couldn't drown him out herself, she used the remote control to turn up the TV volume to maximum. Karam immediately stood up and turned the machine off at the mains. He stepped in front of the blank screen and pointed at his wife. 'If you don't put an end to the constant ranting and raving, your voice is bound to pack up again – maybe permanently.' Sarna continued to jab at the remote control, as if the instrument might have the power to manipulate men as well as machines. When that didn't work, she started to cough.

Karam ignored the first feeble bout and continued with his sermon. Sarna forced out a croaky command, 'Bas! Enough!' Immediately the coughing worsened. Within a couple of minutes she appeared to be choking: tears streamed down her reddened face and she gasped wildly for breath. Nina, who'd been watching, rushed to her side and asked Karam to fetch some water. It took a good half-hour to calm Sarna down. When she began breathing normally again, she opened her lips and mouthed some words. Despite her seemingly strenuous efforts, these remained inaudible. The whisper of a voice she had brought back from the hospital seemed to have vanished altogether. It was Karam and Nina's turn to be dumbstruck. They looked at each other in panic.

Sarna kept on trying to speak, but with no success. Karam turned pale. For most of their married life he had tried in vain to curb Sarna's tongue; now he had unwittingly succeeded and the victory felt scarily criminal. Suddenly Sarna grabbed the pen and paper. In Hindi, she wrote: *Gone*. She clasped her throat to confirm what was gone. Then she tore the page from the pad and, on a fresh sheet, drew a large, incriminating arrow pointing directly at Karam. And voilà! The situation had been transformed to absolve Sarna of all responsibility for her vocal malady.

'Shall we call the doctor?' Karam nervously rubbed a finger against one of the buttons on his shirt. But Sarna shook her head decisively.

'Maybe it will come back.' Nina gave the mirror on the

wall a quick wipe – Sarna had managed to spray the room during her coughing fit. Nina was heartened by her mother's refusal. If Sarna suspected that her voice might be permanently gone, she would be insisting they call an ambulance. The fact that she didn't made Nina wonder if she was acting. It was quite possible that for Sarna the argument, which Karam had started, was still going on, and that by not saying a word, she was winning it.

Both Nina and Karam spent the next couple of days watching Sarna carefully, waiting for her to slip up and speak. They did not openly confess their doubts but reassured each other that she would be fine. Both felt guiltily complicit in consigning Sarna to silence.

Forty-eight hours after the confrontation, Sarna was looking much better. Nina went into the kitchen after a shower and caught her mother meddling with the food she'd made earlier that morning. She stood in the doorway for a moment, amused by the sight of Sarna stealthily adding more lemon to the toor dhal and dipping her fingers in and out of the saucepan several times, licking them approvingly. Nina had long ceased to be upset by this habit of respicing anything she cooked. Indeed, at this particular moment she was glad – for if Sarna was interfering it was a sure sign that she was on the mend.

Sarna was startled when Nina stepped into the kitchen. Turning around, she blurted, 'I thought you were in the shower.' The words came out dark, husky and slightly cracked, like overbaked cookies. Sound had been cooking in Sarna's throat for some time now, awaiting its delayed ejection. Her hand shot up to cover her mouth. The gesture of regret confirmed Nina's belief that she had been pretending.

'Your voice is back, Mother! Unbelievable! What a

miracle!' Without waiting for Sarna's reaction, she called Karam. 'Bhraji! Bhraji! Her voice is back. She's speaking again. How lucky we are!'

'Thank Vaheguru,' said Karam as he entered the kitchen.

'Well, Mother, your voice sounds fine, like it's been sitting there, ripening, just waiting to be used.' Nina was disgusted by her duplicity.

Sarna, who'd started off looking rather sheepish, now blithely displayed surprise at her renewed vocal function. She began to speak slowly, as if trying out her new voice. 'It's not normal yet,' she grunted.

'Well, the surgeon said it would take a few weeks to normalize. Just take it easy now. Don't "lose" it again,' Karam said.

After the operation, Sarna's speech was never quite the same. She had to clear her throat regularly when talking. Her sentences were therefore interspersed with a thick gravelly neighing. Her voice, which had always been her sharpest weapon, had become blunted by illness, by the metaphorical cancer which was eating away at her being. Sarna's words ended up having to fight through the sticky mucus of denial to be heard.

37

Oskar and Nina's relationship developed backwards. Usually people grow closer the more time they spend together, but their closeness was fostered by the fact that they had lived too long apart. Years before, they'd been wed without speaking more than a sentence to each other – a union in which conversation was rare and touch inconceivable. Then fate had thrown them together again and evoked the desire for a closeness that had never been. They had started seeing each other every day. Within weeks they had shared all their secrets. After a month they had slept in the same bed. It was meant to be, they told themselves. Their bond seemed to receive further endorsement when Nina became pregnant after they had been together for just one year. They never imagined that the accelerated nature of events might be the sign of a fast-approaching conclusion.

The prospect of a child wasn't something they'd even discussed, because it seemed impossible. They had planted a whole garden without considering that the most precious seed might be sowed somewhere else. Nina was supposedly infertile. What were the chances of them becoming parents? Perhaps Nina's capacity to have children had been disabled by the lie she had been forced to propagate about her own birth. As long as she could not acknowledge her true self, it seemed fitting that she should not create another in her false likeness. Maybe the long denial of her real identity had caused some kind of short-circuit in her system so that life essentially bypassed her reproductive organs. Perhaps with Oskar, for the first time, that concealment stopped and her circulation returned to normal. What else could it be? Science had no clear answers. Even the doctors were shocked. They advised against the birth, emphasizing the risks for the older mother and baby. For Nina their suggestions were abhorrent. 'No. I want this baby. I'm having it, no matter what.'

Oskar understood her determination. She had always longed for children. And he wanted the baby too. The wondrous knowledge that their merging had created another life was a revelation, a gift he had never dreamed of receiving. So he did not fret about the pregnancy. He was concerned about the health implications flagged by the doctors, but he let himself be swept away by Nina's optimism. And after a while, he too couldn't imagine any outcome other than that of them as a happy family. However, he did consider that the impending birth of their child made it more critical that they should let the world know about their love.

'Maybe it's time to tell your family now,' Oskar suggested a few days after the news had sunk in. Nina looked across the table at him and hunched her shoulders. She knew what he meant: it was time to tell Karam and Sarna about their relationship and that they were expecting a baby. 'You can't hide it any more. In a few months it'll be obvious.' He pointed at her belly. Still she did not reply, but chewed on her lower lip. She had made a decision.

'What's going on? What are you thinking?' He ran a hand through his silver-flecked hair.

'I don't want them to know,' Nina said.

'What? You can't be serious! This is crazy, Nina. They'll find out. It was just about acceptable to keep the truth about *us* from them, but where are you going to hide a baby?'

'They won't find out. They rarely visit now anyway.'

'Nina, think about what you're saying.' Oskar put his mug of tea to one side and reached for her hand. 'People will see you. Someone might mention it to them. What about your friends? Are you going to hide it from them as well? It doesn't make sense. You have nothing to be ashamed of. We're going to get married. You should be able to share this happiness with your family.'

'I don't want to share it!'

The vehemence of her reply made Oskar sit back abruptly.

'All my life, everything has been decided by someone else: where I live, how I marry, what job I do. It was even decided I couldn't call my own mother "ma". For the first time ever, my life feels like mine. This is *mine*.' She clutched at her stomach.

It's mine too, thought Oskar, suddenly feeling a little left out of her affections. And anyway, you didn't choose to get pregnant – that just happened to you as well. Nina seemed so wrapped up in herself, so perfectly content now there was a child growing inside her. He was disappointed that she'd never looked so satisfied with just him. 'So what do you want? Are we supposed to bring up this child in secret?' He forced himself to be calm and reached for Nina's hand again.

'No. I know we have to tell. But we can do it *after* birth. I want to have this time for just me, just *us*. You know what Mother is like. Soon as she knows, she'll try to take credit. "Oh ho, I always knew it. That was why I married you two off in first place." I bet she'll say something like that. I don't want her interfering and back-biting. I want these months to be peaceful and perfect.'

Oskar doubted Sarna would respond that way. He imagined she'd be mortified. He knew Nina had doubts herself, which had already prevented her from disclosing their relationship. 'Widows my age are not s'posed to have love-fairs. What will people say? Mother would be so shamed,' Nina had said months before, to justify keeping their attachment secret. Oskar now realized that fear of disapproval was still preventing her from telling the truth. The fact that they were going to get married did not diminish the ignominy of her predicament – anyone who did some simple maths could work out what she had been up to.

'Why can't you at least tell Pyari?' Oskar tried to quell the impatience in his voice. He could see that Nina heard it too, because she looked away. The split second of visual disconnection reminded him of the immense gap of experience and culture between them. It was a divide usually bridged by love, but from time to time a vast chasm would become exposed. At first Oskar had tried to coax Nina across from the other side, where he saw her sitting in a dark, narrow valley of archaic beliefs and suffocating expectations. Come here, he would plead. Come to where the mountains roll gently to the sea and the horizon is a sparkling place of possibility. Come to where the sand warms your feet and the wind whistles a song of acceptance. Come to my carefree country – at least, it seemed carefree when he considered the restrictions in hers. Mostly, his mental territory was too different a place for her even to contemplate, but occasionally his appeals worked and Nina would slowly venture over.

'I told you, I don't want to tell anyone.'

'But why not her, at least?' Oskar got up and came around the table to sit next to Nina. 'She'll be so happy for you, I'm sure of it. She could even help you if necessary – maybe break the news to Karam and Sarna. Come on, Nina, will you just think about it?'

'No. Please. *Please*.' She took his hand.

'Please what?'

'Why don't you understand? This is all I've ever wanted. Why can't I just enjoy without anyone trying to spoil things? You know everything will be ruined if people find out.'

She *was* afraid of people's reactions. But she was more concerned about the effect their negative responses would have on her. She couldn't abide the idea of rejection or criticism because it would detract entirely from the jubilation of her pregnancy.

'Nina, how will it be ruined? No one can come between us.' He kissed her. 'I'll still be here, no matter what, and if people see that they'll start to come round. You've got to give them a chance to accept your new life. As long as no one knows about it you'll keep living like a thief, stealing happiness. Sometimes people change because they're forced to. Maybe something good would come out of getting things in the open. What if something goes wrong? At least we'll have done the right thing.'

'What can go wrong?' She searched his face anxiously. Wrinkles rippled like waves along the shore of his forehead, moving to the current of his thoughts.

'Anything can go wrong.' Seeing the panic in her eyes, he quickly changed tack. 'But of course nothing will, because we're together. It'll be fine. It will all be perfect.' He took Nina into his arms. He felt she was making everything harder than necessary. Feeling his tension, she whispered consolingly in his ear, 'We *will* tell them. After the birth, we can surprise everyone.'

The months of Nina's pregnancy were the happiest of times for the couple. They delighted in the changes taking place in Nina's body, revelled in their now-remarried status, took pleasure in planning ahead. It seemed as though they had all the time in the world. Photographs they took were left undeveloped, because there was no hurry to see themselves immortalized on paper – after all, they had each other. They picked up holiday brochures offering discounts on breaks for the following summer. They started looking at new areas with good schools and contemplated moving in a few years.

All the while, Oskar was an unwitting accomplice in history's crime of serial repetition. He didn't see this. Perhaps, like Nina, he didn't want to see. He overlooked the horrible ironies of their situation: another hidden love affair, another undisclosed pregnancy, another secret birth.

Should Oskar have questioned Nina more, steered her to face her demons? Perhaps. But old habits are reluctant deserters from the battleground of life. His years as an observer had diminished his instinct for action. He was still better at listening than arguing. He still found it easier just to go with the flow. He thought he was making Nina happy but maybe it was illusory. Love conceived in a prism of denial can never refract pure light.

Later, Oskar would wish again and again that he had helped Nina break the cycle of silence. It would be his biggest regret, and a painfully hollow one at that – because what would it have changed? Everything and Nothing.

38

Karam sat at the dining table in his house with Guru, Mandeep and Sukhi, sipping Sarna's ambrosial masala tea and playing cards. As usual, Guru was winning. He looked disdainfully at the colourful mug to his left emblazoned with the words BEST GRANDMA IN THE WORLD. Sarna had provided this to hold the silver change that constituted Guru's winnings, because his aversion to coins still prevailed. Fortunately for Guru Big-Bucks, his substantial bank balance enabled him to keep indulging this peculiarity. His brothers were obliged to handle any coins they bet and lost to Guru on his behalf. Tradition had it that the money was scooped into a mug.

Tonight Karam had irritated Guru by trying to play with coppers, despite the brothers' long-established rule that all bets must be made in silver.

'Come on! I don't have enough change,' Karam said when Guru objected. 'Besides, you never touch the coins you win anyway, so what difference does it make?'

'It makes a difference to my mood.' The words emerged from behind Guru's long white moustache. He was one of the few Sikhs of Karam's generation in the UK who refused to trim any of his body hair. 'You knew we were playing, you should have been prepared.' Karam grumbled, but went off to scour his trouser pockets and desk drawers for silver coins.

In the hour since they'd started playing, Karam hadn't made a single bet over five pence, and the other two were also being overcautious. Guru was unimpressed but unperturbed. He didn't play to win, anyway. He played to enjoy the crisp feel of the notes sliding through his fingers each time he placed a bet or won it back. He played to feel the curious pleasure of his own indomitable good luck. And he played to sense the amiable frisson of envy at his good fortune.

'Bhraji, I have a great story for you.' Mandeep directed his words at Guru in the vain hope that a good yarn might disrupt his brother's winning streak.

Guru grunted.

'I heard this on the radio recently,' Mandeep said. 'There's a Sikh taxi-driver, Harpreet Devi, in India who's been driving around backwards, in reverse, for a couple of years. He's trying to break various records for reverse driving at high speed.'

'Achah? *Very* good,' Guru growled sarcastically.

'Ah, the Sikhs . . . always distinguishing themselves in the most edifying ways.' Karam straightened his collar over his cardigan.

'No, listen, will you? That's not the point. He's got a master plan, this Sikh.' Mandeep shuffled his cards.

'Does he have a special car?' Sukhi asked.

'No, same bloody car as everyone else, but he's changed the gears around so they all work in reverse. He sits facing the normal way, then twists himself around and cranes his neck to see backwards in order to go forwards.' Mandeep swerved to demonstrate.

469

'Ingenious,' muttered Guru, who made it a point never to be impressed by anything.

'What for?' Karam asked.

'If you let me speak, maybe I could explain.' Mandeep put down his cards. 'He started off driving backwards because after an accident his car wouldn't move forwards. Then, I guess, he was rather affected by the new perspective on things and decided to stick with it and make it his life's philosophy. Apparently he's now telling everyone that "you can improve a situation by going into reverse"'

'Sounds clever, but I don't think it's a very useful idea. You couldn't apply it successfully to every situation.' Karam looked at his small pile of coins.

'*I* think Harpreet Devi might have a point,' Mandeep insisted.

'So what? Are you planning to start this backward stunt with your cab, huh?' Sukhi said.

'People would probably pay more for such a gimmick. You know what they're like in London. Pretend it's fashionable and everyone will want to jump on for a ride,' said Karam, tossing five pence on to the table.

'No, yaar, I'm just interested in his idea. I think sometimes it *is* more helpful to turn around and consider another approach to something. This Devi guy is planning on reversing all the way to Pakistan. He wants to apply the reverse philosophy to Indo-Pak relations—'

'Good idea!' Guru was suddenly animated. Any discussion on India and Pakistan always got him worked up. 'In this case I say yes – let's reverse. Let's reverse right back to 1947 – *before* Partition. Since then it has just been downhill.'

'I don't think that's what Devi's suggesting.' Mandeep

peered over Sukhi's shoulder in an effort to see Guru's cards.

'Well, that's what he *should* suggest. He should forget the reverse-driving business and instead try to turn around the decision that put a stupid border through India.' Guru was getting worked up. Karam and Mandeep exchanged a wary glance.

'Come on, Bhraji, you can't reverse history,' Mandeep said.

'Then don't talk to me about reverse philosophies.' Guru slapped ten pounds on to the table.

'Well, maybe Karam can make something of Harpreet Devi's efforts.' Mandeep declared his hand with a sigh of defeat. 'Maybe you could include him in that manual of Sikhism you've got. You're still working on it, aren't you? The one your Masterji left you?'

'Ah, that's finished.' Karam put ten pence on the table to match Guru's bet. Whatever Guru bet in pounds, the brothers were obliged to match or top in pence, and vice versa.

'What? You've completed it?' Mandeep was impressed.

'No. I mean it's finished as an idea – there's no hope for it. At least, I can't do anything with it.'

'I can't believe you've given up. Come on – I'm sure you've been working on it secretly all these years,' Mandeep teased. 'It must be huge by now – a proper encyclopedia.'

'I'm telling you, I haven't done anything.' Karam wished he had more to show for all the hours of thought he'd dedicated to Masterji's treatise over the years. But the truth was he never felt he'd come up with an original idea that was worth putting down on paper.

'You must, at least, have added the odd fact to Masterji's

work?' Mandeep thought Karam was being modest.

'I tell you, I wish I had, but really I've done nothing except think about it, and that alone usually wears me out.'

'Well, it's a big task. I mean it obviously overwhelmed Masterji in the end.' Mandeep tried to reassure his brother.

'And it's too late anyway.' Karam glanced at the brass map of Africa ticking away on the wall. 'I should have done more sooner. Even if I could start now, I'd never finish.' All those hopes of making history, being a part of it . . . They'd come to nothing, really.

'Well, fear of not finishing is never a good reason not to start. Did I tell you about the man who's working on a dictionary of Sanskrit?' Mandeep said. 'He's been at it for fifty-five years and he's still only halfway through the letter A. Just think of that! There's something like two hundred and fifty thousand words that start with A and the fellow's got about eighty thousand left to do. Now *that's* what I call an endless task, Bhraji. Your little treatise is nothing in comparison.'

'I suppose.'

'Although it doesn't bode well for the future of Sikhism if even you, who are so active in the faith, can't complete a comprehensive paper on it,' Mandeep said.

'I'm only active in a small way. Who am I to make predictions?'

'You're entitled to have an opinion.' Mandeep started to build a tower with the coins in the middle of the table.

'Everyone has opinions – what good are they? We need some direction if Sikhism is going to survive and grow. We need leadership, we need collective action.' Karam wagged a finger. 'I fear Sikhism is a dying religion. Islam is growing and even Christianity is strong. Meanwhile, at our gurudwara the congregation is made up almost entirely of pensioners and the numbers are dwindling. What is the future, I ask?'

'It's the youngsters, they're not interested.' Sukhi declared his hand and withdrew from the round.

'Ah, that's too simple.' Karam flicked at his coins. 'Maybe the elders haven't been the best example of how to practise the faith. We need to modernize – and instead people want to go backwards.'

'*Someone* was just saying backwards is the way forward,' Guru interjected coolly.

'Well,' Karam said, 'the gurudwara committee is definitely in the wrong gear, I can tell you that much. As you know, just last year they were voting on a motion to get rid of all the tables and chairs and revert to sitting on the floor to eat, like they do in Amritsar. In this day and age, in this country.' His palm smacked down on the table. 'Even holding a vote on such an issue is absurd!'

'Nobody agreed to it,' Guru reminded him. He was a little wary of Karam's progressive stance on things since Pyari's divorce.

'Well, they agreed to ban mixed marriages from taking place in our gurudwara.' Karam shook his head. 'That was a giant step backwards.'

'I'm with you on that one, Bhraji. It was a big mistake.' Mandeep was even more liberal than Karam. With his cut hair, unmarried status and host of non-Indian friends, he was considered quite a renegade.

'*I* think they made the right decision,' said Guru, thumbing his wad of notes.

'This is why the youngsters don't come to the gurudwara.' Karam pointed at Guru. 'They see the faith as inflexible and out of touch. Mixed marriages are common these days. I don't know how our bunch became so orthodox.' He was starting to feel despondent and his mood crept around the table like a contagious disease.

'Well, I think they made the right move. And can *you* make your move now, please, Bhraji? You've been analysing those cards for too long. Come on, place a bet, be a man,' Guru said.

'I'm just considering . . .' Karam felt confident about his cards, but was, as ever, inclined to caution.

'Considering what? Whether or not to bet another five pence?' Guru asked. 'Hurry up, don't be so tight.'

'I'm not tight.'

'Come on, loosen up, play the game,' Guru goaded, and managed to provoke Karam into betting fifty pence.

'This game is better with more players,' said Karam. 'I phoned Rajan and asked him to join us. I left a message on his mobile. He must have been too busy with work.'

The brothers nodded to allow Karam the illusion that they believed Rajan would have come if work hadn't prevented him.

'It might get more exciting if you two upped the stakes a bit.' Mandeep tried to lighten the mood.

'How much more can they up them?' Sukhi inclined his head towards Guru. 'Bhraji here just bet *fifty pounds* to match Karam bhraji's fifty pence. You can't get much higher than that.'

Without a word, Guru put down five twenty-pound notes.

'Ohh,' Sukhi murmured admiringly. He reached out, picked up the pile of notes and counted them carefully.

'Eeeh – don't crease them.' Guru frowned.

'What's wrong with you?' Mandeep was amused by his brother's quirk. 'It's just a piece of paper. You should have been born in North Korea. Apparently people there are forbidden to fold a banknote! It's that Kim Jong whatever – he doesn't want his picture defaced by the manhandling of notes. Probably the coins are polished every day as well to keep his tyrant face looking shiny and new.'

'Your cards can't be *that* great.' Karam looked at his own, which were so good he almost dared to think they were unbeatable.

'You just bet or show,' Guru said. 'Stop all these delaying tactics.'

Karam wondered whether to bet or declare. The hand he held was the best he'd drawn in a long time. Winning would be a real coup. Guru had placed almost two hundred pounds on the table – a marked contrast to Karam's own meagre bets, which barely amounted to a pound. The loss wouldn't be great, even if he was defeated. Nevertheless a niggling lack of conviction in his ability, and perhaps even his right, to win made him declare his hand of tricks. He revealed two aces, a king and a queen, and watched in disbelief and disappointment as Guru took the winnings with lesser cards: two aces and two queens.

'How do you always manage it?'

'Luck.' Guru smiled.

'Ah, I don't believe in luck,' Karam said crossly.

'Maybe that's why you don't have it.'

'More tea anyone?' Karam suddenly craved the comfort of Sarna's thick, sweet drink.

They all nodded. No one ever said no to another cup of Sarna's brew.

'Sarna? Sarna?' Karam shouted.

She did not hear him. She had the TV on loud and was crying contentedly in front of it, dabbing her eyes with her chuni as the credits rolled up over the thoroughly satisfying end of a Bollywood film, *Ma di Himat* or *Mother Courage*. Villainous sons, errant husband, evil mother-in-law, long-lost sister, corrupt uncle – everyone had been redeemed in the end. All had returned to the fold of the long-suffering heroine – a model mother, sister, wife – a saint – and fallen to her feet begging forgiveness. Sarna's heart was expanding in her chest as if she was the benevolent protagonist. She was full of love and goodness. She wanted to take the world into her arms and ease every last atom of suffering. She might have done so if it had been possible in that instant. She might even have forgiven herself. But filmy feelings are prone to fade at the slightest prod from reality.

High on the intensity of her affections, she picked up the telephone and dialled Nina's number. No answer. She left a sweet message, hoping Nina was well. She tried the mobile. No answer. She left a neutral message, asking to be called back. She called Nina's pager. No answer. Sarna put down the receiver, her elation in free-fall like a sky-diver with a faulty parachute. Happy endings always happened to other people. She had the most ungrateful family in the world, how could things turn out right in the end?

They had drifted away, her children, despite her best intentions. She had tried not to love them too much for fear she would lose them. She *had* loved them too much, denied it, and lost them anyway. The path had been the same, only each estrangement had left a different pattern on the gravelly surface of time. Sarna kept raking over the tracks of each relationship, trying to smooth a way to some satisfactory end, offering them her food and infirmity as substitutes for real intimacy. But they continued walking in the opposite direction. Now, when she wanted them close, all of her nearest and dearest were heading for some place she couldn't be. Even Nina phoned less regularly, and her visits were petering out like the last gasps from an emptying bottle of soap. She had not been to London for over six months, claiming she didn't feel too well and was busy with work. Sarna blew her nose. Tears throbbed under her diaphanous lilac eyelids. She picked up the phone and redialled Nina's number. It would be a rather different sort of conversation if she answered now. Luckily, or maybe unluckily, she did not. Sarna then tried Pyari, but there too she got through to voicemail. Where were they? Ten o'clock on a Wednesday night, both single women – they ought to be at home. Sarna pressed the palms of her hands over her eyes to dam the tears. No one was there for her. No one cared. And she had lived only for her family, her children, measuring her every action by their needs. Where were the ungrateful wretches?

Pyari *was* at home. Seeing her parents' number flash up on her phone, she'd refrained from answering.

Nina was in hospital. Not working her night shift, but doing a rather different sort of labour.

39

At 10.02 p.m. Nina gave birth to a daughter. She held the baby and said, 'This was my umeed, my hope. This was my greatest hope.' The baby was taken by a nurse and Nina leaned back on the hospital bed. She was exhausted but content. Oskar clasped her right hand, relieved that everything had gone well. Then the doctor injected something into Nina's left arm and Oskar raised his eyebrows questioningly.

'Oh, common procedure,' the doctor said. 'Just something to make the uterus contract again so that the placenta is fully ejected. Nothing to worry about.'

Around them in the small delivery room, although the birth was over, there was still a buzz of activity. A nurse instructed Nina to push again. 'That's it, good girl,' she encouraged. 'Just another couple and then it's over. Good, we're almost there.'

Oskar watched Nina's face scrunch up and wondered where the strength, after twenty hours of labour, continued to come from. He found himself breathing in the same rhythm as her again, fervently willing her along as if the force of his wishing might translate into some kind of useful physical impetus.

All of a sudden, the nurse called out for help. The white sheets were rapidly turning red. Oskar couldn't believe how quickly the colour was spreading: the circumference of this giant pool of blood had already extended halfway up Nina's back and was creeping towards the edges of the bed. The medical staff were suddenly frantic.

'Is it hurting?' Oskar asked. What he really wanted to know was, 'Is something wrong?'

Nina shook her head and replied weakly, 'Not really. Not worse.' She didn't seem to be aware that she was bleeding so heavily.

'Hook her up to O minus. Quickly!' someone ordered.

'She's tachycardic,' a voice reported.

'And hypotensive.'

Oskar listened and watched in confusion, not wanting to interrupt or slow them down by asking questions. There seemed to be blood everywhere: the gloved hands of the medics were deep crimson, their green gowns splattered almost black. Nina's thighs were covered in blood and more continued to leak out of her, bringing with it thick, dark clots like raw liver. Oskar felt sick with fear. Was it just the placenta coming out? What was going on? In minutes, things had gone from being normal to being horribly, horribly wrong.

And then somebody said, 'She's haemorrhaging.'

'She's lost almost two litres.'

'Haemoglobin's below eight . . . below five!'

'Nina? Nina? Can you hear me?' The nurse who'd been supporting her through the labour earlier came right up, leaned over Oskar, and looked into Nina's eyes. Nina blinked and nodded a response. 'Good, stay with me now, Nina. Just stay with me.'

One of the doctors asked an assistant to show Oskar

out. 'We need to operate, I'm afraid you can't be here. We'll keep you informed.'

The heavy doors of the theatre swung behind him. Their swaying quickly slowed and the view between them reduced to a thin white line of light. With a final shudder, like a heart that briefly races before ceasing to beat altogether, the doors closed and became still, but not before Oskar heard the faint murmur: 'She's shutting down.'

All night Oskar's mind switched at whim between clarity and chaos. His heart faltered – rushed – became numb – according to alien design. He could not rely on his limbs to respond as directed, they flailed or became immobile as they pleased. His skin turned angry and red as if it, too, had been wounded – it screamed loudest just below his underarms, which is where she loved to kiss him.

He knew he had to contact Nina's family. What would he say? How could the facts, which refused to sink into his own consciousness, be communicated and made real to anyone else? He dreaded revealing not just the death but the deception that preceded it.

When he eventually made his way to one of the public phone booths in the maternity ward, Oskar was nowhere near comprehension. He expected, somehow, to fumble through the necessary conversation. He called Pyari, believing she would be the most understanding. He should have realized it was too soon for anyone to understand anything. He told her who he was and explained that he knew Nina well.

'Oskar? OK? Oh my goodness. She never said . . . she never mentioned anything . . .'

Ignoring the unspoken questions in her reply, he

moved on quickly to say he'd brought Nina to the hospital the previous day.

'Why? Isn't she well?'

Oskar resorted to medical speak. It came out automatically, as though someone had pressed a first-aid alarm. 'She suffered from a post-partum haemorrhage.'

'What?'

'She died . . . she died,' he managed to whisper. The words came out tiny, as if they didn't want to be. Oskar swallowed and squeezed out a voice, though his throat had tightened sharply as if trying to choke off further revelations. 'While giving birth, there were complications. It just . . . it was so unexpected.'

'What? What are you saying? Nina wasn't pregnant. She can't even have children. You've got the wrong number. Who are you? What are you saying? Where's Nina?'

'I'm sorry . . .' A warning bleep told him to put another coin into the phone box. 'You can call the hospital if you want to confirm things. I'll give you the number.'

'No!' Pyari's voice trembled. 'Wait . . . no. What's going on? Is this a prank call?' She seemed to be talking to herself. 'Where are you?'

'At Trafford General Hospital, in Manchester.'

'Give me the number,' she said. 'And *your* number? Do you have a number?'

'I . . . no, but you can call me on Nina's number.'

'Are you *sure*?' Pyari said, and he knew she wasn't talking about the phone.

'I'm sorry.'

She put down the receiver.

A flurry of investigative phone calls followed. Pyari called Rajan, he rang the hospital, then he phoned Oskar, then

Pyari rang him again. Later brother and sister met up and interrupted each other down the line to Oskar. So it went: a morning of trying to piece together the facts and fashion them into a palatable fiction which could be presented to Karam and Sarna.

Neither Pyari nor Rajan were interested in the romance of how Nina and Oskar had met; they couldn't imagine the two had been deeply in love. They focused on trying to limit the blow to their parents. But they soon realized that the facts could not easily be altered or mitigated. It would be difficult to ignore Nina's marriage or the existence of her baby daughter.

'We think it'll be better if *we* tell our parents,' Pyari proposed at one point.

'Fine, as you please,' Oskar said.

A short while later, Rajan implied the opposite. 'Maybe you should be around when we speak to our parents. It might help, if they have questions . . .'

'If that's what you want.' Oskar wondered what Nina would have wanted. 'But I need to be around the hospital for a few more days because of the baby. And then, I don't know about getting there – I mean travelling with the baby.' He suddenly wondered how he was going to manage now – without Nina but with a baby.

'Oh God, of course. Sorry, I'd forgotten about that.' Rajan considered, for the first time, that Oskar too might be suffering. 'I'm sorry . . . I guess this isn't easy for you either.'

Oskar looked at the people sitting around him in the hospital café. He saw people wringing their hands and remembered others doing the same on public transport or in the waiting room of the doctor's surgery. Wringing, he had imagined, in anxiety or idleness. Now he understood it was the language of loss that their fingers spoke, just as his own twisted and knotted around each other, pressing the knuckles to release the pain that seared them.

The arguing voices of Pyari and Rajan filtered down the phone, like echoes from another age.

'I don't think we can tell them how this happened. It's not fair on them. I don't think they could take it,' Pyari told her brother.

'Don't be silly, you can't hide anything. They'll find out. One of the first things Mum's going to be interested in is Nina's final will—'

'Rajan! That's awful. How can you say such a thing?'

'It's true. Come on, she knows Pritpal left Nina comfortably off, that she owned her house. Of course she'll be curious about where it's all going. You know what Mum's like. So she's bound to find out that Nina was married and everything goes to Oskar and the baby. Sorry about this, Oskar, we're just thinking out loud here.' Rajan suddenly acknowledged his aural presence. 'I think it's becoming clear that we have to come clean about the whole thing.'

Oskar half listened as they discussed him. It was as though they were talking about someone else, someone he'd left behind and wouldn't recognize again for a long time. He didn't want to get involved in their conspiracies. Let them resolve this as they wished. But then Pyari lashed out, making apathy impossible. 'Why did you do this? You shouldn't have let her!'

Her words came at him like an arrow, echoing the guilty castigations of his own heart.

'Nina was an adult. She chose to have this baby.' He wanted to convince himself as much as Pyari.

There was silence for a few moments, broken only by the muffled sound of weeping.

'How is she – the baby?' Rajan broke the silence. It was the first time either of them had asked.

'Fine.' Oskar recalled the warm weightlessness of her in his arms. She felt like a bubble of air. 'Perfectly fine.'

'Good, that's good . . . does she have a name yet?'

Oskar was about to say no, when it struck him that, yes, she did have a name. 'Umeed.'

'Umeed?' Rajan echoed.

'Umeed. Hope,' Oskar confirmed – to himself as much as to them.

'Umeed,' Pyari repeated. The cave of grief that had yelled open inside her swallowed the word with a gulp.

Karam and Sarna didn't know what was more harrowing: the fact that Nina had died, or the fact that she had lied. In a way, they had been confronted with a double death.

Sarna shrank back in her seat, drew her legs up and crossed her arms over them as if she was locking herself up. She crouched there, a compacted version of herself, staring at the wall through wide unblinking eyes.

Sarna had always thought death was the end. Now she saw that Nina's death was a war cry from the past – but she felt too spent for more battles. Nina's death wounded her, hurt her so deeply it stirred an old wail which had been silenced decades before below the creaking decks of the *Amra*. Sarna dared not express her anguish, for it was a grief disproportionate to the image of bereavement she needed to give the world: that of a sister mourning a sister. The love between siblings is different to the love of a parent for a child. Sarna had lost two sisters – she knew the pattern of that mourning. The loss of a child is a heightened and unnatural agony – and she was familiar with its trajectory too. She felt again the sensation of being wrenched apart and crushed at the same time; she felt the blood slow in her veins and pulse haltingly in sickening flushes of hot and cold; she felt the choking constriction in her throat. She felt the blades of regret poking through her ribs and scratching at her soul. Worse, she felt her heart beating – false and jerky. Why did it pump on? She had no wish to live. She should have died years ago in the same circumstances that had just claimed Nina – then none of this would have happened.

Despite the tyrannical exertions of her mind to forget and reinvent the past, Sarna's body remained subject to the time lines of truth. She struggled to keep possession of herself, fearing that to let out just one cry could unhinge and destroy her. She had spent a lifetime making herself the woman who had not given birth to Nina; to mourn that child now would be to acknowledge the end of the part she had acted. And who would she be if she were no longer what she'd become?

Karam's eyes were milky with cataracts and something else. That which inexplicably rides the line between regret and relief, loss and gain, the spoken and unspoken. He stood up and said, 'We must put things in order.' There were rituals to be commenced, customs to be followed. In his meticulous arrangement of these was a discreet expression of love. He called the gurudwara and asked one of the granthis to begin reciting the sadarahan paat for Nina. The prayer involved the priests reading the Granth Sahib from beginning to end without a break, all 1,430 pages of it. He requested that they try and complete the prayer within three days so Nina's cremation could take place on Sunday. But it wasn't possible for Oskar to get down to London with Umeed so soon. Finally they agreed to have the cremation the following Thursday, just over a week after Nina's death.

Later that night, Sarna had a minor stroke. After being taken to hospital, she had a second, more severe stroke. By morning she was in intensive care, hooked up to a ventilator and a CVP monitor. Surprisingly, despite the trauma, she finally looked calm.

The prognosis was curiously ambivalent. Doctors began by emphasizing that Sarna might never regain consciousness. They explained that although she was still showing vital signs, her blood pressure remained high and she was at risk of suffering another stroke. If this happened . . . well, there was really very little hope of recovery. In the present circumstances, however, *if* there were no further complications, Sarna would survive. But if she did pull through, she might not be the same. There could be permanent paralysis or she might have lost her facility for speech or even have amnesia. (None of the family dared inform the experts that she'd been suffering from a selective form of the latter condition for years.) Obviously, the medics pointed out, the longer she took to come out of the coma, the less likely it was that she'd have a complete recovery. The next forty-eight hours were critical. Though, of course, there were instances of extraordinary revivals. Miracles did happen, even in science – but, mind you, they were rare.

The family didn't know what to think. They had been presented with every possibility on the spectrum from pessimism to optimism. All they could do now was wait and see where the quivering hand of chance would choose to rest.

Rajan telephoned Oskar to update him on what had happened.

'Oh God, I'm so sorry. Is she . . . ?'

'She's stable. In a coma, but stable, they say. Whatever that means.'

'What happened? Is it because of what you told her, about Nina? Was it the news . . . ?'

'Possibly. She has a history of high blood pressure. The doctors suspect the bad news may have triggered this stroke, but they can't say so for sure.' Rajan had his own theories about what had happened.

'What a shock this must be for all of you.'

'Yes . . . no. It's not exactly out of character for my mother to overreact,' Rajan said.

'Sarna must have been really shaken by the news.' Oskar wanted to be fair.

'Probably the facts hit her and hurt her, and this stroke is a way of avoiding dealing with the whole issue.' They all knew that Sarna's physical maladies had often reflected her mental state. 'My mother has always excelled at the art of avoidance. I just never believed she could go this far.' Rajan was frustrated that Sarna had once again managed to slip the net of her past actions, and this time she'd left them all messily entangled in the consequences.

'Maybe it's not about telling Sarna any more,' Oskar said. 'Maybe you just need to clear things up between the rest of you – to tell your father, for instance.'

'Well, that's what I thought, but Pyari says we should leave things as they are now. She's concerned about Dad's reaction, which I can understand. I'm certainly not keen to be responsible for ruining the health of both my parents. Pyari feels getting the truth out can no longer change anything for anyone. She's asked me to tell you that we're not going to say anything more.'

'But the truth still has the power to change everything for Umeed,' Oskar said. 'Don't you see? If she cannot know Nina was Sarna's daughter, then she can't know you are her closest relatives.'

'Of course we will always be her family, regardless of who does or doesn't know.'

'Nina never felt like a real part of your family precisely because of the uncertainty about who did and didn't know.'

'Well . . .' Rajan wasn't sure that family feeling was only forged by complete openness. Sometimes quiet complicity was very effective in tightening bonds. He felt tied to his family by dint of all the things he wasn't supposed to be aware of.

'I don't want to have any part in silence if it could later hurt Umeed,' Oskar said.

'What about my dad?'

'Your father has a right to know the truth as well. You shouldn't underestimate his capacity to deal with it,' Oskar said. 'Look, Rajan, it's also about Nina's memory. I think she deserves, finally, to be acknowledged for who she was. According to what she told me, everyone knows anyway – but someone needs to say it out loud. If the silence isn't broken now, Umeed will grow up under the same yoke of false identity as Nina. Can't you see that?'

40

When Oskar arrived in London just after midday on Wednesday, he learned that Karam still had not been told. 'Please don't say anything. He doesn't know yet,' Pyari said as they drove to the hospital, where Karam was with Sarna.

'My goodness! You've aged!' Karam eyed up Oskar critically. So grey! The hair, the eyes – the man was even wearing a grey jacket.

'Mr Singh.' Oskar extended a hand. Karam had aged too, but elegantly and gracefully – not dramatically in fast-forward like him.

'But . . . it is you. It's really you.' Karam shook his hand.

There was an awkward silence. Pyari broke it by reaching out to take Umeed. She held the baby, exclaiming with sadness and wonder, 'See, Pithaji, she looks just like Nina.'

Oskar's heart leaped at the affirmation. He had noticed the strong resemblance but thought it might be a cruel trick of his beleaguered imagination. Karam gave the child a cursory glance before turning to his wife. 'Oh, she's opened her eyes again!' he exclaimed and rushed to Sarna's side. By the time they'd all crowded around the bed, she seemed to be peacefully asleep again. 'She opened them earlier as well. Nurse said it might be a good sign,' said Karam, smoothing the sheet. Through the cotton he felt the curve of Sarna's arm. Now, once again, he could caress her without reproach.

Oskar could not believe that the pale woman in the bed was the culinary seductress he had once known. The bedside table was crowded with bouquets of flowers standing in jugs of water. Oskar nudged his offering of lilies into one jug. Their white heads nodded sadly and cried a shower of orange pollen over his hand.

That evening they sat in the living room at Elm Road waiting for Rajan. 'He's very irritable at the moment,' Pyari warned Oskar. 'I think the pressure's getting to him. He knows we have to tell Pithaji today. He thinks it's harder for him just because he has to say the actual words.' It was clear she was anxious. She couldn't sit still and even her brow danced with worry, arabesquing through various degrees of tension. She and Rajan had finally agreed to reveal everything to Karam, but had found excuses to put it off. Oskar was not pleased to have arrived just in time for their confession.

'How's Mum?' Rajan asked after he had arrived and greeted Oskar.

'Have you come from the office?' Karam scrutinized his son. Didn't he have to wear a suit to run a company? Rajan was dressed casually in blue jeans, a green T-shirt and a brown sports jacket. He was unshaven and in need of a haircut. He looked attractive, but in a neglected, exhausted sort of way.

Sensing his father's disapproval, Rajan ignored the question. 'How's Mum today? Was there any change?'

'She opened her eyes for one second,' Karam reported.

'I suppose she couldn't resist having a peek at little Umeed here.' Rajan touched her cheek. 'She looks so much like Nina.'

'Come and help me with the tea.' Pyari drew her brother away.

Oskar perched on the sofa, put Umeed's rocker beside him and set it swaying with a gentle nudge. Karam leaned back in the big armchair Sarna usually occupied. He looked at the Africa clock. For so many years it had been a reminder of where he had come from – how far he had come. Now its shining, ticking form had become an artefact of love. It was the shape of the continent where he and Sarna had been happiest.

Rajan walked into the room carrying a tray of mugs. Pyari was just behind him. 'Milk, no sugar?' Pyari handed Oskar a mug. He felt like weeping at the question. The secret sweetener of his life was gone.

'Pithaji, something's leaking in the kitchen.' Pyari sat down on the other side of Umeed.

'Really?' Karam stood to go and investigate.

'It's not a big deal.' Rajan waved him down. 'Just a puddle of water which I've mopped up. We can check it out later.' He looked at his watch, thrust his hands into his pockets and walked up to the mantelpiece. 'Dad, we need to tell you—'

'I know,' Karam interrupted.

'You *know*?' Rajan frowned.

'I know what you want to tell me.'

Rajan swallowed hard, as if physically trying to ingest Karam's words.

'About . . . Nina?' Pyari leaned forward.

'I know she was your mother's daughter.' Karam ran a finger along the sharp crease that went down the front of

491

his trousers. It was a strange and remarkable irony that the man who loved history, who had chased it across the globe, had avoided and denied *his* story. Perhaps he'd sought out large-scale dramas in the hope that they'd eclipse all knowledge of his wife's troubled past.

'How long have you known?' Pyari's hands were cupped around a steaming mug of tea.

'Ah, I've always known. For years now, since the days in Kenya.' He glanced at the ticking brass map. 'I overheard Biji and Persini talking once.' Their words still played in his mind with the irritating stubbornness of a tune that hums on in your head against your wish.

'She's a real chalaako, as cunning as they come. I always knew something was going on there. You can tell – when people are too suspicious of others you know they have something to hide.' Persini had been exultant.

Biji was more restrained. 'This is what happens when you send sons off to find wives. They get duped by beauty. Such a mistake letting him go alone. That family of Sarna's could fool you into marrying a monkey. Such talkers. Real motor-mouths, I tell you. They could fill one of those big sky balloons with their hot air faster than you can puff up pooris in your frying pan. You should have heard the mother while I was there. "Father was SDO. Daughters are pure as kyo." Oh ho, what a joke. They've made fools of us. No doubt about it. And Karam, poor man, he's the biggest fool. Completely hoodwinked.'

'Well she hasn't managed to deceive the rest of the world. Everyone knows. Really, *everyone*. Juginder at Textile Mart knows – so you can be sure she's spread the word,' Persini said.

Biji's head shook fatalistically. 'We can't stop what's

already in motion, but we can influence its path. People can speak amongst themselves, but they can't talk to us about it if we don't ask or listen. We won't repeat the shameful facts between ourselves either. Is that clear?' Seeing the disappointment in Persini's eyes, Biji added, 'I hope you haven't said anything to Karam's brothers?'

'No, no of course not,' Persini lied. 'But,' she tried to cover her tracks, 'you never know, they might have heard it from somewhere else, like I did.'

'I doubt it,' Biji said. 'They weren't out looking for scandal, like you. And anyway, I'm sure they would have said something to me. The important thing now is *you're* not to say a word, *ever*. Not even to Sukhi, OK?'

Persini had been hoping for a full-on confrontation with Sarna so that they could set the record straight and put the woman in her place. She had been looking forward to a showdown. Instead, Biji was sentencing them all to a lifetime of false pretences. It didn't make sense to Persini, but Biji had her reasons. 'I don't want Karam to find out. He made a mistake and he has to live with it, but he doesn't have to know. What good will knowing do? It's too late to change anything.'

'You could throw her out – sali shenzi woman!' Persini swore.

'Hai – hold your tongue! Have you lost your senses? What kind of disgrace would that cause? I won't have it!' Biji said.

'But what about *her*?' Persini burst out. 'How can she just get away with it? What do we do? Pretend that we don't know she's a chalaako? Act like we've got no clue she's had an illegitimate child?'

'Heh – sshhhh!' Biji grabbed Persini by the shoulders. 'Promise me you won't ever say anything about Sarna's secret. Promise? Swear!' She squeezed harder and her nails dug into Persini's skin.

'OK!'

But Biji wasn't convinced. 'Swear it on your mother's life. Go on, swear!'

'I swear,' Persini vowed again. The words tasted so bitter that she came towards the door and spat on the gravel outside. Hearing her approach, Karam had quickly slunk away.

'I can't believe you never said anything.' The tea in Pyari's hands had gone cold.

Rajan was still too stunned to speak. He had spent days and sleepless nights working himself up to the task of enlightening his father. Instead, Karam was calmly flashing the torch of truth in their eyes.

'Why should I have said anything? It wasn't a fact I was happy to advertise. I just put it out of my mind. I followed Biji's reasoning about keeping silent.' Karam seemed composed.

'Yeah, but what about Mee? Why didn't you tell *her* when you found out?' Pyari wondered.

Karam had never expected to have to justify the reasons behind his most critical life choices. It had been a long time since he'd reflected on them himself. 'There were different reasons, I suppose. Duty was one. I felt a responsibility to maintain the status quo that Biji wanted. And then I didn't know what telling your mother would do – to us, to the family. The longer I left it, the harder it became to say anything.'

'Is that when you went to London on your refrigeration course?' Pyari set her mug aside.

'It was a bad decision.' Karam nodded. 'There was

494

another sister, you know. Phoolwati, your twin. Your mother doesn't like to talk about her. Anyway, it was even harder to say anything when I got back from London. Your mother was in a terrible state. She'd been mistreated by my family and she was grieving. I couldn't confront her. It would have been too cruel. And moreover . . .' Karam couldn't bring himself to say, 'I loved her.' He remembered the tremendous, consuming love he'd had for Sarna. That love had been only marginally dented by his shame and pain at the revelations about her past. There had been moments when Karam had despised himself for continuing to love her so deeply, as though it was a weakness to know the darkest details of someone's past and still desire the person. 'In my mind,' he said, 'I developed an image of the two of us struggling together against my family and the world. I allied myself to her and we went on. We survived.'

'It's so sad.' Pyari was crying. 'If you'd just said something . . . it might have been easier . . . you might have been happier. The secrecy seems so unnecessary.'

'Maybe.' Karam closed his eyes for a moment. 'Yes, it is a tragedy that we struggled together yet alone – without sharing and telling. That's probably what started to destroy us in the end – the silence. It's easy to see these things now. It's easy to imagine that if we'd told each other we might have managed better, we might have made it through with some dignity. But, you know, all this talking business wasn't the way in those days. Also, you must realize, your mother probably couldn't have admitted anything to me even if she'd wanted to – such issues were a social blight in those days, an abomination. A couple couldn't discuss such things. We certainly didn't talk.'

'No, you shouted at each other.' Rajan found his voice.

'About *feelings*, I mean. You know, fears, worries – such things weren't discussed. It was all hush hush, pushing things under the mat. Shouting, fighting was different – that was your mother's speciality. But did she ever rant about anything important? She always let herself be sidetracked by the superficial. There are many subjects your mother and I never even touched on. You won't believe it, and even I find it strange now, but, for example, we never spoke about the death of our child. Never. Not a word. And yet, you couldn't say we weren't close. We had something. But it was different. It was different . . .'

'Yes.' Rajan's hands flew out of his pockets and collided with a snap. 'It was all a big lie.'

'Rajan!' Pyari said.

'You make it all sound very noble, Dad, but I can't help feeling there was a lot of cowardice in all your actions: not facing up to the facts, running away to London when things got tough, sticking in this loveless marriage based on deception.'

'This is not a way to speak.' Karam raised his voice. 'You think your modern solutions are better? You would have liked me to divorce your mother? Kick her out, have you grow up in a broken home?'

For Rajan it had been a broken home anyway. But no one was allowed to see or say it.

'It is quite possible that in some ways I was a coward.' Karam fixed his eyes on a carpet stain as though that might keep his voice steady, the way a dancer focuses on a spot for balance. 'But my instinct has always been to do the right thing. You think I haven't wanted to blurt out the truth? There have been countless occasions when I've had to restrain myself from shouting it out to your mother. Don't you see? Time has also put me in the wrong. *I* chose her. I had the option and I picked *her*. Biji thought I should have known better. But I made the wrong choice and was implicated by it. Then, because I lived silently with the knowledge of the truth for so many years, I became guilty by association. If I had said anything I would have been accusing myself as well.' He looked up at Pyari, then Rajan. 'How could I just stand up and tear down my whole life? What would people say?'

'*People say, people say*,' Rajan repeated. 'Who cares what people say?'

'We're not all as independent as you. No,' Karam wagged a finger, 'some of us still have consideration for friends and family. It's a shame *you* didn't learn the prudence of holding your tongue.' For the millionth time, he wished he'd never allowed the boy's hair to be cut.

'No, Dad, you know what the shame is? That I admired your patience and restraint until just a moment ago – when I learned it's been a farce. And I can't stand it, because I feel ridiculous too – as if everything between us has been a travesty.' Rajan's voice cracked.

'Raj, don't do this,' Pyari said.

'You let us believe you were someone you're not. That's the worst part of it. With Mum, we knew there were hidden sides, but I thought you were . . . you. All these years we've protected you: bitten our tongues, put up with Mum's nonsense and let Nina suffer – because we thought, At least Dad doesn't know. Poor Dad shouldn't know.' It seemed to Rajan that they had all carried around this burden unnecessarily, each of them trying to be martyrs to a non-existent cause.

'*All these years?* What are you talking about?' Karam's eyebrows clashed in confusion.

'Yes, all these decades.' Which suddenly felt like pitiful

aeons of secrecy. 'Ever since Nina first arrived from India to live with us. That's how long we've known, Dad – and tried to protect you.'

Karam's lips twitched uncertainly. Pyari shot another warning look at Rajan, who was too angry to be affected by the change in his father's countenance.

'Everyone knows.' Rajan forced himself to calm down.

'Everyone?' Karam said.

Rajan looked him in the eye. 'Yes, Dad, apparently everyone knows. Mum's whole family, your whole family – all your brothers, your friends, people at the temple. The whole Sikh community, in fact.'

Karam's face contorted.

'No, not every single person. Just those with East African connections, probably – and I'm sure most of them have forgotten by now anyway.' Pyari hastily tried to mitigate the effect of Rajan's words.

Karam shuddered and reached for the armrests to steady himself. 'My brothers? Not my brothers.'

Rajan saw his vulnerability and refrained from speaking.

Karam's mouth fell open as he contemplated the awful reality: *everyone knew*. They had always known. He clutched at his collar. The fabric of his white shirt tightened around his chest as he pulled it into his fist. 'How stupid I've been.' He stared into his lap. 'How simple, to think that no one else would ever know or suspect. I've been no less deluded than your mother really, in my own way. The world has been laughing at me behind my back—'

'No, Pithaji!' Pyari interrupted.

Umeed stirred and Oskar, who had been sitting like a

statue with his fingers knotted in a lattice of pain, came to life. He bent over to pick her up.

'We have to make it up to Nina,' Rajan said.

'What about your mother?' Karam let go of his shirt, leaving a crushed flower of creases at his chest. He sat tall and put his hands on his knees.

'What about her?' Rajan asked.

'She couldn't face it if there was a public announcement,' Karam said.

'She's not going to be there anyway . . .' Rajan hesitated. He wanted to say that no one bounces back to perfect health from a deep coma, but he stopped himself. If anyone *could*, that person would be Sarna. She'd always had extraordinary powers of endurance. All the medical evidence pointed to the fact that she had suffered a stroke, but Rajan still could not shake off the suspicion that the attack had been self-induced and its after-effects exaggerated. It was not difficult for him to imagine that his mother was conveniently biding her time in a coma. There were moments when he almost believed that Sarna was just waiting for the awkwardness and pain of Nina's funeral to pass before she admitted herself back into the world again. 'I wouldn't be surprised if she did recover,' he said. 'But we shouldn't be so naive as to expect her to pick up life exactly where she left off. She'll probably emerge with even more selective amnesia and claim to have no recollection of anyone called Nina at all—'

'Heh, hold your tongue,' his father interrupted. It seemed that although Karam knew about Sarna's past, he'd never really divined the extent to which keeping that past hidden had corrupted his wife. He still took most of her words and actions at face value.

'I don't know then, Dad. What do *you* want to do? Shall

we tell Mum we're going to announce the truth at the funeral tomorrow? Shall we tell her we know?'

'*Tell* her? What are you talking about? She's not even conscious!' Karam said.

'The doctors say she might be able to hear us. And if not, it can just be a sort of symbolic confession,' Rajan replied.

Karam shook his head. 'No! You cannot tell her. We can't say anything to her.'

'Why not?' Rajan demanded.

'Why, Pithaji?' Pyari echoed.

'Your mother can never know any of this.' Karam's arms folded definitively across his chest.

'No! No way!' Rajan raised both his hands, like a policeman at a roadblock. 'I'm not keeping up this charade for her sake. That's not an option. We shouldn't even consider it. I'm sick of all this secrecy and double-dealing. We need to tell all and get it out of the way.'

'You might as well kill her then.' Karam pulled a pen out of his breast pocket and offered it to his son. 'You might as well sign her death warrant yourself!'

'Pithaji!' Pyari cried out.

'Her world is a certain way,' Karam tried to explain.

Umeed's cries got louder and Oskar took her out into the hallway.

'Yeah – an extremely twisted way!' Rajan said.

'But that's the only world she can see – and the only way she can be,' Karam said. Sarna's whole life had been a negation of the fact that Nina was her daughter. It was the untruth on which her existence depended. Take that away from her and you might as well take a knife to her throat.

'What the hell are you defending her for, Dad?' Rajan asked.

'Because she won't change,' Karam said.

'You don't stand up to people because you think they might change, you do it because everybody should have to face up to the consequences of their actions. That's what justice is. You don't avoid trying a hardened criminal because you're convinced he'll never reform,' Rajan said.

Now he wants to play the lawyer. Karam shook his head.

Rajan threw up his hands and flopped on to the sofa.

Oskar came into the room with the wailing, wriggling bundle of Umeed in his arms. 'I think she's hungry. Can we warm up some water for her formula?' He fished in a bag for a bottle while Pyari headed to the kitchen.

'Oh my God!' She ran back into the living room. 'The leak – it's worse. There's water everywhere.'

Karam stood up immediately and followed her out of the room. Rajan dragged himself off the sofa. It was one thing after another in this family.

The kitchen floor was covered in water. 'Where's it coming from?' asked Karam, stepping gingerly over the wet grey lino. This wasn't good for his shoes.

'I don't know.' Pyari rolled up the sleeves of her purple top, exposing the yellow lining. 'It's hard to tell because it's everywhere now.' She started mopping.

'There's a funny smell.' Karam's nose wrinkled up like a dry fig.

Just as Rajan came in, the door of the freezer swung open. 'Uh!' His hand flew to cover his nose. The pungent smell of hundreds of different dishes filled the room.

Karam inhaled deeply. His stomach rumbled. He could smell all his favourite dishes. He turned to Pyari. 'The freezer has packed up. Did you turn something off by mistake – the mains?'

One by one, the drawers in the freezer began to slide

open as if pulled by an invisible hand. They leaned creakily out of the machine, dripping their defrosted contents on to each other and the floor.

'Oh my goodness.' A fresh assault of Mushq stabbed at Rajan's nostrils. It was a concentrated smell – an eau de parfum of everything Sarna had ever cooked. 'We're going to have to chuck all this.' He swallowed. For an instant he craved his mother's coconut chicken.

Oskar appeared in the doorway. 'Wow.' He took a few steps back, pushed by the potent smell. 'Sorry, but she needs this now.' He held out Umeed's bottle, into which he'd spooned the powdered milk. 'Could you fill it to the twenty mark? Tepid water – but boiled first, please.' Rajan took the bottle and passed it to Pyari. 'Do you need a hand?' Oskar asked, even though his hands were full with Umeed.

'We're going to have to get rid of all this,' said Rajan, looking at his father.

'Your mother will be very upset. It's such a waste.' Karam was still balancing on his toes. 'Can't we eat any of it?' He thought of everything Sarna had put into making that food.

'I don't think it's safe, Pithaji,' Pyari said. Who knew how long some of that food had been in there?

Karam bent to get some bin bags from the cupboard under the sink. His hand went unconsciously to his lower back.

'I'll tell you what,' Oskar said. 'I'll help here if Mr Singh can feed Umeed.'

'That's a good idea,' Rajan said.

'Er . . . well . . .' Karam had not held a baby for years. Not since Amar and Arjun – and they were now teenagers.

'Yes, Pithaji, that would be better.' Pyari handed him the

bottle of milk. Unable to say no, he tiptoed out of the kitchen.

'I'll put her in here and you can just sit beside her,' Oskar said, laying Umeed in the rocker and starting to feed her. He sensed Karam's ambivalence towards the child. 'All you have to do is hold the bottle.' He moved to let Karam take over.

Karam looked into Umeed's green eyes and his heart lurched. He watched the child sucking hungrily at the teat. How we all survive! This little one gulping up the milk, even though it did not come from her mother's breast. He and Sarna persisting in silence – enduring, enduring. He and Sarna. Even after everything, he could not imagine himself without her.

Rajan and Oskar emptied the freezer. Sodden bundles of vegetables, dribbling cartons of dhal, meat biryanis discoloured by freezer burn, soggy handfuls of curry leaves and coriander wrapped in clingfilm, sticky balls of dough – the leftovers of Sarna's sumptuous meals soon filled the big black bins outside the house. The smell crept out from under the lids and drifted down the street. It wafted over the Common, through Wandsworth and across the Thames. Hints of Mushq even straggled into central London. Trees lifted their heads and leaned northwards to catch a whiff of the travelling scent. Pedestrians stopped mid-step and sniffed at the air. Across the capital that evening, Indian takeaway orders rose threefold.

In the kitchen, Pyari rinsed the freezer drawers stained with oil and turmeric. Oskar got down on his knees and scrubbed the inside of the empty freezer, which was scattered with random halves of green chillies that looked like the lost ends of lizards' tails. Rajan finished mopping the floor and glanced at the wooden India clock. Its hands indicated seven forty. Sounded about right, for a change. He looked at his wrist and his own watch confirmed the hour and the minutes. 'Did you fix that?' he asked Pyari.

She turned from the sink and followed his finger to the clock. 'No. It's been behind for years. Only Mee can tell the time on that clock.'

'Well, it's working now.'

Sarna's time had finally caught up with real time.

Karam had finished feeding Umeed and was sitting beside her rocker with the empty bottle in one hand. The thumb of his other hand was clasped by her tiny fist. 'She just grabbed at me and then fell asleep,' he explained as the kitchen cleaners returned. 'Now I can't move in case she wakes up and starts crying again.' He tried to sound annoyed as the gentle pressure of Umeed's hand reached his heart.

Rajan cleared his throat. 'So, have you decided what you want to do?'

A stream that a boy must wade across is easily straddled when he becomes a man. Karam was feeling the peculiar inversion of this natural order. The torrent of truth, whose currents he had avoided almost all his married life, seemed suddenly to swell. He could no longer hop from bank to bank, avoiding the gushing flow of facts about Nina's identity. He was like a boy again, wading uncertainly through a turbulent reality, wondering how to reach dry land. Which side should he approach? How could he remain true to Sarna and uphold the truth?

Oskar watched Karam struggle while Umeed slumbered peacefully and pulled at his finger. Tiny child, born of silence into a cacophony of confession. Her lips puckered as if she was blowing her father a kiss. He had to say something. 'If no clear statement about Nina's identity is made, then her daughter will inherit the legacy of deceit. I saw what that did to Nina and I don't want the same for Umeed.' His words roamed the room like swallows looking for somewhere to nest. They hovered hopefully over Karam. 'In death, at least, Nina should be allowed to be herself.' Oskar felt a stabbing sadness that she'd had to die to get the recognition she'd craved all her life.

Karam thought how Nina had entered his world against his will and left it the same way. Yet she bound him to Sarna more deeply than their own offspring. 'We will refer to Nina as daughter of Karam and Sarna Singh,' he said.

'What? No!' Rajan's left fist slammed into the palm of his right hand. 'This funeral is supposed to set the record straight, not put a whole new gloss on the truth.'

Karam was not going to publicly pair Sarna's name with that of some other man. 'No child is born of just one person. We must state mother and father – it's the custom. But if we mention your mother then we have to mention *me*, that's the meaning of wedlock – your fates are sealed. These days you think nothing of picking the lock and sneaking off when you get bored, or breaking it altogether when you're fed up. In my time, even when the wed bit no longer had any meaning for two people, the lock remained fastened tight.' Slowly Karam was completing a journey he had been on his whole life and was arriving at the point where he would, finally, make history. Family history. 'I'll continue to stand by your mother. I'm the closest thing Nina had to a father, so it's no great falsification to say that I am.'

'I think it's a cop-out,' Rajan said. 'Don't you agree, Oskar?'

'Actually, Nina always wanted to be acknowledged as a part of your family. Mr Singh's proposal would certainly bring her into the fold. As for Umeed, *you're* the people that count – not any deceased biological ancestors.' He turned to Karam. 'I think Nina would have liked to be your daughter. She always spoke of you with respect and affection.'

Karam looked at the child again and saw her mother and her grandmother. He saw what had not been realized and all that was still possible. 'Yes,' he said. 'Tomorrow we will refer to Nina as daughter of Karam and Sarna Singh, sister of Rajan and Pyari, wife of Oskar and mother of Umeed.'

Afterword

People who have lost limbs through accidents or disease sometimes continue to feel pain in the non-existent body part. They call this phantom pain. The name suggests an imaginary suffering and yet science confirms the pain is real. I used to find this bizarre but it does not seem so strange to me now. Since I have lost Nina, I understand the possibility of an ache where there is an absence. Like an amputee who leans forward to scratch the big toe that is no longer there, I still turn in my sleep to hug the emptiness on the left side of the bed. At nine o'clock every Thursday evening, I almost call out to remind Nina that her favourite programme is on TV. When I go to clean my teeth, I still thoughtlessly put toothpaste on the brush that nestles next to mine: the force of habit overriding the force of absence.

Morphine cannot dull the phantom pain in amputees, just as time, which is deemed to be a great painkiller, cannot always heal the hurt of those severed from a loved one. Forgetting is the other great narcotic for the human heart. But sometimes you don't want to forget, even if it means holding on to pain.

Science claims to have a solution for phantom pain.

The motor cortex is the part of the brain that controls all our movements. Within it there is a complete representation of our body. If anything about the body alters, the motor cortex will change or shrink correspondingly: the higher the level of shrinkage, the more intense the pain. In users of prosthetic limbs, scientists believe there is less shrinkage because impulses for movement continue to be sent to the brain and these trick it into thinking the limb is still there. So amputees are now being advised to imagine their missing limb and to visualize it moving. By simulating normal motion, impulses are sent to the brain convincing it that all is well, all is as it should be. Shrinkage in the motor cortex is halted or reduced, and pain subsides correspondingly. Who would have thought that relief could lie in a clever and simple deception?

I have used a similar approach to deal with my loss of Nina: recalling and visualizing the lost one. The tea I drink no longer contains the sly dash of honey from her hand, but as I sip it I think of her and the taste is altered by my memory of sweetness. I also ease my pain through imagining what I cannot quite remember or could not know about Nina. So that place in my being, the cortex of love, where the essence of her resides, is not shrinking because it continues to receive the vital impulses of imagination. It is not just for my own preservation that I pursue this treatment – it is for *you*, Umeed.

You, who do not even know what you have lost. (Or do you? Somewhere in that small body have you felt it already?) Perhaps that is the greatest tragedy – to lose what is yours without ever having it; to lose a mother before you have been mothered. I cannot bear the thought of something within you shrinking away because of this loss and then causing you pain. So I have tried to put your mother into words, tried to create a core text of her, a sort of prosthetic parent. I have put the past on to these pages that they may send vital impulses into the core of you, to deceive your brain into a knowledge of your mother and thereby reduce your hurt.

Take these words. Visualize what they tell you. Feel them. Please, handle them carefully, my Umeed, for the story they tell is your story too. Because the stories of our forebears are inevitably ours as well, and until we know them we can never completely be ourselves.

THE END

Acknowledgements

I am grateful to all who supported me in the creation of this book.

In particular, I must thank:

Bobby and Vicky, both dear friends and generous emissaries of this book on my behalf. Laura Sherlock, for magnanimously speeding the book along its journey to publication. Natasha Fairweather, for her warmth and insight. Jane Lawson, whose vision for *Ishq and Mushq* exceeded my own and whose gentle but incisive editorial guidance brought out the best in me. Everyone at Transworld Publishers who believed in the book and helped prepare it for publication. And everyone at A. P. Watt who has rallied behind me.

I am indebted to my family – inveterate storytellers and fantastic cooks. Mumji and Papaji, who are my second parents. Seema and Agam, who make me laugh at my own foolishness as only siblings can. Rowan and Eliott, who are lovely reminders of how young and how old I am. Nef and Sarah, who have been my guardians and role models. Pa, who knows what it is to work for your dream. Above all, my mum, whose goodness and good food inspire and sustain me.

And then there is Matti. To him, I can say only: Without you, my love, I would not be as I am and this book would not be.

DANCING WITH THE TWO-HEADED TIGRESS
Tina Biswas

'LIKE MONICA ALI'S *BRICK LANE*, BUT FUNNIER'
Elle

Her boorish father is dead, and fat, unsophisticated Mousumi is on her way to visit her cosmopolitan relations in London. For the glamour of the Western world, she leaves behind both her forlorn mother and an amorous shopkeeper.

She is welcomed by the Majumdar family: Prakash, a doctor with too much heart, and Tuhina, an investment banker. But it is Darshini, their nonchalant eighteen-year-old daughter, who really fascinates her.

Darshini and Mousumi are total opposites, and Mousumi just can't beat Darshini's Princess credentials. The two of them form a love-hate relationship, until one day Mousumi's feisty personality begins to assert itself.

Tina Biswas' first novel is an exuberant comedy of cultural misunderstanding and people who simply don't get on. Whose side will you be taking?

'BISWAS MIXES DASHES OF MAGICAL REALISM WITH INSIGHTS INTO WHAT FAMILY LIFE CAN REALLY BE LIKE, AS THE ACTIONS OF GRANDPARENTS ECHO DOWN THE GENERATIONS'
Marie Claire

'TINA BISWAS IS A NATURAL WRITER'
Guardian

'A COMEDY OF MANNERS . . . CHARMINGLY TOLD'
Financial Times

'A BEAUTIFUL DEBUT THAT MIXES HUMOUR WITH BITING SOCIAL COMMENTARY'
Cosmopolitan

9780552773232

BLACK SWAN